Eileen Merriman's three young adult novels, *Pieces of You, Catch Me When You Fall* and *Invisibly Breathing*, were finalists in the New Zealand Book Awards for Children and Young Adults in 2018 and 2019, and all three are Storylines Notable Books. Her fourth young adult novel, *A Trio of Sophies,* was published in 2020 to huge critical praise and was also published in Germany. She released the first titles in the Black Spiral Trilogy in 2021. Her first adult novel, *Moonlight Sonata*, was released in July 2019 and longlisted for the Jann Medlicott Acorn Prize for Fiction 2020, with reviewers calling it 'skilfully crafted', and a 'carefully layered and thoughtful drama, with beautifully observed and believable Kiwi characters'. Eileen's second adult novel, *The Silence of Snow*, was published in September 2020.

Her other awards include runner-up in the 2018 *Sunday Star-Times* Short Story Award, third for three consecutive years in the 2014–2016 *Sunday Star-Times* Short Story Awards, second in the 2015 Bath Flash Fiction Award and first place in the 2015 Graeme Lay Short Story Competition. She works full-time as a consultant haematologist at North Shore Hospital in Auckland.

Double Helix

Eileen Merriman

BLACK
SWAN

BLACK SWAN

UK | USA | Canada | Ireland | Australia
India | New Zealand | South Africa | China

Black Swan is an imprint of the Penguin Random House group of companies, whose
addresses can be found at global.penguinrandomhouse.com.

Penguin
Random House
New Zealand

First published by Penguin Random House New Zealand, 2021

1 3 5 7 9 10 8 6 4 2

Text © Eileen Merriman, 2021

The moral right of the author has been asserted.

Design by Cat Taylor © Penguin Random House New Zealand
Cover photographs by Linus Nylund (background) and
Jonas Weckschmied (couple) on Unsplash
Author photograph by Colleen Lenihan
Prepress by Image Centre Group
Printed and bound in Australia by Griffin Press, an Accredited ISO AS/
NZS 14001 Environmental Management Systems Printer

A catalogue record for this book is available from the National Library of New Zealand.

ISBN 978-0-14-377520-1
eISBN 978-0-14-377521-8

The assistance of Creative New Zealand towards the production of
this book is gratefully acknowledged by the publisher.

ARTS COUNCIL OF NEW ZEALAND TOI AOTEAROA

penguin.co.nz

MIX
Paper from
responsible sources
FSC® C009448

For Charlotte,
who once gave me a home —
thank you for letting me use it in more ways than one.

Prologue

WHANGĀREI HEADS, 2019

Jake lay on top of his board, feeling the swells move beneath him, like the air moving in and out of his lungs, like the blood surging through the four chambers of his stubbornly beating heart. *Thirty-four*, his heart beat. *Thirty-four, thirty-four.* He watched as, one by one, his fellow surfers took their turn, riding the cresting waves in to shore.

Today I am thirty-four years old, and I know this: there are no certainties in life, not even death. I have helped people to live. I have helped them to die. Sometimes I feel as though I'm seventy-four, but I'm not ready to let go. Not yet.

Jake breathed in, breathed out. Listened to his heart accelerate and slow, *thirty-four, thirty-four*. Listened to the voices echoing in his ears, *I promise I promise.*

'I promise,' he whispered, and began to paddle.

PART I

2007, DUNEDIN

Chapter 1: Boulevard of Broken Dreams

After strapping his surfboard to the roof of his car, Jake drove two blocks to Thompson Street. He parked two houses back from number fourteen, and began a slow stroll past his old house — old, but not as old as it had looked when he'd left three years ago. The weatherboards had been painted black, the window frames ivory.

'Huh.' He halted, taking in the closely cropped lawns and surgically trimmed roses. Next door, the Walsh house was the same as ever, apart from the Toyota Prius parked in the driveway.

Time moves on, sometimes slowly, often quickly.

Before *he* could move on, a tall man with a shaved head appeared around the side of the house. Once he'd reached the driver's side of the Prius, he glanced up and frowned.

'Hi, can I — Jake?' Emily's father moved towards him. 'Oh, it *is* you.' His mouth curved up, but his eyes didn't crinkle at the corners.

Jake gave him a tentative smile in return. 'Thought I'd drop by, have a look at the old house.' He shielded his eyes. The February sun was even more intense than it had been in Auckland, if that were possible.

'They've done a good job of it, haven't they?' Jim jiggled the car keys. 'Well. It wasn't as if your family were able to — anyway. Nice to see you.'

'You too.' Jake shuffled his feet. 'Um, I heard Emily's at med school?' Jesus, here he was, twenty-one years old, but Emily's father was making him feel like a schoolkid all over again.

'Fourth year this year. How about you?'

'Second year.' Jake was still finding that a little hard to believe and wouldn't have been at all surprised if a letter or e-mail arrived soon to rectify the error. *We regret to inform you . . .*

Jim's brow wrinkled, then smoothed out again. 'Graduate entry?'

Jake nodded. 'I didn't get in the first time, so I did a BSc.' He'd been so close. Ironic, really, that Emily had gained entry straight away, considering she hadn't even wanted to go to med school before.

Before we—

'Well, you clearly did well with your degree to get straight into second year.' Jim pressed on his electronic key, and Jake heard the locks slide in the car doors. 'I'd better get going. I might see you around the hospital.'

'Sure.' Jake started towards his station wagon. No *are you planning to catch up with Emily* or *how's your family?*

Well, what did he expect? As for Emily, she probably never wanted to see him again. Probably she hated him.

No, surely you're exaggerating. You've just lost touch . . . right?

Jake waited for the Prius to drive past before leaning against the bonnet of his car and taking his phone out of his pocket. After selecting a message he'd received the day before, he hit reply and typed: *Sure, swing by your place around seven?*

Ian's reply came as he was driving back into the city: *Sweet, see you then. Bring beer. We've got a LOT of catching up to do.*

———

Ian's flat, nestled in North East Valley, was only three houses away from the steepest street in the world. They sat in saggy chairs on the front porch, drinking beer as the sun began its slow descent behind the hills.

Ian clinked his bottle against Jake's. 'Long time no see, Mr Heremaia.'

'Long time,' Jake agreed. 'You look the same, though.'

'Good genes.' Ian smirked.

Jake swiped at a sluggish fly. 'Yeah, that's it.' Jake wished he could say the same about his own genes. He might have had his father's surname, but they were like strangers — Jake more a Wilson than a Heremaia. He felt like an imposter when his relatives addressed him in te reo. And yet, who'd want to be a Wilson? He cleared his throat. 'How are things going with Lucy?'

'Ah, we finished up for good last year.' Ian sipped on his beer. 'She was moving to Wellington for her new job and I still had a year to go on my BA, so we decided to go our separate ways. How about you? Anyone special?'

'Not really. There was this girl I hooked up with last year off and on, but it never came to anything.' Jake fell silent. Sienna and he had some fun, but they'd never had much in common.

Ian let a hiss of air out of the side of his mouth. 'Shame.'

'Kind of.' Jake prodded at a hole in the arm of his chair. 'So, Emily's flat-warming . . .'

'We can cruise over whenever.' Ian tilted his wrist, showing Jake his watch. 'It's only half-seven now, though.'

'Yeah, not yet,' Jake said, but his heart was hammering. *Three years, three years, three years.* 'She's got a boyfriend, right?'

'Lucy? Not that I've heard, but guess I'd be the last to know.'

'Not *her*, Emily.' He'd seen photos on other people's Facebook feeds of Emily with a blond guy, although he'd been nursing a hope they were just friends. The guy looked older than her, by three or four years, he was guessing.

'Oh, right.' Ian set his bottle down. 'She's been going out with another medic, Adam, for at least three years.'

'Adam.' Jake had the feeling he sometimes got when he was about to wipe out in the surf, a plunging that went from gut to groin. 'Don't think I know him.'

'He's a first-year doctor. Apparently they met when Emily was doing ward rounds with her dad, when she was still at high school. Sweet, huh?'

'Really sweet,' Jake echoed.

Did you think she was going to wait for you?

She could at least have replied to my letter.

If she even read it. Sometimes, often, he wondered about that.

Jake forced a note of cheer into his voice. 'So, what about her flatmate?'

Ian shrugged. 'Mandy? She's single, as far as I know. Kind of feisty. She's a dental student.'

'Dental, interesting.' Jake drained his beer and stood up. 'Want another one?'

'If you insist.' Ian draped his legs over the side of his chair. 'This is just like old times.'

'Old times,' Jake said, and sloped into the kitchen. Except everyone had moved on, and here he was, still trying to be a doctor, still trying to act as if he were normal.

He popped the cap off a bottle of beer and took three large swallows. *Shut up, brain. I don't need you. Not tonight.*

———

By the time Jake and Ian reached the flat warming it was nine pm, and the sky was just starting to fade. Jake had missed the long Southern evenings.

He hadn't missed the cold, though. It couldn't have been more than fourteen degrees. Jake walked into the shadowy hallway, and felt someone clap him between the shoulder-blades.

'Heremaia!' Turning, Jake saw it was Blake, an old mate from school. Blake grinned. 'Back for a visit?'

Jake fist-bumped him. 'Back for good.'

'He's a med student now.' Ian waved at someone in the periphery of Jake's vision. 'Hey, Mandy, where's Emily? Got an old friend of hers here.'

A petite Asian girl halted in the doorway. 'An old friend?' Mandy adjusted the oversized straw hat perched atop her glossy hair. 'What's his name?'

'His name is Jake,' Jake said, feeling as though he were an object in a museum.

Mandy nodded. 'Nice to meet you, Jake. Emily was outside, last time I saw her. Do you want a drink?'

'We've got lots.' Ian shoved a can at Jake, although Jake didn't want any more beer. He'd had three already, and things were starting to look a little blurry around the edges.

Still, the prop was welcome. Clutching the can, Jake left Blake chatting with Ian and continued into the back yard, where at least thirty people were milling around on the lawn. Just like old times, but the world had shifted. People seemed to be having actual conversations rather than yelling at each other or making out, and they didn't seem half as drunk as they'd been at the parties he used to go to. Loitering by the fence, Jake raised the can to his lips.

'Oh, *hey*.' A guy with a pierced eyebrow swayed in front of him, slopping beer over Jake's shoes. 'Jason Heremaia, right?'

'Jake,' he corrected, and peering closer, 'Roddy?' The student was chunkier than he remembered, and had gained several piercings since he'd last seen him.

'Roddy I am.' Jake's former classmate leaned heavily against the fence, managing to spill the rest of his beer on Jake's jeans in the process. OK, so maybe not *everyone* had grown up all that much.

Shrinking away, Jake took another sip of his own beer. 'How's it going?'

'Awesome, mate. What are you up to?'

'I'm getting drunk,' Jake said, which would be the truth, if he kept drinking.

Roddy laughed and yelled in his ear. 'Got something stronger if you want it. Of the chemical variety, if you know what I mean.'

'Yeah, nah, this'll do.' Jake surveyed the yard. Someone had turned up the music, Eminem's 'Lose Yourself'. Jake was starting to wish he could lose himself too. Maybe he *should* get pissed, even though he hardly ever let that happen.

Tuning in again, he heard Roddy say '. . . doing Law', which seemed ironic, considering.

'That's awesome,' Jake said, just before he saw a whippet-slim pair of denimed legs wander past. The blonde hair was shorter, to her shoulders rather than her waist, but her mannerisms hadn't changed, such as the way she lowered her eyes when she smiled.

And his heart kept beating, *three years, three years, three years*.

'Three years,' he said, and Roddy said, 'huh?'

'I mean, s'cuse me.' Jake took off after Emily, hurtling inside and — where had she got to?

'There you are.' Ian bailed him up in the kitchen, where a couple of girls were cooking up God-knew-what in a massive pot. It smelt like baked beans, or something just as foul. 'What are you doing Sunday morning?'

'Surfing?' Jake said, distractedly, because now he could hear her voice drifting out of the hallway.

Ian snorted. 'Yeah, OK, stupid question. I'm driving out to Tomahawk, want to come?'

'Absolutely.' Jake's t-shirt was sticking to him, even though the temperature must have dropped a couple more degrees. Emily was saying, *long bike ride* and *cycling widow* and laughing. Her voice grew louder. Jake tensed, his eyes flicking towards the doorway.

'Hey Ian, did you see—' Emily's smile faded. 'Oh. Hi.'

'Hi.' Jake swallowed. 'I was just trying to . . . find you.'

She crossed her arms. 'Well. Here I am.'

'Jake's going to med school too.' Ian took his phone out of his pocket. 'Hello? Yes, you are missing the party of the year. So?' He wagged his fingers at them and wandered outside.

'Med school?' Emily was wearing a white shirt over dark jeans and a completely unreadable expression.

Jake chewed his lower lip. 'Think they made a mistake. Letting me in, I mean.'

'Right.' Emily was looking everywhere but at him.

'Look,' he raised his voice over the music, The Black Eyed Peas singing 'Don't Phunk With My Heart', 'can we go somewhere a bit quieter?'

Her eyes met his for the first time. 'What for?'

'Well, I wanted to — just for a few minutes?'

'Fine.' Emily moved into the hallway. Jake followed her onto the porch, across the lawn and out onto the street. Emily wrapped her arms around herself. 'When did you get back?'

The streetlights flicked on. Jake inhaled. 'Yesterday.'

'Right.'

'And I was kind of hoping we can catch up. For coffee or something?'

Emily glanced down the street. A group of students was wandering through the intersection, laughing and waving wine bottles around.

'I don't know if that's such a good idea,' she said. 'Do you?'

'I don't know. I just wanted to—'

Her voice rose. 'Why bother talking to me now, anyway, after three years of nothing?'

He gritted his teeth. 'Well, it's not as if I didn't *try*.'

'What? When?'

He said, 'I wrote you a letter. Remember?'

Emily went very still. 'A letter?'

'Six pages. I sent it a couple of weeks after I got to Auckland.' His breathing quickened. 'Didn't you get it?'

'No.' Her eyes, beneath the cold glow of the streetlight, were glistening. 'I think I would have remembered.'

'I think you would have.' And now Jake was remembering how he'd re-written the last page four times to try and get it right, the words forever etched on his brain. He barely registered the whirr of the bike, didn't even see the cyclist until he halted beside them.

'Hey.' After removing his helmet, the cyclist kissed Emily before squinting at Jake. 'Have we met?'

Emily took a deep breath. 'Adam, this is Jake. We used to be neighbours, when we were kids.'

'Nice to meet you.' Adam was wearing Lycra shorts and cycling shoes. His bike looked expensive. His watch looked expensive. Every fucking thing looked expensive.

'Nice to meet you too,' Jake said. 'I'll leave you guys to it.' Then he began walking — away from the flat, away from Emily, away from the memories flooding into his consciousness.

I think I would have remembered.

I think you would have.

And his brain went *what if, what if, what if.*

Chapter 2: Here Comes the Sun

Adam passed Emily the IV and rested his arm on the table.

'Pull the skin tight,' he said. 'It helps anchor the vein. Ow!'

'Sorry.' She took the needle out. 'If I keep missing *your* drainpipes, then how am I supposed to get an IV into an eighty-nine year old with spidery veins and tissue paper skin?'

Adam pressed gauze over the puncture wound. 'In a couple of years, you'll have no choice. You'll be on night shift with no other doctors around, and that little old lady will need her antibiotics ASAP.'

'Did I ever tell you how much I hate sticking needles in people?' Emily yanked the dining room curtain across, partly to block out the early morning sun, and partly because she didn't want her neighbours to think she and Adam were shooting up.

'I think you did.' Adam bumped his foot against her ankle. 'Try again.'

Clenching her jaw, Emily prodded the rubbery vein coursing across Adam's wrist and pushed the IV in. A second later, she felt a pop and saw a red flashback in the lumen of the catheter.

'Nice.'

'Nice,' Emily echoed, concentrating on advancing the cannula off the end of the needle and into the vein. After taping the cannula flat against Adam's skin, she picked up a syringe and flushed it with saline.

Just fill the syringe with water. That'll work, right?

'Perfect,' Adam said.

'Perfect.' She blinked away the image of Jake's mother, her limbs contracting, her eyes rolling up.

Why did you come back, Jake? Couldn't you have gone to med school in Auckland?

It was two weeks since Jake had turned up at her party. Emily had been in a tailspin ever since. He'd texted her two days later to ask if she'd meet him for coffee. She'd replied *no, are you kidding?*

'Don't fret, Em. You wait, in a few months you'll be doing these with your eyes closed.'

'I hope not. For the sake of the general public.' She peeled the tape off and placed a square of gauze over the end of the IV. 'Coming out now. You'd better get going, or you'll be late for your ward round.'

'Track marks and all.' Adam bent forward to kiss her. 'Do you want to come to indoor soccer tonight? We're having drinks afterwards.'

'No, think I'll get an early night.' She stood up, picking up her empty coffee cup. 'I'll see you at lunchtime, maybe.'

After kissing Adam goodbye at the front door, Emily went to retrieve her phone from her room. There was a newly arrived message on the screen; the third text Jake had sent her in the past two weeks.

How about a walk on the beach after dinner?

Emily contemplated fobbing him off again. *No, I don't want to meet you in a café. No, I don't want to meet you on the beach. I never want to talk to you again.*

And yet, it would be a lie.

OK, she replied. *Meet you by the Surf Club, 8pm.*

———

Two hours later, and Emily was wishing she were anywhere rather than in a hospital room with a patient, five other medical students and a professor staring at her.

'The pulse was slow-rising, and seventy-two beats per minute,' she said. 'And the blood pressure was . . .' Shit, what had the patient's blood pressure been? She'd have to make it up. 'One hundred and forty-two over sixty.'

Prof Wagner, who was so old he still wore a white coat, didn't say anything. Emily felt a tremor begin in her knees.

'Um,' she said, struggling to remember what came next. 'The JVP was four centimetres.'

Prof Wagner's bushy eyebrows went up. Wringing her hands together, Emily carried on.

'Heart sounds were dual with a four over six ejection systolic murmur the chest was resonant with faint bi-basal crepitations no spleen or liver felt and mild pitting ankle oedema,' she blurted, aware the tremor had reached her larynx. *Damn it, damn it.*

'Is that all?' Prof Wagner's voice was soft.

Emily gulped. 'The examination is consistent with mitral regurgitation with early signs of congestive heart failure,' she mumbled.

The professor peered at her through the bottom of his glasses. 'Are you sure?'

'Um . . .' Her heart raced. 'I mean . . . aortic stenosis?' Or should she have said mitral stenosis?

'That's better. There's no need to be so nervous,' he added, before giving her what he probably thought was a kindly smile, but for Emily it might as well have been the kiss of death. That was all she needed, to know that everyone else could see how she was fighting for breath, how she was counting her own rapid pulse.

Which, for the record, is currently ninety-six beats per minute.

They moved to the next patient, a jaundiced fifty-something-year-old woman with the lines around her mouth common to all smokers, as if her lips were the opening of a drawstring bag.

'Doctor Coburn.' Prof Wagner stroked the lapels of his white coat. 'Could you please examine Ms Duke and present your findings.'

A long-faced student with thinning hair stepped forward.

'Hi, Ms Duke,' Thomas said smoothly. 'Is it OK if I examine you?'

Why, Emily thought despairingly, *is everyone else so confident?* It wasn't just that she couldn't get the different heart murmurs straight in her head. The minute she had to speak in front of a group of people, her body went straight into a fight-or-flight response.

More commonly known, a dry voice said in her mind, *as a panic attack.*

I know what it is, she snapped at the voice, which sounded a lot like her father's. But she had no idea what she was meant to do about the episodes, short of taking a Valium or downing a couple of stiff drinks before class.

Zoning back in, she heard Thomas say, 'Consistent with decompensated cirrhosis.'

'Very good,' Prof said. 'Can you name three causes of cirrhosis for me?'

'Um, alcohol.' Thomas stroked his chin. 'And um . . . hmm, let's see.'

'Anyone else?' Prof nodded at Emily. 'Doctor Walsh?' He seemed to like addressing the students as doctor, even though they wouldn't be qualified for three years yet.

Or in her case never, if her heart exploded from anxiety before then. Her mind blank, she shook her head.

Prof's pale eyes moved to the student standing to Emily's left. 'Doctor Wu?'

'Hepatitis?' Grace asked.

'Good. Let's have one more — who was listening in the tutorial last week?'

I was, Emily thought-shouted. So why couldn't she remember anything? Or perhaps it was more that she was scared of getting it wrong. How did doctors live with that kind of stress every day? She stayed mute, right until the end of the tutorial, when Grace asked if Emily wanted to join her for coffee.

'God,' Grace said, not looking flustered in the slightest, 'that was a grilling, wasn't it?'

'Uh-huh.'

'Can you believe that woman drank two bottles of wine every night?' Grace said, as they plodded down the stairs. 'No wonder her liver's screwed.'

'I could do with a bottle of wine right now,' Emily said, and Grace laughed, as if Emily were joking.

Emily zipped her jacket to her chin. The sun was still high in the sky, but the wind blowing off the sea was wintry, even though it was only the first day of autumn. She bent over the railing, watching the lacy foam slide over the surface of the water. *Five to eight, damn it.* If only she weren't so pathologically early for every occasion.

Should have kept him waiting.

Shouldn't have come at all.

She heard footsteps behind her. Jake's gait hadn't changed. Neither had his habit of clearing his throat when he was nervous.

I knew you so well, and now I barely know you at all.

'Hey.'

Emily pivoted, turning away from the railing. 'Hey,' she said, taking in his faded jeans and the unbuttoned checked shirt worn over a white t-shirt. 'Thought you'd have been out on those waves.'

'They're not that great today.' Jake gripped the railing. 'Too close together.'

'True.' She began down the steps. The tide was out, the packed sand bone-white and gritty beneath her sneakers.

'Do you still come down here to sketch?' Jake asked.

'Not for ages. I've been too busy studying.'

Jake cut his eyes towards her. 'That's a shame.'

Emily concentrated her gaze on her feet. 'Med school's busy. You'll find out.'

'Guess I will. Are you enjoying it?'

She hesitated. 'Of course,' she said, and when he didn't say anything, 'it was kind of an accident. Getting into med school, I mean.'

'Imagine that,' Jake said, a faint edge to his voice.

Emily's neck felt hot. 'Not like that. I still had to work hard. Adam tutored me in chemistry.'

'Perhaps I needed an Adam.' Jake gave her a half-smile and she mirrored his expression, unsure whether to be embarrassed or annoyed.

'You always got better marks than me at school.'

'My first year at uni wasn't that great.' Jake stepped to one side to avoid an enthusiastic Labrador, his elbow brushing against hers. He smelt the same but different too, like shaving cream and wood smoke. No cigarette smoke, she realised, wondering if he'd given up. And now *she* was looking sideways at *him*, taking in the more defined contours of his face, the stubble on his chin.

'Too much drinking?'

'Something like that.'

Emily chewed the inside of her cheek. 'How was med camp last week?'

'It was fun. My class seems like a good bunch.' A jogger ran past them, emitting a warm whiff of sweat. 'Hey, um.' Jake rubbed the back of his neck. 'I need to talk to you. About what happened.'

Unease stirred in her gut. 'Why? It's not going to change anything now.'

'But,' he halted, and she did too, her arms crossed, her gaze on the undulating horizon. 'I want you to know I'm sorry. For dragging you into something that was nothing to do with you.'

'It's a bit late for that, isn't it?'

'Maybe.' His eyes were dark, unfathomable.

The words tumbled out before she could lose her nerve. 'It wasn't that I didn't want to help you. It's the way you manipulated me that hurts.'

His mouth fell open. '*Manipulated* you? What?'

'You know what I mean.' *You knew how I felt about you.* 'I had *no one* to talk to about it. I had nightmares.'

And the panic attacks, do you want to hear about those?

Because looking back, that was when they'd started.

Jake's face was wide open, his pupils huge. 'The letter . . .'

'I didn't get the *fucking* letter!' Emily pressed her palms to her eyes. He clasped her wrists, his voice reverberating into her ear.

'When you didn't reply, I thought you hated me. I thought you wanted me to leave you alone.'

'I *did*.'

He said, 'There were so many things I wanted to tell you.'

She drew away, swiping the tears away with her sleeve. 'Such as?'

'I can't tell you three years' worth of stuff in one evening.'

'Tell me about your first year at uni,' she said, relenting a little, but only a little. 'Why don't you start there?'

She started walking again, and Jake fell in beside her. He began to speak. And for the first time in three years, she listened to him.

———

'I had nightmares too,' Jake said, slowly, haltingly.

Emily gripped the buzzing phone in her pocket. Adam, probably, seeing if she'd changed her mind about the after-soccer drinks. She made a mental note to text him later. *Sorry, only just saw your message . . .*

'The letter you wrote me,' she said. 'What did it say?'

'I didn't mention what happened exactly. I mean, anyone could have read it, right?'

'Yeah,' Emily said, unable to suppress a shudder. What if the letter had fallen into the wrong hands?

'I said thank you, and sorry. And . . . well, other stuff.'

Emily, glancing at him, decided not to press him further. What if the other stuff was *I wish I could kiss you again?* She'd rather not know. Besides which, she was with Adam now. By next year they could be living together. *That* thought made her feel as though she were on the edge of another panic attack.

What are you scared of, Emily?

Everything, everything.

'Who knows where that letter ended up?' Emily asked. 'Maybe I'll finally get it in five years, with postmarks from Germany and Madagascar.'

'Yeah,' Jake said, after a brief hesitation. 'Maybe.'

'So you lived with your aunt?' Emily prompted.

'Yeah. I couldn't afford to live in a hall, or go flatting. I got a part-time job at a service station, pumping gas. Got drunk nearly every night of the week that I wasn't working.' He gave her a thin smile. 'Not really a recipe for getting into med school.'

'I got drunk,' Emily said. 'Sometimes.'

'My grades were close enough that the advisor at uni said if I kept up my A- average in a BSc, then I'd probably get graduate entry into med school. And she was right. I got into both Auckland and Otago medical schools.'

'Wow.' Emily bit her lip. 'So, why did you come back here?'

Jake was silent for a moment. Then he said, slowly, 'Do you really have to ask?'

Her heart thudded. 'Three years is a long time.'

'It's a long time.' He bent to pick up a stone, and flicked it into the water. 'People move on, right?'

'Yes,' Emily said, a confusing mixture of emotions knotting in her chest. 'They do.'

Jake cleared his throat. She turned, swiping her hair off her face.

'It's getting late. I've got study to do.'

'Me too,' he said softly.

Chapter 3: I Don't Want to Miss a Thing

Jake dumped his pack on the bed and rubbed his left shoulder. 'Thanks again.'

'No, thank *you* for rescuing us from having to pay extra rent.' Ian leaned against the doorframe. 'Sodding Gazza. Should've known not to trust a JAFA.'

'Hey,' Jake said, feeling a vague sense of loyalty towards the city he'd been living in for the past three years.

'Just kidding, you'll never be a JAFA.' Ian clapped him on the back. 'You're a Southern man, through and through.'

Jake glanced around, taking in the desk by the window and the smears of someone else's Blu-Tack on the walls. 'I'm from the Far North, remember?'

Jake's other new flatmate, Nathan, wandered past holding a spatula and a can of V. 'They breed them feral up there, man.'

'Feral, yeah, you should see my dad.' Not that Jake had seen his father in over a year. No point when they just wound each other up.

'Roster's on the fridge,' Nathan called out. 'You're on bathroom this weekend.'

Jake began unfastening the clips on his pack. 'Bathroom, sure.'

'Nate's anal like that.' Ian loped off, leaving Jake alone in his new room. After upending the contents of the pack on top of the duvet, Jake went to get his textbooks out of the car. Mid-March and the sun was only just setting at eight pm. Back home, it'd probably be dark already.

But I am back home, he thought. Except his mother was dead, his grandma too after one final stroke last year. As for Northland, that had never really felt like home, the family up there more like strangers than whānau.

After checking his brake was yanked up as high as it would go — if it failed, his car would end up in a crumpled heap at the bottom of the hill — Jake staggered through the front door of the flat holding a pile of textbooks. Anatomy, Biochemistry, Physiology; thank God for student loans, though he'd probably be paying his loan off for fifteen years after graduation at this rate.

If you make it that far.

In his room, Jake sat on the bed and stroked the glossy photographs in his Anatomy atlas. Dissected cadavers flayed open to expose grey-brown organs pickled in formaldehyde; metre-long spinal cords with spaghetti-like nerves radiating in all directions; sections of brain. Why did so many internal organs resemble food? Or maybe it was food that resembled internal organs. Brains like cauliflower, kidneys like beans, liver like . . .

'Cheese,' he said aloud, flopping onto his pillow. Maybe Emily would find the food comparisons funny. At the very least, she'd understand.

By the time Emily replied to his text, Jake was sitting in the lounge, watching *Intrepid Journeys* with his new flatmates.

Wait until you start dissection classes . . . you'll never eat creamed corn again.

Thanks for ruining a staple food group, he replied. *Just leave the 2 Minute Noodles out of it, OK?*

His phone beeped. He groaned.

'No wait, it gets better,' Ian said, his eyes on the TV.

Jake, staring at his phone, said, 'Helminthiasis *Toxocara canis*.'

Nathan slurped on his Milo. 'What's that, an STD?'

'Jeez, you wouldn't want these crawling out of your Johnson.' Jake held up his own phone. 'It's a parasite, otherwise known as roundworm. They look like Two Minute Noodles, see?'

'You're sick, Heremaia.' Ian draped a leg over the side of the couch. 'Fancy a surf before class tomorrow?'

'Sure.' Jake sent another text to Emily. Her reply was swift.

Should be done by four tomorrow, see you then.

The next morning, Jake lay on his board, bobbing out behind the breakers at St Clair Beach. Behind him, the sun was oozing across the horizon like a runny egg. The world was perfect at dawn, glassy and new. He turned his attention to the ocean moving beneath him, like the ebb and flow of his heart, until he felt as if he and the sea were one and the same, no beginning and no end.

Out of the corner of his eye, he saw Ian take off and cruise all the way to shore. The next wave began to roll towards him and Jake started paddling, faster and faster. Then he was up on his board, the surf roaring in his ears and his chest, and there was nothing better, *nothing*.

'Mate,' Ian said forty minutes later, when they were sitting in the sand, catching their breath. 'That was better than sex.'

'Better than sex,' Jake agreed, although it had been a few months since he'd been able to make *that* kind of comparison. Thoughts of last night's fantasy loomed — the faintly freckled skin, the full, pouting lips, the familiar curve of her long, long legs.

I hate being tall, she'd told him more than once.

I can't imagine you any other way, he'd replied.

Ian's voice cut into the semi-erotic thoughts scudding around Jake's brain. 'I saw Mandy the other day,' he said. 'You know, Emily's flatmate.'

'Yeah, I remember.' Jake had seen Mandy a couple of times around the campus since the girls' flat warming. 'She's friendly enough.'

'And kind of cute, don't you reckon?'

'Not bad.' Jake stood up. 'Going to ask her out, are you?'

Ian pursed his lips. 'Sort of.' They began ascending the concrete steps, holding their boards at waist height. 'I was thinking we could have our own flat warming to celebrate you moving in. We could invite the girls around, what do you think?'

'Sounds like a good plan.' Jake propped his board against the side of the car. 'Do you think Nathan will agree to a party, though?'

Ian grinned. 'Majority rules, right? It'll give him something to moan about for the next two months anyway.'

'You're on,' Jake said.

Later that morning, Jake sat in a darkened lecture theatre, listening to the first radiology lecture of the year. He was sitting next to Craig, another graduate student he'd become friendly with at med camp, and Kylie, a medical student with flaming red hair and a hyena-like laugh.

Jake was trying to concentrate, but the lecturer had dimmed the lights, and it was practically impossible. Nine am, a darkened room and an early morning surf; a perfect recipe for slipping into a comatose state.

Should have got a coffee. Or a Coke. He picked up his pen and set it spinning across the top of his knuckles with a flick of his thumb. Seconds later, the pen shot across the desk and onto Kylie's lap. *Shit.*

'Think you lost something.' Kylie passed it to him.

'Yeah, sorry.' Jake waited until Kylie was looking forward again before holding his hand out in front of him. Had his arm jerked just then? It remained still, not a trace of a tremor. *Steady as a surgeon.*

'And this,' the radiologist said, 'is an example of brain atrophy in a man with dementia.'

Jake sat upright, his eyes fixed on the screen as the radiologist showed them examples of CT and MRI scans of patients with Alzheimer's disease, multi-infarct dementia, and finally, Huntington's disease.

Slumping in his seat, Jake massaged his temples. What if his brain was shrinking? How would he know? Distracted, he picked up his pen, and began to twirl it through his fingers.

The pen clattered onto the top of the bench.

Kylie let out a guffaw. 'Are you just clumsy, or are you trying to pick me up?' Jesus, she was so *loud.*

'Definitely trying to pick you up,' Jake said, deadpan, even though he felt hot all over.

Stretching across him, Craig pressed his pen into Kylie's palm. 'My one's bigger than his. Just saying.'

Kylie's guffaws intensified. Jake let out a snort before withering beneath the lecturer's steely gaze.

'Is there something you'd like to share with us?' The radiologist's tone was icy.

'Nope,' Jake mumbled, hunching his shoulders.

'You guys are funny,' Kylie whispered, once the lecturer began flicking through PowerPoint slides again. 'Want to go to the pub after this?'

———

Emily dropped a marshmallow into her mug. 'So what did you say?'

'I said, no, I'm meeting my girlfriend.'

Emily frowned. 'Really?'

'No, I didn't. Would you stop freaking out?' Jake glanced around the crowded café. They'd been lucky enough to nab a couch at the rear, the one with the board games stacked beneath the battered table.

'I'm not freaking out,' Emily said, but she was chewing her thumbnail the way she always did when she was agitated.

'What's Adam doing anyway, saving lives?'

'Actually, yes. He's on a long day. Fifteen hours.' At least, that was what Adam had told her, although it was his second long day that week, which was more than he usually did.

'Ugh.' Jake was beginning to wish he hadn't asked. 'That'll be you in two years.'

'And you in five.'

'Five years is forever.'

He cut a wedge off the piece of cake between them. It was the third time they'd met at the café in the past two weeks, and he couldn't get enough of the New York cheesecake.

'Time is relative.' Emily frowned at him. 'Did that hurt?'

Following the line of her gaze, Jake touched the whorled koru on his right biceps. 'You mean the tattoo?'

'No, I was referring to your multiple piercings.'

He rolled his eyes at her. 'Of course it hurt. I might have been kind of trashed at the time.'

'That's not like you.'

'Like I said, first year was,' he shrugged. 'You know. I don't regret the tattoo, though. Do you like it?'

'I do.' For a moment Jake thought Emily was going to touch it, but she picked up her teaspoon and dipped it into her hot chocolate. 'How's your family?'

Jake looked out of the window. The wind was coming up, leaves and pieces of paper scuttling in circles around the pavement.

'My uncle shot himself,' Jake said, his tone casual but his nerves stretched taut. 'A couple of years ago.'

Her mouth fell open. 'God, that's horrible. How old was he?'

'Thirty-eight.'

'How come?'

'Do you have to ask?'

Emily set her spoon down. 'Was that your mum's brother?'

'The youngest one, yeah.' And now he was regretting telling her, because Emily's eyes were shiny, as if she were about to start crying. He exhaled. 'Let's talk about something else, shall we?'

'Such as?'

'Such as whether I'm going to beat you at chess.' He levered a box out from the pile of games beneath the table and lifted the lid off.

'Do you know how much study I've got to do?'

'Me too. Black or white?' Jake picked up a black bishop.

'Black,' she said immediately.

'You always say that.' He felt a sudden rush of nostalgia. It didn't help that the café was playing one of his favourite Aerosmith songs, 'I Don't Want To Miss A Thing'. He and Emily had been in their last year of primary school when that song came out. His mother had still been able to string a sentence together, just. That year, he'd learned to catch a wave and taught Emily how to wolf whistle.

'Then why did you ask?' Emily smiled at him, gently, gently, and he felt something unfurl inside in his chest.

Don't go there, Jake.

But of course, it was already too late.

Chapter 4: Should I Stay or Should I Go?

Emily picked up a book and sat on the couch. 'How about *Hairy Maclary*? That's one of my favourites.'

The toddler pouted. 'Not *Hairy Maclary*.' Charlotte's fine blonde hair was tied up in pigtails, her doll-like feet encased in Minnie Mouse sandals. Emily checked the kitchen clock. Twenty-five minutes until seven pm, and her half-sister's bedtime. At least it was dark outside. Trying to get Charlotte to bed in the summer had been a nightmare.

In a month, it would be winter, Emily's least favourite season. And yet, she thought this winter might be better than the last.

'OK, how about *Doctor Dog*?' Emily took the dog-eared book off the coffee table.

Charlotte brightened. '*Doctor Dog*.' She climbed onto Emily's knee. 'Grandad farted and blew the roof off the house.'

'He sure did.' The weight of Charlotte in her lap was strangely comforting, soporific even. By the time she reached the end of the book, Charlotte's blinks were getting longer, her breathing heavy.

'Time for bed, chook.' Emily set the book aside.

'I'm not tired,' her sister said.

'Not at all,' Emily agreed, taking her through to the bathroom to brush her tiny teeth. Charlotte's eyes were closed even before Emily tucked her into bed.

'Thank you, *Doctor Dog*,' Emily murmured and returned to the lounge, just in time to hear the rap of knuckles on wood.

'Perfect timing,' she said, opening the door to her boyfriend.

'I'm marvellous like that.' Adam kissed her. 'I brought Massaman chicken, and Beef Korma.'

31

Emily took the plastic bag from him. 'That *is* pretty marvellous.'

'And this.' Adam held up a bottle of wine.

'Even better, drunk and in charge of a two-year-old.' Emily closed the door behind him and wandered through to the kitchen.

'I'm sure Steve and your mum do the same all the time.' Adam perched on a barstool. 'Did you have to change any nappies?'

'No, I — shit.' Emily glanced toward the hallway. Silence. Was it worth waking Charlotte up to change her nappy, which she could have been wearing for the last several hours? 'Rule number one,' she said. 'Never wake a sleeping toddler.'

'Or boyfriend. How was your day?'

'I went to Mum and Steve's for lunch.' Emily took a pair of wine glasses out of the cupboard. 'Spent most of the afternoon studying. How was your bike ride?'

Adam crossed an ankle over his knee. 'Never went for a bike ride in the end. I caught up with Holly from med school days, do you remember her?'

'I remember.' Emily poured a measure of buttery wine into each of the glasses. How could she forget? Holly was an ex-girlfriend of Adam's, although he always insisted that six weeks was hardly a relationship. 'So . . .'

'So we got to talking about junior doctor things, decided to go for a walk for some fresh air, lost track of time and ended up most of the way to Port Chalmers.'

'Port Chalmers?'

He shrugged. 'We didn't realise we'd gone so far. We ended up jogging the last few ks, because we were so sick of walking.'

'That must have taken hours.' Emily hadn't touched her wine. Adam took a large sip of his.

'No longer than your study session, I'm sure.'

She looked down, flicked the side of the glass. 'Maybe we should go on a walk sometime.'

'Yeah, sure, whenever you want.' Adam took his phone out his pocket. 'How about tomorrow arvo?'

Emily hesitated. 'I'm meeting Jake. For coffee.'

'Right.'

'Is that OK?'

'Why wouldn't it be?'

'I don't know.' A perverse part of her almost wanted Adam to be jealous. At least then she'd know he cared. She began assembling plates, forks, serving spoons. 'Has Holly got herself a boyfriend yet?'

'Not that I know of.' Adam chuckled and began tapping on his phone.

'Well, I thought you *would* know, since you had such a heart-to-heart today.'

'Methinks someone is a little bit jealous,' Adam murmured, before finally meeting her gaze. 'Come on, Em, how would you like it if I had a cow every time you met up with Jake?'

'That's different. I've known him since primary school.' Two months since she'd started hanging out with Jake again, and she felt as if she'd rediscovered a lost part of herself. Was it wrong to think that? She plucked a leaf off the pot plant at her elbow. 'Well, anyway. It'd be nice if we could go on a walk like that sometime.'

'Like I said,' Adam replied, 'any time you're free.' He removed a takeaway container from the plastic bag between them. 'Say hi to Jake for me, won't you?'

———

'Where's Adam?' her father asked the following lunchtime, once she'd met up with him at a café. Sometimes she felt like a yo-yo, moving to and fro between her parents. 'You did tell him he was welcome, didn't you?'

Emily prodded at an egg yolk. 'He's going on some mega bike ride.' It wasn't a lie, but it wasn't an honest answer to her father's question either.

The truth is, I never asked him. I didn't really want to know the answer.

'He really loves that bike,' Jim said, just as Bradley said, 'hey, can I have an advance on my pocket money?'

'What for?' Their father set his coffee cup down.

'Damien and I were going to catch a movie this afternoon.'

'Have you finished your homework?' Jim nodded at an elderly couple squeezing past their table before turning his attention back to Bradley.

Bradley scowled. 'I've got all night for that.'

Their father's eyebrows drew together. 'This is an important year, Bradley.'

'Every year is important.'

'Especially when you're trying to get into uni.'

'Who said I wanted to go to uni?'

Jim set his fork down. 'I thought we'd talked about this.'

'*You* talked about this.' Bradley ran a hand through his blond mop-top. 'I don't see the point.'

Here we go, Emily thought, glancing around the café to see if anyone else could hear her brother and father sniping at each other.

'The *point* is that no one will hire you as a computer programmer without a degree,' Jim said.

'Why go to uni for three years and spend heaps of money to learn what I already know?' Bradley sucked the remnants of his milkshake through his straw, the gurgling so loud Emily had to restrain herself from kicking him beneath the table.

'Do you have to do that?' Emily arranged her serviette over the remnants of her lunch, hoping her father hadn't noticed that she'd barely touched her eggs Benedict.

'Waste not, want not.' Bradley dragged her plate towards him before the waiter could clear it away. 'Why do you always hide your food under a serviette?'

'Why didn't you ever learn any manners?' Emily snapped.

'Why can't you stop bitching at each other?' Jim balled up his serviette, and threw it onto his plate. 'Christ, anyone would think you were still seven and ten rather than . . .' He gestured at them. 'Twenty-one and seventeen.'

Bradley swallowed loudly. 'I'm not seventeen until next month.'

'Whatever. And stop changing the subject. If you don't go to uni, you'll regret it for the rest of your life.'

'I think you're wrong.' Bradley shovelled the last of Emily's bacon into his mouth. 'You wait, in ten years I'll be better off, rather than — how big is your student loan now, Em?'

'None of your business.'

'I rest my case.' Her brother stood up, still chewing, and pushed in his chair. 'Gotta go, Damien's picking me up in ten. About that advance . . .'

Their father gave him a steely look. 'I'm not sure you've earned it.'

'God, do you have to be such a—'

'Don't say it,' Jim said, his voice taut. 'Or I'll be deducting pocket money, do you hear me?'

'Whatever,' Bradley said, shooting Emily a filthy look.

Jim exhaled. 'Do you think he winds me up on purpose?' He asked, once the door had swung shut behind Bradley. Outside, the tops of the trees were swirling in the wind, like the poi Emily had swung around her wrists at school.

'Probably.' Emily wasn't in the mood to talk about Bradley's future. Her own was frightening enough. 'Um, Dad?'

'Hmm?' Her father's focus had shifted to an article in the Sunday newspaper, which had the horrific title of 'Sex Begins At Forty'.

'Did you always want to be a doctor?'

Her father took his glasses off. 'Well, yes. I couldn't imagine doing anything else. Why?'

'Because,' Emily chose her words with care, 'I'm starting to think I'd rather do *anything* else.'

His brow furrowed. 'We all feel like that sometimes. It can be a bit unsettling when you first start rotating around the wards, but I'm sure things will settle down for you soon.'

'But what if they don't?' *What if I make a mistake and kill someone? What if someone else wants me to end their life and I'm not strong enough to resist, just like last time?*

'They will.' Her father stood up. 'Are you going to come home for a bit?'

'No, I said I'd meet up with Jake to help him with his anatomy.'

'Really? What does Adam think of that?'

'Why should he think anything of that?' Emily snapped, before realising her father was joking.

'You really do have a short fuse this morning, don't you?' her father said. They exited the café. The air was damp, thick clouds hanging low in a colourless sky. 'Is everything OK with you and Adam?'

'Everything is fine,' Emily said. 'Just fine.'

'So you want to quit?' Jake asked. They were sitting on the floor of the lounge in his flat, an atlas of human anatomy between them.

'I don't know. I mean, I liked learning about this stuff,' Emily gestured at the atlas, open to a picture of a cadaver's grey-brown abdominal organs, 'but I don't like sticking needles in people, or having to recite lists of differential diagnoses in front of everyone. It's like I get stage fright.'

Jake leaned against the wall. 'You could be a psychiatrist.'

'I don't want to be a psychiatrist. Anyway, it's not just the stage fright thing. I'm scared I'll get it wrong and kill someone.'

'Some people die no matter what you do,' Jake said, and they both fell silent for a moment. He cleared his throat. 'Research?'

'Boring.'

'Right, so how about . . . Oh yeah, you could quit.'

'You make it sound so easy.'

'But isn't that what you're thinking? Should I stay or should I go?' Jake plucked a Rubik's Cube off the hearth beside him and began to rotate the coloured squares around each other.

'That's a song, isn't it?'

'The Clash,' Jake said. They smiled at each other, and Emily felt a lightening inside her chest.

'I've got a mnemonic,' she said. 'To memorise the cranial nerves. Well, it's not mine. I think it's been around for years.'

'*Oh, oh, oh.*' Jake looked up at the ceiling. '*To touch and feel a virgin girl's—*'

'So you *do* know it.'

'Olfactory, optic, oculomotor,' he recited. 'Trochlear, trigeminal, abducens, facial . . . how am I doing?'

'OK, OK.' Emily pushed the atlas towards him. 'I don't think you need my help at all.'

'I'd much rather recite pornographic mnemonics than stare at photos of dead people's insides.' He stroked the embossed letters on the front cover. 'Don't want to hold you up, though.'

'You're not holding me up.' Emily stood up and moved to the window.

The rain had come and gone, and the sun was sinking fast. 'Do you want to go for a walk?'

Jake stretched. 'A walk,' he said. 'OK.'

———

By the time they reached the top of the steepest street in the world, the sun was setting, the clouds ablaze.

'Red sky at night,' Jake said, sitting in the middle of the road. No cars at the top, just houses that appeared as though they were about to slide off the side of the hill.

'Shepherd's delight.' Emily perched beside him. 'Do you think that's true?'

'I dunno. Red sky in the morning makes sense. Rain coming.' His face was aglow, his eyes dark. 'What's Adam up to?'

'I have no idea.' Her voice was measured, but her heart had sped up. Adam might have texted her. He might have, but Emily hadn't checked her phone since she'd arrived at Jake's flat three hours earlier. She was happy to be caught in a time warp, a bubble of impossibility.

'Some of us are going to the rugby next week, if you and Adam want to come.'

'I'll ask him,' Emily said, knowing she'd do nothing of the sort. 'Have you spoken to your dad recently?'

'No, why would I do that?' Jake rolled a pebble down the gradient. They watched it bounce a few times before disappearing into a shrub. 'We only talk to each other at weddings and funerals. Haven't had one of those in a while.'

He picked up another stone, and she watched him balance it on the tip of a finger before flicking it away. She held up her own hand.

'Steady as,' Jake said, nudging her.

'It's not.'

'You should stop thinking so hard.'

'You can talk.'

'You're not the one with maggoty genes,' he said, and she laughed. Jake let out a low chuckle and nudged her. She gave him a playful shove, and

37

he grabbed her by the arm, and before she knew it, she was lying beneath him. Beneath him, but the only part of his body that was touching hers was his hand, pinning her wrist to the road. She felt her pulse beneath his fingers, her blood surging through her ears.

'Say mercy.' His breath was warm on her cheek.

Emily tilted her chin up. 'Never.' What would she do if he tried to kiss her? Hit him, probably.

'You suck.' Jake released her and turned onto his back. They lay like that for several minutes, watching the stars wink on, one by one. Emily imagined the earth turning beneath her, imagined spinning off into space.

'Jake,' she said after ten minutes, maybe more, 'do you believe in fate?'

There was a brief silence. Then Jake said, 'No, not at all. Do you?'

'No,' she said. 'I don't.'

Chapter 5: Scar Tissue

Not everyone enjoyed dissection classes, but Jake loved them. Entering the lab, lined row upon row with gurneys on which white-sheeted bodies lay, made him feel as if he were being inducted into a secret club. Even the scent of formaldehyde didn't bother him. And when he drew the sheet back, his scalpel ready, he felt as though his dreams were in reach at last.

Doctor Heremaia.

No, *Mister* Heremaia, because once he was a surgeon, then he wouldn't use a doctor title anymore. He remembered Emily's father telling him why this was so, when he was twelve — something to do with barbers being the earliest surgeons, no medical degree required — and then he remembered the exact moment when he'd decided to become a surgeon, too, when watching a deliciously gruesome heart transplant on the grainy TV in his grandmother's lounge.

'What do the instructions say?' Jake asked, without looking up. He knew William Koo would be standing right behind him, just as he knew William would be quite happy to stand aside and let his classmates do the dissection.

A squawk behind him made him jump. Jake gave his red-haired classmate an acid look. 'Jesus, Kyles, I nearly sliced my thumb off just then.'

'Oops, sorry.' Kylie sidled up next to him. William read out, 'Make a vertical incision from the xiphoid process to the pubic symphysis.'

'Xiphoid process.' Jake prodded the protuberance at the base of the breastbone with his gloved finger before pressing his scalpel down. The leathery skin parted beneath the blade, like peeling a banana. Saving the food reference to tell Emily later, he followed William's next instruction to *make four horizontal incisions in the skin and reflect it laterally*.

Kylie peered over his shoulder. 'Did they say to leave the belly button behind?'

'I think so.' Jake took the instruction sheet off William to check before passing it to Kylie. 'Do you want to go next?'

'No, I can wait a few minutes,' she said. 'Are you going to the rugby tomorrow night?'

'Hell, yeah,' Jake murmured, exposing the abdominal muscles. 'Otago versus Canterbury, can't wait.'

'We're having pre-drinks at my flat, if you want to come over.' She nudged William. 'You too.'

'Thanks, but I have revision to do.' William was so predictable.

'Don't we all?' Kylie peered into the abdomen. 'Ugh, look at that fat.'

'Creamed corn,' they all said in unison, and Kylie let out another squawk.

'Has anyone ever told you that you sound like a chicken?' William asked, and Jake started laughing, until he realised his phone was vibrating in his pocket. He peeled his gloves off, but didn't manage to answer in time. A missed call from Auntie Ngaire, what was she calling him for?

His phone beeped: *Call 707 to hear one new voice message.*

'Are you OK?' Kylie asked.

'Yeah, won't be long.' After washing his hands, Jake left the lab and dialled his voice mail.

'Kia ora, Jake.' Auntie Ngaire's panicky tone alone was enough to set him on edge, even before he listened to the rest of the message. 'Just letting you know your dad's been admitted to Whangārei Hospital. He blacked out, and they said it's his heart, pretty serious I think. Give us a ring, eh? Or call your dad.'

'Fuck.' Jake glanced longingly toward the tall double doors at the end of the corridor. He could pretend he hadn't received the message yet and return to his dissection class. Or he could pretend he'd *never* received the message. How would she know?

Auntie Ngaire *would* know, though. And then what? He'd look heartless, like he didn't care about the old man.

I don't *care.*

I don't.

Fuck.

He sank onto the top stair and called his father's sister. Auntie Ngaire answered on the fourth ring, damn it, before he could hang up and congratulate himself for his cursory efforts.

'Kia ora, Jake. Thanks for calling back.'

'How is he?' Jake wasn't sure what he wanted the answer to be.

'Ah, they want to transfer him to Auckland, said he needs urgent cardiac bypass surgery. Four vessel disease, they said.'

'It's all that smoking.'

'Well, it hasn't helped.' Auntie Ngaire sounded close to tears. 'Doc said it was lucky he came in when he did.'

'Yeah, lucky.' His head and heart thudded in unison, blood coursing through his ears. He imagined all the blood vessels in his brain dilating, an instant migraine. 'Um, is he OK? Did they say—'

'He's on a heart monitor, but they think he'll be OK. As long as he gets his vessels replumbed, that is.' She let out a barking laugh.

Should I come up? The words formed and burst before he could release them. He couldn't afford it, anyway. Financially. Emotionally.

'I'll call him,' he said. 'But I can't right now, so can you tell him I said . . . Anyway, I'll ring him. Later.'

His auntie's voice softened. 'He'd love that. How are you, anyway? Things going OK down there?'

'They're good. I've got to go — talk soon, OK?'

Jake ended the call and sat staring at his phone. He heard Kylie's distant cackle, the echo of voices down the corridor to his left. Flicking through his messages, he found the last text from Emily.

Sure, happy to help with the anatomy. Shall I bring snacks?

That had been Saturday, five long days ago.

Jake's thumb moved over the keypad, quick strokes. He sent the message, checked his watch. Thirty minutes until the lab finished. After jogging down the stairs and outside, he walked into the nearest supermarket and bought a packet of cigarettes. Then he wandered around the block as he smoked two cigarettes, one after the other.

His phone buzzed. It was Emily.

Sure. See you around 4.30.

———

'So, are you going to call him?' They were sitting in the kitchen at Emily's flat, a plunger of coffee on the table between them.

Jake poured more coffee into his chipped mug, which said, somewhat ironically, *World's Best Dad.* 'Tonight. Maybe. I dunno.' He added milk and two teaspoons of sugar. 'I wish there was a way of making him think I'd called him without talking to him. Or making Auntie Ngaire think I called him.'

'Is that the aunt you stayed with in Auckland?'

'No, that was Auntie Huia. Auntie Ngaire's Dad's youngest sister. She lives in Whangārei, about fifty ks from Dad.' He watched the granules dissolve into the liquid. 'They don't get on. Dad and Huia, I mean.'

'Sounds like it runs in the family.' Emily passed him another gingernut biscuit. 'OK, so let's say your aunt — Ngaire — thinks you called him. Would you feel guilty if something really bad happened and you hadn't contacted him?'

'Like if he died?' Jake dipped the biscuit in his coffee. 'Good riddance.' He slouched into his chair. 'Yeah, nah. I don't know. Fuck it, why do parents have to be so complicated?'

'What's that saying, blood's thicker than water?' Emily moved into the lounge. A moment later, he heard 'Scar Tissue' emanating from the stereo.

'Ah, Red Hot Chili Peppers.' He tipped his chair back against the wall.

Emily reappeared. 'We used to listen to them in the park, remember?' Her leg was bent, stork-like, her foot planted on the doorframe.

'I remember.' He remembered blood. He remembered water.

Just fill the syringe with water. That'll work, right?

'If you phone him,' she said, 'then you'll feel better. Even though it's hard. You'll be the bigger person, right?'

'You haven't seen my dad's beer gut.' Jake smirked into his coffee. He felt like another smoke. He felt like kissing Emily. Both seemed equally inappropriate right then. 'I haven't asked you how your day was.'

Emily shrugged. 'Pretty standard.'

'As in, you hated every moment of it?'

'Not every moment.' She took a seat again. 'Just the bit when I had to present my clinical case to the class, and I got so nervous I forgot my differential diagnosis. Bet I lost at least half my marks for that one.'

'Maybe you should talk to Prof what's-his-name?'

'Wagner. Are you kidding? This is surgery, survival of the fittest. Weaklings get weeded out quick-smart. I'm surprised I haven't been already.'

'Survival of the fittest, really? Jesus, I'd be a failure before I even started.'

'You don't know that.'

'Well, anyway, is there someone else you can talk to?' He took another gingernut out of the packet and rolled it across the table towards her. 'Maybe not an old-school doctor. There must be some younger doctors around. Or your dad?'

'He wasn't so receptive the other day,' Emily mumbled.

Jake touched her wrist. 'Hey,' he said. 'I think you'll make a good doctor.'

'I think you're lying.' A tear rolled down her cheek. Crap, now what? He pulled his chair closer and gave her a sideways hug.

'You know what? It's not the end of the world if you decide to quit med school. Really.' And now he was close, so close, and he could smell the apple scent of her hair, the salty scent of her distress.

'Tell my dad that, then.'

'I will if you want me to.'

She lifted her chin. 'Maybe not such a good idea.'

'I don't even know if he likes me actually,' he said, and she frowned at him, and then someone said, 'Am I interrupting something?'

Jake shifted away. Emily said, 'No, we were just . . . talking.' Her eyes, Jake knew, were red. And wet. And not looking at him, or Adam. As if they'd been doing something wrong.

'I can come back.' Adam's syllables were clipped. 'If you like.'

Jake sensed Emily tense; could almost feel his own muscles coiling, ready to strike. 'She's upset,' he said, standing up. 'You might want to do something about that.'

'Jake,' Emily called after him.

Pretending he hadn't heard her, Jake loped down the hallway and into the woodsmoke-scented air.

———

Nine pm. Jake on the desk in his room, blowing smoke rings out of his window. Nate would kill him if he found Jake had been smoking inside. Still, what Nate didn't know wouldn't hurt him.

You're wrong. What you don't know can hurt you. A lot.

He held up a hand, watching the fine tremor with a dispassionate eye. Steady as, until he started thinking about his old man.

Jake stubbed the butt out on his empty Coke can and picked up his phone. As he stabbed his father's number into the keypad, blood began to rush through his ears, thud-thud-thud. Too much nicotine. Too much caffeine. *Too much, too much, too much.*

The phone rang. It rang and rang and rang. Eventually, his father's voice came over the line.

Hey, it's Willie. I can't come to the phone right now. Leave a message.

Jake cleared his throat. Put the Nokia down. Picked it up again.

'Hey,' he said. 'I heard about the heart attack. I was . . . thinking about you. Guess you must be asleep.' Or having a cardiac arrest.

What if he was?

What. If. He. Was.

'Um, so I'll ring later,' he lied, and ended the call. Lit another cigarette. Listened to a pair of cats fighting outside. Thought about studying. Thought about the difference between want and need, and how sometimes the two were completely inseparable.

Long minutes later, he texted Emily: *Everything OK with you and Adam?*

She didn't reply.

Chapter 6: Street Spirit (Fade Out)

Mandy tapped her pen on her dentistry textbook. 'So, I just made a major decision.'

'A major decision?' Emily asked, not looking away from the TV, where a man and a woman who had only met ten minutes ago were about to get married. 'Has this got anything to do with Ian?'

'Ian? No, God, that's still . . .' Mandy frowned. 'Work in progress. Anyway, I got an e-mail from a friend of a friend in Christchurch today. I was asking him about maxillofacial surgery — he's halfway through his training — and I'm going to apply.'

'Whoa.' Adam was sitting next to Emily on the saggy couch. So close, but so far away. They'd barely spoken since their heated discussion in the ten minutes they'd had alone before Mandy had arrived home.

Why couldn't you talk to me about that? Did you think I wouldn't understand?

I didn't mean to start crying in front of him. And I'm sorry, but I don't think you do understand.

Emily zoned back in to hear her flatmate say, 'Three years of medical school once I finish my dentistry degree, but I think it'd be fun. What do you reckon?'

'I think you'd make a great max fax surgeon.' Adam laid his arm across the top of the couch. 'High heels and all.'

'I can't imagine those would be very comfortable to operate in,' Emily said, unable to help noticing how Adam's gaze had strayed to Mandy's legs just then.

Nothing wrong with a bit of window shopping, Adam had said, when Emily had caught him eyeing up one of the freshers the other day. *You do it all the time. Movies don't count*, she'd retorted, but Adam had already stopped listening. As usual.

'I wouldn't wear them to theatre.' Mandy stretched. 'But on ward rounds, sure. What do you want to specialise in, Emily?'

'No idea.' Emily stood up. 'Excuse me.'

Emily didn't really need to go the loo. She did need to go to her room afterwards though, where she spent at least ten minutes searching for her sketchpad. Eventually she found it beneath her bed, along with several used tissues and a shoe with a broken heel. Sitting on her haunches, she wiped dust off the cover with her sleeve and turned to the first page.

'Double helix dragon,' she murmured.

'Were you planning on returning to the lounge?' Adam was standing in the doorway.

Emily bit her lip. 'Sorry, I kind of lost track of time.'

'Looks like it.' Adam pushed away from the doorframe with his foot. 'I'm going to take off, might catch you tomorrow night.'

'I'm going to the rugby,' she reminded him, but he was already gone. She sat very still, staring at the dragons in her last sketch. Then she flipped to a blank page, found a pencil on her desk, and began to draw.

———

Ot-aaa-go. The crowd was drumming their feet on the ground, the home-team fans waving yellow and gold banners and scarfs.

'When did you last go to the rugby, Jake?' Emily exhaled, watching her breath hover before dissipating into the almost-freezing air. The air was crystalline, mist forming ghostly haloes around the stadium lights.

'Not since I left here.' Jake raised his cup to his lips. On the other side of him, Mandy raised her arms in a Mexican wave, and Emily and Jake joined in.

'You spilt beer on my shoes,' Emily complained to Jake, although she was pretty sure she'd have worse spilt on her by the end of the night.

Ian yanked his curly gold and blue wig over his ears. 'Lick it off, dude.'

'I'm not that desperate,' Jake murmured, adjusting his own wig. Hugging herself, Emily stamped her feet, wishing she'd thought to wear another layer beneath her jacket. Stupid, what had she been thinking?

'You cold, Walsh?'

'A bit.' Emily touched Jake's neck.

'Jesus, that's colder than a—'

'Please don't say "witch's tit",' Mandy said, huddling closer to Ian. 'I hate that saying.'

'I would never.' Jake sounded wounded.

'Witch's nipple, then,' Ian said, gulping on his beer, then yelped. 'That's abuse, that is.'

'Some call it foreplay,' Jake said, dodging Mandy's scarf when it came flying towards him. Emily took her buzzing phone out of her jacket pocket.

Adam: *Sorry about last night. Work must be making me grumpy. Want to go for a drive tomorrow?*

Emily hesitated. *I would but have study ++ to do. Can we catch up tomorrow night? A movie?*

Her phone buzzed again: *OK . . . Got a movie in mind?*

Not worried, you choose. She pressed send and turned her attention to the field, where the Highlanders were running on.

'Ot-aaa-go,' she bellowed, before joining in on another Mexican wave.

———

Two hours later, they joined the throngs of rugby fans streaming down the streets of South Dunedin. Emily was wishing she hadn't drunk so much beer. She was busting for a pee.

'Man, it's cold,' she said, for about the twentieth time that night.

'Come to the pub.' Mandy hooked an elbow through Emily's and dragged her towards a very long line outside the Fox and Hound. 'Bound to be warm in here.'

'I think I've had enough to drink.'

'Have a Coke, then.' Mandy glanced at the guys, who were ambling towards them, having a heated debate about whether cats were better than dogs.

'Dogs are so needy,' Jake was saying.

Ian took a swig from his can of beer. 'Yeah, but they're really loyal. Cats will just turn around and stab you in the back.'

'Cats don't have hands.' Jake's eyes were glittering, his speech slightly slurred.

'Whatever,' Ian said, draining the can and crushing it before drop-kicking it across the road. 'Cats will love you and leave you. Dogs are always there for you.'

'I agree.' Mandy wrapped her scarf around her neck. 'And they keep you fit, because you have to walk them every day.'

'Yeah, but you have to pick up their turds,' Jake said. 'What do you reckon, Em?'

'Sorry, I'm siding with the dogs.' Emily shuffled towards the front of the line. Her bladder felt as though it had swelled to the size of a watermelon.

Ian belched. 'Well, that's it then. You're incompatible.'

'Damn it.' Jake gave Emily a sideways grin.

'Foiled again,' Emily bantered, her face suddenly warm.

There was a cackle from behind them and someone threw their arms around Jake's neck. 'Hel-lo, where have you been hiding?'

'Right here in this line.' Jake clinked his bottle against the girl's. 'Guys, this is Kylie from my med class.'

'Hey,' Emily said, wondering if Kylie was always that loud.

Swaying slightly, Jake said, 'Meet Emily, Ian and Mandy.'

'Hi, nice to meet you,' Kylie squawked before tugging on Jake's elbow. 'Come up the front, we're nearly in.'

'Oh, I don't want to push—'

'It's OK, I know the bouncer,' Kylie said, dragging him away.

'I know the bouncer,' Emily mimicked in a low voice, and Mandy laughed.

'Meow,' Ian said. 'Ow! Why is everyone always hitting me?'

Emily scowled at the front of the line, where Jake was disappearing inside with the loud redheaded girl.

'I had to hit *someone*,' she muttered.

Once inside, Emily endured another long line for the women's toilets, which smelt of vomit. Afterwards, she found the others standing by a window overlooking the street.

'Oh, I'm definitely a dog person,' Kylie was saying, so loudly that everyone else in the crowded room could hear her. 'Just ask my sister, she's always calling me a bitch.' When she started laughing, everyone joined in — everyone except for Emily, who snatched Mandy's cider off her and drained a third of it in one go.

'You all right?' Mandy asked in a loud whisper.

'Never been better.' Emily checked her phone. Perhaps she should ask Adam to pick her up. He could be asleep, though, and he hated being woken up. 'Here, I'll get you another one of these.'

'Don't worry, I think I'll save myself the hangover.' Mandy squinted. 'Where are the toilets?'

Emily pointed and Mandy took off.

Letting the conversation flow over her, Emily slumped against the windowsill. Kylie really was quite funny. Emily might have joined in on the laughter if she weren't feeling—

What?

I'm not.

'What do you do, Emily?' Kylie asked during a brief lull in the conversation.

'I'm a med student too,' Emily said. 'Fourth year.' For the first time, she noticed Kylie was wearing yellow buckle shoes with blue bows.

Kylie adjusted her glasses. 'Are you enjoying being on the wards?'

'No.'

'Emily's boyfriend's a doctor,' Jake said, giving Emily an odd look before brushing past her and heading in the same direction Mandy had gone.

Kylie twirled a fiery lock around her finger. 'What's he specialising in?'

'He's still a junior doctor.' Emily relented a little. 'He wants to be a plastic surgeon.'

'That must be a really hard speciality to get into.'

'I guess.' Was it too early to make an excuse to go to the loo again? Surely not. 'Um, I'll see you soon.'

'Sure.' Kylie beamed at Ian. 'How about you, Dog Boy?'

'I don't think anyone's ever called me that before,' Emily heard Ian say as she wound her way between several groups of loud, inebriated, students. Once she'd reached a quieter spot she called Adam anyway, despite the late hour. It went straight to answerphone.

After going to the toilet again, which used up another ten minutes, Emily looked around and saw that the others had claimed a table and chairs opposite the bar. Mandy and Ian were facing away from her, while Kylie was perched sideways on Jake's lap. They were all in hysterics, as if Kylie had just said something hilarious. Did she ever stop?

Emily whirled around and hurried past the bar, past the bouncers at the door, and outside. The cold air slapped her cheeks. She crossed the road without looking right or left, and began the long walk home.

———

She'd barely walked a block before she heard footsteps behind her and a familiar clearing of the throat.

'Hey.' Jake jogged to catch up. 'Could have told us you were leaving.'

'Sorry. I didn't want to interrupt.'

'You shouldn't walk home by yourself.'

'This is Dunedin, not Auckland. It's perfectly safe.'

'Hmm.' Jake gazed up at the sky. 'I can see the Southern Cross.'

'Well, that's a surprise.'

'Are you pissed off at me?'

'Why would I be pissed off at you?' Emily tried to keep her voice even. 'You should go back to the pub. Kylie might be missing you.'

'*Kylie?* I don't think so.'

'Are you blind? She was sitting on your lap, for God's sake.'

'There were only three chairs.'

Emily gritted her teeth. 'So why wasn't Mandy sitting on Ian's knee?'

'Sorry I didn't consult you for a seating plan first.' Jake kicked at a stone, sending it flying into the gutter.

'You don't have to walk me home.'

'But I am,' Jake said, and they continued in silence for the next three kilometres, all the way to her flat.

'Shit,' Emily said, digging around in the pockets of her jacket, her jeans, and finally, in an exercise of complete futility, beneath the doormat. Mandy *never* left the key outside.

'You've lost your key?'

'I think I left it inside.' *Great, a perfect end to a perfect night, not.*

Jake wandered around the side of the house. 'Any windows open?'

'Of course not, Mandy's a security freak.' They checked anyway. No windows open.

'No way through,' Jake said helpfully. Emily groaned and sank onto the doorstep.

'Think Mandy will go to your place tonight?'

'I have no idea.' Jake held up his phone. 'Could text Ian, except — my phone's flat, have you got his number?'

'Why would I have his number?' An all-over body shiver had set in. Emily was pretty sure her lips had turned blue. She tried to ring Mandy instead, but there was no answer.

Jake took off his jacket and hung it over her shoulders. 'Come to my flat. I'll sleep on the couch, no big deal.'

Emily wanted to resist. Would have, if it were ten degrees warmer.

———

It took another fifteen minutes to get to Jake's flat, by which time Emily was busting, *again*. After peeing, she brushed her teeth with her finger and someone's toothpaste before going to Jake's room. Jake was sitting on his bed, wrestling his shoes off.

'Here.' He took a spare pillow off the bed and stood up. 'I don't have an electric blanket, sorry.'

'I'll be fine.' Emily crawled beneath the blankets, clothes and all, and pulled the duvet up to her chin. 'Thanks.'

'Any time.' Jake hovered. 'Do you need anything else?'

'No . . .' Emily turned onto her side, gazing at the CDs stacked on the floor beside the bed. 'Oh. Hey.' She took the top CD off the pile and held it out. 'Haven't listened to them in ages.'

'Thought you didn't like Radiohead.'

'I never said that. I like "Creep" anyway, can we listen to that one? If it's not too late for you, that is?' What was the time? After midnight, for sure.

'It's never too late to listen to Radiohead.' Jake fed the CD into the stereo and pushed play. 'Shuffle over, Walsh. Light on or off?'

'Definitely off.' Emily yawned.

Jake flipped the light switch and lay beside her. 'Jesus, it's cold.'

'Have some duvet, I won't bite.'

'Yeah, right, Dog Girl,' he said, and they both got the giggles.

'You could have stayed at the pub,' Emily said, after they'd listened to three songs. 'I didn't mean to ruin your thing with Kylie.'

'There's no thing with Kylie.' Jake sounded drowsy, as if he were on the verge of falling asleep. 'She's just a friend.'

'Like me?'

'No,' he said softly. 'Not like you.'

Her cheeks burning, Emily stared into the darkness until 'Street Spirit (Fade Out)' had drawn to a close. 'Jake?'

'Hmm?' Had she woken him up?

'Did you talk to your dad?'

'I tried,' he said, sounding more awake now. 'But he never rang back. Auntie Ngaire said he needs a quadruple bypass.'

'Whoa. Will you visit him?'

'I dunno. Don't think so.'

They fell silent again. Emily closed her eyes, drifting. She woke an indeterminate time later, shivering, and felt the mattress shift as Jake rolled towards her.

'Cold?' He draped a long arm over her chest.

'Not now,' she said, a heady sense of déjà vu washing over her as his warmth seeped into her, as his familiar scent filled her nostrils; musk and smoke and Jake, Jake, Jake.

What are you going to do now?

I'll call the doctor. When it's light.

'I'm not trying to take advantage of you,' he murmured. 'For the record.'

'Never thought you were,' she said, not sure whether to feel disappointed or relieved.

'That's not to say—' he began, and halted.

'What?'

'Nothing,' he said. 'Go to sleep.' But she felt his heart pounding against her back, and she wondered. She wondered, she wondered.

Eventually her brain began to slow again. When she woke next, a cold dawn was breaking, and Jake wasn't there.

Chapter 7: Creep

Ian dumped three teaspoons of coffee in his mug and filled it with boiling water. 'So Emily spent the night in your bed and nothing happened.'

Jake contemplated his own coffee and added another teaspoon. 'We listened to Radiohead. That was a happening.'

'Did you not even slip her the tongue?'

Jake balled up a piece of paper and flicked it at his flatmate. 'No, I didn't slip her the fucking tongue. What about you and Mandy?'

'Well, we weren't being all *platonic*.' Ian made quotation marks with his fingers.

'Emily has a boyfriend, in case you hadn't noticed.' *Who treats her like shit, but who I am to say anything?*

'You're such a gentleman.'

'Piss off. It doesn't pay to screw your friends, anyway.' Jake gulped on his coffee, removing at least half the lining from his throat. 'Anyway, Radiohead. It was a beautiful thing.'

'You're deluded, mate.'

'It helps.' Jake checked his phone. It was two o'clock, five hours since Emily had left, and she hadn't texted him yet. Had he done something wrong? She hadn't seemed annoyed before she left.

'I was thinking of doing an overnight hike in the Catlins, are you keen?'

'When?' Jake re-read the most recent text he'd sent to Emily: *Need some fresh air? Off to the beach later if you want to come.*

'Next week?'

'Next week?'

'It's the holidays, remember? Unless you've got something better to do, that is?'

'I don't think so. I mean sure,' Jake said, jumping when a reply came through at last.

Emily: *OK, pick me up on your way past?*

Sure, Jake replied. *See you in about an hour.*

'You'll need your winter woollies. Might get snow.'

'Can't be any colder than this flat.' Jake went to have a shower.

———

Jake had just climbed into his car when his phone started ringing. Was Emily cancelling on him? Maybe she'd had a better offer from Adam. He wrestled the Nokia out of his front jeans pocket, his heart sinking when he saw the caller ID.

He didn't feel like talking to his old man right now. Not now, not ever.

'Hey, Dad.'

Willie Heremaia's voice boomed into his ear. 'Missed your call the other night.'

'Figured you must be busy.' Jake watched a pair of dreadlocked students trudging past holding a crate of beer between them. His stomach squirmed. He'd had way too much to drink last night, and why?

Because of the arsehole on the other end of this phone, that's why.

'Got transferred to Auckland Hospital last night.'

'Auckland, why?'

'Have to stay here until I get my bypass. I'm on the urgent waiting list.'

'Congratulations,' Jake said, and winced. He hadn't meant to sound . . . Well, maybe he had. 'I mean, that's good, I guess. Did they tell you to give up smoking?'

Willie snorted. 'What do you think?'

'And have you?'

'I'm wearing nicotine patches,' his father said, which was probably about all Jake was going to get out of him. 'When are you coming for a visit?'

'I only just got here.'

'Really? Thought you left four months ago.' His father started coughing.

'Costs heaps to fly up there. I'll come at the end of the year.'

His father hurrumphed. 'Might be dead by then.'

'That's a bit melodramatic, isn't it?'

'Mel-o-dram-atic,' his father mocked. 'Are those the kind of big words they like to teach you at uni? I had to get shocked back to life a few days ago, did your Auntie Ngaire tell you that?'

'So you've already returned from the dead then,' Jake said.

Why am I being such an arsehole?

Takes one to know one.

'More's the pity,' his father said, and the phone line went dead, *Jesus.* Snarling, Jake threw his phone onto the passenger seat, turned the key in the ignition and planted his foot. The car jumped.

'Take the handbrake off, you dumbarse,' Jake said, doing just that before peeling down the street and around the corner. Seconds later, he heard the whoop of a siren, and saw red and blue lights flashing in his mirror.

His day just got better and better.

———

A short time later, Emily and Jake strolled along the beach holding their coffees. Not that Jake could afford the coffee. Not that he cared right then.

'Eighty bucks for eleven ks over the speed limit?' Emily asked. 'That sucks.'

Jake took a morose sip of his coffee. 'Well I couldn't flash him a bit of leg, could I?'

'What, you mean you didn't try?' When Jake didn't return her smile, she shrugged. 'Just add it to your student loan.'

'Yeah, why not?' He squinted into the watery sun. 'I need a job.'

'Isn't study keeping you busy enough?'

'Sure, but I won't finish med school if I can't afford my rent.' He exhaled. 'Or flights to Auckland.'

'You're going to see your dad?'

'Suppose I should.' Jake was still smarting from the conversation with his old man. *Are those the kind of big words they like to teach you at uni? I had to get shocked back to life a few days ago, did your Auntie Ngaire tell you that?*

Why *hadn't* Auntie Ngaire told him that? Would it have made a difference? Apparently it did, as there was no way Jake would be considering flying up there otherwise.

'He nearly died a few days ago,' he said. 'Had to get defibrillated, apparently.'

'Whoa.' Emily slid her sunglasses on. She was looking remarkably fresh for someone who'd been somewhat pissed the night before. Jake wished he'd thought to bring *his* sunglasses. His vision was starting to shimmer around the edges with the tell-tale wavy lines.

'Well,' she said. 'I think you're doing the right thing.'

'I don't know if I ever end up doing the right thing.' Jake felt suddenly, inexplicably, close to tears. He hadn't cried for years, not since *that* night.

I think we did it.

Yeah. I think we did.

'Who does?' Emily took the lid off her cup and darted her tongue out to the foam on the rim. 'You stopped me from freezing to death last night.'

'True.' He wished she'd stop running her tongue around the cup like that. Migraine aura or no, it was really quite distracting.

'Where did you go this morning?' Emily asked.

'I needed a walk. To clear my head.'

'Like now?' Emily snapped the lid on.

'Yeah, sort of.' He massaged his temples. 'Also, you were snoring.'

Her mouth fell open. 'I was *not.*'

'How would you know? You were asleep.'

Emily elbowed him and Jake elbowed her back before sinking onto his butt in the sand.

'Urrgh,' he said, watching the flashes in the periphery of his vision.

'What's up?'

'Migraine,' he said, and threw up.

———

Emily indicated and turned right. 'I didn't know you got migraines.'

'Only for the last three years or so.' Jake's vision was all jagged edges, green and yellow flashes of light. He closed his eyes. 'Thanks for driving me home. You can take the car if you want, return it tomorrow.'

'It's OK, I can walk home.'

'Seriously. I'm not driving anywhere like this.'

'I'm not sure having your car at my house is such a good idea.' She slowed for a roundabout. Jake decided he didn't like roundabouts very much. Or going around corners. Or anything apart from a darkened room. He wound down the window.

'Because of Adam?'

'You guessed it.'

'S'pose you haven't told him where you spent last night, then?'

'Would you, if you were me?'

'Maybe not.' He wanted to ask her why she was with Adam. He wanted to ask her what she'd have done if he'd kissed her last night. But now even his speech was turning to mush. Christ, he hadn't had one this bad in ages.

'Are you sure you're all right?'

'Just need to lie down,' he mumbled. His left eye was streaming. If only he'd replaced the migraine medication he used to keep in the car. By the time they reached his flat the throbbing in his left temple had started, so intense he chucked up again in the gutter.

'Been on the turps?' He heard Ian say as Emily led him to his room.

'No, he's got a migraine. Do you need a bowl, Jake?'

'Curtains,' he mumbled. 'Dark. Injection.' He yanked open his top desk drawer and flopped onto the bed. Every heartbeat was an explosion behind his eyes.

I blame you, Dad, you you you.

Also, the beer.

Emily sat beside him, inspecting the syringe. 'What is it, sumatriptan?'

'Uh-huh. I can do. It.' Yeah, who was he kidding? If only he'd been able to inject it before the migraine sank its claws into him.

'I'll give it to you.' Emily said, suddenly sounding very professional. She touched his shoulder. 'Here OK?'

'Uh-huh.' Jake barely felt the needle go in. She pressed over the injection site.

'Do you want me to stay for a bit, make sure you're OK?'

'No.' *I do, I do.*

'I'll get Ian to check you in a bit then.'

'Thanks.' He heard her draw the curtains, plunging the room into blessed darkness. 'Em?'

'Yeah?' Her voice sounded further away, as if she were standing in the hallway.

'Love you,' he said before he could lose his nerve. There was silence, followed by the sound of his door clicking shut. Jake drew his knees up to his chest and rode the wave of his blood, surging full force into his sinuses.

Love you, he thought.

I do, I do.

Chapter 8: Purple Rain

On the second weekend of the holidays, Mandy travelled home to Christchurch.

'I can't wait to get into a warm house,' she'd said, lugging her suitcase out to her car.

'Me neither,' Emily said. She had the flat to herself. She could have Adam over. Or she could go home as well, why not? At least her father's lounge would be warmer than the ambient temperature outside.

'Is this part of a staged return home?' Jim asked when Emily arrived on Saturday afternoon, clutching a suitcase and her pillow.

Emily kicked her shoes off. 'Just felt like some home cooking and blobbing in front of the TV for a couple of days.'

'Is that all you think I'm good for?' Jim gave her neck an affectionate squeeze. 'Just kidding. It'll be nice to have you home for a couple of nights.'

Bradley wandered past, clutching a box of crackers. 'Did you have a fight with Adam?'

'*No*.' Was it possible her brother got more obnoxious as time went on?

'So why aren't you staying with him?' Bradley asked.

'Why are you so nosy?'

'Just like old times,' her father said.

'That wasn't sarcastic at all,' Emily said, before escaping upstairs to her old room. Her bed was still covered with the patchwork duvet her grandmother had made when Emily was twelve, her teddy bear sagging sideways on the pillows.

Emily took her sketchpad out of her suitcase and sat on the bed. There was the dragon's den she'd sketched three years ago, nestled high in the

Lupine Mountains. Emblazoned into the cave roof was a shield with a pair of dragons spiralled around each other in a configuration reminiscent of a —

Dragon double helix. Jake's voice echoed in her ears. *Or double helix dragon.*

I think you just found a name for my graphic novel.

Emily touched the blurred colour in the top corner, remembering a spring day at the beach; remembering a three-years-younger Jake, fresh out of the surf, spilling briny droplets onto her drawing.

Love you.

It had been more than a week since she'd driven Jake home and injected him with sumatriptan. She hadn't heard from him since. Was he embarrassed? Did he even remember what he'd said?

He was delirious.

But migraines don't make people confused . . . do they?

What if it wasn't just a migraine? What if . . . ?

Emily pressed down with her pencil, so hard it broke through the water droplets and into the next page.

'Emily?'

'Hmm?' Emily glanced up. Her father was standing in the doorway.

'What's Adam up to?'

'I don't know.'

'He can come for dinner if he likes. I've made plenty.'

'Thanks, but I think it might be good for us to have a night off from each other.'

Jim perched on the end of the bed. 'How *are* things between you and Adam?'

'I don't know.' It was as honest an answer as she could give. She truly *didn't* know.

'All relationships go through bad patches.'

'Is that what happened with you and Mum?'

'Not sure being cheated on qualifies as a bad patch.' Her father's voice had become equally terse.

'I'm not cheating on Adam.'

'I never said you were.' Jim held her gaze. 'But Adam might be a little jealous of you and Jake. You've been spending a lot of time together since he arrived back in town.'

'Yeah, well . . .' Emily rubbed the black-rimmed puncture she'd made in the page. 'We've always been good friends.'

'Just be careful, huh?'

'Of what?'

Her father glanced out of the window, where the first drops of rain were starting to slide down the glass.

'Adam has been good for you,' he said. 'And Jake, well, he's had his fair share of problems, hasn't he?'

Emily focused on the dragons, coloured in royal blue and gentian violet. 'Hardly self-induced.'

Jim cleared his throat and stood up. 'Dinner will be ready soon. I'm having a glass of wine, if you want to join me.'

Emily listened to her father's footfall on the stairs, her mind awhirl.

Dragon double helix.

Love you.

Do you still think you can get something?

I'll get it. I'll find a way.

Double helix dragon.

She picked up her phone and texted Jake. After waiting for a few minutes, and with no reply from him, she went downstairs to join her father.

———

Emily woke the next morning to the percussive beat of the rain on the roof, and the creak of the metal chimney that ran through the corner of her room and up to the ceiling, venting the fire from the lounge below. Yawning, she rolled onto her side and dozed off to sleep again — only to be woken by her phone beeping, an incoming text message.

Mandy: *OMG did you hear about the flooding in the Catlins?*

Emily groaned. *No, but thanks for the weather update*, she replied, resisting adding: *Why am I meant to care at eight o'clock in the morning?*

She was sliding a dressing gown over her shoulders when Mandy's next text came through: *Hope Ian and Jake are OK.*

Ian and Jake? Emily's brain whirred into gear. Mandy had mentioned last week that Ian was going on a hiking trip, but she hadn't said who he was going with. After donning a thick pair of socks, she padded down the stairs.

'Cripes, look at the flooding down south,' her father said as soon as Emily entered the lounge. Jim was sitting in his favourite chair in front of the TV, the Sunday newspaper on his lap.

'I heard.' Emily sat cross-legged onto the couch. 'Crap, is that a bridge?'

'*Was* a bridge,' her father said. 'Considering half of it has been washed away.'

'Shit.'

Her father shrugged and picked up a section of newspaper. 'Nothing like a good old dose of Mother Nature.'

'Bet that's not what the boys are saying,' Emily said, texting Mandy: *Crap. When did you last hear from Ian?* 'Why do people even go tramping at this time of year?'

'Don't ask me.' Her father frowned. 'Don't tell me Adam's gone tramping?'

'No, Jake and Ian. God.' Emily could barely stand to look at the screen, at the creek that had turned into a raging torrent. 'Is that a *tree*?'

Her phone dinged again: *Not since yesterday. No cell phone reception where they are though.*

'I'm sure they're fine,' her father said. 'But . . .'

'But what?'

'When are they due back?'

'I don't know.' Emily dialled Mandy. 'Hey. When are they due back?'

'Yesterday afternoon, I think. Do you think I should call the police now?'

'Yeah,' Emily said. 'I think we should.'

———

By six pm Emily wanted to scream for all sort of reasons. The ceaseless rain. The almost gleeful news reports of the washed-out bridges and roads, and slips. The endless inane comments from Bradley, her father, Adam, even Mandy, for God's sakes.

Bradley: *They'll be hiding out in a bivouac eating possums, ha ha.*

Her father: *They're not stupid. They'll just be waiting it out.*

Adam: *Would you stop freaking out? It's not going to help.*

Mandy: *What if they tried to cross a river? You know what guys are like, they think they're bullet-proof.*

The TV newsreader, with her hot pink suit and matching lipstick, was making Emily want to scream too. 'A search and rescue team are searching for a pair of twenty-one-year-old men who were last seen walking into a hiking track in the Catlins Friday afternoon, hours before the worst storm in five years hit the region.'

'At least she didn't say the *mother of all storms*,' Adam said. Jim had invited Adam for dinner when he'd dropped around after work. Emily wasn't in the mood for Adam. She wasn't in the mood for anyone.

Bradley grunted. 'Every storm is the mother of all storms, isn't it?'

'Why does it have to be the mother of all storms? Why can't it be the father of all storms?' Jim peered into the lounge. 'Dinner's served.'

'Yum.' Adam, sitting beside Emily on the couch, clasped her knee before she could follow Bradley into the dining room. 'Hey. Why don't you come to my place tonight?'

'Thanks, but I think I'll stay here.'

'I've got a TV at my house. A radio too.' Adam spread his hands. 'What?'

'It's not a *joke*, Adam.'

'Did I say it was?'

Fighting tears, Emily said, 'I could do without the funny comments from everyone, including you.' What if Mandy was right? What if Jake and Ian had tried to cross a river and been swept away? They could have been dead for hours already.

Adam stood up. 'We're just trying to cheer you up,' he said in a fierce whisper.

'Well, don't bother.' Emily didn't even try to lower her voice. 'Look, I'm not very good company at the moment, OK?'

'No kidding.' He strode into the dining room. Suppressing a scream,

Emily escaped into the toilet and sat on the lowered lid, shivering in the cool breeze coming through the window.

Love you. What if those had been Jake's last words to her? And what had she said? Nothing, not until the text she'd sent yesterday, which clearly he'd never received: *We need to talk.*

There was a knock on the door. 'Emily?'

Adam, God, why couldn't he leave her alone?

When Emily entered the hallway, Adam's expression was unreadable.

'No,' she said, before he could ask. 'I'm not OK.' She sagged against the wall. 'We need to talk.'

———

Emily barely slept that night, feeling wretched and yet relieved at the same time. In between listening to the news bulletins on the radio, she tossed and turned, unanswerable questions tumbling through her mind. *Did I do the right thing just now? What if Adam was the best thing that ever happened to me? What if he was the worst thing that ever happened to me?*

No. Adam was *not* the worst thing that had ever happened to her. If it weren't for Adam, she'd have been floundering, adrift.

But now Jake was back.

Was back.

And yet, she must have slept eventually. Must have, because it was her phone ringing that woke her, and Mandy's elated voice spiralling into her ear. She heard *found them.* She heard *helicopter*, and *Dunedin.*

Emily jumped out of bed, threw on yesterday's clothes, and ran down the stairs. After checking the time — twenty past nine, what the hell? — she pulled her jacket off the coat stand and ran out of the door.

———

Twenty minutes later, Emily raced through the front entrance of the hospital and into the Emergency Department.

'I've come to see Jake Heremaia,' she said to the disgruntled-looking triage nurse.

'Are you a relative?'

'I'm a medical student.' Emily held up her ID badge, wishing she'd thought to brush her hair or at least tie it up. 'My registrar asked me to come and see him.'

The nurse waved her through, her sour expression not changing in the slightest. 'Cubicle six.'

'Thanks.' Emily brushed past her, trying to look professional. Perhaps she should have asked for his chart. No, perhaps that was inappropriate.

More inappropriate than pretending to be part of the surgical team? It was only mid-morning, but every bed appeared to be occupied with wheezing, crying, coughing and vomiting patients.

She wasn't sure if she'd ever get used to vomiting patients. Or to patients, full stop.

'Emily?' It was Ian's voice that caught her first, emanating from a cubicle to her left.

'Hey.' She took in the sling on his right arm, the scratches on his face, the Bair Hugger blanket filled with warm air. 'Are you all right?'

'Yeah.' Ian's skin was pale, dark smudges beneath his eyes. 'Think I broke my wrist, though.'

'Oh. God.' She hovered.

'Jake's over there.' Ian nodded at a cubicle diagonally across from him. 'That's who you're really looking for, right?'

'No, I — well, I'm glad you're OK, it must have been — I'll catch you soon, OK?' Emily pivoted and hurried towards the cubicle with the curtains drawn around it. Hearing low voices, she halted, just before a nurse came bustling out holding a kidney dish.

'You can go in,' she said, after a quick glance at the ID around Emily's neck.

Unable to speak, Emily gave her a curt nod and entered the cubicle. Jake was barely visible above the Bair Hugger, his dark hair sticking up in all sorts of directions.

'Hey,' she said, moving closer. 'Are you—? Hey.' His face was smeared with dirt, and was that dried blood on his temple?

'Em,' Jake said, clasping her wrist. 'Hey, don't cry, I'm fine.'

'Fucking idiot,' she whispered.

'Sorry,' he whispered back, his eyes roving over hers. She raised her fingers to his cheek, feeling how cool his skin was, but when she moved her hand to his bare shoulder beneath the Bair Hugger it was warm, so warm. And when she slipped her arms around his neck, he pressed his lips to her ear and murmured 'I'm so glad you're here,' and she said 'Love you, Jay', and felt him tense and relax before kissing her.

'Love you too, Em,' he said, and neither of them mentioned Adam.

Chapter 9: I Think We're Alone Now

It was the pain in his toes that woke him. That, and a fierce thirst. Trying not to move his feet, wincing, Jake reached for his cell phone, which someone had helpfully plugged into a charger. A sticky note was attached to the front.

Went home for a shower. Rest up, will see you after lunch. E x.

The display on his phone told him it was ten past one. Man, he must have been asleep for the past couple of hours. Maybe it was the painkillers, or the fact he'd barely slept the night before.

He read the note again. Had what happened before been a dream? He'd kissed Emily. He'd kissed her, and she'd told him she loved him. The memory of *that* gave him a swirly feeling in his chest.

She must have split up with Adam.

Must have, but Jake didn't dare to ask in case he broke some sort of spell. When had that happened? Before he went away? If so, why hadn't she contacted him?

Does it really matter?

The curtains parted and a nurse ambled in, pushing a blood-pressure machine on wheels.

'Let's see what that temperature's up to,' she said, inserting a probe into his right ear.

'What's it say?'

'Thirty-five.' She clipped an oxygen probe on his ear. 'Getting there. How are the feet?'

Hurting like a bitch, Jake wanted to say, but he settled for 'Eight out of ten.'

'That sounds bad.' The nurse hooked him up to the blood-pressure machine and pressed a button. 'I'll get you some pain relief, shall I?'

'That'd be great.' Jake had barely closed his eyes when he heard rapidly approaching footsteps.

'Jake Heremaia?' A guy in scrubs halted at Jake's bedside. He looked young, late twenties maybe, and was wearing what looked like a Chux cloth knotted around his head.

'That's me,' Jake said, as the blood-pressure cuff began to deflate.

The doctor plucked a chart off the end of the bed. 'I'm Tim Jackson, surgical registrar. Want to tell me how you ended up with hypothermia?' As if Jake was some kind of dumbarse.

Bristling, Jake said, 'My mate and I went on an overnight tramp. We knew it was going to start raining in the morning, but we thought we'd be out before the worst of it. Then it really started hosing down, and Ian — my mate — slipped on a washed-out bit of track and busted his wrist, rolled his ankle too.'

'Slowed you up, huh?'

'Yeah. By the time we got to the river crossing, it was in flood, so we had to go up again. We were aiming for a ridge, but it got dark so we had to camp out for the night. We heard the helicopters this morning, set off some flares.' Thank God Ian had thought to pack those.

'It must have been freezing.' Jackson peeled the Bair Hugger back to reveal Jake's feet. 'Those look pretty sore.'

'Uh-huh,' Jake said, glad to see the nurse had returned with his painkillers and a glass of water. He swallowed them down. The water was warm.

'You've got frostbite, mate,' the doctor confirmed after a brief examination. 'We'll dress your feet once they've thawed and get you up to a ward.'

'Oh.' Disappointment curdled in his belly. 'I was hoping I could go home.'

'Not yet, mate. Best to keep an eye on those toes for a day or two, make sure the tissue's still viable.'

'Viable?' Jake gulped. 'You're not going to chop them off are you?'

'I hope not.' The doctor tapped on the IV bag hanging on the side of his bed. 'We'll keep going with the warm fluids, dress your toes. I'll bring the boss around to look at you tomorrow.'

'Have you seen my mate?'

Jackson frowned. 'Your mate? Oh yeah, we're taking him to theatre this afternoon, needs an ORIF.'

'Open reduction and internal fixation,' Jake said.

The doctor nodded. 'Had one before, have you?'

'No, I'm a medical student.' Jake took an almost sadistic pleasure at the abashed expression on the registrar's face. 'Which bone did he break?'

'Head of ulna.' Jackson took a tendon hammer off the bench and swung it at his side. 'What year are you?'

'Second, just a beginner.'

'Time goes fast. I'll get the house surgeon to admit you soon.' Jackson took off. Jake squinted at the text message that had just arrived from Emily.

Want anything from home?

Jake typed: *Fresh clothes. My toothbrush. You.* He pressed send and lay down, waiting for the painkillers to kick in.

———

Emily arrived an hour later, wearing a blue jersey that brought out the colour in her eyes.

'How did you manage to get a single room?' She peered out of the window.

'No idea,' Jake said, wondering if and when she was going to kiss him again. 'I'll just enjoy it while it lasts.'

She turned. 'They let you have a shower, did they?'

'How could you tell?' His stomach flipped when she sat beside him. He'd been hanging out with Emily half his life, but suddenly everything was different. Suddenly everything, *anything*, was possible.

Almost.

'Because you no longer have dirt from here,' Emily touched his temple, 'to here.' She moved her finger to his lips.

'I had dirt in other places too,' he said, and she laughed and let him kiss her on the mouth, let him slip his hand into the gap between her jeans and her jersey. Three years since he'd kissed her like this. Just. Like. This.

Do you promise?

I promise.

'Holy cow,' someone said from the doorway.

Emily started. Clasping her thigh, Jake blinked at Ian.

'You're dreaming, mate,' Jake said, affecting an Australian accent.

'Why am I not surprised?' Ian sat in a chair by the window, cradling his arm, which was encased in a temporary cast and sling. 'Tell you what, I'm starving.'

'Nil by mouth for theatre?' Emily asked.

'That's it.' Ian glanced between her and Jake. 'What happened to Adam, did you give him the flick?'

Jake watched the colour rise up Emily's neck.

'Actually, *he* broke up with *me*,' she said.

Oh. Jake let go of her thigh, irritation needling him. 'Anything else you want to know?'

Ian crossed his legs. 'Just wondering.'

'How come *you* don't have frostbite?' Emily asked.

Ian contemplated his fingernails. 'I didn't wade into a river, for one thing.'

Emily narrowed her eyes at Jake, while he plucked a plastic cup off his bedside table and aimed it at Ian's head.

'Oi!' Ian looked wounded. 'I'm injured, you know.'

'If it weren't for me, you'd still be stumbling around freezing your arse off.'

Ian bent forward. 'If it weren't for *me*, you'd have frostbite on your Johnson as well.'

Emily spluttered. 'Is that what you call it?'

'*There* you are.' A nurse appeared. 'I need to prep you for theatre.'

'Ooh, are you going to shave me?' Ian asked as she led him away.

'I feel really sorry for that nurse,' Emily said.

'Yeah . . .' Jake hesitated.

Emily said, 'I kind of made Adam break up with me. Do you get what I'm saying?'

Jake sank into the pillows. 'I think so.'

She brushed his hair off his forehead, kissed him between the eyebrows. 'Are you sore?'

'No.'

'You're sweating.'

'It's your fault,' he murmured, and after she kissed him again, 'Actually, I am pretty sore.' Someone was sticking red-hot pokers into his feet.

'I'll get your nurse.' Emily took off. Minutes later, a nurse came back with stronger pills than before. Minutes after *that*, the pain in his feet became an abstract, vaguely interesting phenomenon.

'Catch you later, space cadet,' Emily said, squeezing his shoulder.

'It was a stream,' he muttered, 'not a river.'

'What's done is done.' He felt her lips on his. 'I'll be back.'

Jake dozed. *Four years ago*, he thought. *Four years.*

———

It had been the first Friday in September, and two months before school broke up. Jake was sitting in the park, leaning against a tree. His eyes were closed, Red Hot Chili Peppers warbling 'Otherside' through his new earbuds. Between his fingers was a cigarette, his second for the day.

He'd give up the smoking when he left home. That's what he kept telling himself.

He was listening to the final chords of the song when an earbud was yanked out and someone said, 'What are you listening to?'

Jake jumped. 'Jesus, Em. You're so sneaky.'

Emily flopped down beside him. 'You wouldn't have heard a stampede of elephants through this. Did you bunk off early?'

'It was a study period.'

Emily plucked a daisy out of the grass. 'Looks like you got a lot done.'

'I studied the anatomy of my eyelids. Which, I'll have you know, are quite complex.'

'Whatever.'

'Whatever.' He stubbed out the cigarette. 'How was school?'

'Bearable. You?' Emily tucked the daisy into her ponytail.

'Fantastic. What are you up to this weekend?'

She amputated another daisy. 'Dad's going to a conference. Bradley and I are going to stay with Mum and Steve for the weekend.'

'Lucky you. It won't be that bad, will it?'

'You have no idea what it's like to see your mother and her boyfriend behaving like horny teenagers.'

'Spare me, I just ate.' Jake stretched out in the grass and passed her an earbud. 'Want to listen?'

Emily lay beside him. The Chilies had moved on to 'Californication'. Jake had moved on to the thoughts that had been occupying his brain for the past several months.

This can't go on. It can't go on.

Help, help.

'Em?'

'Hmm?'

'Did you talk to your dad?'

'Yeah.' She took a deep breath. 'I told him I was writing a story for English. He was really into it.'

Jake propped himself up on his elbow. 'So what did he say?'

'Insulin or potassium chloride. They'd both be pretty hard to trace, because your body produces them naturally.'

'How do you get hold of those?' He'd never listened so intently to anyone in his life.

Life or death, this is a matter of life . . . and death.

Emily hesitated. 'You could get insulin off a diabetic person, if you know any. Potassium chloride — a hospital, I guess.'

Jake nodded, his eyes swinging around the playground.

Emily said, 'You wouldn't, though . . . would you?'

'Don't know.' His voice came out shaky. When he looked down at his hands, they were shaking too, and his heart was thundering in his chest. 'I just don't think I can watch her suffer anymore. And I—' He gulped.

'You what? Oh — Jake, it's OK.' She put an arm around him.

Jake swiped a hand beneath his nose. 'No, it's *not*. Every night, she's calling out in pain, or fear, or I don't know what. Every day is a nightmare. She didn't want this. I promised her she wouldn't have to go through this, and now I'm just too fucking weak to help her end it.' He pounded a fist on his thigh.

Emily clasped his wrist. 'You're not weak.'

He shook his head. 'I said I'd help her, and now I don't know if I can.'

She hesitated. 'I could — help you. If you tell me how.'

Jake chewed his bottom lip. Should he ask her? What if she said no? What if she said yes?

I can't ask her to do this.

What other choice do I have?

He counted heartbeats, one, two, three, then said, 'You could go visit your dad at work, couldn't you?'

She hugged her knees to her chest. 'I haven't been on a ward round with him since I was a kid.'

'But you could?'

Emily gave him a slow nod. 'I could.'

'OK.' He began plucking at the grass, creating a bare patch beside his thigh. *I wish I didn't have to ask you this. I wish . . .*

Emily took his hand and squeezed it. 'I'll do it,' she said. 'I promise.'

Jake squeezed back. 'Promise,' he echoed.

———

Jake jerked into wakefulness. No park, no Emily, just off-white walls and a window he couldn't see out of because his bed wasn't high enough.

The pain in his feet was almost welcome. He didn't want to think about the promise.

What's done is done.

He held up his hand, lowered it to his side again.

But . . . what if it isn't?

Chapter 10: Lose Yourself

On Tuesday afternoon, Emily drove out to Sawyers Bay in Jake's car. The clouds were thick and close, the sea grey and still. When she stopped in the driveway, she saw that her mother was sitting in the bay window, a book on her lap.

'Brian, *down*.' Emily stopped to give the hyperventilating Border Collie a pat before walking up to the front door. It was unlocked, as usual.

'Hi, love,' her mother called out.

'Hi.' Emily entered the lounge and flopped into a chair. 'Where's Charlotte?'

'Having a nap.'

Emily took a coaster off the table beside her. 'Thought she'd grown out of those.'

'She still has one every now and then. Thank God. How are your holidays going?'

'Well, Adam and I broke up,' Emily said, studying the unfunny joke on the coaster, something to do with forgetting to get married and have children.

Lisa set the book aside. 'Thought you might,' she said, as if they were discussing the weather.

Emily looked up. 'Really? Dad's acting like it's the biggest shock ever.'

Her mother's lips twisted. 'What he wants and knows to be the truth are two entirely different things, I'm sure. He liked Adam, didn't he?'

'Yeah, guess they have a lot in common.' Emily scratched Brian behind the ears. 'And um, Jake and I . . .'

'You and Jake,' her mother said. 'I wondered whose car that was.'

'At least *you're* smiling.'

'Why wouldn't I be?' Her mother had always liked Jake. 'When's he getting out of hospital?'

'Tomorrow.' Emily moved to the floor to tickle Brian's belly. 'Hey, I was wondering if I could put in an early request for my birthday present?'

'And what would that be?'

Emily nudged Brian's muzzle away from her crotch. 'Jake's flying up north to visit his dad in September and he asked if I'd come along. I can't afford the flights by myself.'

'Hmm,' her mother said. 'This is all moving quite fast, isn't it?'

'It's an emotional support visit, not a marriage proposal.' Emily shuddered. 'Not that I ever want to get married.'

'Well, you *are* only twenty-one.'

'Twenty-two in August.' Emily leaned against the couch, letting Brian drape himself across her lap. 'So about those flights . . .'

'I'll talk to Steve, but I don't see why not.'

'Great.' Emily yawned. 'Bradley said he's coming to stay here while Dad's on conference.'

'Yes, Steve said he'd pick him up on his way home from work tonight. Do you want to stay for dinner?'

'Um . . .' Emily fished her beeping phone out of her bag. 'Actually, maybe not.' She held up the phone. 'Jake's been given the all-clear for discharge. He needs me to pick him up.'

'He can come for dinner too if he likes.' Her mother gave her a calculating look. 'Perhaps we can even book your flights at the same time.'

Emily got to her feet. 'OK,' she said, trying to sound enthusiastic, when all she really wanted was a night alone with Jake. *It's our first night together as a couple, are you kidding?*

'Dinner will be served at six,' her mother said. Emily gave up on trying to think of an excuse, and left.

———

Jake angled his crutches into the back seat and sat next to Emily.

'I didn't mean to crash your family dinner,' he said. 'Just drop me home if you like.'

Emily twisted the key in the ignition. 'Mum invited you. Specifically.' She eased the car out of the park, joining the line of traffic. 'She's just being nosy.'

'Nosy? It's not as if she's never met me before.'

'Yeah, but not as my boyfriend.'

'Well,' he said, touching the nape of her neck. 'There *is* that.'

Her stomach began to tingle. 'We don't have to stay late.'

Why, why did I agree to going over to Mum's tonight? How many hours until we can finally be alone, with no I've-already-got-a-boyfriend *guilt?*

'That's OK. We've got all the time in the world, right?'

'Sure,' Emily said, not so sure *that* was true.

After a brief silence, Jake said, 'Did you ask your mum about the flights?'

'She said that would be fine,' Emily said, which was an approximation of the truth.

'Great.' Jake turned up the radio. '"Lose Yourself". Love this one.'

'Me too.' Emily nudged him. 'Just don't make it your theme song, OK?'

———

It was dark by the time they arrived at her mother's, a frigid wind swirling around the bay.

'Brian, *down*.' Emily bent to pick up Charlotte, who appeared as frisky as the dog. 'What's that you've got there?'

'It's my tiger,' her little sister said.

'Nice mane,' Jake observed, tottering on his crutches.

'Good strategy,' Emily muttered. Tantrum diversion was an important skill, she'd learned.

Inside, Steve was standing by the stove, his greying hair as wild as ever.

'Hi, guys.' He turned. 'Jake, is it? Have a seat, mate, your feet must be killing you.'

'They're OK.' Jake lowered himself into a chair.

Charlotte sidled up to him and deposited her toy into his lap. 'Tiger wants a kiss.'

'Where does Tiger want a kiss?' Jake picked up the lion. 'On his tail?'

Charlotte regarded him thoughtfully. 'No.'

'On his paw?'

'On his *lips*,' Charlotte said.

Steve laughed. 'Do lions have lips?'

Charlotte balled her tiny fists. 'He's a tiger!'

'Clearly,' Jake said, kissing the tiger/lion, while Emily turned to hide her smile from her irascible sister.

'Hello, hello.' Their mother trudged in from the lounge, carrying a stack of tea towels. 'Jake, long time no see. How are your toes?'

'Could be worse,' he replied, letting Charlotte clamber onto his lap. 'Thanks for inviting me for dinner.'

'It's lovely to see you. Charlotte, leave him alone, he's got sore feet.' Lisa dumped the tea towels on the bench and reached for her youngest daughter.

'She's fine,' Jake said. 'So, Charlotte, what does your tiger like?'

Bradley sloped into the kitchen, clutching a laptop. 'Can I borrow the car?'

'What for?' Steve took a pan out of the oven.

Bradley shrugged. 'Gaming thing.'

'Aren't you staying for dinner?' his mother asked.

'Nah, don't worry about me.' Bradley glanced at Emily. 'Don't know why Dad had to take his car to the airport.'

Emily huffed. 'He's hiding it from you after last time, isn't he?'

'Last time?' Lisa asked.

'It was nothing. A scrape.' Bradley gave Emily the evils. From the corner, Emily heard giggles from her little sister and a chortle from Jake.

'Not a doggie!' Charlotte said.

'Fine,' their mother said. 'But make sure you return it tonight. I'm driving to Ōamaru tomorrow.'

'No worries.' Bradley snatched the keys off the counter and slipped out of the door.

'Emily, can I interest you in a glass of wine?' Steve asked.

Emily sank onto a barstool. 'Sure, why not?'

'Jake?'

Jake peered around Charlotte. 'Um, no thanks.' He hesitated. 'Well, maybe just one.'

'Great.' Steve poured white wine into four glasses and passed them around with paint-splattered hands.

'According to Emily, you're an artist,' Jake said, once they were seated at the table.

Steve passed him a bowl of vegetables. 'In my spare time, if there is such a thing. I teach Art at the high school down the road. But I'm not the only artist around here, am I, Emily?'

'I'm not really,' Emily said.

'I wouldn't be so sure,' her mother murmured.

Steve lifted his wine glass. 'Methinks there's a frustrated artist inside you trying to get out. What do you think, Jake?'

'I was going to get Em to design my next tattoo.'

'Are you kidding me?' Emily asked.

Jake shrugged and picked up his fork. 'I'll even let you pick the tattoo.'

Steve laughed. 'Be careful what you wish for, mate.'

Lisa began cutting Charlotte's chicken into tiny pieces. 'Jake's mother was a teacher too. Ballet, is that right, Jake?'

'Yeah,' Jake said, and Emily felt him tense beside her. 'Before she got sick.'

Steve opened his mouth, and Emily, dreading the inevitable next question, said, 'So, about those flights.'

'Flights,' her mother said. 'Oh yes, Steve said that would be a great idea, didn't you, Steve?'

Steve rolled up his sleeve. 'I got this one when I was sixteen,' he said, angling towards Jake. 'Thought my parents were going to kick me out of home.'

'*Michelangelo*,' Jake read out. 'Interesting.'

'My dad thought it was a sure sign that I was gay.' Steve topped up his wine glass.

Charlotte jiggled in her high chair. 'Jake put me bed?'

'Of course,' Jake said.

'Your little sister's pretty cute,' Jake said as they drove towards the city, three hours and several painful lines of conversation later. *How are you liking med school, Jake? How's your dad? Where are you flatting?*

'I think she thought *you* were pretty cute too.' Emily imitated Charlotte's piping voice. 'Jake put me bed?'

'I was going to ask the same of you,' he teased, and her stomach flipped once, twice. 'Want to stay over?'

Emily slowed for a corner. 'You didn't think I was going to go back to your place tonight, did you?'

'Well, I . . .'

She squeezed his knee. 'What I mean is, I was planning to take you somewhere warmer.'

'Your place?'

'Better.'

'A swanky hotel?'

'Settle down. I was going to take you home, I mean to Dad's.'

'Ah. Nice,' Jake said, but he didn't sound as though he were smiling anymore.

'Relax. He's away. And Bradley's staying over at Mum's, remember?'

'I remember. Sounds good.'

The house was in darkness when they arrived, the interior cool. Emily switched on the heat pump in the lounge and peered into the wood basket on the hearth.

'Shall we light a fire?'

'We could.' Jake perched on a chair, his crutches beside him. 'Although I'm kind of wrecked, to tell you the truth.' He scratched the stubble on his chin.

'OK.' Emily slung his bag over her shoulder. 'Are you all right to walk up the stairs?'

'I'll manage.' Once in her room, he limped over to the window. 'How are the new neighbours?' He gripped the windowsill, shifting from one foot to the other.

'They're OK.' She leaned next to him. 'Not so new anymore.'

'No . . .' He sat on the end of her bed. 'The last time I was here . . .' He chewed his lip. 'Remember that?'

'Of course,' she said, remembering the longest night of her life, a blood-red dawn.

What are you going to do now?

I'll call the doctor. When it's light.

She sat beside him. 'Shall I turn the heater on?'

'Could.' He looked back at her. 'Am I sleeping in here?'

Emily ducked her head. 'Do you want to?' What was with this new awkwardness around a guy she'd known half her life, a guy she'd twice shared a bed with? Both times, nothing had happened — once, after the rugby, because she already had a boyfriend, and once because . . .

Because we'd just done something wonderful and terrible. Emily still didn't know if they'd done the right thing. She wasn't sure she'd ever know.

'I want to.' He touched her cheek. 'You're shivering.'

'Cold,' Emily said, not wanting to admit it was nerves more than anything. 'Think we need to get under the blankets?'

'Absolutely,' Jake said. So they did just that, stripping down to their underwear and singlets before sliding between the sheets, where they lay nose to nose.

'Should have turned the light off,' Emily said.

'No.' He trailed his fingers down her arm, his touch butterfly-light. 'Not yet.'

Emily breathed in. Jake breathed out. She closed her eyes, felt him push his temple into hers.

'There are so many things I want to tell you,' he said.

'Like what?'

'I don't know where to start.' His breath was warm on her lips.

Emily kissed him. 'Tell me about the letter.'

'The letter.' He hesitated. 'Maybe we should turn the light out after all.'

Emily didn't ask why. 'The letter,' she said, once she'd returned to bed.

'The letter.' Jake's eyelids fluttered against hers. 'You know, I wrote it so many times to try and get it right, I can almost remember it off by heart.' He stroked the side of her breast and she felt a tugging sensation deep within her belly. 'I said, *I need to thank you for what you did for me* and Mum. I'm really sorry I had to leave. This sounds dumb but I didn't realise how much I would . . .' His chest inflated, deflated. 'Miss you. And I hope we can still see each other.'

'I can't believe that went missing,' Emily said, tears pricking her eyes.

'I haven't finished yet.' He kissed the corner of her mouth. 'And I said, I just want you to know that I—' He broke off.

After several long seconds, Emily said, 'Are you OK?'

'I'm . . . no.' There was a tremor in his voice she hadn't heard since that night. 'But what I said at the end of my letter was, I just want you to know that I don't think I'll ever feel about anyone the way I do about you. Love you, Jake.'

'Love you,' she echoed, a tremor rippling through her. 'I would have written back. I would have said . . .'

'What would you have said?'

'I would have said, Love you, Em,' she whispered before kissing him slowly, deeply.

'Do you know what the best treatment is for hypothermia?' Jake asked after an interminable time.

'I think I've got some idea,' she said, and they began to move together — slowly, deeply, inevitably.

Chapter 11: Paranoid Android

Jake was sitting in his favourite spot in the library, at the rear by the window. The oil heater on the wall provided welcome heat in the depths of winter, and it was a good place to study or nap in between lectures.

Yet in just over a week, it would be spring and he would be flying to Whangārei with Emily — a visit he was anticipating with a mixture of excitement and dread.

He looked at his notes. The kidney, while a vital organ, was hardly very exciting. Yawning, he lowered his head until it was resting on the desk and began to doze, random thoughts flitting through his mind.

Must get warrant for car . . . e-mail Auntie Ngaire about that lunch . . . find Emily a birthday present, but what . . . Emily, Emily . . . maybe we could catch a movie tonight . . . text her soon . . . soon . . .

'Uh.' His limbs jerked and he sat up with a start, his heart thumping.

What was that? A myoclonic jerk, happens to people all the time, doesn't mean anything.

'Jake!' Someone yelled, causing him to jump again.

'Jesus.'

'No, it's Kylie,' she chortled, sitting at the desk in front of him. 'What are you looking at? The kidney — ugh, isn't it horrid?'

'But strangely useful.'

'You only need one.' Kylie was wearing a lime green cardigan over a black dress, and had completed her outfit with black-and-white striped tights. She looked like a character out of one of the books Jake's mother used to read him, and that gave him a strange feeling, like homesickness.

He'd have to look up myoclonic jerks, once Kylie was facing forward.

'What are you up to for the mid-semester break?' Kylie started removing items from her bag — books, a water bottle, and what looked like at least three different flavours of bubble gum.

'I'm going to Whangārei.'

'Is that home?' Kylie picked up the bubble gum and fanned the packets out, as if she were holding a hand of cards.

Jake plucked the grape flavour. 'Sort of.'

'Well, it's bound to be warmer than here.' Kylie popped a Cola square into her mouth and proceeded to blow a bubble almost as big as her head.

'Jesus,' Jake said again, and Kylie guffawed, resulting in a chorus of shushing from the three people sitting in front of them. 'Watch this,' he whispered and blew a bubble that ended up mostly on his face. They were giggling uncontrollably, while trying to ignore the evil stares of those around them, when Jake heard someone say, 'Getting lots of study done, are you?'

'Emily!' Kylie yelled.

'Oh my God, would you either shut up or leave?' The guy sitting in front of them waved his pen in a threatening way.

Jake stood up. 'I think we should take his advice,' he whispered.

Emily rubbed at his nose. 'What is that, gum?'

'Uh-huh.'

'Right. I'm going to grab a coffee in the Med Café, are you keen?'

'Definitely.' Jake slung an arm around her shoulders. 'Want to join us, Kylie?'

'Definitely.' Kylie slammed her book shut. 'Don't worry,' she announced. 'We're leaving now.'

'Thank God,' the pen-waving guy called after them.

'No, it's *Kylie!*' she yelled.

Emily wriggled away from Jake. 'See you there,' she said, and took off toward the toilets.

Several minutes later, Jake sat drinking bad machine coffee in the café, wondering if Emily was ever going to show up.

'Maybe you should go check on her,' Kylie said. 'In case she's sick or something.'

'Yeah . . .' Jake checked his phone, but there were no messages or missed calls. What the hell, was Emily pissed at him? And for what? Surely she wasn't jealous of Kylie? He'd just begun typing a message when someone dumped a bag at his feet and flopped down beside him.

'Hey.' He frowned at Emily. 'You all right?'

'Yep,' Emily said, but her eyelids were pink.

'Want a coffee?'

She nodded. Jake walked to the machine.

When he returned to the couches, Emily was, miracle of miracles, laughing at something Kylie had said. Jake deposited the cup on the table. 'Not sure if there's any real caffeine in there.'

'It'll do.' Emily picked it up.

Kylie stood up, gesturing at the counter. 'Anyone else want a Chupa Chup?'

'Nah, I'm good,' Jake said. Once Kylie had disappeared from earshot, Jake clasped Emily's knee. 'Are you sure you're OK?'

'Fine.'

'You don't sound fine.'

'It doesn't matter, OK?'

Kylie sat opposite them and began tearing the wrapper off her lollipop. 'What are you guys up to tonight? Want to come to the pub?'

Jake tensed, waiting for Emily's reply.

'Sure, why not?' she said.

———

Jake propped his elbow up on the bar, wishing he were anywhere but in a crowded room with sixty-odd jiggling, sweaty bodies. He wanted to go to bed. He wanted to wake up to Emily and the promise of a good swell at St Clair Beach.

'Want another one?' Ian yelled in his ear.

Jake contemplated his nearly empty glass of Coke. 'Nah, this one's gone to my head already.'

'You're so weird.' Ian signalled the barman and pointed at his pint glass. Jake turned his attention to the dance floor, where Emily and Kylie were gyrating with a bunch of med students. Emily beckoned him over. Jake narrowed his eyes at her. Emily pouted. Jake sighed.

'Gotta go,' he said to Ian.

'Under the thumb, dude,' Ian replied. Jake wandered onto the dance floor, extending a middle finger behind his back.

'At last.' Emily's breath was wine-sweet, her eyes glazed. 'How can you resist this song?'

'I don't know,' Jake muttered, restraining himself from telling her he couldn't stand Justin Timberlake. What the hell, at least Emily was in a better mood than she'd been earlier.

Drawing him closer, Emily kissed him on the lips. 'You hate dancing, don't you?'

'No, I don't.'

'*Only when I'm pissed,*' she said. 'That's what you told me last time.'

'Did I?' When was last time? Was his memory that bad?

Myoclonic jerks, I need to look that up.

Everyone has those now and then, Mr Paranoid.

Only fifty per cent paranoid.

'At the school formal,' she said, the tips of her fingers sneaking beneath the waistband of his jeans. 'Remember that?'

Jake cupped the curve of her hip. 'I remember,' he said, but when she went to kiss him again he said, 'Not here.'

'Always so shy,' she teased.

He pulled away. 'Let's go home.'

'Now? It's only eleven.'

Kylie lurched towards them. 'Who's up for a cocktail?'

'Not me.' Jake slipped out of her grasp. 'I'll catch you tomorrow, then?'

'Tomorrow,' Emily said, not looking at him.

———

Jake jerked awake, his heart galloping. The rapping started up again. It sounded like knuckles on — glass?

'Urgh.' Jake threw his blankets aside and moved to open the window. 'Do you know what time it is?' He undid the sash, letting the window swing free.

'One am.' Emily said, clambering across the windowsill. Jake caught her by the elbow and helped her swing her legs onto the carpet.

'You're cold,' he said. Her hands were like ice blocks.

'Lost my jacket.' Emily collapsed onto his bed. 'Sorry.'

'Don't apologise to *me*.' He drew the blankets over them. 'Please don't tell me you walked home by yourself.'

'No, I got a taxi.' She wriggled closer to him. 'You're nice and warm.'

'Mmm.' He kissed her, felt her tongue flick over his lips. 'You're pretty drunk, aren't you?'

'Pretty when I'm drunk, is that what you're saying?'

'Pretty whenever.'

'Whatever.'

'Forever.'

'Flatterer.' She slid off his t-shirt, and Jake helped her out of her jeans and top. Skin on skin, tongue on tongue; his head was whirling, and he hadn't consumed a drop of alcohol.

'I love you even when you're inebriated,' he whispered afterwards, as they lay slotted together.

'Even when.' Her voice wobbled.

'Hey,' he said. 'Hey, what's up?' His mouth touched her moon-cool skin, her tears salty pearls on his lips.

'Nothing,' she whispered.

'I knew something was wrong,' he said, but she turned away from him, let him curl around her.

'I'm just drunk,' she said. 'It happens sometimes.'

———

When he woke the next morning, he was alone. Jake stretched, touching the still-warm patch beside him. The display on the alarm clock said seven fifty-five. He sat up and peered through the gap in the curtains. The day was still and blue.

'Hey.' Emily padded in and set a cup of coffee on the desk. 'Thought you might want one of these.' She was wearing his dressing gown.

'Thanks.' Jake shuffled over so she could sit beside him. 'How's your head?'

She grimaced. 'It's been better. Found some Panadol in your bathroom cupboard, hope that's OK.'

'Probably Nathan's, he's got pills for everything. I'm sure he won't miss a couple.' He brushed aside the hem of the dressing gown, kissed the side of her neck. 'You smell good.'

Emily tensed. 'Hey, um . . . we shouldn't. Unless you've got condoms, that is.'

'What? Why?'

'I forgot to take my pill yesterday.'

Jake's chest plunged, his heart coming to rest somewhere in his nether regions. 'You forgot? But . . . last night . . .'

'Yeah, I know.' She inhaled. 'It's the middle of the packet, so it's probably fine, but we should still take extra precautions for the next week.'

'Hang on, hang on.' *Shit, shit, shit.* 'This could be — Jesus, a fucking disaster.' Not just a disaster, an atomic bomb.

'Jake, it's not a big deal.' Emily began gathering up her clothes.

'How can you be so casual about this?' Thick fear climbed up his throat.

She rolled her eyes at him. 'Would you stop being so fucking dramatic?'

'Is that what you call it?' Jake jumped out of bed. 'Maybe you wouldn't think it was so *fucking dramatic* if you had to live with it every day of your life.'

'I *am* living with this,' Emily yelled back. 'Every day of my life. And you know what? It's not all about you.'

'What?' Jake stared at her.

'You heard me.' She balled her clothes. 'Thanks to you, I've been living with this since I was seventeen years old.'

'Em.' *What the hell?*

'Don't you think I worry about this?' Emily carried on. 'About what this might mean for you, for us?'

Jake tried to force some words out, but couldn't. His tongue was a leaden weight in his mouth.

'I know you don't want to talk about it,' she said. 'But sometimes it would really help if you did.' She left, slamming the door behind her.

Go after her. Go after her.

But he couldn't, and didn't.

The following morning, Jake sat on his board on St Clair Beach, watching the sets roll in. The waves were glassy, the sun warm on his wetsuit. He'd go in soon. But first . . . first . . .

He pivoted, gazing up at the boardwalk. *There* she was, blonde strands of hair lifting in the breeze, her feet on the steps leading down from the promenade. Jake dug his toes into the sand and waited.

'Hey.' Emily sat beside him, releasing her grip on her bag. Tucked inside, he saw, were her sketchpad and pencil case.

'Hey.' Should he kiss her? What if she pushed him away? They hadn't spoken since yesterday, but she'd texted him to ask if he'd be on the beach that morning and he'd replied immediately. *Sure, see you around nine.*

'Surf looks good,' she said.

'Yeah, it was going off yesterday too,' he said, then felt guilty for suggesting he'd been out having a good time after their argument. Truth was, he'd needed to wind down in the only way he knew how. 'Um. I'm sorry I . . . over-reacted yesterday.' Had he? He still wasn't sure about that.

Emily lowered her eyes. 'Me too.' Jake thought she was going to say something else, to talk about *it*, and the contents of his gut curdled in anticipation. As much as he wanted to talk about *that* night, and everything that came before and after, it was just too fucking hard.

Denial, he'd once read, was a form of coping. It was all he had. He wound back to a couple of days ago, to the image of Emily pink-eyed and struggling to maintain her composure in the café.

'You seemed pretty upset on Friday,' he ventured. 'In the café, I mean.'

She nudged the toe of her sneaker into the sand. 'I was having a crap day. I wanted to talk to you about it but then . . .'

But then I invited Kylie, Jake thought. 'You had your viva, right?' Examining patients in front of others, he knew, was one of Emily's biggest fears. No wonder she had been acting oddly.

Emily's nod was barely perceptible. A single voluminous tear curled beneath her chin.

'It probably wasn't as bad as you think,' he said, daring to embrace her.

'It was *worse* than you think.'

'How?'

She swiped another tear away. 'I walked out before it had finished. As in, straight after the first case.'

'What happened?'

Emily took a ragged breath. 'I f-froze in front of everyone. The examiners, the patient and — my heart was going so fast, and I was shaking so badly I thought I was going to faint. I just had to get out. And once I left, I couldn't go back.'

'Jesus, that sounds really awful. But Em . . .' He hesitated. 'Don't you think you need to see someone about this?'

'I can't.'

'Why not? Lots of people have panic attacks.' He gave her a gentle smile. 'Like every time I get on a plane, for instance.'

Emily turned to him. 'You're scared of flying?'

'Shit-scared. I try and avoid it wherever possible. But when I can't, I often end up in the bar downing a few drinks beforehand.'

She sniffed. 'Maybe I should try that.'

'Yeah, that's one way to get kicked out of med school,' he said, and they looked at each other for a moment. 'I don't recommend it,' he added, suddenly worried she might act on his suggestion.

'Don't think I haven't thought about it,' she muttered.

'Maybe,' he said carefully, 'you could go to Student Health, see if they can sort something for you. What's the worst that can happen?'

'I don't know.' Her voice was so flat it scared him. 'Maybe it hasn't happened yet.'

'Promise me you'll go and see someone, even if it's not until the holidays.' He kissed her tear-swollen lips. 'I know you can get through this.'

'Maybe,' Emily said, 'I'm not as strong as you think.'

'I think you're wrong,' Jake said.

Chapter 12: Better Be Home Soon

Emily closed her eyes, savouring the salty breeze stirring across her brow. The air seemed softer in Northland, the lines blurred — and a world away from the cold interior of Jake's bedroom only a week ago. They'd never really resolved things, although she had promised Jake she'd seek professional help for her panic attacks. *To do what, some breathing exercises?* She'd tried that. It didn't work. Still, she'd made an appointment for when they returned to Dunedin. She wasn't looking forward to it.

'Cup of tea?' Ngaire, Jake's aunt, offered her the thermos. She'd picked Emily and Jake up from the airport the previous morning and driven them an hour north. It felt like several days ago.

'No, thanks.' Emily squinted at the horizon. 'There they are.' The boat was rounding the point, a white dot on a shimmering canvas. Jake had asked if she'd wanted to go fishing with him and his dad. *In that, are you kidding?* Emily had answered. She didn't like to sail in anything smaller than a ferry.

Ngaire drained her cup and screwed it onto the thermos. 'Hope they've caught some kai.' She shot a grin at Emily. 'Or I'll be sending them straight back out.'

They wandered down to the water's edge, waiting as the whine of the outboard motor grew louder. Willie was sitting at the rear, steering, his arm hanging over the side of the boat. Jake was sitting towards the front with Jimbo, Willie's Jack Russell.

'Hope you like fish,' Willie said, wading towards them.

Emily peered into the bucket. 'What are they?' The fish were lying with their mouths open to their last gasp, their scales chrome-shiny in the sunlight.

'Snapper.' Willie's eyes crinkled up in the corners when he smiled, just like Jake's. His skin was a shade darker, though, his beer gut protruding over the waistband of his shorts. He slipped a cigarette out from behind his ear and placed it between his lips. 'Big feed at our house tonight, sis, are you staying?'

'I am now.' Ngaire pointed at him. 'Didn't the doctor tell you to stop smoking?'

Willie sniffed. 'Ah, too late now.'

'Not now you've got new plumbing for your ticker. You tell him, doctors.' Ngaire frowned. 'Where's Jake off to in such a hurry?'

Emily gazed after Jake. He was already halfway up the beach, his shoulders hunched. 'Maybe he's going to the toilet,' she said, but thought that probably wasn't it.

Willie shrugged and let a curl of smoke out of the corner of his mouth. 'Yeah,' he said. 'Maybe.'

———

The grassy area in front of Willie's bungalow was almost completely obscured by scrap metal — rusting car bodies, a disembodied car roof and an old fridge, among the items Emily could recognise. The aging Triumph parked in the driveway didn't look much better. In fact, she thought the exhaust pipe might have fallen off while they were at the beach.

'Well,' Ngaire said, sipping water out of a mug and surveying the tiny kitchen, with its teal blue and orange cupboards, pot-bellied stove and freestanding pantry, 'hasn't changed much.'

'Suits me.' Willie took a flagon out of the fridge. 'Want a beer?'

'No, I'm fine,' Emily said.

'Jake?' Willie glanced around. 'Where's he?'

'He's gutting the fish.' Emily looked out into the yard. Jake was sitting at a small table in the shed, grimly intent on his task. She picked up the glass, which looked like a recycled Marmite jar, and stepped outside. The sun was sinking behind the hills, the temperature dropping rapidly with it.

She set the glass at his elbow. 'Escaping, are we?'

'No, I'm getting our dinner ready.' Jake's eyes were dark. Emily leaned against the corrugated wall of the shed, the sun's trapped heat radiating through her jersey.

'Did you have an argument?'

Jake tossed a fish head in the bucket. 'Not yet.'

'It's only one more night.' Emily looked through the kitchen window. Ngaire was attacking a cauliflower with a very large knife. A thin line of smoke snaked out the chimney and drifted over the abandoned house next door.

Jake slapped another fish on the table. 'One night too many.' After making a long, thin incision on the ventral surface, he cut the head off. Emily watched with a vague sense of revulsion as he removed the guts with a flick of the wrist.

'Maybe bite your tongue,' she said.

'Not *my* tongue you should be worried about,' Jake muttered. 'I'll see you inside, shall I?'

When Emily returned to the house, the potatoes and kūmara were roasting in the oven, and Ngaire was making a cheese sauce for the cauliflower. Jimbo was standing on the couch, barking at a horse on the TV. Willie was making rapid progress through his beer flagon and chain-smoking. No wonder there was a yellow patch on the ceiling above him.

'Move over, will you?' Willie pushed Jimbo aside and patted the cushion beside him. 'Here, love — found those photos I was telling you about.' He reached down the side of the couch and came up with a large, yellowing envelope.

'Great.' Emily took the envelope and sat beside him. The first photo she came across was an image of a couple leaning against a Volkswagen Beetle. Willie was tall and lean; if it weren't for the moustache, she'd have easily mistaken him for Jake. The woman, presumably Christine, was dreamy-eyed, her slender legs emerging from a short floral dress. The next photo was of Christine in the same dress, but with her hand cupped over her rounded stomach. Behind her loomed the biggest kauri tree Emily had ever seen.

'Wow, where's that?'

Willie peered over her shoulder. 'Waipōua Forest. It's on the west coast, about an hour from here.' He touched the tree. 'That's Tāne Mahuta, separator of heaven and earth. His feet are in the sky. His shoulders are on the earth.'

'That's cool,' she said, looking sideways at him. Jake had said his father was good at telling stories.

'Beautiful,' Willie said, but he was looking at Christine. Emily moved on to the next photo. A boy, no older than four years old, was running towards the camera; all sun-burnished limbs, pot-bellied and shiny-eyed. His mouth was wide open, his lips curved towards the sky.

'Jake,' Emily said, her heart thudding. If she *had* accidentally got pregnant, then maybe their kid would look like — but no. She wasn't pregnant and didn't want to be either — not now, not ever.

'He was a cute kid,' Willie said, a trace of wistfulness creeping into his voice.

'Ah jeez, not another one.' Ngaire wandered through from the kitchen. 'I always knew they shouldn't have lowered the drinking age to eighteen.'

'Huh?' Emily looked back at the TV.

Ngaire gestured at the screen. 'Another fatality on the roads. Teen-agers.'

'I'm with you, sis.' Willie topped up his glass.

'Older people are the worst offenders.' Jake deposited the tray with the filleted fish on the bench and rinsed his hands under the tap, the water running to pink.

'Ah,' his father said with a dismissive wave, 'we all make mistakes.'

'And some of us even learn from them.' Jake set his still-full glass of beer on the bench. The head had dissipated, leaving a thin scud of foam on the top, an outgoing tide.

Willie lit another cigarette. 'My boy's switched on. Must have got all his brains from his mum.'

'Do you need help?' Emily leapt up from the couch and turned Jake towards the stove. 'Settle down,' she whispered, feeling his muscles twitch beneath her palms.

'I will if he will,' Jake muttered, but he opened the fridge and found

94

the butter. Someone turned up the TV. Jimbo started barking again. The sun fell behind the hill.

———

The temperature inside the house rose rapidly, with the oven and the fire in the lounge. Emily felt as though she were in a pressure cooker, in more ways than one. She opened the back door for some fresh air and joined the others, who were balancing their dinner plates on their laps in the lounge.

Ngaire held up her mug. 'I think we should have a toast.'

'I'll have to recharge my glass.' Willie's words were slurred. He reached for the flagon but knocked it over, sending a thin stream of amber onto the floorboards. After picking the flagon up, he shrugged and tipped the remaining dribble of beer into his mouth.

'What shall we drink to?' Emily frowned at Jake, who continued to plough cheerlessly through his dinner.

'Jake getting into medical school, of course.' Ngaire nodded in his direction. Jake looked up at the sound of his name, gave her a blank look.

'Oh yeah.' Willie clinked his glass against Ngaire's and Emily's before shrugging at his son, who still hadn't touched his drink. 'At least I'll have someone to look after me in my old age.'

'Someone to look after you.' Jake got to his feet. 'Imagine that.'

Willie lifted his chin. 'Well,' he said, 'don't forget where you come from when you're rich and famous, will you?'

Emily held her breath, watching as Jake's face flushed and his knuckles turned white, until he said, so low she could barely hear him, 'Not much chance of that, *Dad.*'

'Think you need to relax a little, *son,*' Willie said, his voice soft but his eyes hard. Jake's hands twitched, but he didn't reply. Instead, he loped through the kitchen and outside, slamming the door behind him.

Ngaire cleared her throat. 'Guess I'd better make a start on the dishes.'

'I'll help you,' Emily said quickly. After taking her plate through to the kitchen, she peered outside. The door to the shed was padlocked, the outhouse dark.

'Do they always fight like that?' Emily murmured.

'Yeah.' Ngaire turned both taps on and added a squirt of detergent. 'Jake will never forgive Willie for walking out on him and Christine, I reckon.'

Emily picked up a tea towel. 'How old was Jake?'

'Hmm . . .' Ngaire looked up at the ceiling. 'Guess he was about nine or so. Yeah, that'd be right.' She turned the taps off. 'They were living in Whangārei at the time. Willie was working as a mechanic, and trying to set up his own business. It fell through right around the time Christine started to get sick. So then they were both out of work, and he was drinking . . . a lot. Jake and Christine were better off without him — even Willie admits that.'

'How did they meet?' Emily resisted the urge to wipe the bubbles off Ngaire's spectacles. 'Christine and Willie, I mean.'

Ngaire picked up the scrubbing brush. 'Christine took her car into the garage Willie was working in one day to be repaired. After that, she kept returning for petrol. Willie thought she was a goddess. She was pretty taken with him too. He was pretty good-looking in those days, believe it or not.'

'I can believe it,' Emily said softly.

'They'd only been going out a few months when she got pregnant. Her family weren't too impressed. First of all she was going out with this Māori grease monkey, and then he gets her up the duff.' Ngaire shrugged. 'They got on pretty well, though, for those first few years anyway.' She squinted out of the window. 'Where do you think he's gone?'

'Jake? I don't know.' Emily looked out into the gloom and suppressed a shiver.

'Well,' Ngaire said, once she'd finished the last of the dishes, 'I might get going. I'll come pick you up in the morning to take you to the airport.' She gave Emily a hug. 'Don't worry, they won't have a punch-up or anything.'

Emily forced a smile. 'Thanks.' She finished drying the dishes and walked through to the lounge. Willie was asleep in front of the TV, a cigarette vibrating between his lips. She plucked it out. He didn't stir.

Another hour passed, and Jake still hadn't returned. Emily got into her pyjamas and crawled under the heavy, army-style blankets in the spare room. She tried to read her book but kept scanning the same passage over and over. When she heard the back door open, relief came first, followed by anger when she heard Jake's footsteps in the hallway.

'Where have you been?' Emily asked, once Jake had entered the bedroom.

He unzipped his jeans. 'I was out . . . walking.'

She sat up. 'You've been away for *two hours.*'

'I needed to cool off.' Jake kicked off his jeans and pushed them under the bed with his foot.

'I was worried about you. You could have been hit by a car, for all I knew.'

'Not much chance of that around here,' Jake muttered. Emily lay down and rolled onto her side, so she was facing the wall. 'Hey, I'm sorry, OK?' He touched her, tentatively, on the shoulder. His fingers were cold. Emily ignored him.

Jake sighed and got up to turn off the light before climbing in beside her. 'Good night,' he said. She didn't reply.

Once she was sure he was asleep, she got up and padded into the lounge. Willie had disappeared, presumably to bed. After turning the kettle on, Emily stirred up the remains of the fire and got it going with a couple of sheets of newspaper and a log of wood. Then she made a cup of tea and watched the flames dance up the chimney.

'Couldn't sleep?'

'No.' She didn't look up. Jake sat beside her, his knee touching hers. After a minute or so, he pressed his palm to her cheek.

'Do you think I'm a bastard?'

She shook her head. Jake slid his hand down until it was resting on her neck.

'I'm sorry about tonight. He brings out the worst in me.'

'Yeah.' Emily inhaled. 'I know it's hard for you. Coming here.'

'I always wondered what a normal family was like.' His Adam's apple bobbed up and down. 'I just wanted a father who didn't keep losing his driver's licence, and a mother who wasn't losing it. Sometimes I thought *I* was losing it.'

She shuffled closer to him. 'You're not losing it.'

'I worry I'm going to lose *you*.'

'You're not going to lose me,' she said. 'Why would you think that?' She slid her fingers across his belly. His skin was burning, his abdominal muscles rigid.

'I can't talk to you like this.' He pulled her onto his lap.

'Then don't.' She moved her hand, lower, lower. His lips parted. A thin layer of sweat glistened on his temple. 'Do you want me to stop?'

'No.' His breathing was shallow. The fire cracked and popped as they shed their clothes and seared their skin as they held each other closer, closer, until there was no space between them, none at all.

Chapter 13: A Wolf at the Door

Jake tipped his chair against the wall, inhaling the scent of aged books and freshly shampooed carpet. Outside, the streets were in darkness, occasional students and medical staff scurrying between the hospital and the medical school. He stuck his headphones on, humming along to the opening chords of 'A Wolf at the Door' as he looked down at his textbook.

A double helix is the three-dimensional structure of double-stranded DNA. Jake chewed the end of his pen. *The complementary nitrogen bases are linked by hydrogen bonds.*

Cytosine-guanine. Adenine-thymine. C-G, A-T.

He didn't really need to remind himself about the basics of genetics. They were etched indelibly into his brain, just like the tattoo on his biceps.

And why, why was he drawing dragons on the side of his notes?

Someone lifted a headphone away from his ear. 'Studying hard?' Kylie sat in front of him, ignoring the disapproving stare from the librarian stacking shelves to their right.

Jake flipped the headphones off. 'You know it,' he said, turning the page so Kylie couldn't see what else he'd been writing, over and over. A trio of bases, CAG-CAG-CAG. 'Actually, they're Emily's.'

Kylie's eyebrows shot up. 'Is she having dragon babies too?'

'Something like that.' Jake forced a grin, but Emily missing her pill, although three weeks had passed, was still fresh in his mind; a disaster waiting to happen.

Yeah, that's me, a fucking atom bomb.

'You're hilarious.' Kylie touched his wrist, her rings scraping against his skin. 'How's the job going?'

'It's a gas,' Jake said, provoking a snort from his classmate. Pumping petrol, maybe that was in his genes too.

You'd better not meet the girl of your dreams, Emily had said before Jake's first day last week. She must have been talking to his dad, must have heard the story of how his parents had met over a petrol pump. 'How were your holidays?' he asked.

Unwinding the scarf from around her neck, turquoise to match her rings, Kylie said, 'So, I went home to Christchurch, fought with my mum, went to stay with my ex-boyfriend, pissing off his current girlfriend — God, I slept on the couch, but whatever — and then my ex-boyfriend made things even worse by telling me he wished he'd never broken up with me and then he broke up with Jen — that's his girlfriend — and guess who looks like the bad person?'

Jake spun his pen across his knuckles. 'So what did you say to your ex?'

'Well, that's the thing. I ended up spending the rest of the week with him, and one thing led to another, and now he wants to get back together, but I don't think that's such a good idea.' She offered him a packet of chewing gum. 'So, to summarise, my holiday was an apocalypse.'

'Right.' Jake took a stick of gum and unwrapped the foil.

'And you?'

'Um, similar. Kind of.' He stuck the gum in his mouth. 'Do you think we're meant to hate at least one of our parents? What do they call that, the Oedipus complex?'

'Yeah, but that's just a fucked-up Freudian theory, isn't it? I don't know about you, but I definitely don't want to have sex with my mother.' All of this was delivered at Kylie's usual volume, just as the librarian walked past with another trolley of books. 'Screw it, shall we go for coffee?'

Jake hesitated. 'I think this is turning into a habit.' He had so much revision to do, a presentation to prepare for his tutorial.

'Well, we can't have that. I know, let's go to the pub instead.'

The last thing he felt like was drinking, so why did he say yes?

He was thinking it had a lot to do with double helix dragons.

There were only four other people at the pub, a trio of scruffy guys at the bar, and a woman sitting at a pokie machine, a black Labrador at her feet.

'How do blind people play the pokies, do you think?' Kylie asked, once they were seated opposite each other in a booth.

Jake sipped on his beer. 'There's a difference between legally blind and totally blind, I suppose. Anyway, she mightn't be blind. The dog might be because she has seizures or something.'

'An emotional support animal, I could do with one of those.' Kylie traced a circle in the condensation on her glass. 'Hey, you should text Emily, see if she wants to join us.'

'Nah, she's freaking out about her test tomorrow.'

'What kind of test?'

'She's repeating the viva she walked out of last term.' Should he have told Kylie that? Well, why not? It wasn't really a secret.

'Really? She strikes me as being quite conscientious.'

Jake swallowed more beer, felt a pleasant numbness settle somewhere behind his eyes. 'It's a performance anxiety thing. She has panic attacks.' He thumbed foam off the side of his glass. 'She went to Student Health in the holidays. The doctor gave her beta blockers.'

'Do they help?'

'Guess we'll find out tomorrow.' After a brief hesitation, Jake carried on. 'She keeps talking about chucking it in.'

Kylie's lips formed an O. 'And all they gave her is beta blockers? Aren't you worried?'

'Well, of course I'm—' Jake began, before realising what Kylie meant. 'Oh, hell no, she's not suicidal. She's thinking of quitting med school.'

'Crap. Thanks,' Kylie added, as the waitress set a bowl of chips in front of them. 'Do you think it's just a stage?'

'I don't know.' Was it? What if he hadn't enlisted Emily's help three and a half years ago? Would she be suffering the same sort of anxiety?

'You must have been thirsty,' Kylie said, and Jake realised he'd almost finished his pint. 'Want another one?'

Jake shrugged. 'Yeah, why not?'

Half a bowl of chips and three beers later, Jake was wondering why he didn't drink more often. His limbs were deliciously heavy, his brain in back-up mode.

'What does what's-his-name do when he's not philandering?' Jake asked.

Kylie spun a coaster around on the table. 'You do realise that by calling Hugh a philanderer you are automatically designating me to be a philanderee?'

'I don't think "philanderee" is a word.'

'Are you sure?' She leaned across the table and nearly fell off her stool. 'Anyway. You know what I mean.'

'So if you're not a *philanderee*,' Jake was having trouble getting the word that was not a word out, 'then what are you? His long-lost love?'

'Not long-lost when we'd only been apart for eight months, I don't think. Hugh's doing a Master's in Psychology.'

'Is that how you know about Oedipus complexes?'

'I'm very complex,' Kylie said, before whipping a bundle of paper out of her bag, which was red and furry, like something out of *The Muppets*. 'Have you had a crack at these yet?'

Jake cast an eye over the genetics problems they'd been given in preparation for their tutorial later in the week. 'Not yet. Why, are you having trouble?'

'Just with this one.' Kylie flipped to the last page and showed him the family tree. The males were depicted with squares, the females with circles. 'I've narrowed it down to X-linked dominant or autosomal dominant, what do you think?'

'Looks like X-linked dominant to me.' He pointed. 'See, the affected fathers can only pass on the disease to their daughters, because the sons get an unaffected Y chromosome from their fathers. So, all the daughters of affected fathers are affected.'

'Of course. Like Fragile X syndrome.' Kylie tapped her pen on an ominous black square with a line through it, a deceased male. 'I was reading about anticipation today. Do you know what that is?'

'Sure,' Jake said evenly. 'It's where the disease gets worse with each successive generation.'

'That would suck.'

'Well, you know what they say,' he said, his heart pounding CAG-CAG-CAG. 'The anticipation is killing me and all that.'

Kylie chortled. 'You're hilarious, Heremaia.'

'Hilarious.' Did his laugh sound as fake to her ears as it did to his? Or just hysterical? His phone vibrated, making him jump.

'Shit,' he said.

'What's up?' Kylie drained her glass.

'Emily wants to come over. To my place.' How could it be half-past nine already? 'I'd better get going.'

'No worries.' Kylie slid off the stool and followed him out onto the street. 'Thanks for the chat, Heremaia.' She hugged him. 'Hope Emily's viva goes better than last time.'

'Me too.' He inhaled the crisp, dark air, trying not to think about how he'd much rather be filling his lungs with tobacco smoke.

'Like they say,' Kylie said, punching him lightly on the shoulder, 'it's the anticipation that kills you, right?'

'It really is.' Jake thrust his hands into his pockets. 'I'll see you tomorrow.'

'Catch you tomorrow.' Kylie whirled and took off down the street, her pigtails flying behind her. Jake sagged against a shop front, the glass cold through his shirt.

CAG-CAG-fucking-CAG.

'I need a smoke,' he muttered, before taking off in the opposite direction and making a beeline for the nearest dairy.

Emily let herself in only minutes after Jake arrived home, his nerves newly lit with a combination of anxiety and tobacco. *A fine pair we are,* he thought, greeting her with a kiss.

Emily drew away. 'Ugh, have you been smoking?'

'Just one.' Jake closed the bedroom door. 'But I had three beers.'

'That's not like you.' She sat on his bed and wrestled her boots off. 'Everything OK?'

'Fine. How's the study going?'

'OK.' She flopped back. 'It's not my knowledge that's the problem.'

'I know.'

She frowned. 'What are you doing all the way over there?'

'I don't know.' A sudden melancholy was washing over him, threatening to pull him out in its undertow. He lay down beside her, touched her cheek. 'I think I just remembered why I don't drink.'

Emily's breath flowed over his lips. 'Who were you out with?'

'Kylie.'

'Just you and Kylie?'

'It's not me she's having an affair with, don't worry.'

'I wasn't worried.' She pressed her nose into his. 'What's wrong, Jay?'

'I don't know.'

'You keep saying that.'

Jake closed his eyes. Counted heartbeats. Heard the roar of CAG-CAG-CAG in his blood.

'Turn out the light,' he said, so she did, and they wound around each other like cats, skin to skin beneath the weight of the blankets.

'What's it called,' Jake said haltingly, 'when you can't get a song out of your brain?'

'I think it's an ear worm.'

'I've got one of those. Except it's not a song.'

'So . . . what is it?'

He exhaled. 'Do you ever wish you hadn't met me?'

'What kind of a question is that?'

'The kind of question you don't want to answer.'

Emily was silent for a moment. 'If I could go back,' she said.

Jake waited, thick dread curdling in his gut.

'I *know* I would do the same thing,' she said. 'I still would have helped you.'

'That's not really an answer to my question.'

'That's the *only* answer. I would have done anything for you then, and I'll do anything for you now.'

'Well, that's scary.'

'Yeah,' she said. 'It is.'

Jake went to kiss her, to terminate the conversation in their usual way, but Emily hadn't finished. 'Is that all that's bothering you?'

'Isn't that enough?' *More than enough.* He knew he should have kept his mouth shut. Goddamn beer, loosening his tongue, unhinging his neurons.

'No . . .' Her palm was on his chest. 'Do you think . . . is there ever a time when you'd want to know? To find out?'

Jake's thoughts blurred, eddies and swirls. 'Maybe.' He inched his fingers beneath her breast, felt her heart tapping against his fingertips.

'What would you do if it wasn't the answer you wanted?' Emily asked, her panic tipping into his palm — one hundred beats per minute, maybe more.

'I have no idea,' he said. 'Can we stop talking about this now?'

'Promise me you won't do what your uncle did.'

'Time out,' he said and turned away from her, turned away from the terror that had crept into the spaces between his cells. CAG-CAG-CAG, better not to know, but the not-knowing could kill you too. It could.

He felt Emily's nose between his shoulder blades.

'It's not all about you, Jake,' she said. 'You know that, right?'

'Yeah,' he said. 'That's the problem.'

Chapter 14: I Promise

Emily sat in the tutorial room, pressing over the pulse at her wrist. Sixty beats per minute, one per second. When she held up her hands, there wasn't a trace of a tremor.

'Yes,' she whispered.

'Ms Walsh.' Prof Wagner stood in the doorway, straightening the lapels of his white coat. 'Are you ready?'

'Uh-huh.' Her stomach leaping, Emily accompanied the professor to a single room at the end of the ward corridor.

'This is Mr Harrison,' Prof said, indicating the gaunt elderly man sitting upright in the bed. 'And I think you know Doctor Wong.'

'Yes,' Emily said, giving the middle-aged physician at the foot of the bed a quick, terrified nod before focusing on the patient again. 'Hi, Mr Harrison, I'm Emily. Walsh,' she added, knowing how Prof disapproved of students introducing themselves by their first names only.

The elderly man inclined his head. 'Hello, lass.'

Prof extracted a fountain pen and piece of paper from his coat pocket. 'Ms Walsh, could you please examine Mr Harrison's respiratory system and present your findings.' He nodded at Doctor Wong. 'You can start the timer now.'

Slow down, Emily thought, listening to the metronome beat of her heart. *Breathe.* After making a point of surveying the surroundings, noting the blue inhaler and spacer, and the oxygen prongs curled in the patient's lap, she stepped forward.

'Mr Harrison,' she said. 'Do you mind if I look at your hands?' The room was uncomfortably warm, the air stuffy. She wished she'd taken her cardigan off. Too late now, she was being timed.

'Help yourself.' The patient placed his fingers into her palms, as if laying them on a keyboard. 'Everyone is always interested in my nails.'

'Yes,' Emily said, observing the curved, bulbous nails — clubbing, a classic sign of a lung or heart condition. It was so hot she could barely concentrate. Even worse, her stomach had progressed from fluttering to squirming. She fought the rising nausea. What the hell, was it the start of food poisoning or the flu?

She was taking the patient's pulse when the buzzing began in her ears, her vision to grey. But even then, she didn't grasp what was about to happen, because it had never happened before. *I can get through this*, she thought, clutching her stethoscope. *I can—*

———

Blur. Faces. Blur. Voices crowded in. Her hip was hurting, her shoulder too.

'Just a faint.' Doctor Wong's pageboy-styled hair swung forward as she bent over Emily. 'Would you like a drink of water?'

Emily struggled to sit up. A polystyrene cup appeared beneath her chin and she took a cautious sip before hanging her head between her knees.

'Are you all right, lass?' Great, she was still in Mr Harrison's room. She felt something squeezing her arm, the whirr of an automatic blood-pressure machine.

'I'm OK,' Emily mumbled, even though she was about as far from OK as she could get.

'Did you have breakfast this morning?' Wong asked.

'No,' Emily admitted. Come to think of it, she'd been too nervous to have more than half a glass of water.

The cuff began to deflate. 'Eighty-six systolic.' Prof stepped into her field of view, his bushy monobrow undulating. 'Are you known to have low blood pressure, Ms Walsh?'

'No,' Emily mumbled. So much for the beta blockers. They hadn't just lowered her heart rate and stopped her shaking; they'd socked her blood pressure down as well.

'How about we take you to one of the procedure rooms so you can have a lie-down?' Wong suggested.

'I want to go home,' Emily whispered.

'Not with that blood pressure, you're not, young lady,' Prof said. 'Can someone pick you up? What's your father up to today? Haven't seen him in a while.'

Sharp edges of panic cut into her. 'No, please don't — I don't want to worry him.'

'Let's just get you to a clinic room,' Wong suggested, helping Emily into a wheelchair. 'I'm sure you'll be feeling better very soon. You go, Frank, we'll be fine.' She wheeled Emily down the corridor and into a sterile room with a narrow bed and shelves lined with all manner of equipment — drapes and gowns, chest drains and spinal needles.

'Now,' the physician said, once she'd dropped a sheet over Emily's legs. 'Is there anything else I can get you? A cup of tea?'

Emily drew the sheet up to her waist. 'No, thank you.'

Wong glanced at her watch. 'I'll return in about twenty minutes. I'll get the nurse to check up on you, all right?'

'OK.' Emily bit her lip, watching the physician walk towards the door. 'Um, Doctor Wong?'

Wong turned. 'Please, call me Penny.'

Gripping the sheet, Emily said, 'How long does it take for beta blockers to wear off?'

Wong's brow wrinkled. 'Hmm,' she said. 'Well, that explains a lot.' And then, as Emily began to sob, 'Don't cry, sweetheart, it's not the end of the world.' She sat next to Emily. 'Oh, sweetheart,' she said again, as if Emily were her daughter rather than her student, 'you've been having an awful time, haven't you? But I think I know someone who can help you.'

———

When Emily arrived home, it was eleven am. She wasn't hot anymore. Goosebumps lined her skin. Her eyes were swollen, her throat scraped raw.

After running a bath, she lay in the water for a long time, contemplating

108

the thin blue veins beneath her milky skin. Slitting one's wrists, she knew, was not the quickest or most effective way to end one's life.

She gripped the edges of the bath. Thought of the beta blockers in her bag, and the difference between a therapeutic and a lethal dose. Thought about control, and lack of it. She stood up, water streaming from her elbows, her knees, the corners of her eyes.

I think we did it.

I think we did.

Emily stepped out of the bath.

———

Her father called at eight that evening. Emily was sitting at her desk, a pencil in her right hand, her left arm propped up on a cushion.

She fumbled the phone to her ear. 'Hello?'

'Hi, darling, how are you?'

'Fine.' Emily focused on her sketch, at the winged warrior ascending the double helix staircase. The steps looked, strangely enough, like a diagram of paired nitrogen bases.

'I hear you were unwell this morning.'

Emily pushed her chair away from the desk, the casters bumping over the uneven carpet. 'Who told you that?'

'Frank Wagner,' Jim said, as she knew he would. Goddamn it, she should have known Prof wouldn't keep his mouth shut. Whatever happened to patient confidentiality? 'I have to say, it was rather embarrassing to learn second-hand that you've been struggling like this.'

I tried to tell you, Emily wanted to say, but she remained silent. She'd cried enough for one day.

'Look,' her father carried on. 'Everyone gets a little nervous now and then. But taking beta blockers isn't a coping strategy, is it?'

What the? Emily inhaled. 'What are you implying, Dad?'

'I'm not implying anything. But if you'd come to me sooner, then I don't think you'd be in this situation now. Come on, hon, why don't you let me take you out for dinner so we can have a chat?'

'It's OK,' Emily said. 'I think I'll be all right from now on.'

'Really?' Jim didn't sound so sure about that.

'Yeah.' Emily picked at the edge of the dressing on the underside of her wrist. It was nearly time to remove it. 'Don't worry. I don't think it will happen again.'

'Darling—'

'Dad, I've got to go, OK?' Emily ended the call and removed the dressing to inspect the wound beneath. It hadn't hurt as much as she'd thought it would. 'Double helix dragon,' she whispered.

The phone rang again. It was Jake. She didn't answer. Instead, she crawled into bed and closed her eyes, casting her mind back to almost four years ago, when she'd first stumbled into a world she should never have entered.

Emily leaned back in the passenger seat of her father's car and yawned.

Jim glanced at her. 'Too early for you?'

'You could say that.' The digital clock to her right read 0743. Normally Emily wouldn't have been out of bed before ten am on a Saturday, or any day where she didn't have to go to school.

'Best part of the day,' Jim said, switching on the radio and humming along to Elton John.

'You're making my brain hurt.'

'You wanted to come.'

Emily stifled another yawn. 'I know. Still waking up.'

Her father adjusted the rear-vision mirror. 'What's with the sudden change of heart? I thought you had your sights set on a pharmacy degree.'

Emily shrugged. 'Just thought I'd keep my options open. Maybe I'll change my mind again after this ward round.'

'Maybe,' her father said. But he was smiling, as if he couldn't hide his delight at the thought that at least one of his offspring might follow in his footsteps. 'I thought Jake might have asked to come along too . . . Is he still interested in med school?'

'I think so.' Emily stared out of the window at a jogger, who was wearing bright pink shorts and no shirt. 'Um, Dad?'

'Hmm?'

'How do you get Huntington's disease? Is it like cancer?'

'It might as well be,' Jim said, his pale blue gaze catching hers before returning his attention to the road. 'But to answer your question — no. It's hereditary. You only need to inherit a gene from one of your parents to get it, unlike in some other diseases, where you need to get a copy from each parent.'

'So it's autosomal dominant, then?' Emily asked, recalling her Biology classes.

'Exactly. And it's highly penetrant.'

'And that means . . .'

'It means if you get the gene, then you nearly always get the disease.' Jim stopped at a traffic light. 'I assume you're talking about Jake?'

'Yeah.' Emily said, experiencing a jolt inside her chest. 'When will he know if he's got it?'

'Usually they start getting symptoms in their late thirties or early forties, such as lack of coordination, abnormal movements. Oh, for God's sake.' Jim jammed his fist on the horn. 'Must be pretty tough on Jake,' her father continued, once he'd overtaken the meandering Suzuki in front of them. 'Have you seen him, lately?'

'Once or twice.' Emily's heart sped up. 'He's been busy studying for exams.' She was worried about that too. Jake was one of the smartest people she knew, but with everything that was going on at home, he was struggling to get the grades he needed to get into university, let alone medical school.

'As you are, right?' They were approaching the central city. The moon was still out, a faint half-silhouette in the brightening sky.

'Right,' Emily said, although she had found it hard to concentrate on study herself recently. The conversation she'd had with Jake three weeks earlier kept looping through her mind.

Do you promise?

I promise.

But what if she couldn't keep it?

'Are you coming?'

Emily blinked, realising they were now stationary in the car parking building. 'Yeah.' She followed her father into the stairwell. A bass voice echoed around the concrete walls.

'Putting your daughter to work, Doctor Walsh?'

Jim grinned at the burly man bounding down the steps towards them, holding a takeaway coffee and a copy of the Otago Daily Times.

'I need all the help I can get,' Jim said. 'Emily, this is Walter Gardener. He's one of our orthopaedic surgeons.'

'Going to be a doctor like your old man, are you? Good on you.' The surgeon clapped her on the shoulder, before continuing his rapid descent down the stairs. Catching her father's proud expression, Emily felt a surge of guilt. If Jim knew why she was really there — well, that didn't bear thinking about.

———

Emily woke with a start, wincing as she extracted her left arm from beneath her body. How long had she been asleep? An hour? Two? She reached for her phone, lying on the floor beside her bed. The display told her it was 10.59 pm, and that she had three unread text messages, all from Jake.

9.41: *Hey what's up? I've been trying to get hold of you all day.*

10.20: *Have I done something to annoy you?*

10.47: *Really worried about you. If you get this can you call me? I don't care what time it is.*

Her heart, released from its beta-blocker chains, accelerated. Late, it was so late, but she wanted to talk to Jake as much as he wanted to talk to her. She needed to tell him what she'd done.

Some decisions, she knew, were irreversible.

Chapter 15: September Blue

Jake checked his phone for what seemed like the hundredth time. Ten fifty-seven pm, and still no reply from Emily. He re-read his last message, sent twelve minutes ago: *Really worried about you. If you get this can you call me? I don't care what time it is.* Should he go over and check up on her? She was probably asleep, though, and he didn't want to annoy her by waking her. Still . . . what if she'd done something stupid?

Jake touched the bump on his left temple, thinking back to that morning, when he'd been trudging across the sand with his board, the previous night's conversation with Emily still fresh in his mind.

Promise me you won't do what your uncle did.

Time out.

Time out, time out. He was thinking about black squares with lines through them. He was thinking about CAG repeats. How many repeats had his mother and uncle had? At least thirty-six, maybe more. Jake remembered the first time he'd gone to the medical library to look up the scientific explanation for his family curse, when he was fourteen and fearless.

In an unaffected individual, the CAG sequence is repeated 10 to 35 times through the HTT gene. In people who inherit a mutated HTT gene, the CAG sequence is repeated 36 to 100 times, giving rise to Huntington's disease (HD). As HD is an autosomal dominant disorder, there is a 50 per cent chance that the children of affected individuals will also inherit the mutated gene, and hence the disease.

He'd read on, thinking about how clinical it sounded: *HD is a progressive brain disorder that causes uncontrolled movements, emotional problems, and loss of cognition (thinking ability).* What about, *my fate might as well be decided by a flip of the coin; heads you win, tails you lose?* What about, *HD is tearing my family apart?* What about, *HD is tearing* me *apart?*

And finally, the most chilling fact of all: *the third most common cause of death in HD is suicide.*

Jake set his board down and took his jersey off before pulling his wetsuit up. The world had cracked open, the sun spilling over the horizon. Later that morning, he'd be sitting in a lecture theatre with one hundred and eighty-nine fellow medical students. But right then, he needed to obliterate all thoughts from his mind.

Promise me you won't do what your uncle did.

Pneumonia and other infections are the most common causes of death.

It's not all about you, Jake.

That's the problem.

Jake picked up his board and ran at the waves. The sea roared. Jake roared back.

———

'I am a uterus.' The silver-haired Professor of Anatomy balled his fists and dangled them at his side. 'And these are my ovaries.'

Craig, sitting next to Jake, whispered, 'Is this meant to be some kind of weird sexual fantasy?'

'He's not turning *me* on,' Jake muttered before checking his phone. Half-past eleven. Figuring Emily's exam should have finished by then, he sent her a message to ask her how it had gone before focusing on the lecture again.

'These,' Prof Mountain said, moving the cursor over the diagram on the PowerPoint slide, obviously having decided he couldn't convincingly impersonate a fallopian tube, 'allow the passage of the egg from the ovary to the uterus.'

'I. Am. A. Rectum,' a voice announced behind them. Jake didn't have to turn to see who it was, especially once he heard the familiar cackle, but he couldn't resist. 'And this is my anus,' Kylie went on, puckering her lips. Laughter rippled through the lecture theatre.

'Kylie Flanagan.' Prof directed the laser at her forehead. 'One more word, and you can leave.'

Kylie didn't say anything, just pinched her lips tighter. A squeak escaped. Prof sent her out. Jake checked his phone. No reply from Emily.

————

By mid-afternoon, Emily still hadn't replied. Jake was in a small group tutorial in the Anatomy museum, inspecting preserved body parts — sections of liver with cheesy deposits of tuberculosis, gangrenous sections of bowel, lungs blackened by cigarette smoking.

From the next bench, he heard Kylie say, 'I. Am. An. Appendix,' followed by raucous laughter.

'What does the spleen do anyway?' William Koo asked.

'It stores up little bits of carrot for when you vomit,' Craig said. 'Didn't you ever wonder where those came from?'

Jake wandered around, still holding his specimen pot. 'You're full of it, dude.'

Prof Mountain sidled up to him. 'Mr Heremaia,' he said. 'Tell me about your specimen.'

Jake peered through the glassy surface of the pot, in which floated a once-pink fallopian tube containing an embryo. 'It's an ectopic pregnancy.' Everything turned brown and grey after being placed in formaldehyde.

'Correct. Can you name some risk factors for ectopic pregnancy?'

'Pelvic inflammatory disease, like with gonorrhea or chlamydia.' Jake scratched his chin. 'Or previous surgeries with scarring.'

'Correct.' Prof crossed his arms over his bulging stomach. 'One must always perform a pregnancy test in any woman of childbearing age presenting with abdominal pain. An ectopic pregnancy is a medical emergency.'

'*Pregnancy* is a medical emergency,' Kylie interjected.

Prof's narrow lips quivered. 'You may change your mind about that someday, Ms Flanagan.'

Kylie stuck her pen behind her ear. 'In about fifteen years, maybe.'

Prof gestured at her pot. 'What have you got there?'

'It's a brain.' She tapped the glass. 'A very shrunken one.'

'The word is *atrophic*, Ms Flanagan. Such as is typical in Alzheimer's dementia.' Prof plucked another pot off the shelf behind her and held it up. 'Can anyone guess what kind of dementia this person had? Mr Rothwell?' His ball-bearing eyes lit on Craig.

'Lewy body dementia,' Craig answered. 'Because it's mainly the frontal lobes that are atrophic.'

Fifteen years. Dementia. Atrophic.

Jake couldn't stand it any longer. Muttering 'Excuse me', he picked up his bag and hurried out of the museum — past the shrunken brains, past the scarred hearts, past the deformed foetuses with their swollen heads and buds for limbs, and into the high-ceilinged corridor.

Once outside, he strapped his bag over both shoulders and ran, his feet slapping *CAG-CAG-CAG* all the way home. The day wasn't blue anymore, just grey-grey-grey.

————

At the flat, Ian was lying on the couch, eating crackers and watching *America's Funniest Home Videos* on TV. Jake perched on a chair, watching as some doofus accidentally roller-skated off a roof.

'Ohhh,' they chorused. Next they watched a guy fail a backflip against a wall, followed by an incident involving a gymnastics beam and a poor bugger's nads.

'You're home early,' Ian said, after they'd watched about ten more.

'So are you.' Jake grabbed the box of crackers.

'Yeah, Mandy and I broke up.'

'What?'

Ian snatched the box off him. 'She told me she had feelings for someone else. Turns out her feelings for someone else involves a lot of . . . feeling.'

'Holy crap, who is it?'

'One of her lecturers. Dirty bastard.'

'Fuck.'

'Yeah, I'm sure they were doing a lot of that too.' Ian crammed more crackers into his mouth.

'That sucks, man.' Jake checked his phone again. Still no reply from Emily. 'So, what are you going to do?'

'Get pissed,' Ian said. 'You keen?'

Jake stood up. 'Nah, think I'll go for a surf. Want to come?' The half-hour session he'd got in earlier that morning wasn't going to cut it.

'It's getting kind of stormy out there,' Ian said, his eyes returning to the screen. 'Oooh, nasty, did you see that?'

'I'm leaving in ten, if you want to come,' Jake said, his mood blackening further at the thought that he mightn't be able to let off some steam because of the crappy weather. 'Thought I'd go out to Smaills for a change.'

Ian tossed the crackers on the table. 'Fine. But it's your duty to take me out and get me drunk.'

'Later,' Jake said.

———

Jake was in the zone. They'd rolled into the car park at Smaills Beach just after four. Ian had taken one look at the heavy, barrelling waves, and said, 'I'm not so sure about this.'

Jake snorted. 'Are you kidding? This is fantastic.' The waves were feathering in the stiff offshore breeze, and the sky was gunmetal grey — heavy, unyielding. Soon enough it would start raining. Jake didn't care. All he wanted was to get in that water, to stop the thoughts hurtling around his head.

Ian's brow furrowed. 'It's heaving out there.'

'We'll be right.' Jake jumped out of the car.

'There's a reason why no one else is out there,' Ian grumbled, but he grabbed his board. Once they were on the sand, he laid his board down and sat on it. 'You're on your own, Heremaia.'

'Fine.' Jake fastened his leash around his ankle. 'Watch and weep.'

Now Jake was in the zone, but it wasn't a good one. He was caught inside, trying to get beyond the breakers, but they just kept coming at him; walls of water threatening to pound him into the seabed. His limbs were aching, his eyes stinging, his lungs ready to burst.

Time to die, if you want to go out in style then this is how you do it, Heremaia, you crazy bastard.

Then he was through it, on the other side, thank Christ. Jake straddled his board, trying to catch his breath. The beach looked very far away. He rested for a couple of minutes, the dark swell heaving beneath him. The first drops of rain began to pock the surface of the water.

Once he had the rhythm of it, he began to paddle. The wave began to roll and peak. He held his breath, sure he'd missed it, but it swept him forward and then he was up, sliding down the face of God, all thoughts blown away.

And then he was tilting and falling, falling, and the sky had gone and it was all white and foam and which way is up —

The next thing he knew, he was sitting up in the shallows, and his board had washed up on the sand, and he was grinning. Through the water streaming down his face, he saw Ian jumping up and down on the sand, waving his arms and yelling.

'You're fucking crazy, Heremaia! That was fantastic, but don't you dare go back out there — are you trying to kill yourself or something?'

It was worth it.

———

And now Jake had been sitting at his desk all evening, trying to stimulate his brain with coffee and chocolate. His limbs ached, and there was a bump on his temple that he couldn't account for.

Are you trying to kill yourself or something?

How could he explain to Ian that he was giving fate the finger?

You can't kill me now, not when you've got other plans for me.

If you had the test, you'd know exactly when your number might be up. Or not.

No. No, I don't want the test. What if it's positive?

What if it's negative? You could rest easy for the rest of your life.

He needed to talk to Emily. But for whatever reason, she didn't want to talk to him. When he'd called her, it had rung and rung before going to answerphone. Paranoid thoughts crept in. Why was she avoiding him?

Did it have something to do with Adam? What if she was getting back together with him?

Stop it. She's probably just had a bad day. Still, Emily could at least reply to tell him that. Scowling, Jake read the passage in his textbook for what must have been the fifth time.

The four phases of the menstrual cycle are menstruation, the follicular phase, ovulation and the luteal phase. The follicular phase starts on day one of menstruation and ends with ovulation.

He checked his phone again. Ten fifty-nine. He was about to send a fourth and final message — *OK you've got one more minute to reply before I come and check up on you* — when his phone rang.

It was Emily.

————

Emily's front door swung open before he'd set foot on the first step.

'Hey.' She was in her pyjamas, her hair rumpled.

'Hey.' He kissed her. 'Have you hurt your arm?' She was holding it to her chest, as if to protect it. Anxiety gnawed at him. Christ, she hadn't done something stupid, had she?

'Sort of.' Emily led him into her room and closed the door before showing him the underside of her wrist.

'Whoa,' Jake said, taking in the inked dragons etched into her flesh. 'Is this what you were doing when you weren't answering the phone?'

Emily sank onto the bed. 'Well, obviously *I* didn't do it.'

'It looks a lot like your art, though. Did they copy one of your sketches?' When she nodded, he sat next to her, tracing the reddened outline of the tattoo with his forefinger. 'How long did it take?'

'Three hours.'

'It's awesome.' He lifted his eyes to hers. 'Was that a reward for getting through your exam?' Something wasn't quite right. *Emily, a tattoo?* It was one of the last things he'd expect her to do. Emily didn't say anything; just clasped his hand as if worried he might touch her damaged skin.

'I was worried about you,' he said, when she remained silent. 'When you didn't reply to my messages . . .'

Emily gripped him more firmly. 'I'm leaving.'

'Leaving where?' *Dunedin? Me?*

'Medical school,' she said. 'As of tomorrow.'

His mouth fell open. 'What? Have you thought this through?'

She released him. 'Of course I have. I've been thinking about it for months. God, you sound like my father.'

'Hey, I wasn't — it's just a big decision, you know?'

Emily looked down at her tattoo, and Jake did too, at the dragons twisting around each other in their double helix configuration.

'It's the only decision that feels right,' she said. 'Haven't you ever felt like that?'

He drummed a rhythm on his knee. 'Sure. I get it.' But did he? Three and a half, nearly four years of med school, and she was going to throw it away?

It's my fault my fault my fault.

'It's killing me,' she said. 'Can't you see that?'

Struggling to find the right words, the right answers — if there were any — Jake said, 'Maybe.'

'It is.' Emily sounded so sure of herself, more grounded than she had in months. 'Look. I don't know if I want to give it up forever. But I want to take a year off, to try and work out what I *do* want. You know medicine is what *you've* always wanted to do. God, you did a whole degree first. But I feel like I've been channelled into something I never really wanted in the first place.'

'OK,' he said. 'OK, I get it. But what are you going to do now?'

'Get a job, I guess. I don't know.' She took a deep breath. 'I've got an appointment to see a psychiatrist tomorrow.'

'Yeah?' Relief and terror swirled through him, intersecting currents. What if he was ignoring all the warning signs she was feeding to him? 'Em, I—'

'What?'

'Nothing.' This was not the time to talk about the test, about probabilities and impossibilities. 'I mean, tell me about what happened today.' And when Emily hesitated, 'Do you want me to turn off the light?'

'Yes.' She crawled beneath her duvet. 'Yes, please, turn off the light.'

Chapter 16: Clocks

Emily raised her RTD to her lips and took a swig. 'Look,' she said. 'I'm Switzerland.'

'You'd make a good Switzerland.' Ian yanked his beanie over his ears. 'I've always thought of myself as more along the lines of Alaska.'

'How's that?' Kylie spun into their field of view, the lime green ribbons around her plaits a perfect match for her dress.

'I'm the last frontier.' Ian clinked his beer bottle against hers. 'Happy birthday.'

'Cheers.' Kylie turned and bellowed 'Put the Coldplay on!' before turning back to them. 'I wanted to hire a jukebox, but then I realised I was too poor.'

'That's the problem with being a student,' Emily said, scanning the lounge for Jake. The last time she'd seen him, he was deep in conversation with Kylie in the kitchen, but now here *she* was and Jake was — where?

Ian added his empty bottle to the line-up of empty vessels on the windowsill. 'How about you, Kyles? What country would you be?'

Kylie spread her arms. 'India. Chaotic and vivid, and very noisy.'

Ian grinned. 'And never still,' he said, as 'Clocks' began to play over the stereo.

'Never still,' Kylie agreed, and they clinked bottles again. 'Sorry to hear about your break-up with Mandy.'

'Ah,' Ian said. 'These things happen.' It was very good of him, Emily thought, not to mention *why* they'd broken up. At least, until Kylie said, 'So who's this lecturer? Or should I say *lecherer*?'

'Fucked if I know,' Ian said, glancing at Emily.

Emily shrugged. 'Like I said, I'm Switzerland.' Mandy had told Emily the news last night. *So, I've kind of been seeing someone else. I feel terrible about the whole thing.*

'I think you need another drink,' Kylie said cheerfully.

'I think you're right.' Ian ambled towards the kitchen.

Kylie fiddled with the tangerine beads around her neck. 'So . . . Jake said you decided to leave med school?'

Emily nodded, a slight twinge of irritation needling at her. Did Jake really have to share her news, still fresh and raw, with Kylie? Then again, was it really a secret?

'That can't have been easy.' For once, Kylie wasn't trying to make her laugh.

'No . . .' Emily picked at the label on her RTD. 'It's weird how it's so hard to get into med school, but once you're there, they really don't want to let you go.' The psychiatrist yesterday had talked about *not rushing it* and *you might feel differently after a few months off*. She'd talked about medications to *take the edge off. No*, Emily had said. *I don't want any more drugs.*

'Well, I think you're really brave. I hope you're going to do something much cooler.' Kylie brightened. 'You could pick a skill and perfect it, because you'll have so much more time — like a musical instrument, or hey, you could come to pole-dancing class with me.'

'Did someone say pole dancing?' Ian appeared at Emily's elbow holding two beers and an RTD. 'Hope you're thirsty.'

'Oh, go on then,' Emily said resignedly, while Kylie chortled, 'Thanks, Alaska.'

'Pleasure, India.' Ian slouched against the wall. 'Did you know that chess was invented in India?'

'One of my favourite authors is from India,' Emily said.

Ian pointed his bottle at her. 'Arundhati Roy?'

'*The God of Small Things*,' Emily answered. 'How did you guess?'

He shrugged. 'Figured it had to be either her or Vikram Seth.'

'I *love* Vikram Seth,' Emily said, delighted, and clinked bottles with him.

'Jeepers, this is getting really literary,' Kylie announced as Jake drew near. 'What's your favourite book, Jake?'

'The Edmonds cook book,' Jake said, and they all laughed — even Emily, who'd just had an embryonic thought she hardly dared entertain.

'Peasant,' Ian said, before turning to Kylie. 'Now, about this pole dancing . . .'

Kylie set her bottle down on the windowsill. 'Come outside, and I'll give you a demo, shall I?'

'I don't know whether to be excited or terrified,' Ian said in a stage whisper, before taking off after her.

'Hilarious,' Jake said, loosening Emily's RTD from her grasp. 'How many of those have you had?'

'Not enough,' she said, irritation returning, at least until he murmured, 'Come on, don't be hungover tomorrow, I want to take you for a drive.'

'Where?'

'Surprise.' Jake stroked her behind the ear, as though she were a cat. 'Tomorrow is the first day of the rest of your life, remember?' He'd said the same thing that morning when she'd struggled to get out of bed.

'The rest of my life,' she repeated, watching him insert the RTD between the other bottles on the windowsill. 'Sure.'

'Hey, Jake.' A guy with platinum-blond hair clapped him on the shoulder. 'All better now?'

Jake's brow furrowed. 'All better?'

'You were feeling sick in the Anatomy museum on Wednesday? Well, you took off pretty fast, so I assumed that was the problem.'

Jake fingered his nose. 'Yeah, think I ate something dodgy at lunch,' he mumbled.

'Was it chicken? I never eat chicken.' The guy beamed at Emily. 'Hey, I'm Craig.'

'Emily,' she said, giving Jake a sideways look. *Wednesday?* He hadn't seemed ill, but she'd been so absorbed in her own dramas, she'd hardly have noticed.

'You're a med student too, right?' Craig asked.

'No,' Emily said, a strange mixture of grief and elation knotting in her chest.

His mouth twisted. 'Thought I'd seen you around the hospital, but maybe it was someone else.'

'It was a temporary thing.' Emily brushed Jake's elbow. 'I'm going for some fresh air, catch you soon.'

After squeezing between a trio of students on the doorstep, Emily rounded the corner of the house — and halted. Ian and Kylie were a few feet away, between the fence and the side of the house, standing so close they could almost be — *oh*.

'Guess that's one way to get over your girlfriend cheating on you,' Emily muttered, before taking off in the opposite direction and nearly bumping into Jake.

He clasped her shoulders. 'You OK?'

'Yeah. I'm tired, think I'll go home.'

'I'll drive you,' he said, so she let him take her home, let him kiss her goodbye. But she didn't invite him in, and he didn't ask either.

As tired as she was, it was a long time before she could settle to sleep. Everything was off-kilter, blurred, and she didn't know how to set it right again.

———

The next day, Jake drove them to Taiaroa Head at the tip of the Otago Peninsula. The day was windless, the sea so clear they could see all the way to the bottom.

'Look.' Emily clutched Jake. 'There are seals, can you see them?'

'I see,' Jake said, moving away from the edge of the cliff. Emily stayed where she was, watching the seals twist and turn through the blue.

Jake grabbed the hem of her jersey. 'Get away from there, you're making me nervous.'

'Don't worry, I'm not going to jump.' She tossed him a smile. 'Not today.'

'Glad to hear it. Are you hungry?'

'Starving.' She accompanied him to the checked blanket he'd spread on the grass, still damp with the morning dew, and sat cross-legged beside the picnic basket. 'Ooh, blue cheese.'

'It's pretty stinky.' Jake began extracting more items from the basket — French bread, salami, grapes, a bottle of sparkling grape juice and a pair of plastic wine glasses. 'I thought we could have a French theme,' he said, plucking the last two items out.

'Where did you get these from?' Emily pulled the red beret over her tangled hair.

Jake twirled the black beret on the end of his finger. 'Borrowed them off a friend.' He placed it on his head at a jaunty angle.

She smiled. 'You look . . .'

'Dashing? Suave?' Jake pursed his lips. 'Devastatingly handsome? Why are you laughing?'

'Nothing. You're right. You are devastatingly,' she pushed him over, so he was lying beneath her, 'handsome.' She stroked his stubbly chin. 'Very French.'

'A French Māori,' he said into her mouth.

'A Māori French.' His lips tasted like salt, coffee, hope. 'Jake . . .'

'Mmm?'

'I want to write a book.'

'Mmm.' His pupils were pencil points; his irises were burnt umber. 'I didn't realise you were a writer as well as an artist.'

'As in a graphic novel.' Her fingers danced across his lips.

'I think you've already started that . . . right?'

'Right.'

'You really don't want to be a doctor, then.' Unlike with her father, it didn't sound like an accusation, merely a confirmation. An affirmation.

'I really don't. What do you think?'

Jake touched the tip of her nose. 'I think you'll succeed.'

'With not being a doctor?'

'No, with the book. And not being a doctor.' He kissed her again. 'Think we'd better eat before the seagulls get here.'

'Think we'd better,' Emily said, releasing him. They were halfway through their lunch when, remembering Craig's comment the previous evening, she said, 'I didn't know you were sick on Wednesday.'

Jake peeled a crust off his bread. 'Wednesday, was I?'

'When you had to leave the museum?' She wiped her mouth. 'Well. Maybe I heard wrong.'

'Oh. That. It didn't last long.'

'You're a crap liar, Heremaia.'

'What makes you say that?' Jake threw the crust at a seagull, attracting five more.

'You always do that thing with your nose.'

'Do not.' He held her gaze for a moment before glancing away. 'It was kind of true.'

'Sounds like Wednesday was a bad day for both of us.'

'Uh-huh.'

'So . . .'

'It's all right. I'm over it now.' He plucked a grape off the vine. 'We were looking at shrunken brains in the Anatomy museum and I started thinking about Mum. And then I started thinking about the test, and how I could be negative and not even know it, and how that would be such a relief. But then I started thinking, what if I am positive and do I really want to know, and all of a sudden I couldn't breathe.' He took his beret off. 'You know how it is.'

'I do,' Emily said, but her heart had begun to thud. 'So you're going to have the test?'

Jake gripped his thighs. 'I don't think so.'

'Right,' she said, her heart not slowing one bit.

'Because I could be positive and get all screwed-up about it and be miserable for the rest of my life. Or I could be negative and thinking I'm going to live until I'm eighty and die in a car accident before I hit thirty. Do you get it?'

'I get it.' Did she? She wasn't sure. 'I mean, you always said you never wanted the test.'

'I didn't. I don't know, Wednesday was just a temporary madness, you know?'

Emily stroked the scabbed-over surface of her tattoo. 'Yeah. I know.'

Jake exhaled. 'Did you talk to the psychiatrist about the HD? In your session?'

'No,' she said, which wasn't entirely true, but of course she was a much, much better liar than Jake would ever be. 'I didn't.'

'It wouldn't matter if you did.' His eyes were wandering again. 'If it helps.'

126

'I don't need to.' She shuffled closer to him. 'I'm going to be OK now. And so are you.'

'Yeah.' He touched her arm, just above the twisting dragons. 'I think we are.'

Chapter 17: Every Breath You Take

DECEMBER 2003, DUNEDIN

After walking through the Heremaias' front gate, Emily halted, gazing up at the starless sky. When she turned her attention to the top level of the house, where Jake and his mother's bedrooms were, she saw that the lights were off. Surely Jake hadn't fallen asleep? No, not when they'd been preparing for this all week, ever since she'd procured the insulin.

For seven days, Emily had been waiting for her father to confront her, to ask her if she knew anything about the missing insulin from the ward. But as the days wore on (slowly, inevitably), and her father hadn't even mentioned it, Emily dared to think that maybe, just maybe, she'd got away with it.

So far.

'Hey,' a voice said, and Emily jumped. 'Sorry,' Jake whispered, before leading her into the narrow area between the fence and the side of the house. 'Grandma's been asleep since half-past nine, at least.'

'OK.'

'Do you think you've got enough?'

Emily halted. 'I was talking to one of Dad's patients a few weeks ago, and she told me how many units she took with each meal. So I multiplied it by ten.'

'But do you think that's enough?'

'I don't know,' she snapped.

'Sorry.' Without waiting to hear her reply — she didn't have one anyway — Jake rounded the side of the house and opened the back door.

'Come in,' he said.

———

The musty-sour scent inside the house seemed even stronger that evening. Emily followed Jake up the stairs and stepped onto the landing, halting briefly when a loose floorboard creaked underfoot. Jake was already opening Christine's door. There *was* a light on, Emily realised, but it was very dim, and emanating from a bulb dangling from the ceiling. The sour smell was much stronger now.

Breathing through her mouth, she took in the mahogany dressing table crowded with various medicine bottles, a sipper cup of the type toddlers used, and used tissues. In the double bed lay an emaciated figure, one she hadn't seen for weeks. As always, Christine was writhing, seemingly oblivious to the uncontrolled movements of her head, trunk and limbs.

'Mum.' After closing the door behind them, Jake took his mother's hand and lowered it towards the mattress. 'We've come to help you. Like I said.'

Christine moaned and mumbled.

'What did she say?' Emily asked.

'Help.' Jake's voice wavered. 'That's all she says now. Help.'

Emily stayed frozen by the door, watching Christine's lips and facial muscles move through a series of contortions and distortions. Jake pushed the sleeve of Christine's nightie above her elbow.

'This is it where the medication goes,' he said, and Emily looked at the length of plastic tubing in his palm. Jake prodded the bung on the end. 'The nurses screw the syringes on here.'

'Have you told her?'

Jake gave her a jerky nod. Emily moved closer, clasping the syringe nestled within the inside pocket of her bag. Her father always kept a supply of syringes in the bathroom cupboard — for liquid medications when Emily and Bradley were younger, for squirting water into Bradley's ears when they were blocked with wax. Emily was pretty sure her father would never have guessed what use his daughter was putting the syringe to, on a Saturday night when she should have been out partying or at the movies.

Jake took the syringe and kneeled beside his mother.

'Mum, I'm going to give you some medicine, OK?' His voice was thick. 'To send you to sleep forever, like I promised.' Christine made smacking noises with her lips. Her arm jerked up and Jake lowered it again. 'I can't — can you hold her while I —'

'You should hold her,' Emily said, reaching for the syringe. 'I can do it. She'll want you to hold her hand, right?'

Jake nodded and stayed crouched beside his mother, gripping her at the wrist and elbow.

'It won't hurt, Mum,' he said, as Emily screwed the syringe onto the end of the tubing. 'I promise.'

Emily hesitated. Christine twitched again, and let out a long, low moan. Jake breathed out, loudly. 'Just do it, will you?'

'I *am*.' Fighting tears, Emily depressed the plunger on the syringe. It seemed too easy, the clear liquid inside the barrel disappearing inside the tubing, and presumably, into Christine's vein. She unscrewed the syringe, shaking so badly she dropped it on the carpet. She picked it up and shuffled away, watching Jake stroke his mother's hair.

'It'll be over soon, Mum,' he whispered. 'I promise.'

They waited. And waited. After a few minutes, Jake said, 'Have you got any more?'

'No, but I was sure —' Emily moved forward, squinting at the PICC line. 'Um, do you think it all went in? Because I'm thinking it might be stuck in there.'

Jake bit his lip. 'Shit, a flush. I should have thought.' He looked up. 'The district nurse always — shit.'

'What?'

'She flushes the line with saline after she gives antibiotics. Did you bring any?'

'Of course not,' Emily said, on the verge of tears again.

'Water,' he said. 'Just fill the syringe with water. That'll work, right?'

130

Emily nodded and hurried into the bathroom. It took three attempts to fill the syringe, because she kept dropping it in the basin. Damn it, why couldn't she stop shaking? She returned, mumbling 'sorry', and halted. Christine's head was arched back on her neck, her limbs contracting.

'Oh my God, she's having a—' The thick scent of faeces hit her. Emily wanted to vomit. She wanted to scream. She wanted to run away, *right now*.

'Seizure,' Jake said, a high note in his voice that she hadn't heard before. Oh God, what if Christine didn't die? What if she went to hospital, and someone found out what they'd done?

'She's biting her tongue.' Jake drew in a deep, sobbing breath. Emily tore a wad of tissues out of the box on the dressing table and jammed them between Christine's teeth. She shrank against the wall, and looked away. The grunting and rattling seemed to go on forever. Finally, the sounds grew quieter, and further apart . . . and then ceased altogether.

When Emily dared to look again, she saw Jake kneeling beside his mother. 'I'm so sorry.' His voice cracked.

'Is she . . . ?'

'I don't know. Can you check? I can't.' Jake sat on his heels, running a wrist beneath his nose. 'Fuck.'

Emily drew closer and placed her fingers beneath Christine's nostrils. She couldn't feel any air.

'I think so,' she said, checking beneath her own nostrils, then beneath Christine's once more. Christine's pupils were huge, bottomless. The stench was overpowering. Neither of them moved for a moment. What if they'd woken Jake's grandma up? But the house was still, silent.

Jake exhaled. 'I think we did it.'

'Yeah,' Emily said. 'I think we did.'

Bending forward, Jake placed his thumbs over Christine's eyelids, pushing them closed.

'I love you, Mum,' he said.

And began, finally, to cry.

There was hail rattling against the window — but it didn't sound right. Emily opened her eyes. It wasn't quite dark in her room, but it wasn't quite light either. Remnants of dreams skidded across her consciousness, flying away before she could grasp them. She sat up, frowning as the rattle came again.

Scuttling down to the end of her bed, she peered out of the window. A shadowy figure was perched in the tree outside.

'What are you doing?' Emily whispered.

Jake let the rest of the gravel drop into the lawn below. 'Can I come in?'

Emily unhooked the safety latch, opening the window as far as it would go. Jake hoisted himself over the sill and spilled headfirst into her room. Emily stepped away, watching him scramble to his feet.

'Have you even been to bed?' Jake's eyes were bloodshot, his hair rumpled. He was still dressed in the same jeans and t-shirt he'd been wearing the night before.

'Sort of. Not really.' He sat on the end of her bed.

Emily sat beside him, gripping the edge of the mattress. 'Is she really —' She half-hoped Jake would tell her they'd failed, that Christine was still alive — that she hadn't just done something which could result in them both going to prison.

Jake rubbed his eyes. 'Yeah.'

Emily's chest constricted. 'What are you going to do now?'

'I'll call the doctor. When it's light.'

'Will they be able to tell?'

'I hope not. I got rid of all the stuff, except for the empty vials. Have you got those?'

'Yeah.' Emily gestured towards the jacket lying under her desk. 'I was going to go for a walk later. I'll toss them down a drain, or something.'

'OK.' He touched her knee. 'I'm sorry I yelled at you last night.'

'It's all right. I would have yelled at me too.'

Jake tensed. 'Did you hear that?'

'It's just the wind,' Emily said, listening carefully.

'Yeah, I guess.' He exhaled. 'Do you mind if I stay here for a while?'

'Course not.'

'Thanks.' He shuffled back against the wall and closed his eyes. 'I'd better get home before Grandma wakes up.'

'When does she get up, usually?'

'Around half-six, most mornings.' Jake tipped sideways until his head was resting on her pillow and tucked his hands beneath his chin.

'OK.' Emily lay beside him and drew the duvet up. Jake's breathing slowed and became more regular. She turned onto her side, watching how his eyes flickered, dream movements beneath diaphanous eyelids; touched a finger to his lips. He stirred, but didn't wake. Sighing, she took her hand away again. She dozed.

When she next woke, the display on her alarm clock told her it was quarter to six.

'Jake.' She nudged him. 'Wake up.'

Jake's eyes flew open. He stared blankly at her, then blinked. 'Oh. Yeah. Got to go.' He sat up.

'You look like crap,' she said, and he gave her a ghost of a smile.

'Thanks.'

'Anytime.' She stood up and pushed the window open, listening to the faint roar of the surf.

Jake touched the back of her neck. 'Are you going to let me out?' Turning, Emily stumbled against the sill. Jake gripped her shoulders. 'Don't fall.' His pupils were huge, black with a thin rim of iris around the periphery. Closing her eyes, she moved into him, feeling his heart pounding, the air moving in and out of his lungs; thinking about the not-so-fine line between life and death, as her blood tumbled through her ears and Jake pressed his lips against hers.

She heard footsteps in the hallway, a door opening and shutting. Jake pulled away, his eyes deer-wide.

'Catch you later,' he whispered, before clambering over the windowsill and down the tree.

'Catch you later,' Emily echoed, watching him disappear into the blue dawn. Taking a deep breath, she plucked her jacket off the floor, fumbling in the pocket for the two empty vials of insulin — but found only one.

PART II

2013, MELBOURNE

Chapter 18: Down Under

At the end of the day, they queued outside Lord of the Fries, listening to the trains rumble through Flinders Station. Jake's feet were aching, sweat gathering in the creases behind his knees.

'One hundred points of identification for everything,' he grumbled. 'I thought they were going to ask for a rectal exam when we signed up for our phone accounts.'

Emily shifted from one foot to the other. 'You're not in New Zealand anymore, Doctor Heremaia.'

'No kidding.' Jake was still getting used to being addressed as doctor, even though it was a year since he'd qualified. Perhaps the imposter syndrome never truly went away.

'Did you hear back from Ian?'

'Yeah.' Jake checked Ian's text message. 'He said he and Kylie would come around about seven.'

Emily huffed and shuffled forward with the line. 'To sit on our non-existent furniture.'

'They can share a bean bag.'

Two weeks in Australia, and their container still hadn't arrived in the country. Checking his e-mail, he saw a new notification from the hospital. *Change to run allocation for Jake Heremaia.* 'Oh, man, that sucks.'

'What?'

'They've changed my first rotation to Oncology.' How was that going to help him be a surgeon?

'Might be interesting,' she said, turning to watch a police car whip past, its lights flashing.

'I asked for surgical runs. The last thing I want to do is look after—' He hesitated. 'You know what I mean.'

'Not everyone with cancer is dying,' Emily murmured before greeting the person behind the counter. 'Can I have two of the classic fries?'

'Do you think they're discriminating against me because I'm a Kiwi?' Jake asked once they'd received their order. Even the breeze was hot. He was starting to wish they'd gone for an apartment with air con rather than ceiling fans.

Emily licked salt crystals off a chip. 'Probably. And because you're Māori. Also because you're male.'

'Are you making fun of me?'

'Would I do that?' They walked beneath Flinders Station and emerged onto the walkway beside the Yarra River. Waves of people flowed around them.

'Easy for you to say.' Jake stepped aside to let a cyclist whizz past.

'You're just jealous,' Emily said, her gaze caught by a couple sitting outside a riverside brasserie, sipping from glasses glistening from condensation.

Jake crushed his pottle and lobbed it into an overflowing rubbish bin. 'Totally. Well, tomorrow I'll be out of your hair and you can create to your heart's content.'

'We'll see.' Emily batted away a fly, her skin rippling beneath the tiny spiral tattoo on her shoulder. *A tattoo for every book*, she'd said, when she'd had the second one inked a year ago. *Cripes, you might run out of skin*, Jake had replied.

They strolled past the convention centre and on into Docklands where they caught the lift to the fortieth floor of their apartment building. Emily opened the doors to their tiny balcony. 'I'm going to have a shower.'

'No worries,' Jake said, searching the fridge for a cold drink.

'You sound like an Aussie already.'

'Never,' Jake said, unearthing a solitary bottle of Corona. He'd text Ian and ask him to bring some more beer, wine too perhaps. Seeing old friends for the first time in a year was something to celebrate.

Kylie crossed her legs, her spine ramrod-straight against the wall. 'I can't wait for my obs and gynae run. All those gorgeous babies.'

'And prolapsing uteruses, no thanks.' Jake took another triangle of pizza out of the box.

Kylie's upper lip curled. 'Where do you think you came from, Doctor Heremaia?'

'Yeah, but I don't need to look at where I came from all day. Anyone need another drink?'

'I won't say no.' Ian nestled deeper into the beanbag. 'When's your container arriving?'

Emily groaned and tipped off the inflatable mattress she and Jake were using as a bed/couch/life raft. 'Last week they said it would be this week. This week they said it'll be next week.'

'Sounds familiar.' Kylie pressed the soles of her feet together and lowered her knees until they were resting flat on the floor. While Jake was wondering how she did that, Ian said, 'When do you start work, Emily?'

'In six weeks, once the person I'm filling in for starts her maternity leave.' Emily tore the wrapping off a block of chocolate and passed it to Kylie. 'Get this — I'll be not just a teacher aide, but in charge of the sick bay as well. Half a medical degree gets you everywhere, I say.' So far it had got her jobs not just as a teacher aide, but also manning the counter at a sushi shop and waitressing in a bar, much to her father's disgust.

You're way too bright for that, he'd said on numerous occasions. *When are you going to enrol in another degree?*

When I know what I want to do. Her graphic novels aside, Emily hadn't really found anything she was passionate about, apart from the certainty that she never, ever wanted to be responsible for prolonging or ending other people's lives.

'You could put that on your business card, a MBChB with a square root sign or something.' Kylie snapped off a row of chocolate squares. 'And how's the book going? Or am I not allowed to ask?'

'My book is going fine.' Emily took the empty pizza boxes out to the kitchen. 'Slowly, but fine.'

Ian's eyes lit up. 'Are we allowed to see any of this work in progress?'

'Sure.' Emily nipped into the spare bedroom and re-emerged with her sketchpad. 'Maybe look at it up here,' she suggested, clearing a space on the bench.

'Awesome.' Ian peered at the A3 page. 'Is the whole thing pictures?'

'No, there's quite a bit of text too.' She flipped through a few more pages. 'They complement each other, see?'

Jake moved around the bench to get a better view. He never tired of looking at Emily's artwork. The most recent page showed the main characters standing on the curves of a spiral-shaped landscape as a storm front advanced.

'Do the spirals mean something?' Kylie asked.

Emily nodded. 'It's the symbol of the resistance.'

'Dystopian,' Ian said. 'Cool.' Then he and Emily were off, talking about their favourite sci-fi and fantasy novels.

'Come see the view,' Jake said, leading Kylie onto the balcony. Darkness had fallen but it was still warm, thirty-two degrees Celsius at least.

Kylie pivoted. 'Melbourne at night makes you feel like a grown-up, doesn't it?'

'Is twenty-seven grown-up? I thought I had to be at least thirty for that.' Jake moved to the railing.

'You know what I mean.' Kylie leaned beside him. 'It's a long way from little old Dunedin, isn't it?'

'I didn't mind little old Dunedin.' He watched a winking light in the sky, a plane coming in to land. 'I think it'll be good for Em, though.'

'And you. You'll both get paid more, for a start.'

'True. I'm having surfing withdrawals already.'

'You only just got here, give it a chance.' She lowered her voice. 'How's your family?'

Jake bit his lip, glanced away. 'Dad's still alive. Still smoking and telling everyone it's too late to give up.'

'And your mum's side?'

'I don't know,' he said lightly. 'We don't really keep in touch.'

'Right.' He could tell Kylie wanted to say more, was relieved when she didn't. *That's what happens when you get drunk, Jake, spilling your guts out.*

Not that he'd told Kylie *everything* that night, six years ago. Telling her his mother had died of HD was enough of a revelation. Still, it had been a relief to talk about it with someone who was somewhat detached. He couldn't remember the last time he and Emily had gone anywhere near the topic. What was the point?

Ian stepped through the door and whistled. 'Nice view. Want another beer, Jake?'

'Nah, think I'll keep a fresh head for tomorrow.' Jake watched Emily move through the lounge, holding her sketchpad. She was wearing a filmy sundress that clung to her thighs in a way that had him wishing their friends would leave soon.

'Speaking of which,' Kylie tapped Ian's elbow, 'we'd better get going. Might see you at lunch tomorrow, if you're free, Jake.'

'Sounds good. Maybe we'll even have some furniture next time you come over.'

'I don't mind the minimalist look.' Ian deposited his empty bottle on the bench. 'Good luck for tomorrow, doc.'

'Thanks,' Jake said. 'I think I'm going to need it.'

———

Jake yanked the phone out of his pocket. 'Jake Heremaia speaking.'

A gravelly voice drilled into his ear. 'Are you the new resident? Where are you?'

'Um, in orientation?' Jake stood up, ignoring the questioning look from the woman up the front, who was lecturing the new intake of doctors on fire safety. 'I think it finishes at ten.'

'Can you leave now? Our registrar has called in sick and I need some help on this ward round.'

'Sure,' Jake said, exiting without a backward glance. 'Ward ten, right?'

'Yep, ask for Doctor Patel.' The call ended.

Jake checked the time. Eight forty-five. So much for being orientated. After walking to the completely wrong end of the hospital and being redirected by an orderly, he arrived on the Oncology ward with damp armpits and a bulging bladder.

'Heremaia.' A small man bore down on him, pushing a trolley packed with blue folders. 'Welcome. I'm Sanjay Patel, oncologist. Fresh arrival from Kiwiland, huh? Here.' Patel pushed a folder at Jake. 'We'll start with the side rooms. George Christopoulos is a sixty-two-year-old man with metastatic melanoma. Pretty end-stage unfortunately.'

Jake reached into his pocket and came up empty. 'Have you got a pen?'

Patel frowned. 'A what?'

'A pen. I left mine at orientation.' Jake stepped aside to let an orderly with a wheelchair past. The person in the wheelchair was very thin and very yellow.

'What do you want a pen for?'

'To write in the notes?' Jake asked, his frustration growing.

'Oh, a *pen*.' Patel's brow smoothed out. 'It's that Kiwi accent, thought you'd lost the button on your trousers or something and needed a safety pin. Should be one in here.' He opened a drawer on the side of the trolley. 'Right, let's go, I've got a meeting soon.'

Jake accompanied Patel into a side room, a familiar sour scent assailing him. George Christopoulos was lying on his side, an arm dangling over the bedrail.

'Hi, George.' Patel's voice softened. The patient twitched, but didn't open his eyes. 'Have you got any pain? Nausea?'

George moved his head in what Jake took to be a 'no' gesture. *Patient comfortable*, he wrote in the notes, before searching for the observation chart without any luck.

'We've stopped obs,' Patel said. 'Comfort cares only now.' He tapped the IV bag hanging from the pole at the top of the bed. 'Looks like we've got the mix right here. Morphine, haloperidol, metoclopramide. We're waiting for a hospice bed, hopefully today.'

'OK . . .' Jake wrote in the notes. *Impression: end-stage melanoma. Plan: continue infusion, await hospice bed.*

Patel squeezed the patient's shoulder. 'Nice to see you, George. I don't think it'll be long now.'

Well, Jake thought, as they exited. *That wasn't so bad.* And yet, what did they have to offer a patient like that? Nothing, that was what. The most depressing words in the English language: *what you have is incurable.*

He shuddered.

'Right,' Patel said. 'I'll have to get you to finish the ward round — I've got this dratted meeting. I'll return when I'm done, see what you're up to.' He gave Jake a crumpled piece of paper. 'Here's the list.'

'Great,' Jake said, taking in the number at the bottom of the list. Twenty-one patients; he'd be rounding all day.

'One down, twenty to go,' Patel said cheerfully. 'Try not to call me for the next hour unless it's urgent. Bit of a tense meeting.' He drew his finger across his throat.

Jake blinked. 'Right.' What was that supposed to mean?

'Catch you.' Patel took off with a spring in his step, as if he were happy to be escaping.

Jake looked back at the list. 'Bastard,' he whispered. His phone beeped.

Emily: *How's it going?*

It's shit, thanks for asking, Jake typed, then erased. He sent a more elusive: *As expected* and reached for the next folder. Only one more room before he reached the end of the ward, and hopefully, a toilet. He looked down at the notes. Chrissy Jackson, fifty-three years old, breast cancer.

After reviewing her blood tests, X-rays and recent CT scan on the computer, he took a deep breath and entered the room. A woman with a scarf wrapped around her head was sitting up in bed, a bald man sitting at her bedside.

'Are you the doctor?' The bald man asked. 'Great. I hope you've got some time, because I've got a *lot* of questions.' He unfolded an A4-sized piece of paper.

Jake shuffled his feet. 'I'll see what I can do but it's my first day on the job so I might not be able to answer all of them.'

The woman and the man whom Jake assumed was her husband/partner/significant whatever exchanged glances. 'Is there someone else we can speak to?' the man asked. 'We were told the oncologist does a ward round on Mondays. Where is he?'

'He had to go to a meeting.' Jake gripped Chrissy Jackson's folder. 'But I'll talk to him later about anything I can't answer and let you know what he says.'

Chrissy said, 'Fine. Can you tell me how long I have to stay in this godawful place?'

'Ah . . .' Jake perused the observation chart at the end of her bed. 'From the looks of your fever, it's unlikely you'll be able to leave today.'

Her partner bent forward. 'Can you tell us what's causing the fever?'

'I don't think we've found a cause for the—'

'Do you think it might be the chemotherapy?'

'Um, I — maybe?' Did chemo cause a fever? Jake didn't even know what chemotherapy she was on, and wouldn't have known what the names meant anyway. 'I think it's more likely to be an infection,' he added, starting to feel as if he were treading water, and not very effectively. 'Your white cells are low at the moment, so that makes you prone to infection.'

'Right,' the partner said, etching some sort of symbol on his list — a tick? An asterisk? A skull and crossbones?

'Maybe I could have a read of your list and tell you which questions I *can* answer,' Jake offered. The couple exchanged more pissed-off looks. Jake's bladder felt as though it was nudging the bottom of his ribcage. Surely that couldn't be good for him.

'We want to see the consultant,' the partner said, folding his paper into a lumpy square and shoving it into his top pocket. 'And tell him we are *not happy*.'

'OK, sure,' Jake said, and fled. *Two down, nineteen to go.*

His phone rang. 'Hello,' the voice on the end said. 'I'm Estelle, one of the emergency doctors. Your boss said to ring you about this lass with a neutropenic fever who needs to be admitted.'

'Oh. Right.' Jake abandoned his trolley and hurried to what he hoped was the direction of the toilet. 'I've got this ward round to do first.'

'She needs to be seen sooner rather than later. Blood pressure's a bit saggy,' the emergency doctor said. The phone went dead.

'Fuck.' After ducking through a door with a wheelchair sign — screw it, if he didn't pee soon, he'd rupture something — Jake unzipped his trousers. What the hell was he doing? If they'd stayed in New Zealand, he'd have been guaranteed a surgical run. He'd probably be in theatre right now, learning to take out an appendix or rod a femur. Instead, he was looking after distressed and dying cancer patients, which was the last thing he could cope with. Perhaps he should have put that on his CV: *I'm not good with terminal illnesses. Just saying.*

He was washing up when his phone rang. It was the Emergency Department, *again*.

'Got another one for you,' Estelle said. 'Hope you're good at chest drains.'

'Absolutely.' Resisting the urge to drop-kick the phone into the loo, he returned to the ward to retrieve his stethoscope.

A grey-haired nurse hurried up to him, clutching a kidney dish. 'Are you the new resident?'

'Ye-es,' Jake admitted.

'Thank God. Come with me.'

'I don't think you should sound quite so relieved,' Jake said, trailing after her.

'Have faith, doctor. You know more than you think.'

'I'll remind you of that later,' he mumbled, and she laughed.

'Welcome to Oncology, doctor. By the end of this run, you won't want to leave.'

Jake knew she was wrong.

Chapter 19: Set Fire to the Rain

Melbourne in March was soporific, autumn-ripe days and sun-baked evenings. Emily was sitting outside on the balcony, as she did most mornings unless the wind was up. Over her Bluetooth speaker, Adele was singing 'Set Fire to the Rain', which seemed ironic given she hadn't seen rain since she'd arrived in Australia. Nearby, a crow was cawing, yet another reminder that she wasn't in New Zealand anymore.

Not that she minded. She'd been dying to spread her wings ever since Jake had finished his medical degree. *Just one more year*, Jake had said. *I want to do my first year as a doctor in New Zealand.* It seemed as though she'd spent half her life waiting for someone or something, and at last the waiting was over.

Checking the time, she saw it was quarter to ten, nearly time for her morning walk and espresso. Two weeks since Jake had started work, and Emily had already developed a fixed routine. Trying not to think about how she'd be starting her new job in a month, she turned to a fresh page in her notebook and drew a spiral in the top right corner. Plotting was not her favourite activity. She wanted to draw, ink, paint. But if she could even get started on an idea for the next scene then she could work on the imagery when she went for her coffee.

She wrote *2042* in curlicue writing on the top line. On the bottom line, she wrote *2018*. In between the dates, she drew a series of bullet points, a reverse timeline for her dystopian novel. Beside *2042*, she sketched a tiny row of pods, hospital beds with isolation domes over the top of each one.

That's brilliant, Jake had said, when she'd first told him of her idea — a future society where all vaccinations had been banned because of a fake study published by a corrupt scientist with a political agenda. The result:

a super-strain of measles that caused permanent brain changes in the few survivors of an almost universally deadly encephalitis.

What sort of brain changes? Jake had asked.

Telepathy, but I won't call it that, she'd replied. *More like a . . . collective intelligence. An accessing of ancestral memories.*

Brilliant, he'd repeated, and she'd felt a warm glow inside. Her first book had taken her four years to write, one year to revise to the wishes of a small overseas publisher who'd pulled the plug on her at the last minute, a year to mourn.

Don't give up your day job, her father had said. *It's nice you have a hobby, but don't think you'll ever be able to make a living off it.*

Keep going, her mother said. *Rome wasn't built in a day.*

Jake had said, *I just want you to be happy. That's all.*

Was she happy? Emily closed her notebook and moved inside. Pretty close to it, she thought. If only she could say the same for Jake.

———

The sun was setting when Jake arrived home, the skyline golden. Emily had turned down the electric wok and left the rice-cooker on warm.

'How was your day?' she ventured.

Jake dumped his bag on the table and flopped onto the couch. 'Apparently we might have a registrar by next month.'

'Oh.' Considering next month was three weeks away, Emily figured that was bad. The registrar who'd called in sick on Jake's first day had been *stepped down*, something to do with an undiagnosed psychiatric disorder. End result: Jake was acting registrar, despite only being a second-year doctor, and being extremely grumpy about the whole thing.

'On the bright side, it's ten weeks until I start my orthopaedic run.' Jake laid back, his legs dangling over the end of the couch.

'Shoes,' Emily said reflexively.

'They're not touching the couch.'

It's the principle of the matter, Emily thought, but she swallowed the words. Turning towards the wok, she heard a pair of thuds, Jake kicking his shoes off.

'How about you?' He asked. 'Did you get much done?'

'Not on paper.' But she'd had a breakthrough while out running that afternoon, a new plot twist that had her punching her fist in the air, after which she'd glanced around to see a pair of suits smiling at her. *Broke a record, did you?* one of the guys had called out. *Better than that,* she'd yelled back before breaking into a sprint. She'd realised, then, that she loved Melbourne; that she never wanted to leave. 'Tomorrow I'll start working on my main characters.'

She could see them in her mind now. Violet Black, seventeen years old, petite but toned with snappy black eyes. Emily's fingers twitched in anticipation.

'Good.' He closed his eyes. 'As long as you're happy.'

Emily wished he would stop saying that. 'Kylie said it took nearly a year for her and Ian to settle in.'

'Eleven and a half months to go then. Not long at all.' Jake sat up. 'Can we change the subject?'

'Sure,' she said, wary, but he surprised her next by saying, 'Let's go out for dinner.'

Emily gestured at the wok. 'But I made . . .'

'It'll keep, won't it? We can reheat it for tomorrow night.' Jake reached her in three strides and embraced her. 'Let's go out for dinner, and plan a holiday.'

———

Jake speared a chip. 'Great Barrier Reef? We could take scuba-diving lessons.'

'I don't know if I'd like being seventy feet underwater.' Emily watched a tourist-packed boat cruising down the Yarra River, the city lights reflecting off the mirrored surface of the water. She loved dining alfresco, not something she'd done much of in Dunedin.

'So we could stick to snorkelling then. That's easy.'

Emily took a sip of wine. 'Maybe. I don't know, remember that couple that were left behind by the boat and were eaten by sharks? What was the name of that movie?'

'You're paranoid.'

'I like to call it risk-averse. How about the Northern Territory? We could hire a car and go to Ayers Rock and Kings Canyon.'

'A roadie.' Jake set his fork down. 'That sounds cool. Shall we invite Ian and Kylie?'

'Why not?' The more she thought about it, the more it appealed. 'When?'

He shrugged. 'Early May? I could take the last week of this rotation off. It'd be nice to have a break before I start orthopaedics.'

'Done.' They smiled at each other, and Emily thought about how she hadn't seen much of that from Jake recently. She twirled spaghetti around her fork. 'By the way,' she said, her heart speeding up, 'I was wondering what you think about adopting a cat.'

'A cat?' Jake pushed his plate away. 'From who?'

'Nick, my coffee guy —'

'*Your* coffee guy?'

'Well, he makes it every day. Anyway, the cat's not allowed to hang out at the café anymore because it keeps trying to swipe food off people and I said I'd take her.'

'You want to bring a criminal into our apartment?'

'Would you be serious?'

'Thought you'd had enough of that recently.'

'Maybe.' She slipped her sandal off and ran her big toe along the inside of his thigh. 'So, about the cat . . .'

'We'd better check our tenancy agreement.'

'I already did. Cats are fine.'

Jake's mouth twisted. 'OK, but where's it going to do its business?'

'We'll get a kitty litter box, put it out on the balcony.'

'Fine, as long as she doesn't sleep on the bed.' He clasped her foot. 'Have you finished?'

'No, I was just getting started,' she said, and was rewarded with another smile.

'Me too,' he said, stroking her sole with the ball of his thumb. 'I'll get the bill, shall I?'

Emily stared into the darkness, unsure what had woken her. Something wasn't right.

She pressed over her belly. It was squirmy, unsettled. Turning onto her side, she checked the time and saw it was two thirty-seven am. The not-quite-right feeling was morphing into a sensation she remembered only too well. Yet she'd only had one glass of wine.

The nausea surged, so suddenly she only just made it to the toilet before her barely digested meal was ejected from her unhappy stomach. *Yuck, yuck, yuck.* After washing her mouth out, she went to brush her teeth, but had to run to the loo again. Other end this time, oh great.

'Are you all right?' Jake asked when she finally crawled into bed.

'No.' She huddled beneath the duvet. 'Think those shellfish were dodgy.'

She felt Jake's body behind her. 'Crap. You're shivering, are you cold?'

'Freezing,' she managed. 'Can you find another blanket?'

'I don't think we have one.'

'Or a sleeping bag? I'm so cold.'

'A rigor,' he said, almost to himself.

'I'm going to be—' She bolted out of bed again and sat on the toilet.

'Here.' Jake shoved a bucket through the door. Several ejections and explosions later, Emily sat in the shower, feeling as though her whole gut had been turned inside out.

'Poor thing,' Jake said when she returned to bed, her hair dripping. 'Do you want me to go and get you some ginger ale?'

'It's four am.'

'Five,' he said. God, she must have been spewing and pooing for hours.

She closed her eyes. 'You're on call tonight, you should get some more sleep.'

'Nah, I'm awake now.' He began rubbing her back with slow, circular movements. 'Wonder what it is.'

'Does it matter?'

'Well, yeah. You could have a notifiable disease, like *Salmonella* or *Shigella.*'

'S'pose.' Her brain was sluggish and her skin felt hot all over. 'No wonder pregnant women aren't allowed to eat shellfish.'

'Lucky you're not pregnant then.'

'That's one way of looking at it,' Emily said. 'Glass half full and all that.'

Jake kissed her on the cheek. 'See you soon. Bucket's by the bed, OK?'

———

On day two of her illness, Emily got up at eleven am and sat on the couch with her laptop. She still wasn't up to eating, but at least the uncontrollable emissions had settled, mostly.

When she checked her email, she saw that there was one from her father.

Hi Emily, how's it going over there? Your Facebook posts suggest you're having a great time, anyway.

Translation: *So you have time to post on Facebook but not to ring or e-mail me?*

Funny to think she used to be so close to her father before she'd tuned into his passive-aggressive behaviour. No wonder her parents' marriage hadn't lasted. With an internal roll of her eyes, Emily kept reading.

I'm coming to Melbourne at the end of July for a meeting. Is it OK if I spend a night with you?

Her phone beeped, a message from Jake: *How are you feeling?*

Better, Emily replied. *Is it OK if my dad comes to stay at the end of July?*

Emily went to have a shower. When she returned to the couch, she saw two messages on her phone.

Jake: *For you, anything.*

Nick: *Can I drop the cat off after work?*

After sending *What's the possibility of a massage with all the extras as well?* to Jake and *Any time* to Nick, Emily returned to bed.

———

Kylie gripped a pole as the tram rounded the corner. 'So he declared his undying love for you? That's hilarious.'

'It wasn't hilarious. And it wasn't undying love. He gave me his cat and tried to kiss me.' Emily flushed, remembering.

'Well, you did send him an erotic message.'

'By *accident*.' Sending the massage message to Nick instead of Jake had to go down as one of the most embarrassing things that had ever happened to her. 'Now I'm going to have to find somewhere else to buy my coffee.'

'Because there's such a shortage of cafés in Melbourne. Was he a good kisser?'

Emily glared at her. 'How would I know? I shoved him away and said, *See that guy in the photo over there? That's my boyfriend.* And he said, *Cripes, he's a big fella* and apologised and left me with the cat.'

'Ha ha, that's great.' Kylie's laughter echoed through the carriage.

Biting back a smile, Emily said, 'Let's just say I'm going to triple-check that all my messages go to the right person in future.' A pair of students in striped blazers vacated their seats, and she sat down.

Kylie perched next to her. 'Have you told Jake?'

'Not yet.'

'It was only two weeks ago, after all.'

'I think some things are best left unsaid.' Emily elbowed her. 'So keep it to yourself, will you?'

'My lips are sealed.' Kylie stared straight ahead, her lips still twitching.

Emily dug into her bag, checking she'd brought her copy of *Bring Up the Bodies*. 'Do you think it matters if I haven't read the whole book?'

'Course not. We usually only talk about the book for the first fifteen minutes or so. After that we just sit around drinking and gossiping.'

'Cool. I meant to finish it, but then I got caught up with my drawing.' The tram came to a stop and the doors hissed open. Emily inhaled. The scent of eucalyptus seemed especially strong that evening.

'How *is* the book going?' Kylie asked. 'Your one, I mean.'

'Slowly but surely. How's work?'

'Yeah, not so bad. I'm really enjoying the obs and gobs.'

'For your information, Doctor Flanagan, vaginas are *not* gobs,' Emily said, and she and Kylie burst out laughing. Once she could breathe again, Emily said, 'How about Ian, how's his job going?'

'He's loving it, I think. Yesterday he said he spent all afternoon trying to work out the best way to market a new medication to help sustain men's erections.'

Emily, sensing at least five pairs of eyes swinging their way, said, 'What image did he come up with? Let me guess, couples riding bicycles?'

'No,' Kylie said, feigning indignation. 'They were riding *horses*.'

Snorting, Emily yanked open the window above her. 'It's hot in here, don't you think?'

'We're living in a desert, remember?' Kylie pressed the buzzer. 'Next stop's ours, Walsh. Hope you're ready for lots of intellectual discussion followed by lots of wine.'

'I most certainly am.' Emily stood up. Well, maybe not the lots of wine. Her stomach hadn't quite recovered from the food poisoning yet, she didn't think. She stepped onto the pavement. 'Is that rain?'

'You know, I do believe it is,' Kylie said, and as the intermittent drops turned into a deluge: 'This country doesn't do things by halves, does it?'

I love it, Emily thought. *I do, I do.*

Chapter 20: 2+2=5

Jake pushed his stethoscope into his right pocket, his ID badge into the left. 'Your last week of freedom,' he said, opening the door to let the cat out onto the balcony. Pink loved perching on the barbecue table, watching the activity forty floors below.

'I know. Not sure how I'm going to cope with a regular work day next week.' Emily picked up a piece of toast and set it down again. 'Hey. Did you say the new registrar starts today?'

'Yeah, finally.' He sat next to her, clasping her wrist. 'Did you make that doctor's appointment?'

'I will.' Her skin was winter-pale, even though it was only the end of March. Trying not to let her see the concern thrumming through him, Jake said, 'Just humour me and go today, will you?'

'It's just a leftover from the gastro. I'm sure one's bowel doesn't recover immediately.'

'Sure, but it's been four weeks. I'm sure you're right and it's only an irritation of your stomach lining or something, but you could be iron-deficient or need a scope to check you haven't got an ulcer.' He brushed her fringe off her forehead. 'If it's the cost you're worried about . . .'

'I'm not worried about the cost.' She pushed her plate away. 'I'll go today, OK? Promise.'

'Good.' Jake let go of her wrist — he was sure she'd lost weight — and stood up. 'Let me know how it goes.'

'I will. Have a good day, doing half the work you've been doing for the past six weeks.'

'It'll be like going on holiday.' He kissed her. 'Maybe you should go back to bed for a bit.'

'Maybe I will,' she said, which *really* worried him, because Emily had never been one for lazing around in bed.

After exiting the lift, Jake walked out into the crisp morning, joining the waves of commuters rushing for the next traffic light, the next tram, the next train. Weight loss, reduced appetite, nausea. Jesus, how many red flags was that?

No, surely he'd been working in Oncology for too long. That was enough to make anyone think every pain was a tumour, every mole a melanoma. Shoving the disturbing thoughts away, Jake slipped his earbuds in and selected an album from his phone.

Nothing like a bit of Radiohead, he thought, as he squeezed amongst the other commuters on the packed tram, and the first song, '2+2=5', began to play.

Sometimes, often, life felt a lot like a Radiohead song.

———

The new registrar wasn't there when Jake arrived at ten to eight. By half-past eight, thirty minutes after the ward round was meant to start, Jake gave up and started rounding on his own instead. He was examining the third patient, an elderly man with pancreatic cancer, when a young woman marched into the cubicle.

'Hi, I'm Ingrid Watson, the oncology registrar.' She shoved her hand between Jake and the patient.

Jake stepped away. 'Uh, hi. I'm Jake. I was just listening to—'

Ingrid flipped her dark, glossy locks over her shoulder. 'Don't worry, I can take it from here.' She took the patient's notes off the windowsill and passed them to Jake. 'How are you today, Mr Ricci?'

Ricci tugged on his ear. 'Can you speak up? I can't hear you.'

Ingrid sighed. 'I said, HOW ARE YOU MR RICCI?'

'Like I said, I can't hear,' he repeated, and Ingrid, obviously frustrated, turned to Jake.

'Can *you* ask him how he is? Maybe he'll hear your voice better than mine.'

'He already told me his pain is under control,' Jake said, not looking up from the notes, 'and he's quite frustrated by his hearing loss, as you can probably tell.'

Ingrid Watson, whoever she was, didn't seem to have a very good bedside manner.

'His hearing? What's that got to do with us?'

Jake wrote *Ward Round Watson* at the top of the page and drew a line underneath.

'Side-effect of the cisplatin,' he said.

'Cisplatin,' Ingrid said, expressionless.

'The chemotherapy.'

'I know that,' Ingrid snapped, although Jake was pretty sure she didn't. 'Well, I guess it might take a while for that to get better.'

Jake stared at her. 'It won't get better.'

'I don't think you can know that for sure,' she said, taking her stethoscope from around her neck.

'Possibly,' Jake said, seething inwardly, while knowing she was wrong. In the notes, he wrote: Impression: *(1) Advanced pancreatic cancer (2) Cisplatin-induced ototoxicity.* He was tempted to add *(3) Obnoxious registrar,* but restrained himself. Perhaps she was just new and nervous. He knew what that felt like.

'Where are you from?' Ingrid asked once they had returned to the corridor.

'Dunedin. In New Zealand.'

Ingrid smoothed her hair, which was so long it brushed the top of her buttocks. 'Have you been here long?'

'Couple of months.' Jake slotted Ricci's folder into the trolley and selected the next one. 'I don't know this patient, but it looks like he came in yesterday — mass in his chest, possible germ cell tumour.' Ali Oni, twenty-eight years old.

Emily Walsh, twenty-seven years old.

No, stop it, you're being paranoid.

'Right.' Ingrid yanked the notes off him. 'Let's see . . . shortness of breath, weight loss . . . Where's he from, does he need an interpreter?'

'No idea,' Jake said.

Ingrid huffed and passed the notes back to him. 'Guess we'll soon find

155

out.' She marched into the next four-bedded room. Ali Oni was in a bed next to the window, the curtain drawn around his bed.

'Hello,' Ingrid said super-slowly. 'My name is Doctor Ingrid Watson.'

Oni folded the newspaper in his lap. 'Gidday.' He had a characteristic Australian drawl that nearly made Jake laugh out loud.

'Where are you from?' Ingrid asked, scowling at Jake.

'Melbourne,' Oni said. 'How about you?'

Bending over the notes to hide his smirk, Jake wrote *Ward Round Watson*. In tiny letters on the top right of the page, where no one would read them unless they knew where to look, he added *(1) Kill me now.*

Perhaps it was a bad dream. If so, he needed to wake up *right now*.

———

Kylie picked up a round of sushi with her chopsticks. 'How long do you think she's been a registrar?'

'A year, apparently. This is her first time in Oncology.' Jake prodded his own sushi. So much for having a holiday. Having Ingrid around seemed to have doubled his workload rather than lessened it. Before lunch he'd had to fix up several of her mistakes, including charting one patient not enough morphine, and another patient far too much. 'I think she was having some sort of break.'

'Guess she'll get better.'

'I guess.' He squeezed soya sauce over his sushi. 'How are the babies?'

Kylie nudged her lime green glasses up her nose. 'Well, there's no shortage of them. I helped deliver triplets this morning.'

'Cool,' Jake said, while simultaneously worrying about whether (a) he needed to check all Ingrid's prescribing before the end of the day, in case she'd made any more life-threatening errors, and (b) Emily had seen the doctor yet. Surely (a) Ingrid couldn't be that incompetent and (b) Emily would have messaged him if there was something really wrong.

'Twins are cool. Triplets are a social disaster. I mean, if humans were meant to feed three babies at once, they'd have three breasts instead of two.'

'Were they IVF babies?' Jake bit into his sushi.

'Poorly managed IVF.' Kylie dropped her chopsticks into the now-empty plastic container. 'They were only twenty-five weeks, so tiny I could fit them in my palm.'

'Whoa.' Jake's phone beeped.

'You're jumpy today, aren't you?' Kylie announced at her usual volume, which was about three decibels louder than everyone else.

'Too much caffeine,' Jake muttered, reading Emily's message again. *Can you ring me?* 'Um, s'cuse me.' He moved outside, past a table of rowdy medical students and into the far corner of the courtyard.

'Hey.' Emily's voice alone was enough to make his chest constrict.

He clutched the stethoscope in his pocket. 'How'd it go?'

'Um, I — what're the chances of you getting off early?'

'Early? Why? What did the doctor say?'

'I can't tell you over the phone,' she said, and burst into tears.

'OK.' Jake's heart broke into a sprint. *Shit shit shit.* 'OK, give me an hour, are you at home?'

Emily gulped. 'Yes, I'll see you there.' The phone went dead. Jake stared at the screen. *2+2=5*, he thought. *2+2=5.*

'Sick patient?' Kylie asked when he returned to their table.

'Yeah,' he said. 'I'll catch you later.' After texting Ingrid (*Family crisis, got to go, really sorry*), he left the cafeteria, left the hospital and jumped on the first tram to the CBD.

———

Pink was first to greet him when he entered the apartment, her noisy cries jangling his already fragile nerves. He nudged her away with his foot and continued into the bedroom.

'Em?' She was lying on the bed, the curtains drawn against the mid-afternoon sun, the ceiling fan spinning, whump-whump-whump.

'Hey.' Her tone, in comparison to an hour earlier, was oddly flat.

Jake sat next to her, his thigh touching her hip. 'What did he say?'

'*She*,' Emily said, 'figured it out straight out away.' She drew in a shuddering breath. 'I can't believe I was so stupid.'

'What do you mean?' Jake took her hand. It was warm, slightly clammy. Emily's chest rose and fell, and for the first time, he noted her breasts seemed more prominent than usual.

2+2=5, his brain gabbled. *2+2=*

The words tumbled out of her mouth before he'd had time to assemble his thoughts, but his heart was already clenched like a fist, the blood vessels dilating behind his eyes as the realisation exploded into his subconscious.

Oh fuck, oh fuck, oh fuck.

'Jake,' she said, 'I'm pregnant.'

Jake opened his mouth. Nothing came out.

Chapter 21: Heartbeat

In the seconds after Emily told Jake she was pregnant, he remained silent, expressionless. His pupils were so large there was only a rim of iris around the periphery, his breathing rapid.

She sat up, gripping the sheet. 'I'm not the only person responsible for this. So don't try and make it all *my* fault.'

'I wasn't — Jesus.' Jake stood up, raking his hair.

Emily jumped out of bed and began tugging her clothes on. 'And don't tell me to get rid of it, because I'm not going to, do you understand?'

Jake slumped against the wall. How could he just stand there, saying nothing? Why wasn't he yelling at her or asking how far along she was, *anything*?

'Because it's me who's going to have to deal with it if you won't, or can't,' she carried on.

'Em, can you just calm down for a sec, so we can—'

'No, I can't.' She rushed out, scooped her bag off the table and escaped out of the apartment, slamming the door behind her. After exiting the apartment building, she hurried down the street, thinking back to that morning, before everything had changed.

The doctor had called her in at eleven, by which stage Emily had been sitting in the waiting room for thirty-five minutes.

'Hi, I'm Cathy Liu.' The GP didn't look much older than Emily. She wasn't sure whether to be reassured or worried about that. 'How can I help you?'

Emily sipped on the cup of water she'd brought in from the waiting room.

'I've been feeling sick for the past few weeks,' she said. 'Ever since I had food poisoning.' She relayed her symptoms.

'Hmm.' Doctor Liu typed a few words into the computer. 'Do you take any regular medications?'

'Just the contraceptive pill.'

'Have you missed any doses recently?'

'No. I never miss my pill.' Not since the day Jake had yelled at her, not long after they'd first got together.

'How about when you were sick? You said you had vomiting and diarrhoea for three days, is that right?'

'Well, two and a half. I think.' Emily gripped her bag strap. *No. No, surely not.* 'I take it every day. I've been running the packets together for months so I don't have to have a period.'

'Perhaps we'll just do a quick pregnancy test, shall we?' So casual, as if it wasn't such a big deal.

Emily didn't even try to return Liu's smile. 'I can't be pregnant.'

'Perhaps not, but we should rule it out. There may have been a couple of days or so when you weren't absorbing the pills.'

'No, I mean I —' Emily gave up, not in the mood to explain exactly why she couldn't be fucking pregnant. *No no no.*

But suddenly, finally, everything was slotting into place.

———

Numb, Emily left the clinic with a form for blood tests she wasn't in the mood to have that day, and a prescription for iodine and folic acid.

'We'll book you in for a scan around twelve weeks,' the GP said, before giving her a list of midwives to contact. She didn't talk about termination, and Emily didn't ask. How could she talk about pregnancy? How could she talk about termination? The impossible had happened.

Hurrying home, she went over the impending conversation with Jake in her mind. She could only imagine what he'd say. *How could you be so careless? Don't you know you're meant to use condoms after Ds and Vs?*

Well, Jake, don't you think you have some responsibility in this too? You're the fucking doctor; shouldn't you have been reminding me of that? It takes two to have sex, in case you had forgotten.

After stumbling into the apartment, Emily went straight into the bathroom and turned the taps on. Pink sat on the end of the bath, observing her as she ran hot water until her skin turned pink. Maybe she needed a bottle of gin. Maybe she should book a termination and do it without telling Jake. He'd never know.

Pressing over her lower abdomen, she immediately felt ill again. Six weeks, give or take, Doctor Liu had said. How big was a six-week foetus? Emily stood up and reached for a towel, then headed for the bedroom and her laptop. It didn't take long to find a website about foetal development from weeks one to forty.

At six weeks, she read, *a baby is the size of a lentil. He or she may be wriggling their paddle-like hands and feet, and will soon be sprouting eyes, a nose, ears, chin and cheeks.*

Emily fanned her fingers over her waist. *He or she.* She remembered the photo Jake's father had once showed her of a wee boy with sparkling eyes and a wide smile. Or perhaps the foetus was female, a girl who would have Emily's curls and Jake's dark eyes.

A baby, she thought. *My baby.* Our *baby.*

But I never wanted . . . we never wanted . . .

And yet, suddenly, that was *all* she wanted. How could she get rid of this? What if she never got another chance?

'No going back now,' she whispered.

———

Emily wandered through the subway and into the noise and hustle of Flinders Station. Overhead, loudspeakers announced the next trains for Frankston-Craigieburn-Lilydale. Emily took the escalator to the platforms below and boarded the first train she saw. It was only once the train left the station that she glanced at the destination on the digital display above her. She'd never been to Dandenong before, but whatever. There was a first time for everything.

She unzipped her bag and dug around for a short time before realising she'd forgotten her phone. As if she felt like communicating with anyone right then, although she could have done with some music so she didn't have to listen to the shouted conversation of the teenagers behind her. *Such a slag . . . given blow jobs to half of year twelve, yeah anything that moves . . . fuck off, you loser, you'd be lucky to have this . . .* God, did she used to be like that?

I feel old, she realised. Ten years since she'd finished high school, ten years since she'd made Jake a deadly promise. Ten years since Jake had run away and left her to fend for herself.

No, dial back: that's not fair.

Nothing is fair. Nothing, no one.

Perhaps she'd have to fend for herself again, in time. She stroked the dragons on her wrist. Double helix dragon, dragon double helix. She'd never pushed Jake to have the genetic test. It was his decision, after all, and as he'd always said, *What difference does it make? There's no treatment for HD, no cure. I don't want to hang around waiting to die if I find out I've got the mutation.*

But now . . . Emily touched her stomach, something she hadn't been able to stop doing since the GP had showed her the stick with the two blue lines.

If Jake is positive, then our baby has a fifty per cent chance of inheriting the mutant gene.

If Jake is negative, then we won't have to worry ever again.

But Jake doesn't want to know.

We could test the baby.

But . . . why?

Emily pressed her cheek against the window, the cool glass soothing on her flushed skin. The train gathered speed, propelling them into the suburbs. Her pounding heart felt as if it had too much blood rushing through it, or maybe it was just the effort of beating for two. She closed her eyes, remembering a wind-swept beach, the boy from next door who had grown into a man while she hadn't been watching.

I want you to know I'm sorry. For dragging you into something that was nothing to do with you.

It's a bit late for that, isn't it?

Too late, she thought, thinking of the tiny heart fluttering inside her. *It's always been too late.*

———

It had been dark for a couple of hours by the time Emily returned to the apartment. Her feet were aching, her mouth dry despite the water bottle she'd tipped down her throat on the train ride home. The chips she'd eaten in Dandenong had helped alleviate the nausea, temporarily, but it was creeping up again.

What time was it? When she'd left Flinders Station she'd thought the clock had said nine pm, but she hadn't really been concentrating. All she wanted was to have a shower and crawl into bed. But first, Jake.

When she opened the front door, the TV was flickering, the sound turned down low. Jake was nowhere to be seen. Had he gone to bed early? Perhaps he'd gone out or, God forbid, taken off, never to return.

'Where've you been?'

Emily inhaled. 'You scared me,' she said, as Jake moved in from the balcony, Pink on his heels.

'You scared me too.' He thudded down on the couch. 'I was worried you'd done something stupid.'

'I went to Dandenong,' she said, her voice trembling.

He stared at her. '*Dandenong*? OK, I'm glad I didn't know that.'

'It wasn't as scary as you think.'

'Hmm.' Jake reached out, his hand cool on her wrist. 'Are you feeling sick?'

'A little.'

'Tired?' He pulled her onto his lap.

'Exhausted.' Relief was Jake's embrace, his mouth on her ear.

'Poor baby.' He stroked her stomach, and she felt something unfurl within; something, someone. 'Come to bed.'

'Aren't you angry with me?'

'What makes you think that?'

'I don't know,' she admitted. Had she even given him a chance, this afternoon? Guilt flushed through her. 'Sorry. I'm not thinking straight, I guess.'

He kissed the angle of her jaw. 'Me neither. Come to bed.'

So she let him lead her into the bedroom, where they shed their clothes and lay between the sheets, skin to skin; where she listened to his heartbeat, so steady, and felt her own heart slow and speed up as he stroked her tingling breasts, her deceptively flat belly, her aching thighs.

'I'll take care of you,' he whispered. 'Both of you.'

———

Emily woke to find herself sandwiched between Jake and the cat.

Jake, the cat and an accidental foetus. She squinted at the fluorescent dial on the clock beside the bed. Five fifty-three, annoyingly early, but she was wide awake. The water in her bottle tasted metallic, no doubt due to her hormone-addled taste buds. Pink climbed onto Emily's chest, purring.

'Can't,' Jake mumbled. Emily reached out, touching the knot of his biceps. It was too dark to see, but she knew exactly where the koru was. Ngaire, Jake's auntie, had told Emily the koru was the symbol for new life. *Perhaps that should be my next tattoo*, she thought, *a tiny koru on my hip*.

'Mmm.' Jake turned towards her. Emily rolled onto her side, her back to his chest, two spoons slotted together. 'I had a dream.' His voice was slow, syrupy.

'What about?'

'This.' He fanned his fingers across her lower abdomen. 'But . . . it wasn't a dream, was it?'

'No-oo . . .'

'No.' He fell silent. The fluorescent dial slid from five fifty-nine to six.

'What are you thinking?'

'I don't know.'

'Yes, you do.'

Jake kissed her neck. 'Do you think we should . . . get a test?'

'For the baby?'

'Yeah.'

'I don't know.' Pink climbed over them and nestled against Emily's belly, as if she knew she had competition.

Jake said, 'Would you do anything differently if you found out the baby had a mutant gene?'

'I don't think so. No.' Terminating a pregnancy because the foetus had inherited Jake's deadly legacy? *No. No, because that would be like saying Jake doesn't deserve to be here either.*

'I don't think we should,' she said, more resolute now. 'Do you?'

'I don't know,' he said, but she knew he was thinking of his mother. Christine, her grey skin stretched over her high cheekbones, her limbs twisting around her body in a cruel, endless dance. Who would condemn someone to such a fate?

'I don't think I could stand to find out. Because, if it were positive, that would mean you're also—' Emily broke off.

'Well,' Jake said. 'I'd cope.'

Maybe, she wanted to say. *Maybe* you *would, but I'm not so sure about me.*

'I choose life,' she said. 'I choose *this* life.'

Jake didn't reply, just held her tighter, and they lay like that for several minutes, as time moved on and on and on. When the alarm rang at half-past six, they both started.

Jake sat up, rubbing his chin. 'By the way,' he said, as if he'd only just remembered. 'I forgot to tell you about the new registrar.'

'Oh yeah, are they good?'

'No,' Jake said and left to have a shower. When he returned, he said, 'I think we should call it Nemo.'

'Your registrar?'

'No, the baby. Because it's tiny, like the clown fish in the movie, and because if it weren't for the dodgy seafood . . .'

'Oh, yeah,' Emily said, remembering the food poisoning that had set it all off. 'Nemo. I like that.'

Chapter 22: Lucy in the Sky with Diamonds

Jake spoke into his phone. 'Y-ello, Jake here.' He knew who it was even before the nurse identified herself.

'Hi, it's Petra. Do you know where Ingrid is?'

'No idea.' Did anyone? Ingrid, when she wasn't wreaking havoc on the ward round or in clinic, was often nowhere to be found. After four weeks, Jake's patience, much like the rest of the Oncology team, was threadbare.

'Well,' Petra's tone changed from exasperated to wheedling, 'do you think you could come and drain a couple of bellies? We've got Hershey's Kisses . . .'

Jake ticked the last box on the computerised CT request and sent it into the stratosphere with a click of the mouse. 'Come on, you can do better than that.'

'Got some Bassett's Jelly Babies on the top shelf that Brian brought back from England.'

'Now you're talking. I'll be down in ten.' Jake ended the call and messaged Emily. *Can we do lunch at 1pm instead? I'm CIA on the day ward.*

CIA — covering Ingrid's arse. If he could get through the next week, then hopefully he'd never have to work with her again.

Still, Oncology had kind of grown on him.

His phone beeped. *1pm?? I don't know if we can wait that long.*

Is Nemo being greedy? Jake replied. In two weeks, Emily would have her twelve-week scan. In two weeks, they could tell the rest of the world. He was looking forward to that.

And yet, he was also completely terrified. What if the baby had inherited the gene? What if the baby hadn't inherited the gene, but Jake had, and their child had to witness Jake turning into a writhing, demented mess when other fathers were taking their kids to the park and the movies? What if both Jake and their child had the gene and Emily had to—

As always, his brain clamped down. *Stop worrying about something that may never happen.*

Denial, he knew, would only work for so long.

———

On the day ward, Petra greeted him with a pottle containing sugar-dusted jelly babies.

'Always pleased to see the CIA,' she said, ushering him into the nurse's office.

'That's what they all say.' Jake bit the legs off a purple jelly baby. 'What have you got for me?'

'Mrs Tan is in for her weekly drain. And Cameron Lewis. Remember him?'

How could he forget? Cameron Lewis, a forty-two year old man with widespread adenocarcinoma. Estimated survival, six months. Kid on the way, ETA three months.

'I'll set up a trolley.' Jake took another jelly baby.

'Already done, doc.' Petra bustled off, her blonde ponytail swinging behind her.

Jake glanced at the board — cubicle five — and went to find his patient. Cameron was sitting on the bed holding an iPad, all stick-like limbs and bulging belly. He glanced up.

'Doctor Jake. I was hoping it'd be you.'

'Me too.' Jake parked the trolley at the end of the bed. 'Actually, no. What you want is for your doctor to say they never need to see you again.'

Cameron set the iPad down and reclined against the pillows. 'If only. I'm picking four litres today.'

Jake placed his right middle finger on top of Cameron's abdomen and tapped it with his left middle finger, listening to the dull percussion note that told him the patient's belly was distended with fluid rather than air.

'I'm picking closer to five.' After drawing an X to the left of the belly button with a ballpoint pen, he sterilised the skin with chlorhexidine. 'Sharp prick coming up.'

'I wish,' Cameron mumbled, and Jake let out a barking laugh.

'How's the pregnancy going?' Jake asked, struggling to recall the name of the surrogate Cameron and his partner had chosen to have their baby.

Cameron brightened. 'We saw the baby on a 3D ultrasound the other day. She waved at us.'

After checking to see no one else was in earshot, Jake bent towards the patient. 'Last time I saw ours, she was the size of a kidney bean.'

'Really? Congratulations!' Cameron barely flinched when Jake injected the local anaesthetic. 'How many weeks?'

'Ten.' Jake lowered his voice. 'Still a secret.'

'Of course,' Cameron said, averting his gaze as Jake advanced the catheter into his belly. 'Guess you want to wait until twelve weeks before you announce it to the world?'

'At least.'

'We told everyone straight away,' Cameron said. 'We couldn't help it.' The corners of his mouth turned down. 'Do you think it's irresponsible having a baby when you've got a terminal illness?'

Jake taped the plastic tubing to Cameron's skin. 'That's what you have two parents for,' he said. 'Right?'

'As long as they have someone to love them,' Cameron said, watching the pink-tinged fluid draining into the catheter bag. 'Gareth says he'll always have a piece of me now.'

Petra peered through the curtain. 'Sorry to break this up, but are you ready for the next one?'

'Sure.' Jake shucked off his gloves. 'Might see you next week.'

'I hope so.' Cameron waved. 'See you later . . . Dad.'

'Did he just call you Dad?' Petra asked, as they assembled the next trolley.

Jake flushed. 'It's a running joke.'

'I won't ask you to explain.' Petra unwrapped syringes, needles, a packet of gauze. 'The patients are going to miss you when you leave. Us too.'

'Ah,' Jake said, his blush deepening. 'Bet you say that to all the doctors.'

'No, I mean it. Doctor Patel says you're better than many of the registrars he's worked with. Make sure you come back, OK?'

'I'm going to be a surgeon,' Jake said, but under his breath, because Petra had left the equipment room, and also because he wasn't sure if that were true.

———

Emily poked a straw through her juice carton. 'Linda in the lab says it can get really cold in the desert in winter.'

'Can't be any colder than Dunedin.' Jake tipped salt over his chips. 'I'm hanging out for this holiday. We should have taken two weeks off.'

'Is Ingrid still MIA?'

'Don't know. Don't care.' He glanced up. 'It was easier when it was just me running the ward, so I didn't have to go around fixing up her screw-ups. Yesterday she told a patient the tingling in their fingers was because they were anxious, when it's a known side-effect of the chemo they were on. And do you know why she doesn't know that? Because she's hardly ever here.'

'I don't know why you don't report that kind of thing to your bosses.' Emily had already hoovered down half her lunch, as though she were eating for two already. *At ten weeks*, they'd read over breakfast that morning, *your baby is as big as a strawberry*.

Jake swallowed. 'Maybe, but I'll be gone in a week. I'm sure they know anyway.'

'Hi, guys,' Kylie announced, to half the cafeteria, it seemed. 'How's it going?' She took a seat next to Jake. 'No work today, Em?'

'Yeah, I thought I'd have a day off to work on my book.'

'Maybe I should take more days off.' Kylie peeled apart her chopsticks. 'Do you want this salad? I got a free one with my sushi, but I'm pretty sure the dressing has got gluten in it.'

'Mmm, no thanks,' Emily said. 'I'm pretty full.'

'Jake?'

'Hell, no, that looks far too healthy.' Jake wiped his mouth. 'Got your bags packed for our trip?'

'Of course.' Kylie beamed. 'I've got gin. You like gin, don't you, Emily?'

'Um, yeah, sure,' Emily hedged.

'How's the teacher-aiding going?' Kylie ploughed on, obviously oblivious to Emily's altered dietary requirements.

'It's fine. The little kids come out with the cutest things. I was playing a game the other day, matching the parents arriving at pick-up time with their kids. It's amazing how you can spot the resemblances, even with their mannerisms.'

Kylie smeared wasabi on her sushi. 'Nature trumping nurture, huh?'

'Well,' Emily fingered the dragon tattoo on her wrist, her gaze distant. 'Not always.'

And Jake thought of a double helix staircase, and the inevitability of CAG repeats, and a new wave of fear hit him behind the eyes.

Or, to be exact, one eye.

Crap, he thought, wiping away a tear. *This is not a good time to get a migraine.*

It never was.

———

By the time he arrived on the ward, Jake had lost chunks in his field of vision and was beginning to feel nauseous.

Keith, one of the senior nurses, intercepted him in the corridor. 'Jake, can you finish Mr Demetriou's discharge summary? He's busting a gut to get out of here.'

'Sure, but I just need to get—' Keith disappeared before the words *my sumatriptan* left Jake's mouth. After sloping into the doctor's room, Jake rifled through the inside pocket of his bag and came up empty.

What? He was sure he'd had a spare syringe in there.

'Shit.' Jake moved slowly in the vain hope that would delay the inevitable onset of the headache. Headache, such a stupid word — as if that conveyed the blinding, pulverising pain that was sure to take over half his skull if he didn't get some drugs into his system soon.

After finding a script pad beneath a half-eaten sandwich, Jake stumbled into the corridor. No doctors in sight, of course.

Keith loomed in front of him. 'Don't forget the script for morphine, will you?' Through the kaleidoscope blur, Jake saw Keith's expression morph into one of concern. 'You all right there, mate?'

'Not really,' Jake said, and ducked into the sluice room, just in time to throw up in the sink.

'Eat something dodgy at lunch? I reckon they recycle the sushi.'

Jake turned on the tap and slumped against the sink. 'Migraine.'

'Ugh. Want me to get you something for it? I can call one of the docs.'

'That'd be great.' Jake wiped his mouth. 'Can you get the switchboard to put you through to Kylie Flanagan, see if she can get me some sumatriptan?' The dull throb in his left temple had taken on a new, feral quality. *Here goes.*

After relaying the message to Kylie, Keith said, 'I'm guessing you're not capable of doing a discharge summary, then. Shall I call the boss?'

'That'd be good.' Jake slid down the wall until his butt touched the floor, the pain in his skull accelerating from zero to one hundred. Holding the phone to his ear, Keith shoved a white container at him. Jake couldn't fault his multi-tasking.

After he'd thrown up the rest of his lunch, he tuned in just in time to hear Patel's irate voice radiating from the other end of Keith's phone.

'Where's the registrar, then?'

'The registrar?' Keith snorted. 'What registrar would that be?'

Shit's about to hit the fan, Jake thought, and, *This isn't a migraine, this is a monster.* He angled his body until he was lying horizontal, his cheek pressed against the floor.

'There you are,' a familiar voice rang out. 'What's wrong, Jake, are you pregnant?'

'Something like that,' Jake managed.

Kylie crouched beside him. 'Got some sumatriptan from the emergency department, where do you want it?'

Jake tried to roll up his shirtsleeve, but gave up.

'Here,' Keith said. 'Give us your thigh.'

'Don't worry, we've seen it all before,' Kylie said cheerfully when Jake unzipped his trousers to expose an area of bare skin.

'In your dreams, Flanagan,' he mumbled.

'How about some IV fluids?' Keith suggested.

'And some antiemetics, yes, good idea,' Kylie said, and they hustled him into a spare room. Jake didn't even bother protesting. He was too far gone.

———

Six am. Jake stared into the darkness. Beside him, he heard the hushed sound of Emily's breathing. Slowly, slowly, he turned his head. The wild animal had retreated into the depths of his skull, thank God.

He got up and padded into the kitchen for water, observing the tremor in his hand when he lifted the glass to his lips.

Well, you haven't eaten since lunch yesterday, and you threw that up too. What do you expect? After downing the water, he filled the kettle and flicked the switch to on. Coffee, sugar, Weet-Bix. If only he could have a cigarette.

If you knew you'd inherited the HD mutation, you could smoke as much as you wanted.

Except Emily says she doesn't like kissing you when you've been smoking.

There is that.

Is talking to yourself a sign?

'Are you feeling better?' Emily hugged him from behind.

'Heaps. You?'

'I think this nausea is starting to lift.'

'They say the second trimester is the best one.' He kissed her. 'Want a cup of tea?'

'Love one. Are you staying home today?'

'No, I'm good now.' Also, he had a dim memory of a text message that had arrived on his phone around six last night, something to do with Ingrid being stood down.

Don't want to bother you, Patel had written. *But I wanted to give you the heads-up that we'd had to take Ingrid off the job. We thought we'd give her a second chance but clearly it hasn't worked out.*

But that hadn't been the only message, had it?

'What's up?' Emily asked, once Jake had retrieved his phone from the bedroom.

172

'This.' He held the phone out so she could read it for herself.

'Acting registrar? Isn't that what you've been doing all along?'

'Yeah, but they want me to stay on for another three months until the next registrar starts.' He checked the third message. Jesus, they'd been coming through thick and fast last night while he'd been semi-comatose. 'Patel says I'll get a resident to boss around.'

'Nice.'

'I'll miss out on my ortho run.'

Emily quirked an eyebrow at him. 'So what do you think?'

Jake moved closer, pressed his palm to her stomach. 'I think I'm getting a little attached to Nemo.'

'That's not what I meant,' she said, softening into him. His thoughts drifted to Cameron; forty-two years old with a baby on the way. What was that saying from the Bible? Do unto others as you'd like them to do to you?

'Do you remember those Pick-a-Path books we used to read as kids?' Jake asked. 'Turn to page six if you choose door A, turn to page twelve if you choose door B?'

'I remember.' Her lips were soft. He could smell the almond oil she was already rubbing into her belly to prevent stretch marks.

'This is like that.'

'So what do you choose?'

Jake moved away and plucked a coin off the end of the bench.

'Heads for Orthopaedics, tails for Oncology.' He flipped the coin and they both watched it fall.

'Heads,' Emily said, picking it up. 'Well, there you go. Must have been meant to be a surgeon after all.'

'Ah,' Jake said. 'Best of three.'

Emily looked at him for a moment, then turned the coin over and pushed it into his hand. 'Tails it is.'

Jake curled his fingers over hers. 'Tails it is,' he echoed.

Funny how you could not know you wanted something until it was dumped in your lap.

Chapter 23: Holiday

Emily straightened a tent pole and snapped the joints into place. 'Ugh, those bats are freaking me out.'

Ian peered up at the tree. 'They're just rodents with wings, aren't they?'

'The flapping is gross. And that constant chatter is just creepy.' There were so many of them, all hanging upside down like something out of a B-grade vampire movie.

Kylie adjusted her hat. 'I think they're hilarious.'

Emily said, 'I can't believe you bought a hat with corks.'

'Only thing that works against the flies.' Kylie shook her head. 'See?'

Jake took the pole off Emily and laid it on top of the tent, still collapsed in the grass. 'They *are* uncommonly feral.'

Emily shuddered. 'Do you think they fly around at night-time?'

'I mean the flies, not the bats.' He grinned at her. 'It's the crocs you need to worry about.'

'Do you think there're crocs in that waterhole?' Kylie flapped her dress away from her body. 'I'm dying for a swim.'

Ian crept up behind her and hooked an arm around her waist. 'Famous last words.'

'Kiwi girl gets eaten by croc in Katherine Gorge,' Jake said.

'Only to die after several corks lodge in its larynx,' Ian chimed in.

'Do crocodiles have larynxes?' Kylie asked, and Emily said, 'What's the plural of larynx anyway?'

Ian slung a towel around his neck. 'There *are* crocs in there, but the lady in the office said they've got nets further down the river. Safe as a crocodile-infested gorge, I say.'

Kylie glanced at Emily. 'Are you keen?'

Emily hesitated. 'I guess.' It *was* really hot, sweat and red dust collecting in every crevice.

'It's the salties you need to worry about, not the freshies,' Jake said, watching Ian disappear between the trees.

Kylie shrugged. 'They can all tear you from limb to limb if you piss them off, right? Come on Em, you only live once.'

'I can't believe you just strung those two sentences together and think you're convincing me,' Emily said, but she trudged off to the change rooms. After donning her bikini, she stayed in the shady interior for a minute or so, stroking the soft curve of her belly. Nothing to see yet, or was there?

At eleven weeks, your baby is the size of a lime.

'There you are, thought you'd been eaten by a bat,' Kylie said.

'Very funny.'

Kylie stepped out of her dress and began unhooking her bra. 'How do you stay so skinny? I swear I've gained two kilograms already this holiday.'

'I have a neurotic metabolism.' Emily stuck her feet into her trainers. There was no way she was walking through the grass in bare feet, not with snakes and scorpions and whatever else liked to roam around the Northern Territory.

'I have neuroses.' Kylie wriggled into her swimsuit. 'Like, what if I never get to stay in an ice hotel?'

Emily picked up her towel. 'An ice hotel?' Actually, that sounded pretty tempting right then.

'They've got one in Sweden. It's got a bar and everything.'

'That's not a neurosis, that's a bucket-list wish.' They meandered past the bat tree and towards the gorge. The guys were jumping off the pier already, their legs pedalling through the air. The late afternoon sun felt even more intense near the river, radiating off the red rocks surrounding the waterhole, shimmering across the surface of the water.

'Awesome, that will scare away the crocodiles,' Kylie said, wandering onto the pier.

Jake bobbed up. 'Come on in, the water's boiling,' he said, then squawked and disappeared beneath the surface again.

'Very funny,' he spluttered, once he and Ian came up together.

'You thought I was a croc, didn't you?' Ian chortled, right before Jake jumped on top of him.

Emily ran past Kylie and leapt into the air before she could lose her nerve. She came up with a gasp. The water was colder than she'd thought it would be, and yet she felt instantly refreshed, as if her mind had been wiped clean along with the rest of her body. Something grabbed her ankle, and she screamed and kicked down as hard as she could.

'Jesus, way to break someone's nose,' Jake said, coming up for air.

Treading water, Emily shoved him. 'That's what you get for scaring the hell out of me,' she said, before swimming away from the others so she could float, undisturbed, with her face turned up to the sky.

The colours were so vibrant, red earth and blue sky and eucalyptus green. She didn't think she'd seen a cloud since they'd arrived five days before. The savage yet beautiful landscape made her feel as though she were on another planet. Perhaps she could incorporate that into her next book.

'This is heaven, isn't it?' Kylie said, swimming out to join her.

'Heaven,' Emily agreed.

'I think I'm getting the travelling bug. I told Ian we should take a year off and travel around Aussie in a camper van.'

'What did he say?'

'He said we need to save more money first. And I said, *But it's so much easier to do all this stuff before we get tied down with jobs and fellowship exams and family.*'

'Family, yeah.'

'Why are you smiling like that?' Kylie asked, treading water.

'I'm not,' Emily said, but she couldn't hold it in any longer. 'Hey,' she said, holding onto a rock, 'can you keep a secret?'

Kylie swam closer. 'Ooh, I love secrets.'

'I mean, it's only really a secret for another week.'

'Another week?' Kylie frowned. 'Why?'

'Because,' Emily said, her smile widening, 'by then I'll have had my twelve-week scan.'

Kylie's mouth fell open. 'Oh my God, are you — oh my God!' She clung to the other side of the rock. 'That's so cool. I should have guessed

176

when you started turning down all offers of booze, why didn't I? Was this planned?'

'No,' Emily said. 'But we're — really happy about it.' *Please, please don't ask whether we're going to get the foetus tested for HD.*

But Kylie, as if sensing Emily didn't want to go there, just repeated, 'That's so cool. I'm going to be an aunt! I mean, sort of.'

'You'll be a great sort-of aunt.' Emily, shivering, began treading water again. 'Hey, I'm going in.'

Kylie kicked away from the rock, her dark red locks swirling around her. 'Sure, see you soon. Oh my God!'

'*Ssh*,' Emily repeated, and Kylie, grinning, waved at her before slipping beneath the surface.

Emily swam for the shore and clambered over the rocks. After draping a towel around her shoulders, she massaged the small of her back, which was aching. Perhaps she'd strained it when she jumped off the pier.

———

At dusk, they sat outside their tents, watching the wallabies appear one by one to explore.

'Hope you like beans,' Ian said, opening a can. 'Again.'

'Anything, as long as I don't have to cook.' Kylie yawned and stretched out on her bedroll. 'Don't you think marsupials are so improbable?'

Emily took a sip of water from her bottle. 'They probably think the same of you.'

'An improbably raucous ginger,' Ian said, ducking when Kylie took a swing at him.

Jake pulled a LED headlight on. 'No pouch, though.'

'Don't count on it,' Kylie growled.

Emily strapped on her own LED light before crawling inside the tent and unzipping her toilet bag. Damn it, she was sure she'd packed paracetamol. Instead, there were two blister trays of Brufen, which she knew were definitely *not* safe to take in pregnancy.

A light blazed into her eyes. 'You all right?'

'Whoa, can you turn that around?'

'Sorry.' Jake did as she asked. 'What are you looking for?'

'Panadol, have you got any?'

'Maybe.' He reached into his pack. 'Got a headache?'

'No, I strained my back. When we were swimming.'

Jake passed her a pill bottle and shuffled closer to her. 'Where are you sore?'

'Lower,' she said when he began to knead her muscles. 'Yeah, kind of . . . there.'

'What are you guys doing in there?' Ian yelled from outside.

'What do you think?' Jake called out.

'Stop,' she whispered.

'Stop this?' Still massaging her, he kissed her, once, twice.

'Mmm,' she said, momentarily forgetting her discomfort.

Ian's voice came floating through the nylon. 'Don't hold back on our account, will you?'

'No, you can't watch,' Jake said, tickling Emily. 'Yet.' She let out a squawk, then yelped. Outside, Ian and Kylie descended into hysterics, while Jake, his tone changing from teasing to concerned, said, 'Did I hurt you?'

'No.' Another cramp gripped her. She drew her knees up to her chest.

'It's not your back, is it?' Jake's hand slid over her hip, towards her contracting belly.

She tried to breathe. 'It was before, but now my stomach's hurting too.' The pain was disturbingly familiar, like the worst period pain she'd ever had.

Oh no, oh no.

'Shall I get Kylie?'

'Yes,' she said, and then, as she felt the first rush of warmth between her legs, 'no, no, no.'

———

First rush. First blood.

First blood, last blood.

No, no, no.

Emily curled into her pain, *breathe breathe breathe*, as the SUV sped along the road. Around them, ghost gums rose into the sky, bare-limbed, desolate.

Beside her, Kylie said, 'It might settle down,' but her tone suggested otherwise.

'Shit,' Jake said, slowing then speeding up again.

Emily closed her eyes. She didn't want to know about the roaming kangaroos. Three days ago, a service station attendant had told them not to drive after dusk.

'Last week,' he'd said, 'a lady ended up with a cow through her windscreen, and a horn through her head.' After that, they'd found a road train to stick behind for the rest of their trip to the next town.

Kylie squeezed her knee. 'Hang in there, chook. Not long now.'

'Do you think they'll have ultrasound?' Jake asked.

'I don't know,' Kylie said. 'A sixty-bed hospital doesn't sound that big.'

Emily said, 'It's not like it'll matter if I have an ultrasound tonight or tomorrow, will it?' Either there was a foetal heartbeat, or there wasn't. It wasn't as though anyone could save an eleven-week foetus if it decided to die.

Even a med school drop-out knew *that*.

Kylie hesitated, then said, 'No. It won't matter.'

'Here it is.' Jake turned into a driveway, the headlights illuminating the sign: *Katherine Hospital Main Entrance*. The board looked small, inadequate.

Inside, the bright light of the emergency department flared into her eyes. A nurse showed them into a cubicle, where Emily was subjected to a blood-pressure cuff, a pulse oximeter, razor-sharp questions. *When was your last period? Have you got any other medical conditions? When did you last eat?*

'I'll go find us some food,' Kylie said and left. Emily wondered if Ian was eating the beans by himself, if he'd gone to bed early. She realised she had no idea what the time was.

Jake squeezed Emily's thigh. 'How's the pain?'

'Not as bad as before,' she said, relaxing a little.

'Hey.' The doctor looked young, despite the beard, and disturbingly eager. 'Do you mind putting this on?' He held up a hospital gown. 'It'll help when I come to examine you.'

'I hope he knows his way around a speculum,' Emily muttered to Jake once the doctor had gone, presumably to find his equipment, or preferably an older doctor of the female persuasion.

'Relax,' Jake said, which was easy for him to say, she thought.

'Right,' the doctor said, after returning to perform an unusually speedy vaginal examination. 'The cervix is open. Which means . . .'

'An inevitable miscarriage,' Emily said. 'Right?'

'Unfortunately.' The doctor turned his blood-smeared gloves inside out. Emily tried not to look. 'Is this your first pregnancy?'

Emily nodded.

'We'll get an ultrasound in the morning,' he said. 'In case you need a D&C.'

'OK,' she whispered.

The doctor glanced between her and Jake. 'I'm sorry,' he said, and fled.

Emily tried to breathe past the concrete block in her chest.

Dead, it's dead. What had she done wrong? Maybe it was when she jumped off the pier. Maybe it was something she'd eaten.

Jake climbed onto the bed and held her close. 'Hey. These things—'

'Don't say it.' The words rushed out before she could check them. 'We're never going to have a baby, are we?'

He squeezed her tight. 'That's not true.'

'Isn't it?' The tears came now, spilling into her mouth.

'I promise you,' he said, 'it's not true.'

Chapter 24: Yesterday

Stuffing his stethoscope into his pocket, Jake checked the clock above the ward station. Five minutes to nine.

'I'd better go,' he said to his very efficient resident. 'Clinic starts in five.'

'No worries, I'll get started on some of these jobs.' Rishan took off down the corridor. Jake jogged down the stairs and onto the ground floor, turning right for the café. After five months, Jake had learned that Doctor Patel was always much more genial if presented with a coffee at the start of a long, relentless clinic.

As he waited for his coffee, he scrolled through news items on his phone, wondering if he'd ever stop checking the Stuff website for New Zealand news. *Polar blast on way for South Island*, a headline announced. No surprises there, considering it was late July.

A message flashed up on his screen: *Dad's coming over tonight and I completely forgot!! Dinner in or out?*

Jim Walsh, great, just what he felt like that evening. Jim didn't like him, and Jake didn't like Jim either. Not that either had admitted that to the other, but Jim's body language told him all he needed to know. That, and the photo of Adam and Emily that still graced the sideboard at the Thompson Street house. *It's my best photo of you,* Jim always said when Emily protested. *Look how happy you are.* As if she'd never looked as happy since.

Definitely out, Jake replied before collecting the coffees and continuing around the corridor to outpatients. Perhaps he could swap his evening on call and escape seeing Jim entirely.

Tempting, very tempting.

In clinic, Jake logged onto his computer before taking the spare coffee to Sanjay Patel. Sanjay was dictating into the phone, massaging his temples the way he always did when concentrating. He glanced up, waved Jake in.

'. . . continues in remission. He should have three-monthly blood tests, including CEA, and we will see him in six months. Yours sincerely, etc.' Sanjay slammed the phone down on its cradle. 'Heremaia with the nectar of the gods, what more could I ask for?'

'I could think of several things.' Jake passed his boss the coffee.

'Don't go there.' Patel took a sip. 'There've been a few add-ons to clinic. I couldn't really say no.'

'OK . . .' Last time Patel had said *a few add-ons*, they'd ended up seeing thirty patients between them. 'Maybe I should have made these triple-shot.'

Patel passed him a file. 'We can always send out for more.'

Jake looked at the name on the file. *Cameron Lewis.* 'Don't suppose we've got any new treatments for this guy?'

'Unfortunately not.' Patel tossed him a Fruit Burst. 'I'm surprised he's still going.'

'Ditto,' Jake said, vaguely disturbed to be discussing Cameron's imminent demise so casually. Once in the waiting room, he called out, 'Cameron Lewis?'

A man in a charcoal suit stood up, grasping the handles of a wheelchair.

'Hey, doc,' Cameron said when they moved closer. 'You remember Gareth, don't you?'

'Gareth, of course,' Jake said, but he was looking at Cameron. 'Got a sore stomach?' The patient was clutching his side, his skin chalky.

'Yeah.' Cameron's face contorted. 'Since yesterday.'

'You should have called me,' Jake said gently as Gareth wheeled his partner into the clinic room.

'Thought I could last until today.'

Gareth parked the wheelchair beside the desk. 'He had a temperature of thirty-eight point five degrees before we left home.'

'That doesn't sound good.' Jake sat opposite Cameron. 'Are you passing wind?'

'Am I what?'

'Farting,' Gareth translated.

Cameron's lips twitched. 'Oh, yeah. I think so.'

'Do you think you can get up here, so I can have a look?' Jake helped Cameron onto the narrow bed.

'Ow,' Cameron complained when Jake examined his distended abdomen.

'Sorry.' Jake planted his stethoscope above Cameron's belly button. 'Bowel sounds are normal.' *Not a bowel obstruction, then.* 'I think we should take a sample of the fluid from your belly, so we can check for an infection.'

Gareth hovered at the end of the bed, an alabaster shirt flap sticking out of the front of his trousers. 'Again? He only just finished the last course of antibiotics.'

'It's the most likely problem. If that's clear, we'll ask for a CT scan.'

'Whatever you say, doc. I trust you.' Cameron took his partner's hand. 'Just promise me one thing.'

'What's that?' Jake asked.

'I want to make it to see our baby girl. She's due in four weeks.'

'Four weeks. I'll try my best.' How was it that Jake had become used to these conversations? 'Think we'll get there,' he added rashly, because how did he know Cameron didn't have a life-threatening infection, a dead portion of bowel, or some other fatal complication of his cancer?

'You're awesome, doc.' Cameron brightened. 'How's your girlfriend? She must be at least twenty weeks now, right?'

'Um, no.' Jake moved to the trolley at the end of the bed, assembling syringes, needles, alcohol swabs. 'She, um, had a miscarriage.' His throat constricted. Emily wouldn't talk about it, and he wasn't sure he wanted to either. Almost two months since the miscarriage, and it was still too raw.

'Oh no,' Cameron and Gareth chimed. 'I'm really sorry,' Cameron added.

Jake screwed a needle onto the end of the syringe. 'Well,' he said, thinking of and dismissing several clichés, 'I guess we'll get another chance. Some day.' He glanced up. 'Let's get a sample of that fluid, shall we?'

After aspirating suspiciously murky-looking fluid from Cameron's belly, charting antibiotics and arranging admission to the ward, Jake grabbed the next file. Amanda Rountree, thirty-five years old, breast cancer. At least this one's curable, he thought, then felt guilty. It wasn't Cameron's fault he had a terminal illness.

Besides, there was no guarantee. Amanda Rountree could have her breast removed, followed by chemotherapy and radiotherapy, only to have her cancer return ten years later.

Melanoma and breast cancer are bastards, one of the oncologists told him. *They can come back to bite you anytime.*

Three hours and ten patients later, Jake collapsed into a chair in Patel's room.

'Did you put Basil in my clinic on purpose?'

Patel threw a folder on top of the teetering pile beside his desk. 'I like to torture my registrars. Mad as a snake, isn't he?'

'Worse.' Jake took an aged banana out of his pocket. 'Gave me this, though.'

Patel let out a barking laugh. 'Lucky you.'

'Meanwhile, you got this?' Jake plucked the bottle of wine off Patel's desk, which had a gold ribbon tied around the neck.

'Yeah, man. Do you want a glass? Just kidding. But seriously, we need to organise a dinner to farewell you registrars. Do you like Indian? Good. And by the way, I hope you've changed your mind about this surgical business.'

'I don't know. Ward rounds that finish in ten minutes rather than two hours sound quite appealing to me,' Jake said, but, weirdly, he wasn't looking forward to general surgery as much as he thought he would. 'Although I won't be able to stop wondering what happened to all these patients I've been treating.' He made a note to go and check on Cameron before he went home, see if his pain was under control.

'Believe me, you're not a surgeon.' Patel took the bottle of wine and regarded the label before passing it to Jake. 'Does your girlfriend like Syrah?'

'I think so,' Jake said, touched. 'Thanks.'

'Here's my advice,' Patel said. 'Sit your fellowship exams and apply for a spot in the oncology training programme. I'll give you the best reference you ever had.'

Jake traced the embossed letters on the wine label. 'Is this a bribe?'

'No.' Patel stood up. 'But if you don't return, I'll make you sorry, how about that?'

'I think that's called blackmail.' Jake followed the oncologist into the corridor. 'Seriously, though, doesn't caring for dying people get to you after a while?'

Patel slowed. 'Sometimes,' he said. 'But if I can alleviate their pain and suffering, if I can buy them a few more weeks so they can say their goodbyes, then it's worth it. Death comes to us all, right? It's how you live what you have left that counts.' He entered the stairwell. 'Christ, I'm starving, aren't you?'

'I could eat a crocodile,' Jake said, thinking, wondering.

'What you are up to this weekend?' Patel asked, as they joined the line for hot food at the café.

'Ah,' Jake said, remembering. 'Entertaining my sort-of father-in-law.'

'Sounds excruciating.'

Jake clutched the wine bottle. 'You have no idea.'

———

Emily's father swirled the blood-red liquid around the bottom of his glass.

'Not a bad drop. Did I hear you say one of your consultants gave it to you?' They were perched on bar stools in the dining area at Emily and Jake's flat, looking out over the city lights.

'Yeah, he was in a generous mood.' Jake cut the tip off a wedge of cheese and squashed it onto a cracker.

Jim tutted. 'Oops, cut the nose off.' Emily, Jake noticed, had averted her eyes, as if unwilling to watch the war of body language taking place between her partner and father.

'Whoops,' Jake said. *Evil, Heremaia, you are pure evil.* 'Hope it doesn't ruin the taste too much for you.' He and Jim bared their teeth at each other.

Emily exhaled loudly and began tapping on her phone. 'Where shall we go for dinner?'

'Anywhere you like. My shout,' Jim said. 'So, Jake, I hear you've been working in Oncology for the last few months?'

'Ever since we got here.' Jake gulped on his wine. Nothing else for it, he'd just have to get pissed.

'Don't know how the oncologists do it,' Jim said. 'Charting chemo all day, every day, for what? A ten per cent improvement in survival?'

'We cure some people.' Jake gripped the stem of his glass. 'Anyway, it's not all about cure.'

Jim moved to the window. 'True. How's school, Emily?'

'It's fine.' Emily held up the Entertainment Book. 'How about Molly Malone's? Buy one meal, get one free.'

'Whatever you like.' Jim turned. 'Have you had your iron stores checked recently, love? You look a bit pale.'

'I'm just sun-deprived,' Emily said. 'Melbourne in July is hardly tropical.'

'I suppose.' Jim's gaze lit on Jake. 'How about you, Jake, are you . . . well?'

Jesus. Jake drained the rest of his glass, and reached for the wine bottle. 'Never been better.'

It was going to be a long night.

———

'What's the conference you're going to?' Emily asked, once they were seated in a restaurant on Southbank; Jim facing the window, Jake and Emily facing each other.

'Ah, it's just College of Physicians business, discussing exam formats etcetera.' Jim had ordered another glass of red wine, while Emily was drinking white. Jake had moved on to rum and Coke. Things were blurring around the edges already, and it was only seven-thirty. 'Guess you'll be applying for the surgical training programme, Jake.'

Jake traced the rim of his glass. 'I don't know, I might have changed my mind.'

'Really?' Emily asked. To Jake's annoyance, she didn't even look surprised.

Jim smirked. 'So you've been converted to oncology then?'

'Maybe.' Jake sucked on his straw, taking pleasure in watching Jim's eyes roll at the loud gurgle.

'The fellowship exams are pretty tough-going.'

'So I hear. Can't be any worse than surgical exams, I guess.' Jake considered letting a burp escape, but changed his mind when Emily kicked him beneath the table.

Jim's nose wrinkled. 'Oh, they're much more cerebral, I imagine. How about you, Emily, have you thought any more about further study?' Jim wiped his mouth. 'Remember when you thought you might be a pharmacist? You've probably done a lot of the pharmacology already in your first two years of med school.'

'I don't want to be a pharmacist. And my book's going really well. I just want to concentrate on that at the moment.'

'Right. Well, I should have a look when we return to the apartment. S'cuse me.' Jim got to his feet and walked off in the direction of the toilets.

Emily shot daggers at Jake. 'Oh my God.'

'Yeah, even worse than usual.'

'Not him, you. Do you have a talent for winding up fathers?'

'Me winding him up, are you kidding?' Jake imitated Jim's clipped speech. '*How about you, Jake, are you cracking up yet?*'

'He didn't *say* that.'

'Might as well have.' Jake signalled a passing waiter, and ordered another rum and Coke.

'Don't you think you've had enough to drink?' Emily asked once the waiter had left.

'Definitely not.' Jake leaned sideways to let a waitress deposit a plate of spare ribs in front of him.

'You. Are. Being. An. Arsehole,' Emily whispered, her eyes jerking towards the far side of the restaurant, where Jim was emerging from the toilets, his bald pate extra-shiny in the glow of the ceiling lights.

'What's that saying?' Jake asked, picking up a rib. 'It takes two to tango?'

————

And then it was ten pm, or was it eleven? Jake had lost track. All he knew was that they were back in the apartment, having a cup of tea before Jim pissed off to his hotel. He'd obviously decided that would be more comfortable than a night on a stretcher in their lounge, thank God.

Jim draped an arm across the top of the couch. 'Well, you two have a nice set-up here. Is your mum going to come for a visit, Emily?'

'Maybe in the next school holidays.' Emily's cheeks were flushed. Jake figured he'd be spending the night on the couch — although to be fair, Jake had been trying not to say much for the past hour or so, not since getting baited into a conversation on Māori quotas at medical school.

I don't know why we need quotas when everyone in New Zealand has the same opportunities, Jim had said.

Tell that to the kids growing up in damp, overcrowded houses with abusive parents, Jake had said.

Can we talk about something else? Emily had pleaded.

'So anyway,' Emily said, after a meandering conversation about who-knew-what, because Jake had given up trying to concentrate, 'it must have been a long day for you.'

'Yes, I did get up pretty early.' Jim yawned. 'I should wander back to my hotel, if I can remember what direction it's in.'

'Jake could walk you,' Emily offered. 'Couldn't you, Jake?'

'Happy to.' Jake stood up, trying not to trip over his feet, which suddenly seemed too big.

Jim hugged Emily. 'Take care, hon. Don't forget to ring me, OK?'

Jake and Jim descended in the lift without a word. Outside, the rain had stopped but the wind was icy. Jake zipped his jacket to his chin.

'This way,' he said. They continued in silence until they rounded the corner, and Jim slowed.

'Jake, look, I —' Jim gestured Jake into a doorway.

'Are you all right?' Jake asked, a low-level nausea beginning to niggle at him. All he wanted was to go home and sleep.

'I'm not sure.' Jim thrust his hands into his coat pockets. 'Look, I've been meaning to ask . . . what your intentions are.'

Jake squinted at him. 'My *intentions*?' With what? Emily? Medicine? Life in general?

'Obviously you and Emily are pretty serious about each other. And I don't know if you've thought about — well, whether Emily might want to have a family, and whether you might want to —' Jim's eyebrows drew together. 'I know it's kind of personal, but are you going to get tested?'

Jake gritted his teeth. 'I have no idea.' *And quite frankly, it's none of your fucking business.* He wondered what Jim would say if he knew about the pregnancy and subsequent miscarriage. So far they'd only told Emily's mother, and he was happy to keep it that way.

'It's only fair on Emily, don't you think?'

'It's between her and me,' Jake said. 'Don't you think?'

Jim lifted his chin. 'What I think is that you dragged Emily into something she might not have been able to handle.'

'Dragged her in?' Jake was starting to wish he hadn't drunk so much, or maybe he hadn't drunk enough for *this* conversation. 'I didn't drag her into anything. She's known about the HD from day one.'

Jim fumbled in the inside pocket of his coat. 'And this?' He pressed an object into Jake's palm. 'What about this?'

Jake stared at the glass vial in his hand, unable to process what he was seeing at first. 'Insulin,' he read by the glow of the street lamp. He looked up. 'You're diabetic?'

'Hardly.' Jim plucked the vial back before Jake could close his fingers around it. 'I've kept a hold of this for ten years. For you.'

'Ten years?' Jake's heart began to thud. *Oh. Shit.* But how had he got hold of that? Had Emily given it to him? No, surely not?

'Ten years I've kept my mouth shut about this,' Jim said, as Jake's vision began to blur. 'You think I don't care about my daughter? You could go to prison for this, both of you.'

'She wouldn't have helped me if she didn't want to.' Jake pressed his palms against the wall behind him.

'Oh, I've no doubt of that. But please tell me you're not going to put her through that again. You'll destroy her. You know that, don't you?'

Jake didn't reply. He couldn't. *Hello migraine, my old friend.*

'Just think about it,' Jim Walsh said. 'That's all I ask.' He drew his coat around himself. 'I can direct myself from here.' He walked out into the rain, leaving Jake in the doorway with the discarded cigarette butts and takeaway wrappers and the remnants of memories, flapping around his skull like malevolent bats.

Chapter 25: Life in Technicolor ii

Perhaps Patel was right. Perhaps he wasn't meant to be a surgeon. But right then, swinging on the end of a retractor, looking at the Technicolor world inside the patient's abdomen, Jake felt more alive than he had in weeks.

Possibly it was the distraction of the operating theatre. As soon as he stepped out of the changing rooms and into the theatre corridor, Jake could have been in another world, a parallel universe far away from the tiny Docklands apartment he shared with Emily.

The apartment, lately, seemed smaller than ever. Everywhere Jake turned, there was Emily, needing something from him — a kiss, a hug, conversation, advice.

Had he ever kept a secret from Emily before? He didn't think so. It had been four weeks since her father had confronted him with what he knew. Jake had been spinning ever since.

'Here.' The surgeon gripped Jake's wrist, forcing him to yank harder on the retractor. 'Concentrate, will you?'

Jake's face, beneath his mask and safety glasses, felt even hotter than usual. 'Sorry.' Penelope Watts, colorectal surgeon, didn't suffer fools.

'What have we got here?' Watts asked, prodding a blood vessel.

'The superior mesenteric artery?'

'Are you sure?'

Jake wavered. 'Coeliac artery?'

'It's the superior mesenteric artery. Be confident with your answers, huh?' Watts began running scarlet loops of bowel through her fingers. 'Aha, there it is.' She pointed at a hole in one of the multiple pouches protruding from the bowel wall. See?'

'Perforated diverticulum,' Jake said, with conviction this time.

'Exactly. What do you recommend?'

'I guess you need to resect that part of the bowel.'

'I guess we do.' Watts looked up. 'Koutsis, where have you been?'

The registrar approached, his gloved hands held high. 'Lining up the perianal abscesses in ED.'

'Oh, good. You can show Jake how to drain one.'

'That would be a pleasure.' Theo Koutsis lifted his chin at Jake and Jake mirrored the gesture, simultaneously wondering if he'd have time to nip to the maternity ward at lunchtime.

Cameron and Gareth's baby had been born by C-section the night before. *Mum, dads and baby doing well*, according to Gareth's text. *How's Cameron?* Jake had replied. *He'd love to see you* was Gareth's cryptic reply.

Maybe Jake shouldn't have been giving his number out to patients, crossing the invisible, often grey, patient–doctor boundary — but he hadn't been able to resist.

———

Lunchtime. After a quick dash to the ward to insert a urinary catheter in a man with a bladder swollen all the way to his belly button, Jake jogged to the maternity ward.

'Doctor Jake,' Cameron greeted him. 'You made it.' He was sitting on the bed in a single room, cradling a parcel so tiny it was hard to believe there was a baby swaddled inside.

'Wild camels wouldn't keep me away,' Jake said, taking in Cameron's hospital gown and the IV taped to his hand.

Gareth, sitting in a chair next to the window, stood up. 'Do you want to have a hold?'

'Um, I don't know if I'm very good with — o-kay.' Jake gazed at the baby Gareth had transferred from Cameron's embrace to his. 'Wow, she's gorgeous. What's her name?'

Cameron smiled. 'Hannah.'

'Hannah Rose Lewis-Barton,' Gareth added.

'Pretty.' Jake gazed into the baby's eyes, blue-black, like agates. 'Hello, little one.' His delight had morphed into something else; a gripping sensation in his chest and gut. *Was it a girl or a boy that Emily and I lost?*

Gareth chuckled. 'Think she's hypnotised you.'

'Is this where I'm meant to say she has someone's nose?'

'God, I hope not,' Cameron said, and winced.

'You all right there?' Jake passed Hannah to Gareth.

'It's nothing,' Cameron said, holding the right side of his chest.

'He was admitted a few days ago.' Gareth jiggled the baby, who was starting to fret. 'It's in his lungs.'

Jake didn't have to ask what *it* was. It, metastases, cancer, the big C. The euphemisms didn't make it any easier to deal with.

'Crap,' Jake said, because what else was there to say when there was nothing anyone could do about it? 'Do you need some pain relief?'

'I've got some Sevredol in there somewhere.' Cameron waved at a paper bag beside the bed. 'Gareth, do you want me to hold her while you make up a bottle?'

'Nah, mate, I'm all good.' Gareth moved the baby to his shoulder, then hesitated. 'Actually, Jake, do you mind?'

Jake gave the paper bag to Cameron, and took hold of Hannah again. She was chewing on her fists, her tiny cries growing louder.

'Don't think it's a good idea to eat yourself,' he said, bobbing her up and down, as he'd seen his cousins do with their babies. Hannah held his gaze for a moment before chewing her fists with renewed vigour, crying every time he stopped moving.

'You're a natural,' Cameron said, sagging into the pillows as Gareth went off to heat the formula.

'Yeah, I'm not so sure about that.' Jake paced between the window and the door, patting Hannah between the shoulders. 'How about some oxygen?' He nodded at the taps on the wall behind the bed. 'Could hook you up here. I'm sure no one will mind.' His phone was vibrating in his pocket, no doubt another job to add to his growing list.

'Actually, that'd be great,' Cameron said as Gareth hurried in, holding the bottle aloft.

'I'll see what I can do,' Jake promised, waiting for Gareth to sit in the chair before settling the baby into his embrace.

'I wish you were still our doctor,' Gareth said, when Jake returned a couple of minutes later with the plastic oxygen tubing, 'When are you returning to Oncology?'

Jake jammed the plastic tubing onto the tap, and helped Cameron feed the oxygen prongs up his nostrils before hooking the tubing over his ears.

'I don't know,' he said. 'I'm on surgical rotations for the next six months.'

'Don't be a surgeon.' Cameron closed his eyes. 'You've got such a great patient manner.'

Jake wrestled his phone out of his pocket. 'Maybe not by the end of today. Hello?'

'Hello, stranger,' a voice boomed. 'Where are you?'

'Just reviewing a patient,' Jake told the nurse. 'What do you need?'

Sounding almost gleeful, Carlos said, 'Three IVs, four discharges, and Mrs D is short of breath again, think she might need some more furosemide. There's more. We've left a list on the ward clerk's desk.'

'Awesome, see you soon.' Jake ended the call. 'I'd better go, but thanks for introducing me to Hannah.' The baby was already half-asleep on the end of the bottle, her lips working contentedly.

Cameron and Gareth looked at each other, then at Jake.

'We've got something to ask you,' Cameron said.

'What's that?' Jake's phone was ringing again. Goddammit, could the nurses not wait five minutes?

Gareth said, 'You've been so kind to us, and . . . Well, we were wondering if you would do us the honour of agreeing to be Hannah's godfather?'

'Her godfather?' Jesus, what was he meant to say to that? *This is not appropriate. You're the doctor and Cameron is — was — your patient.*

But they're looking at me like . . . Ah crap, I can't do justice to this right now.

'Um, sure,' Jake said. 'I guess that — well, that's an honour. Thank you.'

Cameron beamed. 'No, thank *you*. You have no idea what a difference your care has made to us.'

'And now we'd better let you get back to your job,' Gareth said. 'Catch you later, Godfather.'

'Yeah, catch you soon,' Jake said, and fled.

'You what?' Emily stacked the plates in the dishwasher and closed the door. 'Isn't that some kind of violation of the patient–doctor relationship?'

Jake threw the dishcloth into the sink. 'Yeah, no kidding. But they were looking at me like . . . well, you know.'

'Right. So what do these godfather duties entail?'

'I don't know. Probably nothing.'

'I think you need to reverse your decision,' Emily said, flopping onto the couch.

'Maybe. But it's not a good time right now, I don't think.' Jake took a squash ball out of the fruit bowl and tossed it in the air. 'Ian's keen on a game of squash tonight.'

'OK.' Emily sat on the couch and took her sketchpad off the coffee table.

'You can come if you want.'

'Is Kylie going?'

'Don't think so.'

'Then no. Squash with three people is just awkward.' Emily bent over her drawings, lost in her world already, Jake figured.

After changing in the bedroom, Jake checked the calendar on his phone. Two-thirty tomorrow. He'd set an alert for fifteen minutes before so he wouldn't forget.

As if I'd forget that.

'Are you all right?'

Jake stuck the phone in his pocket. 'Yeah, just checking Ian hadn't cancelled on me.'

'All right.' Emily hovered, her eyes lowered.

Jake moved closer. 'Are *you* all right?'

'Fine,' she said, but her voice was shaky, her irises shiny.

'I don't have to go to squash.' The gripping sensation was back in his chest, worse than ever. If only he could get Jim out of his head. *Please tell me you're not going to put her through that again. You'll destroy her.*

Emily averted her eyes. 'No, you should go.'

'I won't be late.' Jake kissed her, inhaling her scent, mango-salt-Emily, and wondered how much longer they had. *How can we carry on like this, so close, and yet so far away from each other?*

'OK.'

'And you can show me your progress with your book.' He thought, for the hundredth time, about telling her about his appointment tomorrow, and for the hundredth time dismissed it.

'Sure.' She retreated into the bathroom. Jake shoved his feet into his shoes, picked up his racquet and escaped.

———

The following afternoon, Jake sat fidgeting in an outpatient waiting room. *We encourage you to bring a support person*, the letter had said, a letter he'd asked to be sent to him care of the hospital. A piece of paper with the Genetics Service letterhead was the last thing he wanted Emily to find lying around.

'Jake Heremaia.' A woman in a pink suit was standing outside the clinic room to his left, her silver hair cropped close to her skull. Jake stood up, his stomach twisting. 'I'm Irene Tannin,' she said, beckoning him in. 'One of the doctors.' She gestured at his ID badge. 'And you're staff too, I see.'

'I'm a resident.' He took the chair next to the desk, feeling completely out of place, as if he should be in the doctor's chair rather than the other way around. 'Surgical.'

'And you're from New Zealand?' Tannin clicked on the mouse, her gaze on the screen in front of her.

'That's right,' Jake said, examining his fingernails, which he'd bitten to the quick over the past few weeks.

Jim's voice intruded into his mind again. *Ten years I've kept my mouth shut about this.*

Go away, go away.

Obviously sensing his impatience, the geneticist swivelled, shifting her focus from the screen to Jake. 'And you're here because you have a family history of Huntington's, is that correct?'

'Yeah. My mother had it. And her youngest brother.' He cleared his

196

throat. 'And I — I want to get tested to see if I've got it too.'

'How old was your mother when she was diagnosed, do you know?'

'She was thirty-five.' He gripped the tops of his thighs. 'My uncle was thirty-eight when he found out. He shot himself.'

'I'm sorry to hear that,' she said softly, and when he didn't reply, 'and your mother?'

'She died ten years ago. Pneumonia.' At least, that was what the GP had put on her death certificate. There'd been no reason for him to suspect an insulin overdose, none at all.

You could go to prison for this, both of you.

'That must have been very hard on you and your family.'

Jake cleared his throat. 'That's one way of putting it.'

'And you're worried that could be you one day.'

'Naturally,' he said, impatience pricking at him again. *Can we just get this over and done with?*

Tannin picked up a pen. 'What's the main reason for you wanting the test?'

He swallowed. 'I'm trying to plan ahead.'

'And how do you imagine a test would change things for you?'

'Well, if it's negative then I'd be happy to slog my guts out to specialise as a surgeon, or whatever else I choose. But if it's positive . . .' He picked at a loose thread on the seam of his trousers, 'then what's the point? I might as well take it a bit easier, do some locums or something.'

'So, you're twenty-seven?'

'Uh-huh.'

'And you could have another ten years before the first signs appear.'

'Or earlier,' Jake said.

'Maybe. Maybe not.' Tannin leaned forward. 'You know, you think this test is going to give you certainty, but that's not always true. You could be negative, and hit by a car and get killed while crossing the road after this appointment. You could be positive, and still be hit by a car and killed while crossing the road after this appointment.'

'Sure,' Jake said, his voice steely. 'But what I do know is that if I'm negative, I'm very unlikely to be jerking and pissing in my pants by the age of fifty.'

Tannin didn't even flinch. No doubt she had these kinds of conversations every day. 'Fair enough. Tell me, are you in a relationship?'

Jake met her gaze. 'No, not at the moment.' If he mentioned Emily, he knew, the doctor would want Emily to attend an appointment with him, would want her to come to hear his test result.

You'll destroy her.

Fuck off, Jim. Really.

'Well,' Tannin said after a brief hesitation, 'I'm sure I don't need to remind you about the genetics of HD, but I think we need to go through the implications of getting an indeterminate result.' She angled forward, her expression earnest. 'Do you know what I mean by that?'

Jake nodded. 'Too many CAG repeats, and you'll definitely get the disease. Twenty-six or less, and you won't. In between, and you may or may not get the disease, but you could still pass it onto your children.'

'That's right. So, the next step is to book you an appointment with a psychiatrist. Once we get the report from them, if you still want to proceed, then I'll get you in for another chat. Have you got any questions about that?'

'No,' Jake said. 'None at all.'

Chapter 26: Bloodstream

Emily strolled beside the river, the mid-morning sun warm on her back. It was the third Tuesday in November, and Melburnians were being treated to a string of clear blue days. A day off to work on her book; it was gold. Normally she liked the solitude, loved the clearing of space in her brain that she enjoyed when away from the company of others. But today she hadn't been able to concentrate.

There's something wrong with Jake. Not just with Jake, with me and Jake.

She stepped onto the footbridge, stopping halfway across to gaze over the river. A pair of black swans glided over the mirrored surface of the water. She heard a far-off siren, car horns, music from a nearby café; Ed Sheeran's 'Bloodstream'.

Have a good day off, Jake had said that morning before kissing her goodbye as always. She'd sensed his mind was already elsewhere.

But where?

Emily continued over the bridge and descended underground, through the bowels of the railway station and up the stairs to a narrow street jostling with cafés, bars and quirky shops. As she approached Number 42 Café, she saw a familiar figure in a nearby alley, smoking a cigarette.

'Hey, Emily.' Nick stubbed the cigarette out on a bin lid and ambled towards her, his jeans riding low on his hips.

'Hey.' She flipped her sunglasses up. 'How's your day going?'

'Good now,' he said, and an unsettling mixture of emotions she didn't dare name stirred in her stomach. She and Nick had put the embarrassing mix-up with text messages behind them, but it hadn't taken long for him to start up with the shameless flirting again.

Trouble was, she liked the coffee. And maybe, maybe, the flattery too.

It wasn't as if she was getting much attention from Jake lately.

'How's Pink?'

'Her usual sassy self.'

Nick grinned. 'I miss that cat.'

'I can bring her in for a visit if you like.'

He held up his index fingers in the shape of a cross. 'The boss will kill me. We got rid of her for a reason, remember? Because she kept stealing people's food?'

'Oh yeah,' Emily said. 'She *is* pretty sneaky.'

'Typical cat. Well, maybe you could bring her for a drive-by. Just the usual?' He sauntered inside, and her eye was caught, as always, by the tattoo on the back of his tanned neck.

'Yes, please. I always feel as if that owl is looking at me, you know.'

'That's what everyone says. Day off work, huh?'

'Yeah.' She perched on a stool at the counter. 'I'm meant to be finishing the latest sketch in my book, but . . .'

'You needed caffeine.' Nick wiped crumbs off the section of counter in front of her. 'You should bring your work down here. We get lots of students and writers parking up here, sometimes for hours.'

Emily played with a loose strand of hair. 'Change of atmosphere, yeah, maybe.'

'Your dragons are looking at me,' Nick said, his arm brushing hers ever-so-briefly.

The feeling in her stomach intensified. 'Oh, I don't think so.'

'Why not?'

'Because,' she said, 'they only have eyes for each other.'

'Fair enough,' Nick said, and moved around to the coffee machine.

She really needed to find somewhere else to buy her coffee.

———

That afternoon, Emily sat on the balcony, the spring breeze stirring over her as she sketched a room with a leafy forest floor and cylindrical walls and ceilings.

'His shoulders are on the earth,' she whispered, remembering what

Jake's father had told her about Tāne Mahuta, the largest kauri tree in New Zealand. 'His feet are in the sky.' The hollowed-out interior of a giant kauri was the perfect hideaway for the fugitives in her novel.

The cat leapt onto the table and sat in the middle of her sketch. Emily pushed her away. 'Pink, *no.*'

After giving her the evils, Pink began washing her butt. Emily gave up, and returned to decorating the walls of her kauri room with spirals and eyes.

They only have eyes for each other.

Hopefully Nick had got the message. There was only Jake and Emily, had only ever been Jake and Emily. Adam had been a temporary, albeit three-year, aberration.

Pink descended into her lap, stretching luxuriously before turning around twice and thudding against her bladder.

'You're such a succubus. Or should I say, succu-pus.' Kneading Pink's fur with her left hand, she began to copy the photo of the hypnotic spiral displayed on her laptop. *Space isn't the final frontier*, she thought. *The mind is.* Was that a cliché? She didn't think so. She reached for her notebook to jot the idea down, then wrote *Jake . . . ?* Beneath his name, she made a series of bullet points.

Beside the first bullet point, she wrote *surgical rotation.* Emily was pretty sure Jake (a) wasn't liking surgery as much as he thought he might and (b) was missing oncology a lot more than he'd thought he would. Still, that could be a temporary problem, if he made his mind up.

Next she wrote *pregnancy/miscarriage*, experiencing a sharp pang as she did so. Sure, Jake had been shocked by the accidental pregnancy, but he'd seemed to adjust to it, and had seemed as shaken as Emily had been by the miscarriage. Had he meant the promise he'd made to her at Katherine Hospital, or had he just been placating her?

We're never going to have a baby, are we?

That's not true.

Beside the third bullet point she wrote, *?someone else*, and felt her stomach flip. *No. Surely not.* And yet it might explain a few things, like Jake's on-again, off-again affection over the past couple of months — distant one moment, almost over-the-top the next.

No. She drew a line through *someone else.* Impossible. That would be completely out of character.

Out of character, she thought, and etched two letters next to the fourth bullet point, so firmly the tip of her pencil pierced the paper.

HD??

Beside that, she wrote *too young?* And next to that, *but ?anticipation.*

She slammed the notebook closed. God, the longer she brainstormed, the worse it got. Mind you, what could be worse than an early onset of HD? After dragging the laptop towards her, she typed *genetics anticipation* into the search bar.

Anticipation, she read, *is a genetic phenomenon where a disease increases in severity with each successive generation. For example, affected children of HD sufferers often have an earlier age of onset and experience a more rapid development of the disease.*

As if she didn't already know that. So why did she feel so wound up?

Because Jake is acting really weird. She moved on to *early signs of HD,* even though she could have recited them by heart: *forms of nervous activity, like fidgeting, minor twitching in hands and toes; social withdrawal; insomnia; frequent thoughts of death, dying or suicide.*

'Shit.' Emily pushed the laptop away, yelping when Pink impaled her thigh with her claws. 'That's it, get off, will you?' She moved inside. What was an earlier age of onset meant to mean? Two years? Five? Ten? Should she make Jake see a doctor? Ask him if he was depressed?

Jake's voice dropped into her ear: *my uncle shot himself.*

Anxiety clawed at her. *I need to talk to someone. I need to talk to someone right now.* But who? Kylie was at work, Ian too, and none of her new friends knew about the HD. She checked her watch. Ten past three, which meant it was ten past five in New Zealand.

She plucked her phone off the bench and selected the last New Zealand number she'd called, only one week before. It rang twice before her mother's voice came over the line.

'Hello, sweetheart, how are you?'

'Terrible,' Emily said, and burst into tears.

'OK,' her mother said about twenty minutes later, after Emily had finished going around in ever-diminishing circles, her own hypnotic spiral. 'Let's just try and put this into perspective. I remember you saying how grumpy Jake was when he was thrown into oncology at the start of the year, and now you're saying he's not so keen on the surgery after all. His job is pretty stressful, correct?'

'Uh-huh.' Emily gulped. Twenty-seven years old, but she felt like a teenager again. Did one ever stop needing their mother in times of crisis?

'And you've both suffered a loss,' Lisa continued. 'How long has it been? Six months?'

Emily gripped the phone. 'Five.' Her head felt thick, as if her blood were moving super-slowly through the vessels. 'You haven't told Dad, have you?'

'I told you I wouldn't, didn't I? But that must be weighing on Jake too.'

'I guess. I don't know.' Emily moved into the bedroom and sat down on the mattress with a thud. 'He doesn't talk about it.'

'Well, he *is* a male.' Lisa paused. 'Hon, have you two ever discussed seeing a genetic counsellor?'

'No.' And why hadn't they? *Because we hardly ever talk about the HD, that's why.* 'Jake doesn't want to find out.'

'Sure, but it doesn't mean you can't talk through the issues you're both facing, does it? I would have thought they'd be the best people to guide you through this.'

'Maybe.' Emily took a deep breath. 'But what I'm really worried about is that maybe Jake is—' She broke off, unable to put her fear into words — because what if that made it true?

'Jake is what? Depressed?'

'Yes, because maybe . . .' Emily hesitated before ploughing on. 'I'm worried this could have something to do with the HD. I mean, we don't even know if he's positive and what if these are the first signs?'

'Look,' Lisa said. 'I think the best person for you to talk to is Jake. Tell him exactly what you're telling me, that you're worried about him. Don't you think?'

'You make it sound so easy.'

'Life isn't easy, hon. Now, promise me you'll talk to him tonight.'

'He's on a long day. He won't be home until at least eleven.' Probably later, if he decided to accompany the registrar to theatre.

'Tomorrow, then.'

'Tomorrow.' Emily hugged a pillow. 'Thanks for listening.'

'Any time. You take care of yourself, OK? Call me any time you like. Love you.'

'Love you too,' Emily whispered. After ending the call, she lay down, staring up at the ceiling. How had such a bright blue day been turned inside out? Everything seemed so unstable, so uncertain.

An even scarier thought struck her: *What if this never got better? What if our happiest days are behind us?*

No. No, you're being paranoid, as usual.

———

Emily woke the next morning to an insistent paw patting her cheek.

'It's way too early for breakfast,' she murmured after a quick glance at the clock on her bedside table. Five fifty-three. A tangerine sliver of sky was visible through the gap in the curtains.

She contemplated cuddling up to Jake, but thought better of it. He hadn't come to bed until after midnight and probably needed all the sleep he could get, judging from the number of times he'd jostled her awake with his tossing and turning.

After getting up, much to Pink's delight, Emily padded into the kitchen and tipped biscuits into her bowl, then filled the kettle with water.

A mournful siren echoed below; an ambulance, coming or going, who knew? Perhaps Jake would be tending to whoever was sick or injured in a couple of hours.

'Morning.' Jake sloped out of the bedroom and into the bathroom.

'Morning,' Emily murmured, slipping teabags into a pair of mugs. When Jake emerged several minutes later, a towel wrapped around his waist, she was sitting at the bench with a cup of tea and her laptop.

'Who do you think will be the prime minister next?' Emily ventured, pointing at the newspaper article in front of her, which was lamenting the rapid turnover in Australian leaders over the past year; five at the last count.

'I don't know, haven't really been following it.' He grazed her cheek with his lips, and she caught a whiff of shaving cream and cologne. 'Did you get much done yesterday?'

'Not really.'

'Artist's block?'

'Something like that,' she said, about to elaborate, to launch into the dreaded *talk*, but Jake was already walking into the bedroom. She sat on the bed, watching him put on underwear, a blue-and-white striped shirt, navy trousers.

'How was your long day?'

Jake sat next to her, pulling socks over his feet. 'Long. I ran around the Emergency Department for hours, had to eat lunch and dinner on the run. I was about to come home when Koutsis asked me to stay on and assist with an appendicectomy. Didn't get home until half-midnight.'

'I know.'

'Yeah? Thought you were fast asleep.' He kissed her. 'Better go, the boss wants to start rounding at seven.'

'What? You don't get paid for that.'

'Try telling *him* that.'

'Jay.' She clasped on his wrist before he could rise to his feet. 'It's only twenty past six. At least have some breakfast.'

'I need to chase all the bloods and make sure the patients are ready for the morning list. I'll grab something from Zouki's on the way past.' He yanked on the sleeves of his shirt, his gaze averted.

'OK,' she said, her arm falling to her side. *Fidgety, moody, evasive.* And was that a twitch she'd seen just then, or was she imagining it?

'Are you all right?'

Emily steeled herself. 'I'm fine — are you?'

Jake regarded her for a moment. 'I'm kind of wasted from yesterday. That's all.'

'All right,' she said, sensing his impatience. 'But . . .'

'Look,' he said. 'I'm tired and shitty, and I've really got to go, OK? I'll catch you tonight.'

Emily stayed where she was, frozen, until she heard the door to the apartment slam behind him. *Talk to Jake — yeah, right.* Her mother had no idea how hard that was.

————

After a long shower, Emily trudged into the bedroom to find her phone was blinking, a message from an unknown number.

Left my phone behind, can you bring it to work? Just page me when you get here 93557. Jake.

Sure, will do, she replied to whoever's phone it was. Just Jake, no kisses or hugs, but then why would he send her terms of endearment on a colleague's phone? Rebuking herself for being over-sensitive, she went around to Jake's side of the bed and unplugged his phone from the charger.

And really, she didn't mean to read the message displayed on the screen. But once her eyes lit on it, she couldn't ignore it. It was from Kylie: *I'm really conflicted about this. The longer you leave it, the harder it's going to be.*

Emily went very still, listening to the blood rush in her ears. *OK. OK, so that could mean anything . . . right?* She hesitated for a few long seconds, then pressed on the home button and entered Jake's pin. It was hardly a secret. He knew her pin too. They had no secrets, nothing to hide.

20992, she typed, before reading the string of texts; once, twice, three times; backwards and forwards, forwards and backwards, and still they made no sense, no sense at all.

Jake: *Still OK for 2pm Thursday?*

Kylie: *Sure . . . How long do we need?*

Jake: *I'll try and make sure it's a quickie* ☺

Kylie: *Very funny. Don't you think it's time you told her?*

Jake: *No, best to tell her once we know for sure . . . OK?*

And then, the final text from Kylie: *I'm really conflicted about this. The longer you leave it, the harder it's going to be.*

'No,' Emily said, and then, louder, '*No.*'

You are dead, Jake Heremaia, DEAD.

Jake could have his fucking phone, all right. He could have the phone, and he could have Kylie, and as for Emily, she was done. *Done.*

Shaking, Emily picked up her own phone and rang the only person she could think of who might be able to help her, *right now.*

He answered straight away.

Chapter 27: Secret

At quarter-past nine, sick of waiting for his phone and with no answer to his texts or calls to Emily's phone, Jake exited the hospital building and tried Emily's work number.

'Airdale Primary,' a cheerful voice said.

'Hi, I was wondering if I could speak to Emily? Walsh,' Jake added, when there was no immediate reply. 'She's a teacher aide.'

'Yes, I know Emily,' the woman said. 'Who's calling, please?'

'Jake. Heremaia. Her partner,' Jake added, getting more tongue-tied by the second.

'Jake, right, hello. Well, she's called in sick.' The voice took on an almost accusatory note, as if Jake should have known that.

He should have known that.

'Sick?' He tried to hide his surprise. 'Oh. Right. Yeah, of course, I — I guess she must have got sick after I left.' Why did that sound like a lie?

'Hope she's feeling better soon.' The woman rang off.

'Shit.' Why hadn't Emily texted him?

Because you don't have your phone.

She could have paged me.

So why hasn't she?

He hurried to the ward, just in time to hear an alarm going off opposite the nurses' station.

'Code Blue,' someone called out, and then he was swept into a room on an incoming tide of doctors and nurses. Crap, it was Mr Wilson, an elderly man who'd had half his bowel removed three days prior, along with a very large tumour. Harry, one of the interns, was already pumping the man's chest, while Greta, one of the registrars, blew air into Wilson's lungs with a bag and mask.

'Hey Jake, can you take some bloods?' Greta called out.

Jake lifted a needle and syringe out of the resus trolley. After an unsuccessful attempt on a collapsed vein in the man's arm, he went for the groin instead. *Bingo*, he thought, watching the dark red blood flash into the syringe.

Nurses swarmed around them; attaching ECG leads, a blood-pressure cuff, oxygen probes.

'Stand clear,' a guy in scrubs yelled. They all leapt back, waiting for Scrubs to discharge the paddles on the man's chest before looking at the ECG monitor.

'Is that VF or a flat line?' Greta asked.

'Looks pretty flat to me,' Scrubs said, and they returned to chest compressions and adrenaline.

Twenty long minutes later, Scrubs said, 'Shall we call it?'

Jake consulted his watch. 'Time of death, nine-fifty-nine am,' he said, and everyone began to drift away. Everyone, apart from Jake and one of the nurses, who began to remove the various wires and lines from the man's prostrate, battered body.

'I'll call his family,' the nurse said. 'Can you get going on the death certificate?'

'Sure,' Jake said, but he lingered for some time after she'd left, taking in the needle marks on the man's skin, the smears of spittle at the corners of his mouth, the dull eyes staring at the featureless ceiling. He moved to the head of the bed and gazed into the fixed, dilated pupils.

It wasn't the first patient who had died in front of him and it wouldn't be the last. But for some reason, Jake felt as though he were teetering on the edge of a cliff, ready to launch into free-fall.

Dragon double helix.

Double helix dragon.

He reached out, pushed the man's eyelids closed.

'Rest in peace,' he murmured.

Jake tried to call Emily three times over the course of the afternoon, but each time it went to answerphone. By three pm, worried something could be wrong — *really* wrong — he said to Harry, the intern, 'Can I ask a favour?'

'Sure,' Harry said, through a mouthful of crisps. They were sitting side-by-side at the computers in the doctors' room, going through countless blood tests and X-rays and CT scans. Every result Jake checked seemed to be out of range, much like the rest of his life.

'Could you hold my pager for the last couple of hours?'

'Sure,' Harry repeated, seemingly unconcerned about the reason for Jake's early departure.

Jake slapped the pager into Harry's palm. 'Thanks heaps, I owe you one.'

'I won't forget.' Harry attached Jake's pager to his belt. 'Have fun.'

The heat hit him as soon as he exited the hospital, the sun so bright he didn't see Gareth until he was at his elbow.

'Hey, Jake, in a hurry?' Gareth was wearing sunglasses and a faded Bob Marley t-shirt, his smile strained.

'No,' Jake lied. 'How are you? How's Hannah?' Nearly three months since she'd been born and Jake hadn't been called on for any godfatherly duties. He'd often wondered if Cameron was still alive, but hadn't been able to bring himself to message Gareth to ask how he was.

And boundaries, Jake, remember those?

Yeah, I think we leapt over those some time ago.

Gareth's face relaxed a little. 'She's great, such a good baby. It's like she knows, you know?'

'And Cameron?' Jake asked.

Gareth tensed again. 'He's not good. The doctors reckon he won't last out the week.'

'I'm really sorry to hear that.' Jake glanced towards the road, where the next tram to the city was trundling past. What the hell, he had to ask. 'Is there anything I can do?'

Shuffling into the shadows, Gareth said, 'If you could come see him,

I'm sure he'd love that. Only if you've got time, that is.'

'Of course.' Whatever was up with Emily would have to wait. Chances were that he was stressing over nothing anyway. 'Where's Hannah?' Jake asked once they were in the lift.

Gareth sagged against the wall. 'Jess, my sister, is looking after her. I'll pick her up before Jess starts her night shift this evening.'

'Right,' Jake said, following Gareth to the Oncology ward.

'Jakey, welcome back to the fold!' A burly pair of arms wrapped around him from behind. 'We've missed you so much.'

'I'm just visiting,' Jake protested, wriggling out of Keith's death grip.

Keith's gaze swung between Jake and Gareth. 'Yeah, right. Cameron's in the single room down the end — we moved him a couple of hours ago. If you need anything then let Pamela know, she's his nurse.'

'Thanks,' Gareth said and hurried down the corridor, Jake a couple of steps behind.

'Hey, darling, look who I found in the car park,' Gareth said, his demeanour changing as soon as he sat next to his partner. Cameron's eyes opened and Jake saw his lips twitch, as if he were trying to smile.

Jake walked around to the other side of the bed and touched Cameron's thigh through the sheet. 'Hi, Cameron.'

'Jake, so good to . . . see you,' Cameron managed. Jake perched on the edge of the mattress, taking in Cameron's slate skin and glazed gaze. The on-the-brink sensation had returned, as if all the dead and dying patients he'd seen recently were swirling around him, threatening to suck him into their vortex.

Cameron moaned and mumbled something else. Jake pressed over the rapid pulse at Cameron's wrist. 'Are you sore, Cameron?'

Gareth made a strangled noise. 'I told them he needed more pain relief this morning,' he said. 'I *told* them.'

'OK.' Jake stood up. 'I'm sure we can sort that out.' Returning to the corridor, he found Cameron's nurse rinsing a urine bottle in the sluice room. 'Hey, can we get some more pain relief for Cameron Lewis?'

Pamela pressed her lips together. 'We only increased his morphine this morning. I think it's the partner who needs sedating, myself.'

Jake stared at her. 'Are you serious?'

She rolled her eyes. 'He's been on at us ever since Cameron arrived on the ward. Nothing is good enough; you know the type.'

'No,' Jake said, his tone steely. 'I don't.' Images of his mother bobbed to the surface of his brain. Shoving them away, he said, 'And I would have thought Gareth would be the most likely person to know if his partner was in pain, don't you?'

Help, help.

I promise, I promise.

'Fine,' Pamela said, her syllables clipped. 'If you think Mr Lewis needs more pain relief, *doctor*, then you'll need to adjust the chart. The morphine is currently charted to be given two- to four-hourly, and it's only been an hour since his last dose.'

'Fine,' Jake snapped. 'Coming right up.'

'Chart's in the drug room.' Pamela stalked off, her multiple chins held high.

Jake eventually found the chart in the nurse's office beneath a half-eaten block of chocolate.

'Stupid,' he repeated, crossing off the two- to four-hourly instruction beneath the morphine and replacing it with a simple: *As required for pain.*

'You right, doc?'

Jake rubbed his chin. 'Sort of. Can you do me a favour?'

'Anything for you,' Keith said, batting his eyelids.

Jake, grinning, swatted him with the chart. 'Do you think you could get another dose of morphine into Cameron Lewis? I know he's not your patient, but . . .'

'But certain nurses should have retired last century, yeah, I know.' Keith took the chart. 'You owe me one, Heremaia.'

'I won't forget.'

'No worries, mate.' Keith ambled out. Several minutes later, Jake leaned against the windowsill, watching Cameron's breathing slow, watching the creases in his forehead smooth out.

Gareth, clutching Cameron's hand, said, 'That did the trick.'

'Sure did,' Jake said, wondering what sort of bribe he'd need to convince Keith to look after Cameron for the rest of the shift.

'You know what he said to me the other day?' Gareth swallowed. 'He said, *If I were a dog, you'd put me down.* And I said, *No, I'd never do that.*'

'No,' Jake said, a numbness settling behind his eyes. 'Of course not.' After a couple of minutes, when Cameron appeared to be asleep, he said, 'Do you want to go and get yourself something to eat?' And when Gareth hesitated, 'I'll stay with him for a while.'

'OK, thanks. I won't be long.' Gareth bent to kiss Cameron. 'You're so strong,' he murmured.

'He's wrong,' Cameron mumbled, once Gareth's footsteps had faded away.

Jake, lost in thoughts of what the hell was up with Emily, jerked to attention. 'Huh?'

'I'm not strong.' Cameron's gaze was steady.

'You don't have to be strong,' Jake said gently, and Cameron's eyes began to shimmer.

'I'm done,' Cameron whispered. 'Gareth won't let me give up, but I can't do this anymore.'

Jake touched his shoulder. 'It's OK to let go,' he said. 'I can talk to him if you like.'

'No, I—' Cameron coughed. 'Doc, if there's anything you can do. Anything to . . . speed it up.' He coughed again. Jake took the cup of water off the bedside table and fed the straw between Cameron's lips.

'I'll see what I can do,' he said. Fuck fuck fuck, what was he saying? What was he promising, *again*? Once he was sure Cameron had drifted off again, Jake moved into the corridor and towards the nurse's station.

'You right there, mate?' Keith sloped past, pushing an observation trolley.

'Yeah, have you got Cameron Lewis' drug chart?'

'Here somewhere . . .' Keith rummaged in the basket on the side of the trolley and passed him a blue clipboard. 'Sad case, eh?'

'Sad,' Jake said. 'Um, I'll get this to you soon, OK?'

'Sure, mate, all yours.' Keith continued on his way, whistling. Jake sat at the ward station desk and opened the drug chart. Morphine, check. Metoclopramide and ondansetron for nausea, check. Midazolam nasal spray for agitation, check. Augmentin, an antibiotic for some sort of infection — chest? Urine? Jake took a pen out of his pocket and drew a thick, deliberate line through the antibiotic, then signed and dated the change. *J Heremaia, 20/11/2013.*

He paused, the date registering in his brain. In sixteen days, it would be the ten-year anniversary of his mother's death. Sixth of December 2003, one of the worst days of his life. What if he'd left his mother alone? What if he'd thought he was doing what his mother wanted when, really, all she'd been able to say at the end was *help*?

His vision blurring, Jake went through the rest of Cameron's chart, crossing off everything that wasn't necessary. *Comfort cares only.* Was it enough? What if, despite Jake's best efforts, Cameron died in pain?

After a brief hesitation, Jake turned to a new page and began to write again, charting a script for a continuous infusion of morphine, metoclopramide and midazolam. Remembering Patel telling him once — *don't worry about giving the patient a bit too much when they're dying, as long as you're giving enough so they're not suffering* — Jake doubled the dose of morphine, then thought better of that and revised it to a dose fifty per cent higher than Cameron had received in the past twenty-four hours.

First, do no harm. Somehow Jake didn't think Cameron would object to floating on a cloud of morphine.

You could give him more.

He could.

He could, but he wouldn't. Cameron was already dying. All Jake needed to do was to keep him comfortable in his last hours.

Jake found Keith in a four-bedded room, hooking a breathless patient up to oxygen. 'Hey . . .'

The nurse rolled an eye towards him. 'Let me guess, you need another favour? I like Guinness, if you're shouting. Just saying.'

'It's yours.' Jake followed Keith into the corridor. 'I've charted a subcutaneous infusion for Cameron.'

'About time someone did that.' Keith took the chart. 'When are you coming back, doc?'

'Tomorrow,' Jake said, glancing towards Cameron's room. *If he's still here, that is.*

'No, I mean for good.'

Jake clutched his pen. 'I don't know. Still making up my mind.'

Keith regarded him for a moment. 'You've got a way with dying people, doc,' he said.

'Thanks, I'll be sure to put that on my CV.' Jake started towards the double doors.

'It's not such a silly idea. Don't forget the Guinness,' Keith called after him.

'I'll bring it in tomorrow,' Jake said. 'I promise.'

———

By the time Jake arrived home, it was half-past five, and he was wrecked — physically and emotionally. Pink ran up to him as soon as he entered the apartment, yowling so loud it set his teeth on edge.

'No one fed you yet?' He trudged through the lounge, past the unoccupied bathroom and into the bedroom. No Emily. There was his phone, though, on the floor between the bed and the window. When he picked it up, he saw ten missed calls and three text messages, all from the hospital.

'Huh.' He turned a circle. The bed was unmade, the curtains still drawn. Perhaps Emily had been in bed all day, and had nipped out for something.

But why hasn't she tried to get in touch with me? And why, why, isn't she answering my calls?

He began scrolling through the texts on his phone, finding one from Kylie he didn't recall reading: *I'm really conflicted about this. The longer you leave it, the harder it's going to be.* The text had arrived at six forty-five am, at least fifteen minutes after he'd left for work.

But the text wasn't showing up as unread. Which meant someone had . . .

Oh. Shit.

He rang Kylie.

'Hel-lo.' Why did she always have to sound so fucking cheerful?

'She knows,' he said.

'You told her? Thank God.'

'No.' Jake marched into the lounge. 'I didn't tell her. But I'm pretty

215

sure she read your message this morning. And all the other ones we sent.'

'Right . . . So what did she say?'

'I think she's not talking to me.' Jake exited onto the balcony, watching the pedestrians scurrying along the street below. 'She didn't go to work today. And she's not answering my calls.' *Shit, shit, shit.*

Kylie made a clucking noise. 'Like I said, she had to find out sooner or later.'

'But not like *this*.'

'I *told* you we were asking for trouble. Oh my God, what if she hates me?'

'Why would she hate you?' Jake asked. 'Jesus, Kyles, I—', and then he heard a door slam, heard Emily say, 'If I told you I'd just screwed someone else, what would *you* say?'

'What?' Kylie squawked.

Jake, in a panic, pressed end and faced Emily. '*What?*'

'You heard me,' Emily said, and he waited for the punch line, for the *just kidding*, but it never came.

Chapter 28: Soul Mistake

That morning, after calling Nick, Emily slipped into matching underwear, of which she only had one set. She'd been saving the new underwear for a special occasion. *What the hell*, she thought, thinking of Nick's square, stubbly jaw and full lips, *maybe this is it*. She added a floral sundress and blue cardigan before stepping out into the morning. Another clear day, crows cawing on the power lines above.

A murder of crows, she thought, and, *I'll kill you Jake Heremaia.*

Kylie too. How could she have been so blind? The messages she'd read that morning kept marching across the front of her brain. Two pm tomorrow, oh God, were Jake and Kylie going to have it off with each other in a hotel room? Or at Kylie's, or horror of horrors, in the bed Emily shared with Jake?

Stop, stop. But the images of her man in bed with one of her best friends just wouldn't go away.

It was half-past seven when she reached Number 42 Café. A row of customers sat in the window seats, peas in a pod, focused on phones, laptops, newspapers. Nick was behind the counter, pouring milk on top of someone's coffee.

'Didn't know they did silver ferns in Australia,' Emily said.

'Especially for you, Kiwi bird.' He pushed the saucer towards her. 'On the house.'

Emily didn't reply. She couldn't. Nick signalled to a dreadlocked woman in the kitchen. 'Cath, can you cover me for five minutes?' As he steered Emily up a narrow set of stairs, his palm between her shoulder blades, he murmured, 'Stay as long as you want, OK? I'll come check on you in an hour or so, once the morning rush is over.'

The apartment above the café was tiny — one room with a couch that looked as though it doubled as a bed at night, a folded blanket and pillow at one end, a kitchenette and cupboard-sized bathroom. Emily perched on the couch, uncertain how to feel, what to do. Had Jake really been cheating on her? And for how long?

There was a rap on the door and Nick appeared, balancing the coffee cup and saucer. 'Forgot this. You right there, Kiwi bird?'

Emily nodded. 'Thanks. Sorry.' She drew in a shaky breath. 'I won't stay long.'

'Like I said, it's not a problem.' Nick straddled a low stool. 'Want to tell me what's going on with you and your boyfriend?'

Emily rubbed the dragon tattoo on her wrist, which she suddenly wanted to erase. 'I found something. On Jake's phone.'

Nick mirrored her, his fingers sneaking beneath a copper bracelet around his own wrist. 'Let me guess, there's someone else?'

'Don't.' She blinked, her vision blurring.

'Guys are pricks sometimes, aren't they?' Nick touched her elbow. 'Want me to arrange something?'

'Arrange . . . ?' She swallowed. 'Oh, God. No. Please.' As much as she hated Jake right then, the last thing she wanted was for some thug to rearrange his face or whatever they called it.

'You don't deserve to be treated like that.'

Emily stared at the pattern on her milk froth, which was starting to resemble a pine tree rather than a silver fern, or maybe it was an arrow, pointing towards — what? 'Thanks for letting me crash here.' *Is that what I'm doing? What will I do tonight? Will he offer to sleep on the floor? To sleep with me?*

'Stay up here, or come hang out in the café later, whatever you want to do.' Nick embraced her, quickly, firmly. 'I'm on a break from eleven until twelve, if you want to go for a walk or whatever.'

'Cool. Thanks.' She brushed her lips past his bristly cheek. 'I'll see you then.'

'Catch you,' Nick said, his slate gaze on hers. 'Key code's on the fridge.'

'Key code?'

'For the door.' He released her and clattered down the stairs, whistling.

Emily wandered over to the smudged window and peered into the alley below. A line of overflowing bins, a tabby cat, a blanketed lump that could have been a homeless person. She pivoted, taking in the books stacked on the floor, the dust motes swirling in the oblong of sunshine slanting through the window.

Inspecting the books, she came across many authors she recognised, as well as others she'd never heard of. Bret Easton Ellis, Salman Rushdie, Philip Roth, Margaret Atwood. She wondered what an avid reader like Nick was doing working in a café, and realised she didn't really know him at all. *Not like Jake*, she thought, and she almost, almost wished she hadn't read the messages on Jake's phone.

What you don't know can't hurt you.

No, that's not true. It will hunt you down anyway, when you least expect it.

After drinking the coffee as slowly as she could, Emily decided to do as Nick had suggested. But first, she went to the 7-Eleven on the corner to buy an exercise book and a pencil; something to keep her occupied while she tried to work out what her next step should be.

Don't you think it's time you told her?

No, best to tell her once we know for sure.

Emily sat at one of the outside tables and opened the exercise book. A virgin white page stared back at her. Damn it, she needed her sketchpad. No reason why she couldn't return for it.

But she couldn't bring herself to set foot in the apartment. Not yet.

A new story, perhaps. She pressed down until the pencil broke through the page. Lifting the pencil, she observed the puncture wound, rimmed with lead, and thought of irreversible decisions, of bullets and tattoos and infidelity.

'Another coffee?' Nick deposited a glass of water on her table.

Emily lifted the glass to her cheek. 'No, this is good thanks. Are you sure it's OK, me loitering here like this?'

'Who's going to tell me off?'

'Your boss?'

'He never arrives until afternoon. Sometimes later.' He sat opposite her, crossed an ankle over his knee. 'Starts drinking as soon as he wakes up, I reckon.'

'Really?' Emily was struggling to remember what the other staff looked like. Apart from Nick and the girl with the dreadlocks, she'd never taken notice of the rest of them.

'And that's just the alcohol.' Nick fiddled with his lighter, sparks jumping out of his palm. 'Did you have breakfast?'

'No.'

'What do you want? On the house.'

'I don't want to get you in trouble,' Emily protested.

'Like I said, who's to know?' A flame leapt between his fingers. 'Eggs Benedict?'

'OK,' Emily said, too tired to argue, even though she had no appetite. 'Sure.'

———

Later that morning, Emily and Nick crossed the street, and strolled through Federation Square and towards the Yarra River.

Emily knotted her cardigan around her waist. 'I always love it here. An oasis in the middle of the city.' The scent of eucalyptus wafted towards her, a constant reminder that she was in Australia.

'I often come here in my lunch hour and lie under a tree with a book.' Nick was wearing dark blue jeans and a Talking Heads t-shirt, his dyed-blond hair sticking up in all sorts of directions. She wondered how old he was. Early thirties?

'You've got quite a collection of books in your apartment.' She flushed. 'Not that I was snooping around.'

Nick plucked a leaf off a nearby gum tree. The trunk looked improbable, as if it were wrapped in papier mâché rather than pale bark. 'It's not like you can hide anything up there, let alone swing a cat.'

'A recidivist cat,' she said, thinking of Pink, and he laughed.

'Definitely not *that* cat. Dave would kill me if he knew she was on the prowl again.'

'She's very affectionate,' she said as her phone began to ring.

'That your man?' Nick asked.

'Not any more,' Emily mumbled, pressing the button on the side of the phone to silence it. She wondered if Jake had figured out that she was pissed off at him. Not just pissed off, livid.

I know what you've been doing behind my back for . . . how long? The jab in her chest was so strong she needed to do something, anything, to chase it away. She took Nick's hand, feeling the chunky ring on his left thumb scrape against her skin.

Oh, but you could regret this. You could.

'This way, little Kiwi,' he said, leading her down a side path lined with flowering trees and shrubs of all different colours, violet and yellow and orange.

Her breath short, Emily said, 'It's so lush in here.'

'Lush, huh.' Nick's gaze was so intent she had to look away, but his finger was already on her chin, his mouth on hers. And it was wrong, all wrong, and she slid out of his embrace, out of the inevitability of yet another thing she couldn't reverse, no matter how hard she tried.

'Em, wait,' he called, but he didn't come after her, and she didn't want him to either.

———

Emily walked. She walked and walked. Through the gardens, past the parents pushing babies and toddlers in prams, past the joggers and the dog walkers and the homeless people with their belongings spread out on the grass, then onto the street, following the tram line until her feet hurt and her head hurt and her heart her heart her heart.

After an hour, she turned her phone off, unable to cope with not just Jake but Nick messaging her, their messages a swirling jumble of disembodied words: *where are you are you OK you didn't tell me you were feeling sick I'm sorry if I jumped the gun.*

The sun was still high in the sky when she returned to Southbank, although her watch told her it was just after five. It had been one of the longest days of her life, but she wasn't ready to face Jake, not yet, so she stopped at a riverside bar.

'What would you like?' The waitress couldn't have been a day over twenty, with her unblemished skin and high ponytail.

Emily, feeling old, said, 'I'll have a glass of Sauvignon Blanc.'

'Which one?'

'I don't know, whatever you recommend.' Emily propped her elbows up on the railing, watching a ferry slide past. The waitress returned with the wine. After drinking the glass in three swallows, Emily ordered another.

'Celebrating something?' The waitress asked.

'No, I'm about to break up with my boyfriend.'

The waitress's eyes widened. 'Sorry to hear that.'

'He might be too.' *Or not.* The wine was so refreshing. The more she drank, the clearer her mind felt. A short time later, Emily swayed to her feet and finally, finally, went home.

———

Pink ran up to her as soon as she entered the apartment. From the balcony, she heard Jake's raised voice, and she froze, wondering if someone else were there, before realising he was on the phone.

'She's not answering my calls,' he was saying. There was a pause, then, 'But not like *this*.' Emily gripped the doorframe. 'Why would she hate you?' he said next, followed by, 'Jesus, Kyles, I—.'

Rage bubbling up her throat, Emily slammed the front door and strode across the lounge. Jake was facing away from her, his shirttail dangling free.

'If I told you I'd just screwed someone else, what would *you* say?' Emily spat.

Jake turned. '*What?*' The hand holding the phone dropped to his side. Was *she* still listening? Emily was past caring.

'You heard me,' Emily said, watching the tendons on his neck stand out, watching his jaw contort.

'Where have you been?'

'Out.'

'Where?'

'Why should I tell you?' She gestured at the phone. 'Seems like you've been hiding plenty from me.'

His breath quickened. 'I was going to tell you. When it was over.'

'When it was over? What's that supposed to mean?' Her voice rose to a shriek. 'When you've got sick of having it off with each other?'

'*What?*' Jake's mouth fell open. 'Jesus, is that what you — it's not that, how could you even —' He moved towards her. 'I've been tested, Em. Why the hell would you think it was anything else?'

The rush of blood to her head was so sudden Emily thought she might faint. *Oh my God. Oh my God.* 'When?'

'Six weeks ago.' He reached for her wrist. She shrank away.

'*Six weeks?*'

Jake's Adam's apple bobbed up and down. 'I asked Kylie if she'd be my support person tomorrow afternoon when I get the result. They won't give it to me without one, and I didn't want to put you through all that waiting. I was going to tell you as soon as I heard.' Words, words, but she couldn't, didn't, want to listen.

'You trusted *her* but not me? I'm meant to be the person who's closest to you. *Me*, not Kylie.'

'I was trying to protect you.'

'I don't need *fucking* protecting. You're always so fucking secretive, how am I meant to keep up?'

'I've never hidden anything from you before. Never, never. Look.' He stepped away, as if scared she were about to hit him. 'Please. Come with me tomorrow afternoon. I want you to.'

'No. No, why should I? I wasn't invited to take part in one of the most important moments in your life. And you would think,' she swiped a hand beneath her streaming nose, 'you would think I'd earned it after everything we've been through. Or have you forgotten?' She bolted inside and almost fell over the cat. Pink yowled and ran beneath the couch.

Jake, close behind her, said, 'Em, you're over-re—'

She whirled. 'Over-reacting, am I? Do you want to know where I was today? Do you really?'

He didn't reply. She could see, from his expression, that he was already halfway to the answer.

'I was with Nick,' she said. 'And do you know what we did?'

'No,' he said, his voice suddenly icy, 'but I'm guessing you're going to tell me anyway.'

Emily gritted her teeth. 'Perhaps I'll just leave it up to your imagination. You can discuss it with Kylie when you see her, like you discuss everything else.'

'Don't,' Jake said hoarsely, but she was already opening the door, was already leaving. Again.

Chapter 29: Jump

His world was inside out, outside in. After Emily left, Jake paced the apartment, pinching the skin on the tops of his thighs, his stomach, over his biceps. *Stupid, how could I be so stupid?*

And: *Emily, Emily, what have you done?* Had she really slept with that greasy coffee guy?

I was with Nick. And do you know what we did? No matter which way he turned it around in his mind, Jake couldn't see how he could interpret that any other way.

Then again, Emily had taken his text conversation with Kylie *completely* the wrong way. When he read through the string of messages again on the phone, he could see how that had happened. Yet how could Emily fail to see that he'd been acting with her welfare in mind? Anger and indignation simmering inside him, he wrote Emily a text: *I had this test for you, don't you get it?*, then deleted it. No, clearly she *didn't* get it.

Because you never discussed it with her.

Shut up.

Next he sent a message to Kylie: *So Emily thought we were having an affair.*

His phone beeped almost immediately: *!!! I hope you set her straight.*

Sure did, Jake replied. He didn't have the energy to tell Kylie the rest. What to do now? Get drunk? No, he couldn't cope with the inevitable migraine. If only he could hit the surf, throw his body into the foamy brine until he was too tired to think. Perhaps they should have moved to the Gold Coast rather than Melbourne.

Except . . .

It wasn't home.

After firing up his laptop, he downloaded his e-mail. There it was, the letter from the Australasian College of Physicians welcoming him to the training programme. As of February next year, he could start accumulating credits towards his oncology training, could start studying for his fellowship exams.

Is that what you really want?

He slammed the lid of the laptop closed and sagged against the couch cushions. How could he make any kind of decision until after his appointment tomorrow? If he tested positive, he might as well give up on all his long-term plans.

Including, it seemed, Emily.

Do you think a negative result is going to make her any less angry with you?

Jake's thoughts turned to Emily's father. Damn it, if Jim hadn't forced him into a corner, he probably wouldn't have had the test at all and they wouldn't be in this mess.

He ate a dinner of baked beans straight from the can, then wandered down to Southbank, half-hoping, half-dreading coming across Emily. What if she were with Nick?

Emily's voice jeered at him: *Perhaps I'll just leave it up to your imagination.*

I am, and it's out of control, just like the rest of my life.

After contemplating and dismissing going past Number 42 Café — if he caught sight of Nick, he'd be tempted to deck him — Jake trudged home and went to bed. Alone.

———

That night he had a dream that wasn't a dream, more a version of a memory. In the dream-memory, it was the last Friday in November, and school was out — forever. Jake should have been celebrating, but he wasn't, not yet.

The music was getting louder and louder. Quarter to ten, and the sky was aflame, the sun having slipped behind the hills only minutes before. Jake leaned over the porch railing. He was at Ian's house, perched high on the cliffs above St Clair Beach. On the lawn below, a group of kids from their year were dancing and singing along to 'Let's Get Retarded'.

'Red sky at night.' Emily appeared next to him, her elbow brushing his.

'Shepherd's delight,' he said reflexively, an all-too-familiar twinge of desire and apprehension kindling in his belly.

'Are you all right?'

'I'm fine, are you?' He glanced at her. Emily was staring out to sea, her skin aglow.

'I'm fine,' she said. Lying, just like him. Jake raised his beer bottle to his lips and took a large swallow before passing it to her. 'You all set for tomorrow?'

Emily gulped on the beer. 'I think so.'

'I don't want you to get in trouble.'

'Yeah, you keep saying that.' Emily swivelled and began walking down the porch steps. Jake traipsed after her, waiting until she had reached the hedge at the perimeter of the sloping lawn before clasping her shoulders.

'Em.' He brought his mouth to her ear, closing his eyes against the warmth radiating off her skin. 'You don't have to do this.'

'Don't I?'

'Of course not. Jesus, maybe *I* should have been asking to go on your dad's ward rounds.'

'I wouldn't have gone this far if I didn't want to help you.'

'No . . .' This was where he should tell her to abandon their plan, to abandon him. But he couldn't, because that would mean breaking his promise to his mother. *And I can't stand to see her suffer any longer, not for another year, another month, another day.*

Emily faced him. 'I promise you,' she said, her voice firmer, 'that I'll get it. If not tomorrow, then the next time.'

'*There* you are.' The head girl, Lucy, flashed her teeth at them. 'Oops, was I interrupting something?'

'Not at all,' Jake said, before practically sculling the rest of his beer.

Lucy slung an arm around each of their necks. 'Come and dance,' she bellowed. 'It's not every night you get to celebrate the end of an era.'

'Not drunk enough.' Jake slipped out of Lucy's grip and sloped around the side of the house, peering over the shadowy bank below.

From the front lawn, he heard the heaving mass of no-longer-high-school-students shouting, *jump, jump, jump.*

Jump, he thought. *Jump, jump*, and the ground dropped away before him, and he was falling, falling, falling . . .

Jake bolted upright, the sheet tangling against his sweaty skin. Reached for his phone. Saw a message from Emily, just received, even though it was five past two in the morning: *I really need to talk to you. If you get this can you call me?*

As soon as she answered, he said, 'Come home, Em. I'll come and get you. I don't care where you are, or what you've done, I just want you to come home.' Expecting her to lash out at him, to tell him it was over, once and for all.

Instead, he heard her say, 'Here now.' He heard her footfall in the lounge, felt her move back into his sphere, or perhaps one of the hypnotic spirals she liked to draw, and he sucked in a shattered breath and she climbed into bed and embraced him, and said, 'I'm sorry, I'm sorry,' and he said, 'Me too.'

————

'Nick and I didn't really do anything,' she said, minutes later, or was it an hour, he'd lost track.

'I don't think I want to know.'

'But *I* want you to know. He kissed me and it was yuck and I don't know why I let him near me.'

'Stop.' Jake wound his fingers into her hair, feeling her inhalation in *his* lungs, her heartbeat deep within his own ribcage. 'Just . . . stop.' How long since they'd been this close, in mind as well as body? He couldn't remember. 'I'm sorry I shut you out.'

'Don't do it again,' she said.

'No.' He turned over, stared up the ceiling. *Tell her what Jim said. Tell about the insulin vial.* No, no, he couldn't dump that on her, not now. She was spinning out enough as it was. 'What's the time?'

'Quarter to three.'

'I'm due on the ward in four hours,' he said faintly. *Coward, I'm such a coward.*

'Call in sick.'

'I can't.'

'You're not indispensable, Doctor Heremaia. Except to me.'

'Ditto, Walsh.' He stroked her wrist. 'Double helix dragon.'

'Dragon double helix,' she answered, and when he woke, the sky was red once more.

———

At nine minutes to two, Jake stood by the hospital lifts, hoping no one he knew would wander past. No one except for his support person, of course. His head was aching, his mouth dry. He'd bought a packet of crisps earlier and had managed five before he'd dumped the rest in the bin. Half a can of Coke sat uneasily in his stomach.

'Hey.' Emily appeared beside him and threaded her fingers through his. 'Are you ready?'

He gave her a jerky nod and pushed the up button for the lifts. A very pregnant woman and a man with a beard, presumably her partner, squeezed in behind them. Twenty-four weeks' gestation, give or take, Jake thought, and wondered if Emily was thinking the same thing. The lift stopped at their floor, way too soon, and his knees began to shake.

I don't think I can do this. Too late. He couldn't reverse his decision now, not after everything he'd put Emily through over the past forty-eight hours, let alone the past ten years. He led her into the waiting room on spaghetti legs. The same old magazines littered the waiting room, along with the same old posters, the same old receptionist.

'Take a seat, Jake,' the receptionist said, as if he were an old friend, rather than a patient on his third visit.

Emily gripped his hand tighter. Feeling nauseous, Jake glanced around for the white containers they used for all manner of bodily fluids on the wards, but no such luck, just a bin by the water cooler.

'Jake,' a voice announced. Tannin was standing in the entrance to one of the clinic rooms, clutching a file to her chest. 'Come in,' she said, and smiled at Emily. 'And you must be—'

'Emily,' Jake blurted. 'My . . . girlfriend.' *The one I never mentioned.*

What the hell, would Tannin withhold his test result now? Maybe that wouldn't be such a bad thing.

'Welcome.' The genetic counsellor ushered them in. 'Jake said you've known each other since you were both students,' she added, and he realised Tannin thought that Emily was the old friend he'd mentioned, a.k.a. Kylie.

Emily sat next to him, pulling on the sleeves of her cardigan. 'That's right.'

'Thanks for coming along.' Tannin crossed her legs. 'How are you, Jake?'

'Well, you know.' His palms were clammy, his heart going so fast he thought he'd probably spew the organ up as well when the time came.

Tannin nodded, her lips assuming the neutral position. 'Are you still happy to hear your result?'

'Sure,' he said. 'Let's just get it over and done with.' Positive, negative, he no longer cared. He just wanted the waiting to be over; a clear path, however short that path might be.

'All right.' Tannin turned the computer screen around. 'Here's your result. Thirty-nine CAG repeats. That means you're —'

'Indeterminate,' Jake said, barely able to comprehend what he was hearing. He bent forward, squinting at the screen.

CAG-CAG-you've-got-to-be-fucking-kidding.

'Indeterminate?' Emily echoed.

'It's nothing,' he said. 'It means nothing.'

'I know what it means,' she said quietly, and Jake wanted to scream, or cry, or run. Instead, he sat like a dummy, his fists on his knees, his heart crashing in his ears.

Tannin said, 'It's not a positive or negative, I agree. It means you may or may not develop the disease. But I don't think you should view this as a bad result.'

Jake breathed in. Breathed out. *I'm not positive or negative. I'm . . . nothing.*

He felt Emily's touch on his neck. 'It's OK, Jay,' she said. 'Everything's going to be OK.'

'Have you got any questions?' Tannin asked.

'No,' he said. 'Thank you.' *For nothing, absolutely nothing.*

'I'm going to refer you to a neurologist,' Tannin went on. 'For yearly follow-up, if you'd like that.'

'Sure.' He hung his head in his hands.

'This doesn't mean you can't have a family,' Tannin said. 'You don't have to worry about passing on anything with preimplantation genetic diagnosis.'

'Exactly,' Emily said, rubbing his neck as if he were a dog, or some other animal that would need to be put down eventually.

Jake's stomach twisted. 'I can't talk about this right now.' *What about passing on a legacy of grief? What about that?*

'This is not a bad result,' Tannin repeated. 'You might think that right now, but it really isn't.'

'Sure,' he said, before standing up and bolting towards the waiting room.

It was fortunate he'd checked out the rubbish bin before, because that was exactly where the contents of his stomach ended up.

Chapter 30: Everybody Wants to Rule the World

Emily squeezed Jake's knee. 'I always tell myself that the pilot and airline staff do this every day, so it can't be that unsafe.'

'I always tell myself that most accidents happen on take-off and landing,' Jake muttered. His palm was clammy, his temples shiny. The plane bounced as they began descending through the clouds, and he gripped her fingers so tight it was almost painful. 'Should have had that glass of wine.'

'I'm sure Mum and Steve will be happy to oblige at dinner tonight.'

'Huh.' Jake's eyes were closed.

'Just think of those waves.'

'Uh-huh.'

'Look we're through the clouds.' Emily peered out of the window. Dunedin looked so much greener than she remembered — and really, really small. 'I always know we're pretty close when I can see the sheep.'

'I'm not relaxing until I can see the whites of their eyes,' he mumbled.

The loudspeaker crackled. 'Cabin crew, please be seated for landing.'

'So nice to hear those Kiwi accents,' Emily said.

Jake grunted.

Emily gave up, her thoughts instead turning to the contents of her suitcase. Christmas presents, check. Sketchpad and pencils, check. Oral contraceptive pill, double check.

The plane's wheels hit the tarmac with a jolt and Jake's eyes flew open.

'Jesus,' he said, holding the seat in front of him. 'Thought we'd hit an air pocket or something.'

'*Now* you can relax,' she said, although she thought that would only really be true once they returned to Melbourne. Jake had been extra irritable in the few days leading up to their departure.

No, I don't want to stay at your dad's a whole week, he'd said. *Can we stay with your mum and Steve?* And then there was the impending visit to Northland next week for an obligatory three days with Jake's father, whom he hadn't seen in over a year.

Switching his phone on, Jake said, 'What do you think about me squeezing in a surf before dinner?'

'Sure,' Emily said. 'Get it out of your system.'

Jake smiled for the first time since they'd left home, several hours before. 'Get it back *into* my system, you mean.'

———

'Gosh,' Emily's mother said as they drove away from St Clair, the undulating sea reflected in the rear-vision mirror. 'He was busting to get in that water, wasn't he?'

'It *has* been eleven months,' Emily said. *Pick me up in an hour or so,* Jake had said. *No rush if you get distracted.*

'Mum, when can I learn to surf?' Charlotte piped up from the back seat.

'I'm sure Jake will be happy to give you a lesson,' Emily said, and satisfied with that, the eight-year-old stuck her headphones over her ears and began swaying to her music.

Lisa turned down the radio, on which Tears for Fears were crooning 'Everybody Wants to Rule the World'. 'How *is* Jake anyway?'

Emily squinted into the late afternoon sun. 'I don't know. Ever since he got his test result, he's been . . . God, I can't even talk to him about it.'

'Sounds like a common theme with you two.'

Emily kicked her shoes off. 'Tell me about it. I'm trying to give him some time, but how long is that meant to be? We both thought this test was going to give us an answer, but now everything seems even more uncertain.'

Lisa gave her thigh a squeeze. 'It's an adjustment, hon. For both of you.'

'Maybe you should be a genetic counsellor.'

Her mother snorted. 'I do enough counselling at school, believe me.'

Emily gazed over the harbour. 'I think he's worried I'm going to dump him.'

'Thought he might have figured out by now that you're not going to do that.'

'You'd think,' Emily murmured, although perhaps her episode with Nick was bothering Jake more than he cared to admit. She'd been trying to make it up to Jake ever since, but she wasn't sure how.

Lisa waved at the estuary. 'Get anything this idyllic in Melbourne?'

'It's different.' Emily wound down the window a crack, inhaling the scents of seaweed and salt. 'It's been good for my creativity, anyway.'

'Have you finished your book?'

'Hell, no. Maybe in a few months. I might see if I can apply for a creative grant.'

'Sounds wonderful,' her mother said.

'When can we go to Melbourne, Mum?' Charlotte asked.

'Maybe next year,' Lisa said vaguely. Charlotte huffed and stuck her headphones on again. Emily toyed with her water bottle, wondering how her life would have turned out if she'd gone to live with her mother when her parents had split up, rather than staying with Jim to finish high school in a familiar neighbourhood.

Maybe then Jake and I wouldn't have . . .

But then we wouldn't be together . . . or would we?

You're not together because of what you did for him . . . are you?

'Have you heard from Bradley?' Emily asked.

Lisa huffed. 'No. I can only assume he and his friends have reached Thailand safely.'

'Or been thrown into the Bangkok Hilton.'

'I should hope not. I assume he'll call home on Christmas Day, if nothing else. That's only two days away.' Her mother glared at the rear vision mirror. 'Charlotte, stop picking your nose.'

'I'm *not*,' Charlotte said.

Emily's phone sprang to life, and she frowned. 'Hi, Dad.'

Jim's baritone poured into her ear. 'Well, hello. Are you back in paradise yet?'

'If paradise is Dunedin, then yes I am.'

'Of course it is. Are you free for dinner tonight?'

'Not tonight, no,' Emily hedged. 'How about lunch tomorrow?'

Her father made a semi-exasperated noise. 'I'm working.'

'OK, well . . .' She looked at her mother, who was pretending not to listen. 'I could swing past before I pick up Jake from the beach later, how about that?'

'Perfect, see you then,' her father said, seemingly delighted at the thought that Emily was going sans Jake, but perhaps she was imagining that.

'Your father?' Her mother said after Emily ended the call.

'The one and only.' Emily shoved her phone into the bottom of her bag.

———

It was just after six when she walked down her father's driveway. Jim was sitting on the porch, his pen poised over a sodoku puzzle book, his hat low over his eyes.

'Sweetheart.' He stood up to greet her. 'How was your flight?'

'Just the usual,' Emily said, deciding not to mention Jake's aerophobia, if that was the correct word for it. 'Jake's gone for a surf.' She glanced around, taking in the blooming roses, blood red and butter yellow, and the neatly clipped lawns.

'Good, good. Come in, do you want a drink? Glass of wine?'

'Well, I could have one.' She entered the house. 'Garden looks good.'

'I get a lot done on these long evenings.' Jim poured wine into a glass and passed it to her. 'Although I've been spending a few nights out lately.'

'New hobby?' Emily asked, watching him pour another glass for himself.

'You could say that.' He clinked his glass against hers. 'I've got someone I want you to meet.'

'A lady someone?' Emily asked.

He nodded. 'That's right. Yvette.'

'Is she another doctor?'

'No, she's a fashion designer.' He swirled his wine, took a sip. 'We met at a party.'

'Right.' Emily buried her nose in her glass, unsure what to say next. No matter how long it had been since her parents split up, discussing her father's girlfriends was still really weird.

'She's coming around at seven, which is why I thought you could have joined us for dinner.' He cleared his throat. 'Never mind, we can sort something out another time.'

'We can.' Emily entered the lounge and plucked a framed photograph off the mantelpiece. 'How many times have I asked you to put this away?'

'It's a good photo of you,' Jim said, with a fond glance at the picture of her and Adam standing with their arms linked around each other, the St Clair promenade behind them.

'I'm sure there are lots of good photos of you and mum I could dig out too.' Emily turned the photo facedown. 'Before your fashion designer arrives. What do you think?'

'Her name is Yvette. And no need to be so sensitive,' he added, but he reached over and put the photograph inside the piano stool. 'Come on, let's sit outside and enjoy the sun. How are you, anyway?'

'Never been better,' Emily said, which was and wasn't true. She sat in the swing chair on the porch. Jim perched on a porch step, his hat tipped sideways.

'Things going OK with Jake?'

'Absolutely.'

'Good,' Jim said, his pale eyes flitting to hers, as if he didn't believe her.

Emily took a deep breath. 'He's had the test. We got the results last month.'

Jim set his glass down, his gaze intent. 'And?'

'He's indeterminate.'

'Indeterminate?'

'He's got an in-between number of CAG repeats. So they can't say whether or not he'll get HD.'

Her father frowned. 'That's not very reassuring.'

'Not really. Although . . .' She set the chair rocking. 'It's kind of as if he never had the test at all. Which is not necessarily a bad thing. I mean, he never really wanted to have it in the first place.'

'So now what?'

'We just carry on, I guess.' She took a large swallow of wine, glad for the chemical blunting of her nerves, which were starting to feel jagged, raw. 'There's no reason why we can't have a family. We—'

'Emily.' Her father's voice was like a slamming door. 'Look. I haven't had a chance to talk to you alone about this before, but I really need to express my concern at what you could be letting yourself in for.'

Her breath quickened. 'What?'

Jim leaned forward. 'If Jake ends up developing HD in — what, ten, twelve years' time — where's that going to leave you? He's never going to get income protection or life insurance with a test result like that. He'll lose his income, and you'll be struggling to support the whole family.'

She bristled. 'So what are you saying? Don't have kids?'

'I'm saying, if family is really important to you, then perhaps,' his voice softened, 'perhaps this relationship is not for you.'

'Oh my God.' Emily leapt up, wine slopping over her dress. 'I can't believe that *you*, of all people, are saying that, a medical professional.'

'I'm saying that *because* I'm a medical professional. Because I've witnessed up-close, as have you, the havoc this disease wreaks on families.' He gestured towards the fence, as if Jake's family were still residing next door, rather than scattered to the wind. Christine, dead. Jake's grandma, dead. Jake — her heart thrummed as she remembered Jake's hand on her belly, his voice in her ear: *I choose life. I choose* this *life.*

Jim's insistent tone yanked her into the present. 'I'm saying this because I'm your father and I don't want you to ruin your life.'

Emily gritted her teeth. 'How many times do I have to tell you? This is *my* life. I'm sorry if it's not the one you chose, but Jake and I aren't going to break up, no matter what you say.' She pushed the glass at him. 'Are you going to get your new girlfriend screened too? She could be harbouring all sorts of deadly diseases.'

Her father fell silent for a moment, his fingers tightening around the stems of the wine glasses. Then he said, 'Has Jake told you everything?'

She glared at him. 'We don't keep secrets from each other, if that's what you mean.'

'I mean, has he told you what I showed him on my last visit to Melbourne?'

'What did you show him?' She asked, her tone icy. *What?*

'Why don't you ask him?' Jim poured the wine from her glass into his. 'Don't think I'm acting out of anything other than concern, my darling. But mark my words, Jake *will* leave you, either willingly, or unwillingly. So my advice to you is, get out while you can.'

Emily let out a strangled noise, half-scream, half-cry, and bolted towards her mother's car. After reversing out of the driveway, she drove toward the beach, Jim's words reverberating around her skull.

He will *leave you, either willingly, or unwillingly.*

But how could her father know that? What had he given Jake? Did it have anything to do with Jake's erratic behaviour over the past few months?

I've never hidden anything from you before. Never, never.

But it's not true, is it Jake? It's. Not. True.

Chapter 31: Numb

DECEMBER 2003

Ian had managed to fit a record number of ten people in his VW, six in the back (Emily was in the bottom layer), two in the passenger seat and one on the handbrake. On the stereo, Linkin Park was crooning 'Numb'. Emily had taken several gulps from the bottle of Southern Comfort that was being passed around.

And yet—

And yet—

She still couldn't blank out the memory of *that* evening.

Two weeks since she'd murdered her neighbour, but it felt like yesterday. The sounds. The smell. The contracting limbs.

Murder. Emily had looked up the definition in her mother's old dictionary the other day. *c1300 from Old English mordor (plural morpras) . . . secret killing of a person, unlawful killing.* Well, it *had* been secret and unlawful. Also, *mortal sin, crime; punishment, torture, misery.* Was what she and Jake had done a sin? Was she going to hell?

The previous weekend, Emily had stayed up to watch a late-night horror show with Bradley. The episode had depicted a wagon packed with people being carted around hell, where they would stay in torment for eternity. She didn't believe in hell, she didn't — but what if it *were* true? And yet, hadn't she helped *release* someone from torment?

Next Emily had looked up euthanasia: *the painless killing of a patient suffering from an incurable and painful disease or in an irreversible coma. The practice is illegal in most countries.*

She needed to talk to Jake, but she'd scarcely seen him since he'd left her room the morning after they'd ended his mother's life. There had been an endless stream of relatives coming and going next door, a wake, a funeral that she hadn't been able to bring herself to attend.

She hadn't been able to bring herself to tell Jake that she'd lost one of the empty insulin vials. Countless times, she had retraced her footsteps, rummaging through soil, grass and gravel. She'd found coins, nails, even a cracked baby's dummy, but no glass vials.

Now, two weeks later, no one had come to arrest her, or Jake.

And still she couldn't sleep.

The car shuddered and halted outside a sprawling, two-storey house with manicured gardens. How she'd been cool enough to be invited to Roddy Hamilton's house was anyone's guess.

Her classmates began spilling out of the car; past the freaky-looking bonsai trees, draped with Christmas lights, and through the gigantic front door. Emily stumbled out and nearly fell over, her left leg having lost all circulation beneath Lucy's butt.

'Whoa,' Emily said, once they'd entered the spacious foyer. 'This house has *paintings*.'

'Bet they're worth a few grand.' Lucy looped her arm through Emily's and led her down the stairs. The basement was occupied by at least thirty people, only some of whom Emily recognised, and the indoor pool was shimmering red and green due to the painted light bulbs hanging from the ceiling. She followed Lucy to a spot near the French doors and sank onto the tiles.

'Hey,' Lucy said to a thin but very muscular guy sitting on the ledge behind them. 'I'm Lucy. And this is Emily.'

'Hi. I'm Charles Darke.' His teeth were like piano keys, large and ivory-white against his blue-black skin.

'Seriously?' Lucy giggled. Such a flirt.

'Seriously.' Charles held out the bottle. There was a dirty layer of foam on top of the Coke. 'Do you like rum?'

'I really shouldn't,' Emily murmured, but then Eminem started singing 'Cleanin' Out My Closet', and she was starting to feel deliciously numb all over. After taking a swig, she joined Lucy and Charles, who had begun jostling by the doors, their hips swaying. That is, until Ian cut in, and Charles shifted his attention to Emily.

'Hey,' he said, wriggling his groin disturbingly close to hers.

'Um, just getting a drink,' Emily said, and took off. After squeezing past a group of heavily made-up girls that she recognised from the year below her, she lingered beside the pool. Four guys and two girls were horsing around in there now, in various stages of undress.

Someone touched her elbow and she turned. Roddy Hamilton took his cigar out of his mouth, grinning.

'Hey, Emily. Having a good time?'

'Yeah, it's great.' Emily touched the wall, the concrete blocks cool beneath her skin. Many girls in her year thought Roddy was good-looking, with his thick, coppery hair and sharply defined, unblemished features. Yet on closer inspection, she noted that his nose was slightly pointy, and that his chin receded a bit.

Or maybe it's just that he's not Jake.

Where was Jake, anyway? Perhaps she should text him to see if he were coming.

'How were your exams?' Roddy put the cigar between his lips.

'Oh, I don't know. I'm just glad they're over.'

'Bet you did just fine,' Roddy said as two guys began to strip in time to the music, to the hilarity of those around them. Roddy laughed, his skin glowing green beneath the lights. Emily began to feel, not for the first time, as if she were in a parallel universe, one that had split off at the moment she'd dared to challenge her own.

'Who cares, it's all over now, right?' He held the cigar out. 'Want to try?'

Emily opened her mouth to say she didn't smoke, but changed her mind. After taking the cigar, she sucked some smoke into her mouth and blew it out again. It tasted different from the cigarettes she'd tried, thick and woody. She drew in another mouthful of smoke and felt it whirl through her head.

Roddy nodded at the pool, where his friends were trying to drown each other. 'Been for a swim?' He gave her a mischievous grin, leaned closer. 'Bet you never did anything crazy in your life.'

Staring back at him, floating and buzzing, Emily said, 'I've done crazy things.'

'Yeah?' He blew a smoke ring towards the ceiling. 'Such as?'

Emily didn't reply. A roar went up as 'Smells Like Teen Spirit' started playing, God, where had they dug that up from? But she was reminded of the baby on the album cover, swimming naked through a heavenly pool of aquamarine, and wondered if she could capture that serenity, if only for a short time.

She didn't stop to think. She was sick of thinking. After pulling her jeans off, she unbuttoned her shirt and rolled it up into a ball. The water was tepid, the pool tiles slick and smooth beneath her feet. She pushed off from the wall, the multi-coloured lights moving, kaleidoscope-like, through her fractured vision. Gazing at the blurry distortion of her limbs underwater, she thought that they could almost be someone else's.

Maybe she was going crazy. Maybe what she'd done two weeks ago had unhinged her forever.

A wave of water washed over her face, and she spluttered. She stood up preparing to give Roddy a telling-off, but saw Ian instead.

'Good swim?' Ian's strawberry-blond hair was plastered against the sides of his head.

Emily bobbed beneath the surface, feeling suddenly exposed. 'It was hot.'

Ian laughed and flipped onto his back. Emily followed suit, staring up at the ceiling as they shouted to each other over the music.

'Have you seen Jake lately?' Emily asked after about ten minutes, during which time Ian had managed to cover how his exams had gone, what he was doing over the summer, and which papers he was taking at uni next year.

'About twenty minutes ago.'

Emily stood up and looked towards the window. 'Is he here?'

Ian, still floating, said, 'Yeah, somewhere.'

'Where?'

'He was playing pool, last time I saw him. Are you getting out already?'

'I'm cold.' Emily swam towards the steps. She found her jeans and shirt underneath a wicker chair, and struggled to put them on over her dripping skin. After making a brief pit stop in the bathroom, which smelt of vomit, she went to the rear of the house.

'Ooh . . . the wet look, I like it.' A freckly guy held the door open for her. Emily cast her eye over the group of boys around the pool table, which didn't include Jake, as far as she could see, and carried on, ignoring the wolf whistles.

She went up the stairs, past a group of students playing drinking games in the lounge, and onto the balcony. Jake was leaning against the railing, smoking a cigarette.

'Hey,' she said.

'Hey,' he replied, his eyes still fixed on the city lights below.

Emily moved next to him and rested her chin on her arms. After finishing his cigarette, Jake rested his chin on his arms too. The city lights began to blink off, one by one.

'How was the funeral?'

'It was OK.'

'Did your dad come?'

Jake exhaled. 'Yeah. Didn't stay long.' He frowned at her. 'Did you go swimming in your clothes?'

'Sort of.' Her elbow bumped against his. Jake's skin felt cool. He moved a fraction, so they were no longer touching, and she felt it again, the cracks that seemed to have appeared since *that* morning.

Well, what *had* happened that morning, after he'd climbed through her window? Did he regret kissing her? Maybe he'd just been playing with her emotions all this time, so she'd help him. But now his mother was dead, and he didn't need her anymore.

She pushed away from the railing. 'I'm going home.'

Jake stood upright. 'I'll walk with you.'

'No need.' Emily jogged down the steps and out onto the street. It was dark now, many of the surrounding houses decorated with fairy lights, and in one case, a pair of reindeer leaping across the lawn. Eventually she gave up on trying to ignore Jake and let him fall in beside her.

They were a block from home, just past the Four Square, when Jake broke the silence. 'I'm moving.'

Emily slowed. 'Where?'

'Auckland.'

'What about uni?' Her legs were moving, but they felt as though they didn't belong to her.

'There's a uni in Auckland too. I'm going to stay with my auntie.'

'What about your grandma?' They turned into Thompson Street.

'She's moving into a rest home. She's not been well.'

Emily stopped beside her letterbox. 'When?' Cymbals clashed in her chest. *What the fuck? After all this, after all I've risked for you, you're abandoning me?* But she couldn't say anything, because her tongue seemed to have turned to lead.

Jake glanced up at the second storey, his eyes settling on the one room in her house with a light on — her father's — and sighed.

'Tomorrow.' A car cruised past, its lights illuminating them for a moment.

Emily looked down at her feet. *Don't cry. Don't cry. Don't cry.*

Jake touched her cheek. 'Hey, I—' She heard him swallow hard. She pulled away and walked up her driveway, tasting chlorine and salt on her tongue. As she neared the front porch, she heard him say, 'I'll call you.'

'Don't bother,' Emily said, before slamming the front door behind her.

Her father's voice floated down the stairs. 'Emily? Are you OK?'

'*No!*' Emily yelled and fled to her room, where the tears came at last.

A door slammed, nearby. Maybe it was Jake's, and maybe it wasn't. She no longer cared.

Chapter 32: Welcome Home

2013

Jake floated behind the breakers on his board. His mouth was salty, his limbs aching, and he felt *great*. More than that, it was as though he'd been off-kilter for the past several months and was aligned once more, in sync with the earth's orbit at last.

Welcome home, the wind whispered. *Welcome home, welcome home.*

There was a surfer further out, and Jake waited for him to catch a wave. Behind it was a second one, larger and already feathering. He paddled like crazy to get there, turning just in time, and it gathered him up, propelling him shoreward. Scrambling to his feet, he made the drop — just. After pumping to get around a section crumbling further down the line, he aimed for the lip, but his timing was off and he went down hard with the falling curtain, driven deep by the turbulent whitewater.

Jake struggled to his feet, trying to catch his breath. Damn it, he was out of practice. Tugging his board towards him, he glanced towards the shore and saw a figure perched on a rock. Emily already, how had that hour gone by so fast?

'What's the time?' He asked, trudging up the sand.

Emily slid off the rock. 'It's just gone half-past six,' she said, and he noted that her skin was flushed, her eyes bloodshot.

'You all right?'

Emily opened her mouth and closed it again. Unsure if he should press her further, Jake tilted his board against the sea wall and kissed her instead.

'Mind if I have a quick shower at the Surf Club?'

'Course not.' Her eyes were darting all over the place.

'What's up?' Jake asked, resigned to an inevitable — what? Argument? Was she unhappy that he'd chosen to go surfing the minute he stepped off the plane?

'I went to see Dad.'

Jake leaned against a rock. 'OK . . .' When she didn't respond immediately, he said, 'Did it not go so well?'

'You could say that.' She shivered. 'We . . . argued. Dad said he showed you something in Melbourne. He told me to ask you about it.'

His chest tightened. 'Right.' That prick, what was he playing at?

He's trying to break you up, that's what he's playing at.

Prick, prick.

'Would you stop saying *right*?' Emily flared.

'I didn't think I should tell you,' Jake said, bracing for the inevitable. 'Since it wouldn't have made any difference.'

'Any difference to *what*? God, Jake, when are you going to stop assuming you know what's best for me? How weak do you think I am?'

'That's the *last* thing I think.' The creeping dread he'd been experiencing prior to getting his test result had returned. 'I knew you'd freak out. And there's nothing we can do about it, nothing.'

'Nothing we can do about *what*?'

Jake looked up. Puffy clouds hovered on the horizon, clotted cream. The surf seemed louder, closer. 'He showed me a vial of insulin,' he said. 'An *empty* vial of insulin.'

Emily stared at him. 'Insulin?'

'An *empty* vial of insulin,' he repeated, and watched her eyes widen, watched her raise her hands to her mouth.

'Shit. Oh . . . shit, I . . . I looked for it, but when I never found it, I just assumed . . .' Her words tumbled over each other, faster and faster. 'I thought . . . I thought it was gone . . . forever, I thought it must be buried or crushed or . . .'

'What do you mean, you *looked* for it?' He grabbed her by the wrists. 'You knew we'd lost one?'

Tears began spilling down her cheeks. 'I didn't know Dad found it. When I went to check the morning after, one was m-missing.'

'Jesus.' He released her. 'And you're angry with *me* for keeping things from *you*?'

Emily gulped. 'I didn't know how to tell you. And when so much time passed and nothing happened, I couldn't see how telling you would make any difference.' She sucked in a shuddering breath. 'But that means he's known all this time.'

Jake's brain raced. 'But why did he tell you today?'

'I don't know.'

'Is that all he had to say? You said you had an argument about something.'

'He said — I don't know if I want to repeat it. What did he say to you in Melbourne, when he showed you the vial?'

'Well,' Jake said, a slow fury coming to the boil, 'I imagine it was probably a very similar conversation. He doesn't approve of our relationship.'

'So, screw him,' Emily whispered.

Jake shook his head. Emily shook her head back at him.

'He told me you'd leave me,' she said.

'*What?*'

'He said, *sooner or later, willingly or unwillingly, he's going to leave you.*'

'Is that meant to be some kind of threat?' He let out a short laugh. 'Why, is he going to dob us in? No, wait, he wouldn't drop you in it, but he's got every reason to tell on *me*.'

Her mouth fell open. 'No. No, he wouldn't.'

'Well, here's the thing,' Jake said, his mind beginning to slow in the same way it did when a patient arrested in front of him — cold, clinical, detached. 'If I leave you alone, if I break up with you, he doesn't say anything. If I don't, then he goes to the police.'

'But I'd tell them what I did,' she said. 'I'd tell them where I got the insulin. I'd tell them it was me who injected it, not you.'

'No,' Jake said. 'No, you wouldn't.'

'*Jake.*' Emily stamped her foot. 'I know my dad. He wants to protect me. There's no way he'll let me incriminate myself.'

Jake paced between the rocks. 'I knew it. I knew this was going to return to haunt us, to haunt *you*. But I can deal with this. I can leave you out of it. No one has to know you helped me.'

Emily pointed at him. 'Don't you *dare* do what he wants. Don't you dare.'

'But how do I know what you say is true, that he'll leave us alone if you threaten to confess as well? What if we both end up in prison?' Tremors began to ripple through him. He'd be struck off the medical register for sure, his career over, his life over. And Emily, no, he couldn't let that happen to her.

'As long as we're in this together, he won't touch us.' Emily sounded so certain, growing stronger even as Jake's resolve weakened.

'Is that all?' Emily asked. 'Is there anything else I should know?'

'*No,*' he said. 'No, there's nothing, God.'

Emily took a deep breath. 'I know,' she said.

'You know what?'

'I know what we should do.' And she was smiling. How could she be smiling at a time like this? She dropped into a crouch, plucked something off the ground.

'What are you doing?' Jake asked, when she straightened up and reached for his hand.

Emily held out her palm, in which nestled a bone-white, ring-shaped shell. 'Jake Heremaia. Will you marry me?'

That evening they sat in the lounge, everyone sipping on mulled wine, apart from Charlotte, who was campaigning to stay up past her usual bedtime. The lounge smelt of cinnamon and cloves, pine, roast lamb. Outside, the sky was faded denim, the first few streaks of pink beginning to appear. If only Jake could relax, but it was impossible. All he wanted was to return to the surf, to that idyllic hour he'd had before Emily had dropped the latest bombshell.

No, you're *the bombshell. You always have been.*

'My friends get to stay up until ten o'clock.' Charlotte was standing behind the couch, draped around Jake's neck.

Lisa arched an eyebrow at her younger daughter. 'I don't believe that for a second.'

'It's true,' Charlotte said in unison with Steve.

Her father chuckled. 'See how well I know you? I always know exactly what you're going to say next.'

'Jake, tell them they're being mean to me.' Charlotte flounced over to the Christmas tree and sat beneath it, stroking a gift-wrapped box. 'And stunting my development.'

'Lack of sleep stunts your growth,' Steve said.

'Perhaps *I* should have had less sleep then.' Emily crossed her legs. 'I would have been more comfortable on the plane if these weren't quite so long.'

'I like your legs just the way they are,' Jake murmured and everyone else laughed. The conversation moved on to news about uncles and aunts, cousins, old friends — but Jake had only one thing on his mind.

What did Jim want?

Exactly what you think he wants — for you to be gone from Emily's life, never to be seen again.

'What are you two up to tomorrow?' Lisa plucked a fallen bauble off the carpet and hung it over a branch. 'Are you going to catch up with your father, Emily?'

Emily stiffened. Jake chewed his thumbnail.

'Everything OK?' Emily's mother asked.

'Sure.' Emily's voice had taken on a high-pitched quality. 'Yeah, I guess we need to go and tell him the news.' She touched Jake's thigh.

Lisa's brow wrinkled. 'News?'

'Jake and I are engaged.' Emily gave them a tentative smile. 'As of a couple of hours ago.'

'Oh!' Charlotte leapt up. 'Are you going to have babies now? I can't wait. And can I be your flower girl? I know exactly what I want to wear.'

'Charlotte, stop,' Lisa said. To his relief, Jake saw she was beaming. 'Congratulations, you two.'

Steve stood up to shake Jake's hand. 'Congratulations. When's the big day?'

'Um . . .' Jake glanced at Emily. 'Not sure?'

'At least a year away,' Emily said, flipping her hair behind her ear, and suddenly all he wanted was to be alone with her, skin on skin, her breath in his lungs.

'I want my flower-girl dress to be the colour of Elsa's dress from *Frozen*,' Charlotte bounced on her heels. 'Where's your ring?'

Jake touched the shell in his pocket. 'It's in progress.'

———

Jake held the book above him, trying to focus on the words. He'd plucked the novel off the bookshelf in the hallway minutes before, intrigued by the cover.

'Look,' he said when Emily entered the bedroom wrapped in a towel. 'A book written just for you.'

Emily sat beside him. '*The Girl with the Dragon Tattoo*,' she read. 'Huh, I never got around to reading that. Is it good?'

'No idea.' He set the book aside. 'Do I really need to come and see your dad tomorrow?'

She exhaled. 'I've been thinking about that.'

'And?'

'And I'm not going to visit him again.' She planted her palm on his chest. 'I'll text him tomorrow. That's all he deserves, right?'

'I'm not going to argue with you.' He released her ponytail from the elastic band she'd used to tie it up. 'You smell like strawberries.'

'Mum's body wash.' She bent to kiss him. Jake unfurled the towel, grazed a thumb over her nipple. Her breath quickened. 'I should turn off the light.'

'But I want to see my fiancée,' Jake said, watching her eyes soften and then glaze as he manoeuvred her until she was lying beneath him.

'Someone might come in.'

'Charlotte's in bed. And your mum and Steve would not,' he slipped his hand between her thighs, 'crash in on this *very* private engagement party.'

'Oh, a party,' Emily said, and then she didn't say anything else for some time.

Jake woke later, as he knew he would, staring into the asphalt darkness. When he reached for his phone, he saw it was quarter to two. Four hours until sunrise. Perhaps he could hit the beach early and let the waves pound the anxiety from him, scour him clean.

Was there such a thing as freedom? Freedom from what? Jim? The unreliable DNA twisting through every cell in his body? The memories he'd tattooed into the brain of the girl he loved? The legacies they all carried with them, the fears they projected into the future?

Ten years I've kept my mouth shut about this.

In ten minutes, probably less, Jim could destroy the tenuous shelter Jake and Emily had erected.

Do you really think this is enough, Emily, to bind yourself to me forever?

I don't know, I don't know.

Jake felt his way to the door and padded down the hallway to the lounge. He sat next to the window, gazing over the bay. A single light winked at him from a house below. He wondered who else was awake, and why — another insomniac? A mother feeding her baby?

Something tugged deep within him, a primordial umbilical cord. A new certainty surged into him. When he returned to bed, Emily was lying on her side, facing the wall. Curving around her, Jake murmured in her ear — and heard her breathing speed up, her muscles tense and relax — before she sank, deep, into sleep once more.

In the morning, perhaps, she'd wake and remember his words as if from a dream. By then he'd be skimming across the surface of the sea, his board pointed towards a new horizon.

Chapter 33: Grenade

Emily stretched out, starfish-like; her nose turned toward the sun, her toes pointed toward the sand. It was a typical summer's day in Northland, twenty-eight degrees at least, but she wasn't ready for another swim. Jake had gone out in the kayak, saying he was going to catch some fish, when she thought all he was really after was some solitude.

It's going to be OK, she thought. *It's going to be OK, OK, OK.*

If only she could get her subconscious to believe that, to stop waking her at three am with endless questions — *when is Dad going to text me ring me threaten us go to the police no he wouldn't but what if he does shall I tell Mum* — spiralling around and around until she felt as though she would explode with anxiety.

She placed her hat over her face. Snatches of conversation drifted toward her, *where's the sunblock . . . what a babe . . . theirs for a barbie . . . best I've had in ages.* But as her brain slowed, as she began to doze, it was Jake's voice that she heard.

Let's make a baby.

'You make that sound so easy,' she'd said, once she'd confirmed she hadn't heard his words in a dream. She was impatient to return to Melbourne, to see whomever they needed to consult to make it work.

And yet there was the unfinished business with her father. Not just unfinished business, but an unexploded grenade, a smoking volcano. It had been a week since she'd texted him with the news: *I proposed to Jake today, and he accepted.*

Jim had yet to reply. She wasn't even sure he'd received her message.

I'm sure he did *get it*, Jake had said.

Got it, but didn't get it, Emily thought. So what now? Was her father working out how best to approach the police? But with what? How was an insulin vial evidence of anything? Surely it was all empty threats, an attempt to manipulate them.

She sat up, blinking into the sun-dazzle reflecting off the sea. No sign of Jake yet. She wandered to the water's edge. The water lapping over her toes was tepid, soothing. It wasn't so hard to wade in, not so hard to float on her back, listening to the soft lap of the sea in her ears.

Tomorrow was New Year's Day. She was looking forward to putting the year behind her, looking forward to *looking forward*.

Let's make a baby.

Yes, yes, yes.

———

Jake's father was sitting on the front porch when Jake and Emily returned from the beach, a half-empty flagon of beer on the overturned crate beside his chair. Jimbo, lying on the boards next to the crate, gave out an obligatory yap before relaxing into sleep again. *We're both old dogs now*, Willie had said the night before. *Can't teach an old dog new tricks.*

If only, Jake had muttered to Emily.

'Catch anything?' Willie asked, once Jake had deposited the kayak on the front lawn.

'Just some tuatua.' Jake nodded at the bucket at Emily's feet, and she carried it over to Willie to show him the shellfish, which were immersed in seawater.

Willie gave her a gappy grin. 'Yum.'

'Mmm,' Emily said, not sure about that. After hanging her towel over the porch railing, she continued inside to the bathroom. The shower curtain was hanging half-off and spotted with mildew. *At least the water's warm*, she told herself as she lathered her hair with shampoo. The tank was small, which meant the water had run cold before she'd managed to have a shower that morning.

A pair of arms slid around her waist and she yelped.

'Come on, don't act so surprised,' Jake said in her ear, his chin resting in the hollow behind her collarbone.

'I didn't hear you,' she said, relaxing into his embrace as he ran soap over her breasts, her belly, the tops of her thighs.

'What do you think about this party at Jonesy's?'

'I don't know,' Emily said. 'If you want.' Jake had a seemingly endless supply of cousins; she couldn't keep up with them all.

'It's either that or hang out with the olds.' He scooped her hair up, kissed her on the neck. 'Think I'm done with Dad.'

She turned around, planting her palms on his chest. 'You were done before we even arrived.'

'You know me so well.' He kissed her slowly, insistently.

'Jake,' she said, but she stroked his slippery skin, tracing the tense curve of his biceps, the rigid muscles of his abdomen. *If only we could make a baby the normal way.*

'We could find a quiet spot on the beach,' Jake said, holding her tighter.

'I just rinsed all the sand off.'

'Spoilsport.' He let her go, turned the taps off. 'We don't have to stay late.'

———

Jake's cousin Jonesy shared a house with his girlfriend, Freda, and an elusive boarder named Bjorn.

'I don't think I've ever met anyone called Bjorn before,' Emily said to Freda.

Freda shrugged. 'You probably won't tonight either. He keeps to himself. Hates parties.'

Emily gazed over the scrubby front lawn, where at least forty people were assembled. 'Can't imagine this will finish early. Where will Bjorn go?'

'To his girlfriend's.'

Jonesy appeared holding a can of beer, Jake close behind him. 'Have you not turned your bloke into a Southern Man yet, Emily?' He gestured at Jake's can of Coke with a hand that looked almost as big as Emily's head.

Jake shrugged. 'Drink Speight's, lose your mates.'

Jonesy's upper lip curled. 'I wasn't asking you to drink *that* rubbish. No wonder you got turned off drinking.'

'I don't need to turn him into a Southern Man,' Emily said. 'Considering he's spent most of his life down there.'

Jonesy crushed his beer can. 'Ah, but you're coming back north, aren't you, mate?'

'Maybe,' Jake said, his eyes sliding away when Emily tried to meet his gaze.

'Our people need their own doctors,' Jonesy said, before moving inside.

Jake reached into a passing bowl of chips. 'How's the business going, Freda?'

Freda pursed her plump lips, and Emily wondered if she'd had lip fillers. 'Not bad. Everyone wants a wax.'

Jake grinned. 'Even Jonesy?'

'*Especially* Jonesy,' Freda said, giggling. Checking her phone, Emily saw she'd had a missed call from her father at eight forty-one, twenty minutes ago, and tensed. *Great, he wants to talk now?*

Leaving Jake and Freda to discuss the merits of male waxing, Emily wandered away to listen to the message, halting beside a hibiscus bush when she heard her father's urgent tones: 'Emily, I need to talk to you. Please call me.'

After deleting the message, Emily moved inside to get a beer, her third for the evening.

She would call him. But not tonight. Not on New Year's Eve.

————

Several beers later, Emily lay in the grass beside Jonesy's letterbox, looking for all the constellations she knew, which totalled three. The stereo was blasting yet another of Jonesy's retro tunes, 'Don't Be So Reckless', multiple drunken voices joining in. Emily contemplated getting up to join the dancers. No, too much effort. She wondered how long it was until midnight.

Jake loomed above her. 'You're quite pissed, aren't you?'

'You should try it sometime.' The stars dipped and swayed. The memory of the phone call from her father was a blur. Perhaps she'd dreamed it. Miracles happened, sometimes.

Jake stretched out beside her, his hip solid against hers, an anchor before she spun off into space. 'You might not say that tomorrow.'

'Tomorrow.' Emily closed her eyes. 'Dad called.'

'What did he say?' She wasn't too drunk to notice the edge in his voice.

'Nothing. Left a message.'

'Saying what?'

'To call him.'

'And did you?'

'Not yet.' She rolled onto her stomach. The grass smelt, faintly, of beer — or maybe she was inhaling her own breath.

'Are you going to call him?'

'Might be a good idea, I suppose.' Anxiety began to gnaw at her again. An empty vial of insulin, along with missing insulin from her father's ward. (Had the missing insulin ever been reported? If so, Jim had never said, but then why else would he be so suspicious?) But how was that evidence? It wasn't as if the police would exhume Christine's body now, and what would they find anyway?

Insulin or potassium chloride. They'd both be pretty hard to trace, because your body produces them naturally.

And how, how could she have forgotten that conversation with her father?

If you want to write a story about the perfect murder, darling, then have your murderer use insulin or potassium chloride.

Jake said, 'We should go back to Dad's.'

Fighting a rising panic, Emily said, 'Hey, they're counting down,' and scrambled to her feet. The crowd on the lawn, which seemed to have grown as midnight approached, was shouting out: *five, four, three, two, one . . .*

'Happy New Year,' Jake said, embracing her. Emily kissed him, the leaden certainty of a tomorrow that had become today weighing on her.

'Happy New Year,' she said.

Phone. Ringing. No. Really? Emily groaned. What kind of sadist could be calling her at the crack of dawn?

Dad, oh my God he's called the police.

The perfect murder murder murder.

But when she looked at the caller ID she saw it was her mother. 'Do you know what time it is?' Emily grumped into the phone.

'I know what time it is. Emily, your father's in hospital.'

'Hospital?' Emily sat up, pawing hair out of her eyes. Something wasn't making sense. Her father was often at the hospital. No, but her mother had just said *in* hospital, not *at* the hospital.

Lisa said, 'I went to see him last night after he called me about — well, anyway, I went to see him around ten pm and found him slumped on the porch.'

'Was he drunk?' Emily slid out of bed. 'Did he hit his head?'

'No. I mean, yes he hit his head but not because he was drunk. The CT scan showed a large bleed. The doctors said it caused the fall, rather than the other way around, because it's deep within his brain.' Her mother's voice was shaking. Emily felt a tremor ripple through her. Jake appeared behind her, his hand on her hip.

Anchor, my anchor.

'Is he OK?' Emily's voice rose. 'Can he talk?'

'No,' Lisa said. 'To both of those. Emily, you need to fly down soon. They don't know if he's going to survive the next twenty-four hours.'

Jake drove her to Auckland in Ngaire's car, where Emily had managed to secure a seat on an early afternoon flight to Dunedin.

'Ring me when you get there,' he said when he kissed her goodbye at the gate. 'Or text me.'

'I will.' Emily's heart was galloping, her nerves twanging. *What if it was due to stress over everything that's been going on with us?* she'd asked Jake on the drive down.

Stress doesn't cause intracranial haemorrhages, Jake had said. *He had high blood pressure, right?* So clinical, as if her father was one of his patients.

On the flight, Emily drank two cups of coffee. They didn't do much for her beer headache, or the alcohol-adrenaline twist in her bowels. When she arrived, Dunedin seemed smaller, colder, more hostile than when she'd left three days before.

Her mother was waiting in the arrivals area, her body a series of slim, terse lines. *Is it a sign she's wearing black?* Emily thought, with a fresh surge of fear. But when Lisa hugged her, all she said was, 'Thank you for coming so quickly.'

Emily waited until they were in the car, whipping past endless fields and identical sheep and cars towing trailers, before saying, 'You said Dad rang you last night. Was he feeling unwell then?'

Lisa tightened her grip on the steering wheel. 'He must have been. I mean, he wasn't really making sense. Perhaps the bleeding had already started.'

'He left a message on my phone, but I didn't get around to calling him back.' Guilt crashed in on her anew. What if she'd been able to urge him to seek help just a little sooner? Would that have changed anything? But shouldn't a doctor, of all people, know when something was seriously wrong?

'It's not your fault, hon,' her mother said. 'There's nothing anyone could have done.'

Emily's phone buzzed. It was Jake, asking if she'd arrived safely.

Emily replied with a *yes*, even though she wasn't sure if that was true.

Chapter 34: New Year's Day

When Jake arrived home that evening, his eyes scratchy and his throat dry after six hours on the road between Northland and Auckland, his father was sitting on the porch drinking beer.

'Have you moved since last night?' Jake continued into the house without waiting for an answer. Six-thirty and no sign of dinner. Not that he'd expected anything else.

'Beans on toast it is then,' he muttered. He couldn't rely on his father for much, but there were always dozens of tins of baked beans and spaghetti in the pantry, as if his father were stocking up for an apocalypse, or at the very least a bender.

'A beer apocalypse,' Jake said, and stalled. Talking to himself, the first sign of — what?

Indeterminate, indeterminate.

But what did that actually mean? The articles he'd read online hadn't reassured him much. In one study, four of ten patients with an indeterminate number of CAG repeats had remained disease-free after four years of follow-up. What was he meant to draw from that when he had a whole lifetime to worry about? He'd found a second study of identical twins with indeterminate results where one remained disease-free at seventy-one years, while the other was diagnosed with HD at sixty-five years. Whichever way he looked at it, it seemed his odds of escaping HD, yet again, were no better than the fifty-fifty fear he'd grown up with.

Heads you win, tails you lose.

Jake opened a can of beans and took a fork out of the drawer that never closed before joining his father outside.

'Want a beer?' Willie asked.

'No,' Jake said, and then, 'actually, yes.' He went to the kitchen and returned with a recycled jar.

Willie lit a cigarette. 'How's Emily's old man?'

'Don't know yet.' Jake sipped on the beer, scooped beans out of the can. 'Sounded pretty bad.'

His father exhaled. 'So was I, but they brought me back from the dead, didn't they?'

Jake suppressed a burp. 'Difficult to come back from a bleed involving half your brain.'

'Mmm.' Willie slid a second cigarette out of his shirt pocket and held it out. 'Want one?' Jake didn't even bother trying to resist. His father tipped the rest of the beer into his own glass. 'Got any New Year's resolutions?'

'Yeah, I'm going to quit smoking,' Jake said, and Willie snorted. Jake averted his gaze, hiding his own smile. Once he'd finished his cigarette, beans and beer, in that order, he said, 'So, I had the test.'

Willie frowned. 'And?'

Jake squinted into the evening sun. 'Indeterminate.'

'What the hell is that supposed to mean?' His old man bent forward. 'Did they stuff it up or something?'

'No. Just means I'm in between. I might get HD or I might not.'

'Did you ask if you can get another test?'

'The result won't change.' Jake leaned against a porch post, the sun dappling over his ankles. 'They count the number of CAG repeats in the gene. It just so happens I have an in-between number.'

'Well, that's not very helpful,' Willie said, as if it was someone else's fault that Jake harboured an inconvenient number of CAG repeats. 'Anyway. It's good you're getting hitched. Emily's a nice girl.'

'She sure is.' Jake checked his phone. The only messages he had from Emily since she left were *Yes, Mum's just picked me up* and *Haven't seen him yet, they're giving him a wash*. He got to his feet. 'I'm going for some fresh air.'

'Plenty of fresh air out here,' Willie said, waving his cigarette around.

'You're killing me,' Jake said, only half-joking, and sauntered off.

Once on the beach, Jake perched on a rock, watching the waves batter the cliff to his left. Not for the first time, he felt as though he were peering through a blurred lens, feeling his way blind. Shifting truths, soft euphemisms.

At ten to eight, as the sky softened, he called Emily.

'Hey,' he said when she answered. 'How's it going?'

'He's in intensive care with a tube down his throat.'

'Crap.'

Emily inhaled. 'Yeah.'

'So he can't breathe for himself?'

'Not very well. He's kind of in a coma.'

Jake was starting to wish he'd bummed a second cigarette off his old man. 'Have you seen the scan?'

'No. But the intensive care doctor said he's bled into his brainstem.'

'Oh.' That was bad, bad, bad. He'd never heard of a patient recovering from a bleed into the brainstem, which controlled breathing and consciousness, along with ferrying all the important nerve signals between the brain and spinal cord.

'And that it's unlikely he'll . . .' Her breathing hitched. 'Recover. And even if he does, he probably won't be able to do much for himself. He may not even be able to move his eyes.'

Jake flicked a shell into the water below. 'So what now?'

'We're waiting for Bradley to fly in from Thailand so we can have a family meeting. About switching off—' She halted, and he realised she was crying.

'The ventilator,' he said gently. He wished he'd flown down with her — despite the cost, despite his stupid phobia, despite the fact that her father would have hung him by the balls if he'd had the chance.

'I'm really sorry,' he said, and he really was, despite everything.

If he dies then he can't

But I shouldn't be thinking

I'm a despicable person for even thinking

But how can I not?

He slid off the rock, watched the surf swirl around his ankles. 'Do you want me to fly down?' Jake asked, after counting one, two, three waves.

'Yes,' she said. 'Yes, please.'

———

The things we do for love, Jake thought the following afternoon. After a short flight from Whangārei to Auckland in something not much bigger than a tin can, followed by a two-hour flight to Dunedin, Jake's nerves were shredded. So much for flying straight back to Melbourne from Auckland.

'We're having the family meeting tomorrow morning,' Emily said as they sped away from the airport in her father's SUV. 'Bradley doesn't get in until tonight.'

Jake wound the window down a crack. 'How's he doing?'

'He's no better. Which is no surprise.' She adjusted the rear-vision mirror. 'But Dad's girlfriend thinks we should wait before making any final decisions.'

'His *girlfriend*?'

A pained look flitted across her face. 'Her name's Yvette. I don't even think they've been together very long, but she's being a pain in the butt.'

'Is she a medic?'

'No, she's a fashion designer. She wants to bring in some flake to do reiki on Dad.'

'The laying on of hands thing?'

'Yep.'

'Jesus.' Jake reached for Emily's bottle of water, which was sitting in the cup-holder between the seats. 'So what do the ICU doctors think of that?'

'The reiki?'

'No, the possibility of him coming around.'

'Same as before. They think it's unlikely he'll recover. Meanwhile, Yvette is digging up all these stories of patients who've been in comas for months and have then woken up.'

'Holy cow.' Jake drummed his fingers on the dashboard. 'Did he — *does* he — have an advance directive?'

Emily gave him a contemplative look. 'I never asked. But now you mention it, I don't know why he *wouldn't* have one.'

'Where do you think that would be? In a file?'

'Or on his computer.' Emily indicated and swung out to overtake a caravan. 'I can't believe we're talking about this,' she said, once she'd completed the passing manoeuvre.

'Sorry.'

'It's OK. I mean, we have to. But it's also awful.'

Jake squeezed her knee. 'You all right to drive?'

'Fine.' She took a deep breath. 'I think I know what his advance directive would say, if we find it.'

'And what would it say?'

'To let him go. He's always said he'd never want to be kept alive if he were a vegetable.'

Whatever that means, Jake thought, but he knew what she meant.

'That's probably enough, when it comes down to it,' he said. 'We usually trust families to know what their loved ones would want.'

Emily bit her lip. 'That's fine if you don't have a flaky girlfriend sticking her beak in.'

'So, we'll look for an advance directive,' he said. 'Most people try to leave them in an obvious sort of place. That's the whole point, isn't it?'

'Of course,' she said, and then, 'You know what? Maybe you should drive after all.'

———

The intensive care unit looked familiar and yet foreign at the same time — probably, Jake reflected, because he wasn't used to being on the family's side of the bed. Jim Walsh was situated opposite the ward station, his bare chest covered in ECG dots and leads, tubes and catheters snaking out of various orifices and veins — the tube to protect his airway, a catheter to drain his bladder, a central line in the jugular vein in his neck, an arterial line in his wrist to monitor his blood pressure.

Pointless, Jake thought but didn't say, because that would have been heartless. True, but heartless.

'She's gone,' Emily muttered.

'The girlfriend, you mean?'

'Yes. Thank God.' She approached her father. 'Hi, Dad.'

Jake hung back, watching Emily stroke her father's forehead, watching her use a tissue to wipe the drool from his lips. A strong sense of déjà vu flooded through him.

Mum, we've come to help you.

'I've got Jake here with me,' she said.

Jake cleared his throat. 'Hi, Jim.' No matter what he thought of his almost-father-in-law, it was a sobering sight, seeing the physician reduced to this.

There for the grace of God go I.

A shiver wound down his spine. Maybe he should get onto writing his own advance directive.

'Bradley will be here tonight.' Emily sat in a big blue chair at the side of the bed. 'He booked a flight as soon as he could.'

Jake listened to Emily continue to talk about the weather, news items she'd read earlier that day, the time her father had tied a piece of cotton around her tooth and tied the other end to a doorknob.

'Because I was sick of my wiggly tooth,' she said. 'And you slammed the door, remember? And Mum thought you were being mean to me when really you were just doing exactly what I asked.'

Throughout it all, her father remained still, unmoving. Still, but not silent. Jake could hear the beep of the heart monitor, the blood-pressure cuff intermittently inflating and deflating, the air moving in and out of the ventilator.

A nurse stopped at the end of the bed, holding a kidney dish. 'Sorry to interrupt, but I've just come to give your dad his meds.'

'No problem.' Emily gestured at Jake. 'This is Jake, my fiancé. He's a doctor too.'

'Yeah?' The nurse didn't look much older than Jake and Emily. 'What kind of doctor?'

'Jack of all trades at the moment.' Jake rubbed his chin. 'Um, is it possible to see Jim's scan?'

The nurse screwed a syringe onto the end of the central line. 'I don't see why not.' She flushed the line with saline before attaching a second syringe. 'I'll log onto the computer for you in a sec.'

A few minutes later, Jake sat in front of a computer in the ward station, scrolling through the images.

'Even *I* can see that,' Emily said.

'It's not subtle,' Jake said, staring at the massive white blob in the middle of Jim's brain. He pushed the mouse towards her. 'Do you want to—'

She stepped away, her eyes averted. 'No.'

He shut the programme down and stood up. 'When do you have to pick Bradley up from the airport?'

'Mum said she'd get him.'

Jake drew her towards him. 'You want to go home for a bit? We can look for that advance directive.'

'Sure.' She was crying again.

He held her close. 'Or we could just rest up,' he said. 'No rush.'

'No,' she said. 'I want to find it. It's the least I can do.'

Chapter 35: If I Could Turn Back Time

Her father's filing cabinet was located in the guest room downstairs, the contents arranged in A to Z dividers.

'Huh.' Emily took her year thirteen class photo out of the divider labelled *Emily*. 'Remember Roddy Hamilton?' She pointed to a boy with thick coppery hair standing in the second row, experiencing an odd pang when she remembered his death four years before.

Jake sat on the bed. 'How could I forget? And we all thought he was going to be a hot-shot lawyer.'

'I knew he was into drugs, but I didn't realise he was injecting heroin.' Emily had always wondered if the heroin OD was accidental or deliberate, was guessing no one would ever know. After replacing the photo, she flipped through *Health*, *House* and *Insurance* before arriving at a divider labelled *Personal*. 'OK, so I've got three expired passports . . . a birth certificate . . . and hey, look at this.' She extracted a dog-eared document consisting of three pieces of paper stapled in the top left corner. '*I, James William Walsh, do make, publish and declare this my last will and testament.*'

'Awesome.' Jake kicked off his shoes and stretched out on the bed. 'What else does it say?'

'I don't know, let me wade through the flowery lawyer talk.' Emily scanned the pages, which as far as she could see, split her father's assets fifty-fifty between her and Bradley in the event of Jim's death. She also learned he wanted to be cremated, and that his funeral expenses were to be paid from his estate before any finances were distributed to his beneficiaries. 'But,' she said, after reading for a few minutes, 'I can't see anything that looks like an advance directive.'

'It'll be separate from the will, I would have thought.'

'OK . . .' Emily set the will on top of the filing cabinet and took a second, thinner, document out of the file. 'Aha. Listen to this. *These are my wishes if I have a terminal condition. I want,*' she paused, '*to receive all the life-sustaining treatments that are available to me, until such time as I declare I no longer wish to receive these.*' She glanced up. 'Maybe Yvette is right after all.'

'Surely that's not all he said?' Jake sat up. 'The directives I've seen usually list a few different circumstances.'

'Oh. Right, yeah, here it is.' Emily read on. She was beginning to feel wobbly again. God, why did she have to think about this? '*These are my wishes if I am ever in a persistent and vegetative state. I do not want life-sustaining treatments, including CPR, started. If life-sustaining treatments are started, I want them stopped.*' She took a deep breath. 'I guess that applies to him now, right?'

Jake rubbed his stubbly chin. 'I guess it depends on what the ICU docs say at the family meeting tomorrow. But it's hard to imagine your dad ever being much better than he is now.'

'We should take this in tomorrow. To the family meeting.'

'We should. Does it say who he's nominated as his enduring power of attorney?'

Emily flipped to the start of the document. 'Huh.' She hadn't noticed that detail before, her eyes having been immediately drawn to the words *terminal illness* halfway down the page.

'Who is it?'

She looked up. 'It's Mum.'

His mouth twisted. 'Guess he might have written that a while ago, and saw no reason to change it.'

'Or had no one else he trusted enough to do what he wants.' A wave of melancholy assailed her. Her father had never really found someone to replace her mother, or at least no partner who had lasted more than a few months. She'd never really thought he might have been lonely, or pining for her mother. 'It's dated 2002, so that makes sense.'

'Good work, Em. Now you can be sure you're acting in his best interests . . . right?'

'Right.' She sat next to him, feeling oddly numb. A week ago, she'd been petrified that her father was going to destroy her and Jake with the information he had. Now she felt guilty for thinking that their secret was, most likely, safe forever.

Jake touched his fingers to her forehead. 'Families,' he said. 'It never gets any easier, does it?'

'Don't say that.' Exhausted, she lay back and Jake did too, his breath mingling with hers.

'Think we just made a fatal error,' he said.

'What?' Her heart sped up.

'Lying horizontal. Sorry, bad word choice.'

'Yeah, really.' She snuggled closer, her ear on his chest. 'You must be tired after all that driving and flying.'

'Mmm.' His breathing slowed.

'Do you want to go upstairs?'

'Quite comfortable right here,' he murmured.

'True.' Emily closed her eyes.

———

She wasn't sure how long they had been dozing when her phone rang, but the world seemed to have moved on — the light from outside faded, the sounds muffled. Emily tipped off the mattress and found her phone on top of the filing cabinet.

'Hi, Mum.' She gazed at the bed, where Jake was still lying in a semi-comatose state, his eyelashes fluttering.

'I've just collected Bradley from the airport. Where are you?'

'At Dad's.' Emily wandered down the hallway and into the kitchen, checking the clock above the stove. Quarter to seven already? 'Jake suggested we check to see if Dad has an advance directive.'

'Did you find it?'

'Yeah, in the filing cabinet. He's named you as his enduring power of attorney, did you know that?'

'Gosh.' Her mother gave out a short laugh. 'I thought he would have changed that by now.'

'Guess he never got around to it.' Emily leaned against the bench. 'Are you going straight to the hospital?'

'No, we're just about to stop at the fish'n'chip shop. Thought you might like some too.'

'Sounds good,' Emily said, her stomach growling in anticipation. Hearing her brother's low rumble, she added, 'What's Bradley saying?'

'He's asking if there's any beer there.'

Emily rolled her eyes. 'No idea. See you soon.' She rang off and moved to the lounge, where she sat on the couch, scrolling through Instagram and Facebook posts for a few minutes. Everything seemed so trite, so meaningless. She dumped her phone on the table, just as Jake sat on the chair next to her with a thud.

'Was that your mum calling?'

'Yeah. She and Bradley are coming over with fish'n'chips.'

'Yum, I'm starving.' Jake began flipping through a dog-eared copy of *The Listener*. 'What's the capital city of Kenya?'

'Why do you ask?'

'It's in the quiz.' He took a pen off the coffee table. 'OK, here's another one: which artistic movement came after the Gothic period?'

'Rococo.'

'Ooh, I'm impressed.'

'I did history up to year twelve, remember?' Emily pulled the lever on the side of the La-Z-Boy, reclining into a forty-five degree position.

'Ever thought about doing a Fine Arts degree?'

'What makes you say that?'

'Just a thought.'

'Maybe not such a bad idea. I was thinking . . . last night, when I couldn't sleep . . .'

Jake drew a circle on the magazine. 'About?'

'About revisiting the *Double Helix Dragon* book. There's this competition in the UK I want to enter, but I need to re-jig the last quarter.'

He glanced up. 'How long will that take?'

'A few weeks, if I can get some time off work. Deadline isn't until end of April.'

'So, do it.' He peered out of the window. 'There's your mum and Bradley.'

'Great.' Emily went outside to greet them. She'd think about *Double Helix Dragon* when she returned to Melbourne, once all of this was over.

As for the Fine Arts degree, she'd never really entertained that as a real possibility. But maybe . . . just maybe . . .

———

Bradley suppressed a belch. 'That's the best feed I've had in days.'

'Thought they'd have plenty of cheap food in Thailand,' Emily said, her eyes settling on the photo of her and Adam on the sideboard, which her father had obviously taken out *again*.

'They did, but I got this Delhi belly thing.'

'Is it Delhi belly when you got it in Thailand?' Jake asked.

'Whatever, I've been mostly on the loo for the past three— What?' Bradley shot his mother an irritated look.

'I'm still *eating*.' Lisa reached for the tomato sauce. 'Can you spare us the details?'

'Thought you'd have heard it all before.' Bradley sipped on his beer. 'Anyway, there's some amazing surf beaches there, Jake. You should go. Heaps warmer than here.'

'As long as I don't mind a bout of Bangkok belly, right?'

Bradley took his phone out of his pocket. 'Figure I'll be immune to it next time.'

'I wouldn't be so sure.' Lisa carried her plate out to the kitchen. Emily followed her, taking her father's advance directive off the end of the bench.

'So, I'm guessing you've seen this before.'

Lisa slid the plate into the dishwasher. 'Possibly, although it's so long ago I can hardly remember.'

'He only wrote it twelve years ago.'

'That's a whole life cycle.' Her mother took the document. 'Well,' she said after a couple of minutes, 'it's pretty much what I remember. I don't think his views will have changed much.' She placed it on the bench.

'I think that's what most of us would want, although I'm sure it varies with advancing age. For instance, once I hit ninety, there's no way I'd want someone jumping up and down on my chest, in any circumstance. Whereas if I had a cardiac arrest right at this moment—'

'Then you'd be wanting us to do exactly that.' Jake entered the kitchen. 'Jump and down on your chest, I mean.'

'Unless you're Yvette,' Emily said sourly. 'She might do reiki instead.'

'Or acupuncture,' Lisa said.

'With really long needles,' Jake added, and Lisa snorted.

'Stop.' Emily swiped him with a tea towel, giggling, and then burst into tears. It all seemed so wrong. How could they be joking and laughing when her father was dying?

Her father, with whom she hadn't even been on speaking terms for the past week. Emily felt awful about that too. Maybe she should have tried harder.

But . . . how?

'It's OK, sweetheart.' Her mother hugged her. 'I know you weren't talking when he got sick, but you're here now, and that would be really important to him.'

Emily drew away, wiping her eyes. 'What did he say the night he rang you?'

'He wasn't making sense,' her mother answered, just as she'd done the day before, after picking Emily up from the airport.

'Yeah, but what did he say?' Emily peered into the lounge to see if Bradley was listening, but he was reclining on the couch, engrossed in whatever was on the TV.

'He wanted me to talk some sense into you, thought you were plunging into something you couldn't handle.'

'Doesn't sound as though he was confused to me,' Emily said, glancing at Jake. 'What else did he say?'

Lisa twisted her wedding ring. 'He wanted to talk to me in person. I was worried about how he sounded — it was after that he started sounding confused, muddling his words up — and I drove over.'

'And found him,' Emily said, the nauseating guilt-relief needling at her again. Her father hadn't said anything about the insulin to her mother then, thank God. *No one else knows what Jake and I did, no one, no one.*

'And found him.' Her mother gazed outside, at the porch where, presumably, she'd found Jim two nights before. 'A few more minutes, and the ambulance drivers think it would have been too late to resuscitate him. But now I'm thinking it would have been a mercy if . . .' She trailed off.

If you hadn't come over at all, Emily thought, and her mother gave her a nod, as if to say, *Yes, yes, that's exactly what I mean.*

Lisa said, 'I can't remember if I told you, but the family meeting is at ten tomorrow morning.'

'The family meeting,' Emily echoed. At which, she knew, a decision would have to be made. 'Will Yvette be there?'

'I'm afraid so.'

'But she's not family.' Bradley deposited his empty beer bottle on the breakfast bar. 'She hardly even knows him.'

'You can't shut her out, mate,' Jake said.

'I think we should go and see him before it gets too late,' said Lisa. 'Are you ready, Bradley?'

Emily's brother straightened up. 'Um, sure.' For a split second, he appeared far younger, and Emily experienced an odd sense of déjà vu, as though she'd been transported into the nineties.

Emily, Bradley, your father and I are separating. For good.

'See you tomorrow,' Lisa said, hugging first Emily and then Jake.

'Ten o'clock,' Emily said, accompanying her mother and brother to the door. She lingered on the porch after the car had reversed out of the driveway, the night air cool on her glowing skin.

He only wrote it twelve years ago.

That's a whole life cycle.

Jake embraced her from behind. He didn't say anything at first, and neither did she. But in her mind, she was remembering their conversation in a tiny bedroom next door, when playing Monopoly.

Maybe he could help my mum.

Is she sick?

Not yet.

Would she have changed anything, if she'd known? If she'd never gone next door that day or the next or the next . . .

She turned, pushed her head into Jake's chest.

'I'm tired,' she said. 'Are you?'

'Exhausted.' He kissed her. 'Early night?'

'Early night,' she agreed, and they went inside.

Chapter 36: Let Go

Thank God he'd brought his board with him. The next morning, after numbing his body and mind in the churn and whirl of the Pacific Ocean, Jake trudged up the Walshes' driveway.

Emily was sitting on the porch, her sketchpad on her lap. 'Good surf?'

Jake leaned his board against the side of the house. 'Some good swell out there this morning.' He sat at the barbecue table, enjoying the warmth of the sun on his wetsuit. 'I don't think I knew how much I was missing it until . . .' He trailed off, guilt twinging at him. If it weren't for Jim's devastating bleed, they'd be in Melbourne, with its packed city streets and temperatures ranging anywhere from seventeen to forty-one degrees Celsius.

'Maybe I should have learned to surf.'

'Never too late to start.'

'You know I'm too chicken.' She peeled her cardigan off. 'I told Mum we'd be at the hospital around nine-thirty, so we can have some time before the family meeting.'

'Fine.' Jake touched the dewy petal of a rose, wondering who would look after Jim's garden now.

'Do you really want to come back to Dunedin?'

'I don't know. I like the work in Melbourne.'

'But the city not so much . . . right?'

'I don't mind it,' he said, choosing his words carefully. 'But I miss . . . this.' He spread his hands. 'Not just the surf, but New Zealand. I know everyone says Australia is so similar, but at the same time it's really not. And it's not even homesickness, if you can call it that.' He yanked at his wetsuit zip, the morning air cool on his damp skin. 'I got talking to

Jonesy when we were up north, and there's so much inequity between Māori and non-Māori health care. I feel as though I could make a difference.' He shrugged. 'I don't know. Maybe I'm wrong.'

Her brow furrowed. 'I doubt *that*, Doctor Heremaia.'

'Well, anyway.' Jake moved to sit beside Emily, taking care not to drip on her drawing. 'We've got enough to think about at the moment.' He nudged her ankle with his foot. 'How's the book going?'

'Not so well. I'm itching to get into *Double Helix Dragon* now, but I left it in Melbourne.'

'Your first love,' Jake teased, and she squeezed the back of his neck. 'You got it.'

———

'Is that her?' Jake asked when they entered the intensive care unit, his gaze immediately drawn to the attractive woman sitting at Jim's bedside.

The woman's hair was long, dark and glossy; her taut, smooth features almost certainly doctored with Botox, lip fillers and expensive creams.

'How did you guess?' Emily muttered. 'How old do you reckon she is?'

'I think she's achieved immortality,' he murmured, and she elbowed him.

'Can you be serious for once?'

'I *am* being serious.'

The woman rose to her feet when they approached. 'Hello, Emily,' she said, giving her a hug. 'And you must be Jake. I'm Yvette, Jim's partner.'

'Nice to meet you.' Jake stole a glance at the read-out on the machine above Jim's bed. Blood pressure, pulse and oxygen levels all within normal limits but the ventilator was still breathing for him, IV fluids trickling into the vein in his neck.

'I hear you're a doctor too.' Yvette stroked Jim's brow, and Jake sensed Emily bristling beside him. 'How do you think he's doing?'

'Um,' Jake said, after shuffling through several potential responses, including *I don't know, I just walked in here* and *Pretty horribly, or he wouldn't be here*, 'I guess it's up to his doctors to tell us that.' He gave her an apologetic shrug. 'It's not really my area of expertise.'

Yvette took a hanky out of the capacious bag at her feet. 'Well, it's early days yet. But I really think we need to talk to the doctors about feeding him. It's been three days since he ate anything.'

Emily crossed her arms, looked away. No answer, Jake decided, was probably the best strategy. He didn't think a conversation about futility was going to go down too well. Instead, he said, 'Who wants a coffee?'

'I'd love one,' Yvette said. 'Would you like some money? Tell you what, it's my shout, what would you like?'

Feeling cornered, Jake said, 'Um, a latte would be fine. Em?'

'No thanks.' Emily waited until Yvette's heels were clicking across the floor before muttering, 'Coward.'

'What do you mean?'

'*It's not really my area of expertise,*' she mimicked. 'You've been telling me over and over how horrid the prognosis is. Why didn't you tell her that?'

'Do you really want to be arguing around your dad?'

Biting her lip, Emily moved closer to the bed. 'Hi, Dad.' She curled her fingers around her father's. 'We found your advance directive. I'm assuming you haven't changed your mind about that. Knowing you, you would have altered it if you had.'

Jake stayed at the foot of the bed, listening as Emily carried on talking.

'We're having a meeting soon and we'll show the doctors the directive. I know you wouldn't want to be kept alive like this.' Her voice began to wobble. 'And I hope — I hope you can understand why Jake and I did what we did.'

'Em,' Jake whispered, but she kept talking as if she hadn't heard him.

'I'm not asking you to forgive me. But we love each other, the way you loved Mum, and maybe . . . I don't know enough about you and Yvette to know how you felt about her.' A tear slid down her nose. Jake drew closer, placing his palm in the small of her back. 'I'm sorry I didn't return your call the other night. I don't know what you wanted to say. I guess I'll never know now.'

Jim didn't move, but from the frequency of the beeps coming from the machine, Jake could tell that Jim's heart rate had sped up a little. Not a lot, but a little.

'Do you think he can hear me?' Emily asked.

'Yes,' Jake said. 'I think he can.'

———

At five to ten, Bradley and Lisa entered the unit, Yvette close behind them.

'Sorry we're late,' Lisa said, sidling up to them. 'We had a flat tyre.'

Yvette smoothed her hair with ring-crowded fingers. 'Oh, are you a member of AA? I always find them so helpful.'

'I know how to change a tyre,' Lisa said, and Jake suppressed a smile.

'Shall we go into the family room?' Emily asked. 'Dad's nurse said the doctors would be with us soon.'

The family room was as nondescript as any other Jake had been in over the years, a pile of magazines stacked on the coffee table, a selection of chairs arranged in a semi-circle. He sat next to Emily and reached for a magazine, flipping through photographs of immaculate gardens and houses with massive kitchens.

'Wonder what we have to do to get one of these when we grow up,' he said.

'I aim never to grow up,' Bradley said, intent on his phone.

'That's obvious,' Emily said, just before a pair of women in scrubs entered.

'Hi,' the older of the two, a woman with short silver hair, said. 'I'm Pauline Gilson, one of the intensive care doctors, and this is Sally Chin, one of our registrars.' She gestured towards the young woman to her left, whom Jake recognised from medical school, although Sally had been a couple of years ahead of him.

'Hi, Emily,' Sally greeted her. 'We were in the same class at med school,' she added.

Gilson raised her eyebrows at Emily. 'I didn't realise you were a doctor.'

'No, Jake's the doctor.' Emily clutched her bag. 'I dropped out in fourth year.' There was a short, awkward silence, and then Gilson asked everyone to introduce themselves.

'So,' Gilson said, once the introductions were out of the way, 'can you tell me what you understand of Jim's condition?'

'He's had a bleed into his brain.' Yvette crossed her legs. 'Recovery could be slow.'

'He's had a devastating intracranial haemorrhage,' Emily said. 'And the chances of recovery are practically non-existent.'

Yvette's mouth tightened. 'I think it's far too early to tell.'

Emily, her jaw clenched, said, 'I think we should listen to the people with medical degrees.'

'*Emily*,' her mother said. Jake, his fingers crushed in Emily's grip, didn't say anything. He knew the ICU doctors would speak soon enough.

'Bradley?' The intensivist asked. 'What do you think?'

Bradley gripped his thighs. 'I don't know. He looks pretty bad. To me.'

'That's fairly accurate,' Gilson said, and Yvette's lips almost disappeared. 'Lisa?'

'I'm with Bradley,' Lisa said. 'I don't see how he's ever going to get any better.'

Gilson gave her a nod before turning to her colleague. 'Sally, can you summarise for us?'

'Sure.' Sally, sitting next to a computer in the corner, swung the screen around. 'This is the CT scan on admission. The white on the scan is the blood in Jim's brain. As you can see, it was a very large bleed. This,' she tapped on the screen with her pen, 'is the brainstem. Because of the site of the bleed, even if Jim wakes up, it's extremely unlikely he will be able to move his arms or legs, or possibly even his eyes. He won't be able to talk. We're not even sure if he'll be able to breathe for himself if we switch off the ventilator.'

'But what if he does?' Yvette asked. 'What will you do then?'

'That's up to what you think he'd want,' Gilson said. 'Some — many — families would opt for comfort cares only in this sort of situation. If he got a pneumonia or another complication, we would only treat the symptoms, but we wouldn't give him any treatments to prolong his life.'

'I think we need to give him a chance,' Yvette said. 'Whatever it takes.'

'But what if that's not what he wants?' Emily leaned forward, holding the document Jake knew to be the advance directive. 'What he wants is right here. Do you want me to read it to you?'

Gilson's brow furrowed. 'Is that an —'

'Advance directive,' Jake said. 'He's nominated Lisa as his enduring power of attorney.'

Yvette's expression was stony. 'When was that dated?'

'Does it matter?' Emily asked.

Gilson took the directive. 'I don't think it does, really. If Lisa is his EPOA and believes this is still what he wants, then we should act as per his wishes. Although,' she glanced at her registrar, 'it would be good if we could get some agreement between you all.'

'I don't believe in euthanasia,' Yvette said. 'It's cruel.'

'Withdrawing active care is not euthanasia,' Jake said quietly. 'It's called palliative care. Caring for the dying with dignity.'

'Jake's right,' Lisa said. 'Jim would hate to be kept alive like this. What do you think, Bradley?'

Bradley rubbed his eyes, looked away. 'He's not there anymore,' he mumbled. 'Is he?'

Emily, her expression intent, said, 'What do you think we should do?'

'I think,' Gilson said, 'that it would not be unreasonable to switch off the ventilator at this stage. If your father can breathe for himself, then it's up to you whether you wish for him to still receive IV fluids and antibiotics. You don't have to decide all of that right now.'

Yvette let out a loud sob. Bradley leapt up and strode off.

'*Mum*,' Emily said when her mother got up to go after him. 'Can we make this decision?'

'You know what he wants, sweetheart,' Lisa said. 'You were closer to him than anyone.'

'No,' Emily said, suddenly pale. 'Not recently. And you're his EPOA. You should decide.'

Lisa glanced at Jake, then at the ICU consultant. 'Well,' she said. 'If Jim were in this meeting, I'm pretty sure he'd tell us to stop mucking around. He'd want us to say our goodbyes and switch off the ventilator. The last thing he'd want is to be kept alive as a prisoner in his own body.'

Yvette, still sobbing loudly, rushed out. Jake slipped his arm around Emily's waist, felt her tremble against him. 'Do you want me to go and talk to her?'

'Talk to who?' Emily asked.

'Yvette,' he said. 'Who else?'

———

He found Yvette in the corridor, clutching a sodden hanky.

'Hey.' Jake wished he'd thought to bring a box of tissues with him. 'I um . . . that was pretty hard in there.'

'Hard?' She blew her nose. 'That was me versus the family. David and Goliath.'

Jake rubbed his own nose, which was starting to itch. Yvette's perfume, he was guessing. 'How long have you known Jim?'

'A couple of years.' Yvette brushed a finger beneath her lower lip, wiping away a smear of lipstick. 'But we've only been dating for a few months. He's been so good to me, bringing me flowers and taking care of my garden when I was away last month. He even fills my car with petrol.' She gave him a watery smile. 'The least I can do is take care of him.'

'There are lots of different ways you can take care of people.' Jake stalled. What to say now? Obviously speaking to her as a physician wasn't going to help. 'My mum was sick for a long time when I was a kid,' he said. 'For years, actually.'

'Really?' Yvette wiped her eyes. 'What was wrong with her?'

'She had Huntington's disease.' When she looked blank, Jake added, 'It's a progressive neurological disorder. There's no cure.'

'How horrible. Did she . . . die?'

'When I was eighteen.'

Her expression softened. 'That must have been really hard for you, growing up.'

'It was. In the end she couldn't do anything for herself. Watching her suffer was the worst.'

Help, help.

I promise, I promise.

'You must miss her.'

'All the time. But I like to remember her as she was before she got sick.' Something clenched deep within his belly. It was the same sensation he got when he thought about the baby he and Emily had lost. 'That's how I keep her spirit alive. In here.' He tapped his head. 'And here.' He touched his chest.

'Yes,' she murmured. 'Yes.' Jake could see she was close to tears again.

'That's the hardest part about dying,' he said. 'Letting go. But often it's the kindest thing to do.'

'I know,' Yvette said, her voice wobbling. 'I know, but I'm just not ready.'

'No one is ever ready.' He touched her shoulder. 'See you inside?'

She took a deep breath. 'I'll be there in a minute. They won't do anything before I get there, will they? They won't switch off—'

'No. Of course not. I'll let them know.' He stopped short of hugging her, this woman he'd only just met; this woman he suddenly, surprisingly, felt deeply sorry for. 'See you soon.'

'Soon,' Yvette said, and turned to face the window.

Chapter 37: Go Your Own Way

No one ever tells you how to say goodbye, Emily thought. *No one tells you how deep grief runs, marbling inside you, layer upon layer.*

At four pm, they gathered around her father's bed. Emily didn't know exactly what Jake had said to Yvette before, but she seemed resigned to the course of events. Her father's girlfriend sat on Jim's left, holding his hand. Emily and Bradley sat on the other side of the bed, touching other parts of his body — a foot, a shoulder — while Jake and Lisa stood at the end of the bed. *Like the funeral before the funeral*, Emily thought. Was that an awful thing to think?

At five past four, Sally Chin stepped inside the curtain.

'I've come to take the tube out of Jim's throat now,' she said. 'Is everyone OK with that?'

'I'm . . . OK,' Emily said. Damn it, there she went, crying *again*.

'Uh-huh,' Bradley said. Jake and Lisa nodded. Yvette didn't say anything, just turned away. But when Sally said, 'Is anyone not OK with that?' Yvette didn't object.

Emily didn't watch the tube come out, but she heard the moment the suck and hiss of the ventilator stopped. She heard Sally say 'All done', and when she looked at her father she saw how still he had become. And yet his heart was still beating, because she could see the ECG reading on the monitor, the pulse rate climbing higher and higher.

'Darling Jim,' Yvette whispered. 'I'm right here.' Emily wished Yvette didn't have to be there — yet another thought she was glad no one could hear. She squeezed her father's shoulder, closed her eyes. The sterile atmosphere of the intensive care unit disappeared and she remembered a dimly lit bedroom, remembered placing her fingers beneath Christine

Heremaia's nostrils to check she had stopped breathing. *No air. No air. No air.*

'Oh no,' Yvette said, after an interminable time. It could have been a minute. It could have been five. 'Oh no.'

Emily opened her eyes. Jim's pulse rate was much slower now, only thirty beats per minute. Soon, she knew, it would stop all together.

'Dad.' Bradley bent forward to whisper in their father's ear. Emily couldn't hear what he said, but she could guess. Once Bradley sat up, she did the same.

I love you. I'm sorry.

By the time she straightened up, the ECG tracing was a flat line. It went on and on and on.

———

Emily woke with a stiff neck and a feeling that she'd never really fallen into a deep sleep. The covers on Jake's side had been thrown aside. When she went downstairs, in the morning sun spilling across the bench, she saw a note: *Gone surfing, love J.*

She wandered aimlessly around the garden, yanking some stray weeds out before entering the glasshouse at the rear of the section. The air smelt moist and earthy. She plucked a cherry tomato off a vine and popped it between her lips, the juices exploding onto her tongue. Next she bent to twist a cucumber off its stem, followed by a courgette. She decided to return with a colander that afternoon so she could pick perpetual lettuce for a salad.

This house could be ours.

The thought seemed wrong, mercenary considering her father had died only two days before . . . but it was a thought that wouldn't go away.

Half of this house belongs to Bradley.

We could save up, buy him out.

But we live in Melbourne.

For now.

The fresh, new-day vibe seeped away, replaced by the churning she'd had in her gut ever since she'd arrived in New Zealand. All she wanted was to be back in Melbourne, going about her everyday routine, even if that meant boring things such as trams and grocery shopping.

'There you are.' Jake peered through the door. 'Hot in here.'

'That's the idea.' She moved closer. 'Stick out your tongue.'

'That's what all the girls say,' he said, giving her a cheeky grin, but did as she asked. 'Mmm. Very sweet.'

'That's what all the boys say,' she said, and he pulled her closer for a kiss. 'You taste salty.'

'Is that good or bad?'

'I don't mind salty.' She unzipped his wetsuit and slid it down until the wetsuit lay discarded, snakeskin-like, at his feet. Jake nudged her dress up, her underwear down, and there was no one to see, no one at all. Minutes later, she lay tangled with Jake in the soil, cherry tomatoes nuzzling her face and what she was sure must be a grape squashed beneath her right buttock.

Jake cupped her breast. 'Greenhouse sex, that's a new one.'

'You did say it was hot.' He was still inside her, his weight almost enough to crush the breath from her lungs. She didn't mind. For the first time in days, she felt safe, settled, blissfully languid.

He shifted. 'Did you take your pill this morning?'

'I will.' She kept them by her toothbrush. Every morning, she flossed, brushed her teeth and took her pill. 'But Jake . . .'

'Mmm.'

'Do you still want to have a baby?'

'Of course.' His pupils were pinpricks in the white light, his irises almost black. 'Do you?'

'Yeah.'

'Once all this settles down, we can make an appointment . . . OK?'

'OK.'

'Nothing's changed.'

'Nothing,' she said. Jake got up, helped her to her feet.

'Love you, Em,' he said, and they went inside to have a shower.

That afternoon, her mother came over to help them. The task ahead seemed overwhelming — lawyers, a funeral to organise, property managers, bank accounts and investments, not to mention sorting through the contents of a five-bedroom house with three and a half decades of accumulated books, medical journals, photographs, clothes and —

'Stuff,' Emily said, standing on a stool so she could view the top of the wardrobe in the master bedroom. 'I bet he didn't even remember half of this was here.'

'Half of it probably belongs to you kids,' Lisa said.

'Yeah, but I don't have anywhere to store it.'

'Neither do I. Do you really need all those soft toys in your old room?'

'I don't know. I'll have a look later, maybe just keep one or two.' Emily passed a box to her mother. 'Not sure what's in here — notebooks?'

Lisa dumped it on the floor and peered in. 'Probably the travel diaries he used to keep when we went overseas. I couldn't be bothered, myself.' She paused for a moment, her face averted, before asking, 'Anything else up there?'

'Just these.' Emily reached for a smaller box before climbing off the stool. 'Adaptor plugs for different countries, by the looks of it.' She picked up a plug with two pins. 'Which country do you reckon this one is for? A European one?'

'No idea.' Her mother straightened up. 'Do you want to sort through this box, see if there's anything you want to keep? Otherwise we might as well stick them in the recycling bin.'

'OK.' Emily examined the plugs again. Maybe Bradley would want them.

'I'm going to make a cup of tea. Do you want one?'

'Sure, I'll come down soon.' Once her mother had left, Emily sat on the floor and took the first notebook out of the box. The pages were packed with her father's tall, sloping writing. The first page was titled *Paris, April 1976*. A travel diary, as her mother had guessed. After reading the first couple of pages, which described the view from the Eiffel Tower and how unexpectedly small the Mona Lisa painting was, Emily set it aside and reached for another notebook. What country was next? Poland? Germany? South America?

But the next notebook wasn't a travel diary at all. The first entry was dated *August 21 1985*. Beneath that was a single sentence: *Today I became a Fellow of the Royal Australasian College of Physicians, and we have decided to have a baby.*

And thirteen months later, you had your wish, Emily thought. Her father would have been thirty-three years old when he wrote that.

If only it were that easy for her and Jake. Glancing through more notebooks, she saw that her father had kept a number of diaries over the years, although the entries were often months to years apart. The earliest entry she found was in a battered school notebook dated 1967, when her father would have been fifteen years old. Fascinated, she read about his crush on Lesley Gordon, whomever she was, and how he'd kissed two girls that year and was hoping to make Lesley the third.

Ugh. Emily wasn't sure she wanted to read on.

Picking up a notebook with a burgundy Moleskine cover, she opened it up to find the first entry had been made in January 2003.

2003. As if she'd ever forget anything that happened *that* year. It was the year she'd finished high school; the year she'd helped Jake end his mother's life.

The year Dad found a misplaced insulin vial.

She thumbed through the pages, dog-eared and coffee-stained in places, until she reached November 2003, stopping when she saw her name.

November 29 2003. Emily came on another ward round today. Nice to see her taking an interest at last. She was particularly interested in talking to one of our patients about her diabetes, insulin, etc. At home she's very distracted, though. Perhaps she's worried about her exams, although they're all over now. I've told her there's no point stressing about something she can't change. Guess it's a major life transition, finishing high school.

Asked Penny out for dinner but she said she was 'flat out' this weekend and the next. Not sure if that's just an excuse. Jesus I feel like a teenager sometimes. Never thought I'd have to go through this whole dating thing again.

Emily wasn't interested in her father's struggles with dating, but she remembered twenty-ninth November 2003 very well. It was the last ward round she'd been on with her father, the last time she'd punched in the key code to the drug room. It was a code that she had little chance of ever forgetting: 1993, the year scientists had discovered the mutation that caused Huntington's disease.

Her father's voice echoed through the years: *Can anyone grab me a tongue depressor?*

I'll get it, seventeen-year-old Emily had answered. *Be right back.*

Two tongue depressors. Two vials of insulin.

And then it was Jake's voice she was remembering: *Do you think that's enough?*

I don't know, she'd answered. *I don't know, I don't know.*

Trembling, she turned to the next entry.

Sun 7 December 2003.

The words blurred. Sunday seventh December was the day after . . . the day after . . .

I'm not sure what to do with what I found this morning. Need to talk to Emily. Don't know how. Someone else's? No one has stayed here recently, no one who could have lost . . . that.

And then a series of cryptic jottings:

For: Short story I/K. Access. Tongue biting ?seizure.

Against: IV?

She heard her mother calling to her from below. 'Tea's ready.'

Emily cleared her throat. 'There soon.' Clutching the notebook, she marched into her old room and stuffed it into her suitcase. When she returned to the master bedroom, she began searching through the drawers in Jim's tallboy, in the cabinets beside his bed, beneath the mattress. It didn't take long to find another notebook beneath one of the pillows on the bed, a black Moleskine this time. The last entry was dated *31 December 2013*. The last day of the year. The last day her father had been able to write, to talk, to breathe. She closed the bedroom door and sank onto the bed to read, to get some clue as to why her father might have been calling her that evening.

I only want what's best for her. I thought convincing J to have the HD test would help solve matters. If he was negative, then nothing to worry about; if positive, then at the very least E could re-consider what she really wants out of life. But he's indeterminate, for God's sake. I didn't even realise that was a possibility. So, yet again, there is roughly a 50:50 chance that he could develop HD. The last thing E needs is to suffer through that situation again. I really think it would destroy her.

'You're wrong,' she whispered. 'You have no idea.' The latest entry was nothing she hadn't already gleaned. As for the earlier diaries, she was pretty sure now that she knew exactly how Jim had pieced together what had happened.

I'm writing a short story for English and a man wants to murder his wife . . . what medicine would you choose that had the least chance of being traced?

Insulin or potassium. They're both produced naturally by the body. A big load of potassium will cause cardiac arrest.

I/K. I for insulin, K the chemical symbol for potassium. How naïve she had been. How obvious. But if her father hadn't found that insulin vial, then surely he'd have been none the wiser. As for the tongue biting, he must have got that detail from the GP who'd signed Christine's death certificate. Emily remembered her father chatting to Doctor Reynolds as he left the Heremaias' house; remembered him returning to tell her that Christine had presumably died of pneumonia. He'd paused for a moment after telling her that, his brow wrinkling, but she'd been so relieved at the time that she'd barely noticed.

But she remembered that now. Yes, she did.

Bending over the notebook again, Emily read the last couple of lines. Once, twice, three times — she couldn't make sense of them, or maybe it was merely that she didn't want to make sense of them.

Need to talk to Lisa. We've buried this for so long but it's time to sort this out once and for all.

She heard footsteps in the hallway, a knock on the door.

'Emily? Are you OK?'

Emily shoved the notebook under the mattress before standing up to open the door. Her mother was holding a steaming mug of tea and a saucer with a chocolate biscuit.

'Find anything interesting?' Lisa asked.

'Not really. Maybe I'll just keep one. I'll sort through the rest of them later.'

Lisa nodded. 'Auntie Carol called, said she and Harold will drive up on Thursday. I can help you do something easy for dinner, a big lasagne or something.'

'Good,' Emily said, relieved her mother was taking charge. She'd lost track of how many friends and relatives had called and e-mailed to say they'd be coming for the funeral on Friday.

'Do you and Jake want to come over for dinner tonight?'

'Thanks, but no. Jake and I thought we'd have a quiet one.' And maybe, she thought, trying to resist the urge to glance toward the mattress, she'd light the fire.

Ashes to ashes, dust to dust.

'Oh honey.' Her mother embraced her. Emily hadn't even realised she was crying.

Chapter 38: Lego House

MELBOURNE, JULY 2014

Jake knew something was up as soon as he arrived home from work. The first clue was the pair of champagne flutes on the bench. The second was the music Emily was playing at full volume, which she usually only did if she were really happy. He found her in the shower, singing along to Ed Sheeran, something to do with a Lego house.

'Holy cow.' He shucked his clothes off and stepped in to join her. 'What's the occasion?'

'What's that?' Emily bent to turn down the volume on her Bluetooth speaker, and he couldn't resist stroking her naked butt.

'I said, what's the occasion?' Jake repeated after she'd turned to kiss him.

'I've got news.'

'About what?' He cupped her buttocks. Her naked curves were very distracting, even after seven years together.

'I won.' She kissed him again.

'Won what?' *The lottery? A raffle?*

'The graphic novel competition in the UK, remember that?'

He gaped at her. 'Really? Whoa, how much did you win?'

'A thousand pounds. Better than that,' she added, while Jake tried to mentally convert the amount into Australian dollars, without success, 'they've guaranteed me publication. It's a small printing press, but they're sending me a contract and everything. Can you believe it?'

'Whoa,' he repeated. 'You're amazing.' He twirled her around the shower, as much as he could in a slippery, confined space. '*Double Helix Dragon* by Emily Walsh. Wait, are you going to have a pen name?'

'Better than that.' She was stroking *him* now, in the most distracting way possible. 'By the time it's published, we'll be married.'

His breathing sped up. 'Next January?' Tuesday evening was shaping up to be a lot better than he'd anticipated, especially after yesterday's news.

'Well, *we're* getting married in January, but the book probably won't come out until next July. I think Emily Heremaia would look great on the cover, don't you?'

'Yeah,' he agreed. 'Yeah, it would.' He nudged her against the wall of the shower. 'You're a little tease, you know that?'

'You came in here.'

'Not yet,' he said, 'but close,' and she said 'you're so disgusting', and then neither of them said anything for some time.

———

The celebration continued on Friday night. Ian and Kylie had invited them for dinner at their apartment, the décor of which was in keeping with Kylie's dress sense; the couches accessorised with hot pink throws and electric blue cushions, the lounge wall sporting a painting of a giant sunflower on a blue background.

'So, a published author,' Kylie said after they'd raised a toast to Emily's success. 'When do you get to quit your day job?'

'I don't think the salary's that great.' Emily dipped a carrot into Ian's homemade baba ganoush. 'And we're saving for a wedding. So . . . not for a while, I don't think.'

'Unless someone turns it into a movie or TV series.' Ian brightened. 'Hey, it could be the next *Game of Thrones*.'

'Might need a bit more sex for that,' Jake said.

'Oh, I don't think you'd need to sleep with the director if you paid them enough — ouch, do you have to kick me all the time?' Ian gave Kylie a mock glare.

Emily reached for another carrot stick. 'This dip is really good, Ian. I think your talents are wasted in advertising.'

'Agree.' Ian topped up everyone's wine glasses. 'Although I'm about to expand on my advertising talents. Has Kylie told you our news yet?'

Jake took a handful of chips. 'You got a promotion?'

'Kind of.' Ian sipped on his wine. 'I'm being transferred to the Gold Coast.'

'Ah man, we're coming to visit,' Jake said, not even bothering to try and hide his jealousy. 'Like, forever.'

'Will you apply to work at Gold Coast Hospital?' Emily asked Kylie.

'Yeah, I'm looking forward to some balmier temperatures. Although I suspect I'll be seeing a little less of the grommet here.' She waved at Ian.

'I've told you before, a grommet's a baby surfer,' Ian grumbled.

'You'll be surfing off into the sunset.' Jake raised his glass. 'Here's to the perfect wave.'

'To the perfect wave.' Ian clinked his glass against Jake's. 'Maybe you guys should transfer too. Perfect scenery for your next novel, Em.'

'Yeah, that would be perfect,' she said. 'If it weren't for . . .' She glanced at Jake. 'We had an appointment yesterday.'

'About?' Kylie looked between them. 'Wait, to see the fertility specialist?'

'That's the one,' Jake said, his good humour beginning to evaporate.

Kylie set her glass down. 'So what did they say?'

He sagged against a monster cushion. 'They told us to check our insurance cover, and guess what? We're not covered for PGD.'

Kylie scowled. 'That sucks. I would have thought it was a basic human right.'

'Not according to Medicare,' Jake said, frowning into his glass.

'PGD, what's that?' Ian asked.

'Preimplantation genetic diagnosis,' Emily said. 'So we can pre-select embryos without an HD mutation.'

'I'm pretty sure PGD is funded in New Zealand for serious genetic disorders,' Kylie said. 'Have you checked?'

'Of course,' Emily said, not looking at Jake. 'And it *is* covered.'

'Will you return to New Zealand then?' Ian asked.

'We're going to look into it.' Jake was avoiding Emily's gaze too. 'After the wedding. There's been so much else going on.'

'True.' Kylie opened a box of crackers and arranged a selection in a fan-shape on a plate. 'How are the tenants at your dad's house?'

Emily shrugged. 'They seem OK. We let the property manager take care of most of it. Guess we'd have free accommodation if we move back to Dunedin.'

'Except Bradley owns half of it,' Jake reminded her.

'We can buy him out. Rent to own.'

'I need to finish up the year here.' Christ, were they going to rehash the whole of yesterday's argument in front of Kylie and Ian?

'So,' Kylie said cheerfully, 'who wants to play Balderdash?'

'Balderdash?' Jake asked, relieved at the change in topic.

'Guaranteed to make you laugh,' she said, and, as if to illustrate, let out one of her infamous cackles. 'Or I'll eat this cushion.' She held it up.

'Tempting,' Ian said, 'very tempting. Ow, do you think my shins are made of rubber or something?'

———

Kylie was right. By the time they got home, Jake's facial and stomach muscles were aching from laughing. He hadn't checked his phone in hours, having developed a strange aversion to being contacted after two and a half years of on-call duties. Yet when he went to plug the phone into the charger beside their bed, he saw a missed call and a text message, both from the same number.

Hi Jake. Hope you don't mind me contacting you. I was wondering if you and your girlfriend are free for a coffee tomorrow afternoon? I'd love to show you how your goddaughter has grown. Gareth.

His goddaughter. Hell, he hadn't heard from Gareth since Cameron had died last year. Hannah must be — what, eleven months old? Gareth had texted a photo too, of a button-nosed cherub with wispy blonde hair.

'We've been invited out for coffee tomorrow,' he said when Emily entered the bedroom.

'By who?'

'Gareth,' Jake said, and when she looked blank, 'Cameron's partner. The father of my goddaughter, remember that?'

'Oh, Jake.' She climbed into bed, her feet cold against his legs. 'Don't you think it's time to tell him it's . . . well, you know, slightly inappropriate?'

'I can talk about the godparent thing, let him know that's not a good idea. But he's a nice guy. It'd mean the world to him if we meet up.' He showed her the photo Gareth had sent.

'That's not fair.'

'What do you mean?'

'I mean, she's so adorable.' She peered closer. 'Her parents must be pretty good-looking. Which one do you think is the father?'

'Cameron. She's got the same bright blue eyes.' When he reached for his phone, he saw Emily's eyes were bright too, but for a different reason. A couple of weeks ago Jake had made the mistake of mentioning that one of the interns was pregnant and had been met with a similar response.

'Hey.' He reached for her, but she turned away.

'Don't worry. I'm just being stupid.'

'You're not stupid.' He cuddled her, his chin nestling in the hollow by her neck. 'Em, I never said we shouldn't move back to New Zealand. You know I've been keen on that for ages. But if I swap hospitals halfway through the year, I'll end up on some really crappy rotation.'

'Well, maybe we should get the PGD here then.' God, she was so stubborn; it was one of her best and worst qualities.

'How? Change insurance companies? I don't see how we're going to get covered when I've got a pre-existing condition.'

'We could use the inheritance to pay for it.'

'But it'll cost tens of thousands. We — you — could need that money for something else. Our mortgage, or for you if I—'

'Don't say it.'

'Don't say you haven't thought about it.'

'No, I'm *not* thinking about it.' She faced him again, her expression fierce. 'That's just inviting trouble.'

'It's being sensible.'

'I don't want to be sensible,' she said, and started crying again. He felt like such a shit. Was he being selfish? It was all down to him, after all. If only they'd invented some sort of gene therapy that could strip the mutation from his cells. Hell, he'd have a stem cell transplant if he thought it would help. But every time he checked on the latest research in the HD field, the answer was the same.

There is no cure no cure no cure.

———

Gareth was waiting to meet them when they arrived at the café the next morning, sitting at a table nearest the playpen in the corner.

'Hey Doctor Jake.' He stood up, giving Jake an awkward handshake that morphed into a half-hug, half-backslap. 'And you must be . . .'

'Emily.' She sat down, escaping any bodily contact. 'Is that your little one in there?'

'Hannah, yes.' Gareth beamed at the little girl sitting in the middle of the playmat, who appeared to be playing with some sort of abacus. Her hair was in tiny pigtails, her chubby legs clad in unicorn leggings.

'Is she doing your accounts?' Jake asked, and Gareth laughed.

'Something like that. How's it going, are you still playing surgeon?'

'No, I saw the light, thought I'd aim for oncology.'

'Thank God for that. Do you want a coffee? Emily?'

'I'll get it.' Jake stood up, noting the empty coffee cup at Gareth's elbow. 'Do you want another one?'

'No, I'm good.' As Jake moved towards the counter, he heard Gareth say, 'Jake tells me you're an artist,' and had to resist glancing behind him to check on Emily's response. After ordering the coffees, he returned to the table to find Gareth was alone.

Jake frowned. 'Where's — oh.' Emily was sitting in the playpen with Hannah, building a tower. 'Any excuse to play with Lego.'

'It's Duplo,' Emily called out. 'Lego's dangerous for little kids.'

'Dangerous?' Jake asked.

'Swallowing hazard,' Gareth answered, and Jake was reminded that he didn't know the first thing about looking after small children.

'Just testing,' Jake teased. 'How about you, how are things?'

Gareth played with a teaspoon. 'Oh, you know. Ups and downs. I don't think I'd be able to get out of bed some days if it weren't for Hannah.'

'She looks pretty happy,' Jake said, glancing at Emily, who seemed pretty happy too, right then. 'And super cute, too.'

'Thank God she got Cam's genes and not mine,' Gareth said. 'How about you two, are you planning any family?' He flushed. 'Sorry, was that too personal? You don't have to answer that.'

'S'OK.' Jake waited for the waitress to deposit the coffees on the table before continuing. 'We're really keen. But there are a few things we need to sort out first.'

'Don't leave it too long. You never know what's around the corner.'

'You never know.' Hearing delighted laughter, Jake saw that Emily was playing peek-a-boo with Hannah. 'We didn't even know we wanted one until last year.'

'You can borrow Hannah any time you want.'

'Don't say that too loud.' Jake sipped on his coffee. 'Seriously, though, we could babysit for you one day, give you a break.'

Gareth hesitated. 'Nah, I'd hate to impose on you like that.'

'It's not a problem, as long as you give us a bit of notice. I know.' Jake took his wallet out of his pocket and found a random card advertising a taxi company he never used. 'Here.' He scribbled *Get Out Of Jail Free* on the reverse of the card, and beneath that, *Jake* and his mobile number, even though he knew Gareth already had it. 'When it feels like everything's too much.' When Gareth hesitated, Jake added, 'I'm not just doing this for you. I'm doing it for Cameron too.'

'For Cameron.' Gareth blinked. 'I never thanked you for coming to his funeral. That meant a lot to me.'

Jake didn't know what to say. Instead, he pushed the card towards Gareth.

'It's the least a godfather could do,' he said.

Emily was going to kill him.

Chapter 39: Deleted

That Friday, Emily went for a wander through the Botanical Gardens, a welcome break from the edits she'd been working on all morning. It was the first day of September, the first day of spring, and the gardens were in bloom — scarlet tulips, fluffy pink blossoms on trees that had stood bare all winter.

As she wandered, her eyes were drawn to women with pregnant bellies and parents pushing prams. Babies, babies, babies. Suddenly they were everywhere, or perhaps she'd been blinkered for the first twenty-eight years of her life.

Before she miscarried. Before Jake had a test that made everything even more uncertain.

Emily was starting to wish she hadn't come out at all. Changing direction, she emerged onto the street and began walking towards Flinders Street. There were guaranteed to be far fewer children in the CBD.

We'll have a baby soon enough, Jake had said. *We know we're fertile already, right? There's no hurry.*

And of course, there wasn't — she was only twenty-eight — but now her biological clock had been tripped, she just couldn't stop it. Or perhaps *stopwatch* would have been a better word for it, the feeling that she was running a race with a finish line she couldn't see.

After crossing at the lights, she continued into Degraves Street, half-hoping, half-dreading seeing Nick standing outside the café. When she didn't spot him, she walked inside, the bell above the door announcing her arrival.

'Hey, Kiwi bird,' a familiar voice said, and she jumped. 'Sorry, didn't mean to scare you.' Nick smiled as if it hadn't been ten months since they'd last spoken, ten months since he'd kissed her beneath a gum tree.

Emily smoothed her hair. 'Hi,' she said. 'Long time no see.'

'Coffee?'

'Love one.' She took a seat outside, gazing up into the rectangle of sky visible between the buildings. Muslin clouds, no wind; the summer heat was on its way. Soon, soon.

Nick set a cup and saucer in front of her. 'So, what's new?'

Emily took her sunglasses off. 'Well, I got a publishing contract for my graphic novel.'

'Yeah? Where can I get a copy?'

'It's not published yet. I'll let you know when it is, so you can order it online.' Emily watched Nick glance around before sitting opposite her. There were no customers inside, and only one other patron sitting at a nearby table, reading a newspaper. 'How are you?'

'Ah, same same. Actually, not really.' He fingered the ring through his eyebrow. 'I've got myself a girlfriend since I saw you last.'

'Really?' Emily asked, feeling an inexplicable twinge of jealousy. 'Great. What's her name?'

'Brianna. She's a musician. Plays guitar and sings.'

'Wow. That's awesome.' It was. Still. She'd enjoyed their months of flirtation, even though she hadn't wanted it to go anywhere, as it turned out.

'How about you? Are you still with—'

'Jake, yes.' She showed him her engagement ring. 'We're getting married in January.'

Nick took her hand. 'Diamonds set in . . . what, silver?'

'Platinum.'

'Goes well with your dragons,' he said, touching the tattoo on her wrist before releasing her. Emily felt a familiar flicker in her belly, one she knew she'd never act on again. 'Things going well then?'

Flushing, she averted her gaze. 'Mostly. I mean, they are.' She watched a pair of young men in suits amble past, bantering and laughing. 'We're moving home in the new year.'

'Aw, seriously? Had enough of it here?'

'No.' She picked up her coffee for the first time. The brew was just as good as she remembered, strong and smooth. 'Jake's got a job in Dunedin.' She left out the details about the fertility treatment. It wasn't something she wanted to share with someone she barely knew, someone she'd nearly wrecked a seven-year relationship with.

Nick took a lighter out of his jeans pocket, flicked the wheel. 'Do you have a job lined up too?'

'Actually, no.' Emily wiped milk off her top lip. 'I'm going to be a student again.'

'Yeah? Doing what?'

'I'm going to art school.' Excitement thrummed through her. 'I can't wait.'

'Congratulations. I've always wanted a trip to New Zealand. Maybe I'll drop in, pay you a visit.'

'You should,' Emily said, knowing that was unlikely. A middle-aged couple approached and hovered next to the window for a moment, perusing the menu, before entering the café.

Nick got to his feet. 'Better do some work. You take care, Kiwi bird.' He bent forward and she felt his lips on her cheek. 'I haven't forgotten,' he murmured, and then he was gone.

———

That afternoon, Emily inked an edited sketch from her novel and set it aside to dry while she made a start on dinner. Pink leapt on top of the couch, watching her crush garlic, dice ginger and slice chillies for the curry. She listened to music as she worked, Adele, humming along to 'Rolling in the Deep', breaking into song for 'Set Fire to the Rain'.

Jake wasn't into Adele. He thought she was too soppy.

At five fifteen, her phone beeped.

Hey I said we'd look after Hannah tonight. Sorry, short notice but hope that's ok with you since we're not up to much anyway? Gareth dropping her off at 6. I should be home by then.

What? Since when had they offered to be babysitters? And what were they meant to do with a one-year-old?

Think it's a bit late to be asking me, she typed, but deleted it. Instead, she replied: *OK*. Jake could read whatever he wanted into that. So much for wine, curry and a movie.

Did one-year-olds eat curry? From Emily's memory of Charlotte at that age, that seemed *very* unlikely. What *did* one-year-olds eat? And when — at five thirty? Six?

Emily stomped around the apartment, checking for hazards and breakable items. *Typical Jake. Act first, apologise later. So much for telling Gareth that he shouldn't be the godfather. No, come on in, we'll look after her anytime you like.*

At five fifty-nine, the doorbell rang. Adopting what she hoped was a neutral expression, Emily rinsed her onion-covered hands and went to answer the door.

'Hi.' Gareth seemed to have perfected the art of hanging as many items off his body as possible, including a baby bag, a wheelie suitcase with green horns and a tail, a long rectangular bag and of course Hannah, who was strapped to his front.

'Hi. Come in,' Emily said, wondering if there was something Jake had yet to tell her — a spur of the moment adoption, perhaps?

'Sorry to bust in on your Friday night.' Gareth began depositing various items on the couch and bench. 'Hannah was meant to be staying over at my mum's, but she's got the flu and I had this date arranged which I could have cancelled but it would have been the second time in a row because last time Hannah was sick, and I thought hey, why not use my *Get Out of Jail Free* card . . .'

Emily pushed a box of tissues aside, making way for a plastic container containing an unidentified white powder. 'It's fine.' *Get Out of Jail Free* card, what the hell?

'Ganma,' Hannah announced, and Gareth chuckled.

'No, sweetie, this is Emily. She thinks all ladies are called "Ganma" at the moment.'

'As in "Grandma"?' Emily smiled at Hannah, who was, admittedly, looking adorable in a blue dress with white polka dots and blue tights with soft leather shoes, along with a blue bow in her hair. 'You can call me Em if you like.' She pointed at her own chest. 'Em.'

'Em.' Hannah waved her legs up and down.

'I've fed her dinner,' Gareth said. 'Nappies and wipes are in the bag, and her formula is in that container there. Just make it up to two hundred mls with water and thirty seconds in the microwave. I give it to her just before she goes to bed, but there's a spare one in there, too, in case she wakes up.'

'Right. Thanks. What time does she go to bed?'

'About seven. Oh yeah, I almost forgot.' Gareth unstrapped Hannah and passed her to Emily before bending to unzip the rectangular bag. 'Where shall I put the port-a-cot?'

'Um, the spare room should be fine.' Emily jiggled Hannah up and down, and Hannah's lips parted in delight. 'Would you stop being so cute?'

Gareth laughed. 'I have that problem.' Now that he'd shed the baby paraphernalia, Emily noted that Gareth was wearing a navy suit with a crisp white shirt and dark red shoes.

'So who's your date?' Emily asked, showing him into the spare room.

'His name's Brendon. He's a graphic designer.' Gareth emptied the contents of the bag onto the floor.

'Really? I'm jealous.'

Gareth unfolded the cot. 'Sorry to disappoint you, but he's not into women.'

'No, I mean the graphic design thing.' Emily sat on the spare bed, Hannah on her lap. 'I think I would have liked to have done something like that.'

'Sounds like you're doing pretty well with your art already.' Gareth disappeared into the lounge and returned with the baby bag. 'This is her sleep sack,' he said, taking a striped piece of fabric out of the baby bag. 'She likes to be zipped inside it, makes her feel snuggly.'

'It does look pretty snuggly.' Emily stroked Hannah's cheek. 'Maybe we could watch *Master Chef* together. What do you think, Hannah?'

'Hel-lo.' A door slammed and Jake appeared, his shirttail hanging out, his top button unfastened. 'Am I missing the party?'

'Mate, it's only just begun.' Gareth straightened up. 'Thank you so much. I'll pick her up by eleven, I promise.'

'No problem.' Jake shot Emily a grin. 'We need all the practice we can get.'

———

'Do you think we'll get in trouble for not putting her to bed at seven?' Emily gazed down at the sleeping child in her arms. Eight pm, and Hannah had fallen asleep halfway through drinking her bottle. Was there anything as angelic as a sleeping child?

'Nah, I think he'd be delighted. We should send him a photo.'

'No, don't disturb him.' Emily nudged the teat out from between Hannah's lips and set it on the table beside her. 'So, about this godfather thing . . .'

'It sounds like a mafia movie, doesn't it? Come on, it's a bit late to rescind my acceptance, isn't it?'

'You make it sound like an Emmy award.'

'Maybe.' He stroked the heel of Hannah's foot and they watched the big toe curl upward. 'Babinski reflex,' they chorused.

'See,' Emily said. 'I didn't forget *all* my medical training.'

'I still want to take a photo.' He bent forward to kiss her. 'Maybe this time next year . . .'

'This time what?' Her heart accelerated.

'You know.' He slid his hand between Hannah and Emily's belly, and her vision blurred. 'Sorry. I didn't mean to—'

'It's fine.' She swallowed. 'I should stop being so sensitive.'

Jake moved closer, pressed his cheek to hers. 'You'll be an amazing mother,' he said. 'I know you will.'

'What if it doesn't happen?'

'Then I'll love you anyway.' He stroked Hannah's chubby arm. 'If I'm the godfather, then you must be the godmother.'

'Does it work like that?'

'Don't know why it wouldn't.'

'The word godmother makes me feel old.'

'We're not old.'

'No,' she said. 'Not at all.' She'd read the lifespan of a child born in

2014 was eighty years for a male, eighty-three years for a female. In 1986, when she had been born, it was only seventy-two years for a male but seventy-eight years for a female.

Unless . . . unless . . .

The thought sprung to the forefront of her mind, fully formed, as though it had been waiting in her subconscious for months.

If you had an advance directive, what would you say? What would you want? Do you want what your mother wanted? But how could I . . . ? How could we . . . ?

'Are you sure you're OK?' Jake touched the tip of her nose.

'Of course.' She lifted her chin, inviting him to kiss her again. 'But Jake?'

'Yeah?'

'If a patient ever asks you to be a godfather again . . .'

'Yeah, yeah, I know.' He stood up. 'We'd have a nursery full of children before you know it.'

'And all the boys would be named Jake.'

'And the girls would be called Jakina,' he said.

Emily laughed, looked down at their tiny charge. 'Think I should put her to bed now?'

'No,' he said. 'Do you?'

'I won't tell him if you don't,' Emily said, watching Pink slink towards them, her tail held high.

'Our secret.' Jake walked into the kitchen. 'Cup of tea?'

303

Chapter 40: True Love Waits

Jake looked down at his t-shirt, which had been white and unmarked at the beginning of the evening, but was now covered in the lipstick marks of who knew how many women. He'd lost count of the number of Dunedin bars and pubs they'd been to, but at every establishment, Ian had insisted on asking the female patrons to kiss the buck's t-shirt. Most of them had been happy to oblige.

Ian pounded his fist on the table before standing up and raising his glass. 'I am Spartacus!' He downed the remains of his beer.

'Ah fuck, not again,' Jake protested, contemplating his brimming pint.

'Rules are rules,' Craig, his former med-school classmate, chimed in, before the rest of the guys chanted, 'I am Spartacus!' They drained their glasses, Jake included. Everything seemed blurred around the edges, the colours muted, like one of Emily's watercolour paintings.

'Hey, you know what? Last time I was here,' Ian leaned forward, 'Kylie was sitting on *your* lap. Remember?'

Jake propped his elbows up on the table. 'Um, no?' But come to think of it, perhaps he *did* remember. A rugby game at Carisbrook, an argument outside with Emily. He'd walked Emily home, but she'd been locked out of her flat, so she'd come back to his and then . . . and then . . .

'Actually,' Jake said, lowering his head into his arms, 'maybe I do.'

Emily slept in my bed, and all night I wanted to kiss her but I didn't. I didn't. His groin stirred at the memory.

'Nah, mate, evening's not over yet.' Nathan, whom Jake liked to remember as the grumpiest flatmate he'd ever had, yanked him up by the collar. 'We've got a little something for you.'

'A little . . . what?' Jake blinked. Surely that wasn't what he thought it was?

'Made of the finest materials,' Ian crowed.

'I'm not wearing a chicken suit,' Jake protested. Jesus, it had feathers and everything.

'Relax,' Nathan said. 'This won't hurt a bit.'

———

Light exploded behind his eyelids. Jake sat up, then wished he hadn't. Everything above his groin hurt — his guts, his chest, and most especially, his head, which was pounding in time with his heartbeat.

'Oh my God, can you at least aim in here?' Emily shoved a bowl at him. 'I can't believe how drunk you were last night.'

'Last night?' When Jake retched, all that came out was yellow bile. He took the tissues Emily gave him and wiped his mouth. He had a dim memory of chucking up — but where? In the gutter? In the hallway? In the toilet? He had a horrible inkling it might've been all three. No wonder Emily was livid.

'Technically your so-called friends returned you at five am. Very good of them to put you in the recovery position before leaving you on the lawn.'

Jake raised a tremulous hand to his eyes. 'Can you turn off the light?'

'Only if you promise to have a shower. You stink. And what the hell are you wearing, a chicken outfit?'

'You're making it sound like I had a choice,' Jake said, but Emily had already left. Groaning, he lay horizontal again, nausea rippling through him. His right eye was streaming. Great, a prelude to a migraine — just what he needed on the eve of his wedding day.

Peering through narrowed eyelids, Jake realised that he was in the spare room in the downstairs level of the Walsh family home. He struggled to get his thoughts in order. *OK. Sumitriptan, water and shower, in that order.* Which required assuming an upright position and making it up the stairs to the bedroom he was sharing with Emily.

Not the master bedroom, Emily had said when they'd moved in a couple

305

of weeks ago. *That would just feel weird, at least until we do the place up.*

'Jeepers,' his old man said when Jake limped past the lounge, trailing feathers. 'You're a sight for sore eyes.' Willie started chortling, as if Jake was the funniest thing he'd ever seen.

'*Jake.*' Emily appeared on the landing, holding a bottle of disinfectant. 'Can you please have a shower before you—'

'Migraine,' Jake mumbled, sinking onto a step.

'Oh, great,' she muttered. 'Where's your medication, in your toilet bag?'

'Uh-huh.' Jake slumped against the wall. 'Thanks.'

Less than a minute later, Emily reappeared, holding a syringe. Jake accompanied her to the downstairs bathroom, where he struggled out of the chicken suit so Emily could give him a jab in the biceps, slightly harder than necessary, he thought.

'I hope this works,' she said, 'because we have lots of guests arriving today, remember?'

'I remember.' He sloped into the shower and sat in the pan, the water cascading over his exploding head.

I'm going to kill you, Ian Whittaker, do you hear me?

———

'I'm going to kill you,' Jake said as soon as he saw his best friend coming down the driveway.

Ian straightened his bow tie. 'Come on, mate, that was the best buck's night ever.'

'For you, maybe.' The last vestiges of Jake's hangover/migraine/kiss of death were still lurking in the periphery of his skull, even though he hadn't touched a drop of alcohol since the early hours of the morning before. At least, he thought that was when he'd stopped drinking, but how would he know?

'I think we overestimated your drinking capacity. Sorry.' Ian didn't look sorry. 'But you did a great chicken dance at the Fox and Hound, don't you remember?'

Jake glared at him. 'No, I really don't. Have you got the rings?'

'Of course, what kind of best man do you think I am?' Ian took a pair of boxes out of the inside pocket of his suit jacket. 'I haven't sold them off on Trade Me or anything, if that's what you're worried about.'

'The thought never crossed my mind,' Jake muttered, his nerves settling a little when he saw the rings nestled in the pink fabric inside each box. Now all he had to worry about were his speech, his old man not getting too plastered before the ceremony, and Emily not ditching him at the altar. At least she'd been talking to him by the time she left to stay at her mother and Steve's place the evening before.

Thank God he didn't have to worry about Emily's father as well. Was it wrong to think that? Maybe, but Jake was sure his anxiety levels would be at least eighty per cent higher if Jim were still around to threaten him with insulin vials and God-knew-what-else.

Ian checked his watch. 'It's quarter-past four, do you think we should get going?'

Jake let out his breath. 'Guess we should.' It was a fifteen-minute drive to Glenfalloch, give or take, which would give him half an hour until the ceremony was due to start. Plenty of time.

'Not thinking of doing a runner, are you?' Willie limped toward them, the buttons of his suit jacket straining against his bulging stomach.

'Wouldn't dream of it.' Jake resisted the urge to add something more cutting, something along the lines of: *Because it's not as if you've ever done anything like that, right, like abandoning your eight-year-old son and wife after she was diagnosed with a terminal illness?* A fight with his father was the last thing he needed.

Someone clasped his shoulder. 'See you there, Jake. You look very handsome, I must say.' It was one of Emily's great-aunts, who'd arrived that morning, along with her husband. An inexplicable terror gripped his bowels. What if he was a terrible husband? Would the whole family descend on him, like the mafia?

'Um, just going to the loo,' he murmured to Ian before jogging towards the house.

Once he'd finished evacuating his bowels, Jake flushed and sat on the closed toilet seat. *Deep breaths, deep breaths. You can do this.*

But can Emily?

Jim's words wormed through his brain: *Please tell me you're not going*

307

to put her through that again. You'll destroy her. You know that, don't you?

Jesus, what am I doing? How can I promise Emily anything?

There was a rap on the door, Ian's rumbling voice. 'Twenty past, Heremaia. We'd better get going or Kylie will string me up.'

Jake clenched his fists, opened them again. 'By the balls,' he called out, before flushing again and unlocking the door.

'You'd like that, wouldn't you?' Ian asked as he steered Jake down the hallway like a recalcitrant child.

'I may not remember much,' Jake said, following Ian out to the car, 'but just you wait until *your* buck's night.'

Ian slid into the driver's seat and turned the key in the ignition. 'I'm trembling.' He smirked at Jake. 'Just like you are now.'

'Am not.'

'Are so,' Ian said, and they argued all the way to Glenfalloch, just like old times.

———

Jake started freaking out again as soon as they drove through the gates of Glenfalloch. So many people already, although when he checked the time on Ian's rental car, he saw it was quarter to five. The ceremony started in fifteen minutes, which seemed way too soon and yet a very long time to wait.

'Kia ora, Jake!' Auntie Ngaire swooped on him, giving him a power-hongi as soon as he stepped out of the car, followed by Auntie Huia and her boyfriend, Pete. And there was Jonesy, looking gigantic in a cream suit, and Freda, her lips extra puffy, as though she'd injected extra lip fillers just for the wedding.

'Look at you, just like your dad when he was your age.' Ngaire seemed close to tears already. 'I wish your mum could see you.'

'Me too.' Jake fought a rising tide of emotion. Crap, he hadn't expected that. He wished he could restrict his memories to all the good ones about his mother, rather than the hard years they'd had before she died. But Ngaire was right, if only his mother could have been here. She would have been helping calm him down, straightening his collar and tie while looking amazing in whatever bridegrooms' mothers like to wear.

Huia squeezed his shoulder. 'She'd be so proud of you.'

'And we are too,' Ngaire added, and Jake gave her a fierce hug, Huia too.

'Thanks for coming,' he said. 'It means . . . everything.'

'Think we should assume our positions yet?' Ian was such a nag, but Jake was grateful for it.

'How's my hair?' Jake asked as they stood at the top of the lawn, the celebrant facing them.

'Awful, how's mine?'

Jake eyed Ian's receding hairline. 'Should have had those extensions.'

'Fuck off.'

'That was inappropriate, man. On my wedding day and everything.'

Ian made a chicken noise. Jake shoved him, as surreptitiously as he could. The celebrant gave them a disapproving look.

Feeling as if he were in high school again, Jake turned to look behind him. No car yet. He didn't even know what Emily's family had chosen to hire for the occasion, let alone what she was wearing. His bowel began to twist again, but it was five minutes to five, no time for another mercy dash to the toilet. Trying to think constipating thoughts, he faced the front. *Breathe, breathe, breathe.*

'Before you ask, I've still got the rings.'

'Cool.' Jake shuffled his feet.

Ian squinted at him. 'What's with being fashionably late, anyway? Like, who decided that was a thing?'

'No idea.' Jake was all out of banter, almost out of adrenaline too. Hearing a collective murmur behind him, he checked again, and *there* she was. At least, he assumed that Emily was in the Rolls-Royce Silver Shadow with the silver ribbon on the front.

Ian whistled. 'Nice car.'

Jake didn't answer. His gaze was on the girl in the window.

How old are you?

Eight. How old are you?

Same.

Emily caught his eye, and he saw her lips curve upwards in the special smile she reserved for him, just for him. He lifted his chin, returned her smile.

Love you, Em, he mouthed at her.

Love you, Jay, she mouthed back.

The car came to a standstill. All eyes were on the bride in the window, but no one, Jake knew, saw who *he* saw.

My Emily, the most beautiful person in the world. I promise to look after you until death do us part. And I promise, with all my heart, that I will not destroy you.

I promise.

Chapter 41: Waiting for a Star to Fall

DUNEDIN, SEPTEMBER 2015

'My old house is up for sale,' Jake said when he arrived home from the hospital. It was eleven pm and Emily was in bed. Normally she would have been asleep.

'I saw. Who do you think our next neighbours might be?'

'We could buy it.' Jake sat on the bed and kicked his shoes off.

'Are you kidding me?'

'Leverage. We could rent it out.'

'Since when did you become a property mogul?'

'Just planning for the future.'

'Too risky.'

Jake huffed. 'OK, fine.'

'Jake . . .' But he'd already gone to the bathroom, leaving her to sift through her muddled thoughts. One mortgage was enough responsibility, let alone two.

Jake returned to the bedroom, his toothbrush poking out of his mouth. 'Did you book your scan?'

'Yes, they said Friday afternoon was fine. Can you get off work?'

Jake took the brush out from between his lips and wiped his mouth. 'Of course.' He sat beside her, curved his fingers around her rounded belly. 'Any chance to see my little whetū.' *My little whetū. My little star.*

'Think she heard you,' Emily said as she felt the familiar flutter within, a sensation she'd been aware of for the past two weeks.

'Hey.' He went very still. 'I felt that.'

'Really?' She put her hand next to his. 'Oh. Wow, that was . . . yeah, definitely.'

'She's going for it, isn't she?'

'She can hear you.' Emily leaned forward to kiss her husband. 'How was work?'

'You don't want to know.' He stroked her cheek. 'You look hot.'

'It's this little furnace inside me.'

'That's what happens when you try to catch a star.' Grinning, he stroked her inner thigh. 'Think you're wearing far too many clothes.' He nudged her nightie up to her waist. 'I'm loving these pregnancy boobs. Just saying.'

'Enjoy them while they're still yours. But Jake . . .'

'Mmm?'

'You're wearing far too many clothes.'

'I can fix that.' Before she could blink, Jake was naked, and they were tangling beneath the bedcovers. Unprotected sex was still a treat after months of IVF and PGD. An unplanned pregnancy, they knew, could be disastrous.

Afterwards, Emily lay staring at the darkened ceiling, listening to Jake fall into sleep — and she remembered how they'd laid next to each other, right where they were now, almost twelve years before.

What are you going to do now?

I'll call the doctor. When it's light.

The mattress shifted beside her.

'You all right, Em?' Jake's body curled around hers, his warmth radiating into her.

'Thought you were asleep.'

'I think I was. But then I woke up and remembered I forgot to chase a chest X-ray.'

'Are you going to call the hospital?'

'Maybe. It was just a routine, guess it will be OK.' He pressed his mouth to her ear. 'Why aren't you asleep yet? Whetū still doing acrobatics?'

'No, I think she's asleep too.' Emily held her breath, listening. 'Is that your phone?'

'Probably the hospital. They should know I'm off duty now.' Jake climbed over her to get to his trousers, which were crumpled on the floor beside the bed. 'I'll put it in flight mode, shall — oh.'

'What?' Emily asked, just before she heard Jake say, 'Jonesy?' and then, 'Yeah, no worries, we were awake. Just.' He raised his eyebrows at Emily before wandering into the hallway, closing the door behind him.

'Everything OK?' Emily asked when Jake returned several minutes later.

Jake climbed in beside her. 'Yeah, Jonesy just has no sense of time. He wanted to know if we want to go in for a present for Auntie Ngaire's sixtieth.'

'Oh,' Emily said, relieved. 'What are they getting her?'

'Didn't ask, just said I'd be happy to put in fifty bucks. Is that OK?'

'Of course,' Emily said. Ngaire was her favourite in-law, although she had a soft spot for her father-in-law too, despite his and Jake's tenuous relationship. 'Have you turned your phone off now?'

'Yeah. Except . . .'

'Don't tell me you're still worrying about that chest X-ray.'

'Won't be long.' Jake slipped out of bed again. Emily groaned and closed her eyes.

———

Emily sank into a fold-out chair, cradling her lime and soda. 'Nice evening, isn't it?'

'Lovely.' Jake's father stubbed his cigarette out on the arm of the chair. 'Not a bad spot for a party, is it?'

'Not bad at all,' she agreed, glancing up at the fairy lights strung across the makeshift bar Jonesy had constructed in his garage. 'Several degrees warmer than Dunedin too.'

'It's always warm up here,' Ngaire piped up.

Emily peered around Willie. 'Oh, I didn't see you there.' She went to rise to her feet, but Ngaire waved at her to stay put.

'You should rest up,' Jake's aunt said, making her way over to Emily instead.

'I'm not *that* pregnant,' Emily protested, bending forward to give Ngaire a hug.

'When are you due, love?' Ngaire sat beside her.

'Tenth of January.'

'Awesome. Well, you're welcome to come and stay anytime. We love babies, don't we?' Ngaire looked up at her younger sister, who was wandering past holding a glass of bubbly.

Huia lit up. 'We'll look after your pēpi any time you want. Looking forward to your first mokopuna, Willie?'

'I can't wait,' Willie said, slopping beer onto the front of his t-shirt, which might have once been blue but was now a tired shade of grey. 'Babies love me, they do.'

'It's true.' Ngaire nudged Emily. 'As soon as he picks them up, they go quiet.'

'Because they're knocked out by your smell, bro,' Huia said, and Willie aimed a twisted smile-snarl in his sister's direction.

'Whatever works,' Emily said, glad when Ngaire changed the subject by saying, 'Thank you for my present. I don't think I'm going to get any work done now. I'll be outside swinging in that all day long.'

'I could do with one of those egg chairs,' Emily agreed, startled when Ngaire leapt to her feet.

'They're playing my song! Who's coming to dance with me?' Ngaire clapped her hands.

'I will.' Emily left Huia and Willie bickering about who-knew-what in the corner. Remembering that Tina Turner had been one of her father's favourite singers, Emily felt the usual pang of regret-guilt-nostalgia she experienced whenever she thought about her father. Perhaps he had only been trying to look out her.

But he was trying to sabotage my relationship with Jake. How could Dad not have known that would only drive a wedge between him and me?

Emily had destroyed the incriminating diary the day after she'd found it, ashes to ashes, smoke up Jim's own chimney. As for the insulin vial, there was no sign. Perhaps Jim had already disposed of it. Even if he hadn't, no one else would be the wiser if they'd found it, Emily was guessing.

'Hey.' Jake joined in, spinning her around the dance floor until the fairy lights were a blur. 'You look beautiful,' he said in her ear, once everyone had started singing along to 'The Joker'.

'I think I'm just at the *is she fat?* stage,' Emily replied, and Jake gave her a *I-don't-think-so* look before greeting another one of his many cousins. Emily danced for a few more songs, including 'Eagle Rock', which even got Willie up, although he disappeared outside as soon as it ended, presumably for a nicotine fix.

Emily decided she could do with some fresh air, which meant avoiding her father-in-law. She was wandering past the letterbox, inhaling the intoxicating scent of jasmine, when she heard someone say, 'Kia ora cuz-in-law.'

Hugging Jonesy was like how she imagined embracing the Big Friendly Giant from the Roald Dahl books, with an extra layer of padding. 'Kia ora,' she replied, wishing she'd had the energy to learn te reo with Jake this year. 'Thanks for organising the present.'

'Nah, that was Freda. She's good with present ideas. Can I get you a drink?'

'I'd love a glass of water,' Emily admitted. Being pregnant seemed to be synonymous with drinking and peeing. She gazed up at the starry sky. Perhaps she should pick one out, a star for Whetū, although Emily thought it unlikely she'd remember which one she'd decided to dedicate to her daughter. She gave it a go anyway, picking the star closest to Venus.

This one's for you Whetū, a star for a star. She'd point it out to Jake, later.

'Here you go.' Jonesy pressed a deliciously cold glass into her palm and clinked his beer bottle against the side. 'Cheers.'

'Cheers. Beautiful evening, isn't it?'

'Sure is.' He sipped on his beer. 'Tell me, what do you think I have to do to convince Jake to move back home?'

'Back home?' Emily rolled an ice cube across her tongue. 'Let me see. Good surf. And a bunch of patients with cancer.'

'Got plenty of both.'

'Also somewhere to live.'

'Lots of cheap accommodation up here.'

'Yeah,' Emily said, swallowing the rest of her water, 'but there's the small matter of my Arts degree. And Jake's got fellowship exams to sit.'

'Excuses, excuses.' Jonesy leaned forward. 'There's so much Jake could be doing for our people. You want a bunch of patients with cancer?'

'*I* don't want a bunch of patients with cancer,' Emily said, but Jonesy carried on as if he hadn't heard her.

'If you're Māori, you're more likely to get cancer, and you're more likely to die of that cancer than if your Pākehā neighbour gets diagnosed at the same time. Why do you think that is?'

'Well, that, for one thing,' Emily said, gesturing at a pair of teenage girls smoking by the fence.

'That's part of the reason, sure. But why do you think Māori don't respond as well to treatment?'

Emily bit her lip. 'I guess if someone presents later, they'll be diagnosed later. And . . .'

'And?'

'They might not get the full course of treatment.'

'Or they might not be *offered* the full course of treatment.'

Emily frowned. 'I don't think that happens.'

'Doesn't it?' Jonesy nodded at Jake, who was ambling towards them, holding a can of soft drink. 'What do you think, Jakey? Do you think your dad would have been offered the same treatment as Emily's dad if they both got cancer at the same time?'

Jake shrugged. 'I'd hope so.'

Jonesy's upper lip curled. 'Is that really what you think?'

'That's what I'd *like* to think.' Jake flipped the tab on his Coke. 'But I suspect it doesn't always happen for all sorts of reasons, some of which we're not even aware of.'

'Because why?' Emily asked. 'Are you saying the doctors are biased?'

Jake slipped his arm around her waist. 'Like I said, for reasons *we're not always aware of.* Bias isn't always a conscious thing.'

'There you go.' Jonesy let a hiss of air out of the side of his mouth. 'You want to make a difference, cuz, a real difference? Come up here.

You could make a difference every day of your life.'

'You should go into sales,' Jake said evenly. 'You'd be good at it.'

'But would you?' Emily asked, once Jonesy had wandered off to talk to an uncle.

Jake just gave her a vague smile. 'One thing at a time, huh?' He led her across the lawn. 'That spit roast is making my mouth water — shall we go and check it out?'

Chapter 42: Are We the Waiting

Jake flopped onto the couch in the junior doctors' lounge. 'Please tell me you're not watching *Love Actually*.'

'How can you not like this movie? I watch it every Christmas.' Sasha, his house surgeon, held out a plastic bag. 'Licorice Allsort?'

'Christmas has been and gone,' Jake said, taking two lollies. *Three days ago, to be exact.* 'Seriously, do you really find Hugh Grant attractive?'

Sasha drew a blanket up to her chin. 'God, no. But the whole movie's got that feel-good factor, you know?'

'Hmmph.' Jake, at four am, was not in the mood for schmaltzy movies. He started drifting off as soon as he closed his eyes, his brain already half-asleep.

Get all the sleep you can, other parents kept urging him. Impossible when he was rostered on for a week of nights. In two weeks he'd be a father. *That* thought was enough to temporarily stimulate his fatigued brain.

'Hey.' Sasha's voice sounded very loud. 'You're missing the best bit.'

'There is no best bit,' Jake said in a monotone.

'Such a Grinch.'

'Mmph.' Even Sasha's prattling wasn't enough to stop Jake hurtling into the sleep zone.

When his phone woke him, he realised he'd been having an elaborate dream involving Santa Claus and a little boy who bore an unfortunate resemblance to Hugh Grant. 'Jake Heremaia,' he mumbled into the receiver.

The nurse, who identified herself as Linda from ward whatever, gabbled, 'I've got a ninety-three-year-old patient called Mr Godfrey, do you know him?'

Jake suppressed a yawn. 'Nope.'

'He was admitted with an inferior MI earlier this evening. He's got a blood pressure of seventy-four systolic and oxygen saturations of eighty per cent on air. Can you come see him?'

'Be right up.'

Jake stood up and stretched. 'Want to come and see a ninety-three-year-old who's about to arrest?'

'What?' Sasha tore her gaze away from the TV.

'Well, unless you'd rather watch these two have sex.'

'They don't have sex,' Sasha said, as they walked out into the corridor, 'because her phone keeps ringing.'

'Fancy that,' Jake said.

Mr Godfrey truly did look as if he were about to arrest by the time they arrived on the ward; his eyes glazed, his blood pressure barely recordable. Jake listened to the man's crackly chest and pointed at his distended neck veins.

'He's in heart failure, lungs full of fluid,' he told Sasha before turning to the nurse. 'Let's give him eighty migs of IV frusemide, stat. Sasha, can you ring for a portable chest X-ray?'

Minutes later, Jake, Sasha and the nurse stood by the bedside, watching as the oxygen level and the blood pressure began to increase, and the patient's breathing began to slow.

'I think you just saved my life,' Godfrey gasped.

'Just a little hiccup,' Jake said, although he knew Godfrey was right.

'That was quick thinking,' Sasha said as they left the ward.

'Once you've seen a few heart failures, you know what to do.' Jake yawned. 'What do you think the chances of having a nap are?'

Sasha plucked a beeping pager off the waistband of her scrubs, contemplating it with distaste. 'Nil, I'd say. Look at this.' She showed him the message.

'*Mrs Wang is confused, please review,*' Jake read aloud.

'She's confused every night.' Sasha stomped down the corridor, mumbling beneath her breath.

'Me too,' Jake said and returned to the doctors' lounge. Three hours until eight am and the end of his week of night shifts, *yes.*

He'd just assumed a foetal position on the couch when his phone rang again.

'Chrissake,' he said, his irritation subsiding once he saw the caller ID. What could Emily want at this hour of the morning?

'Hey.' He licked his dry lips. 'How's it going?'

'My waters just broke.'

Jake sat bolt upright. 'What? Are you sure?'

'Well it was either that or a massive — ow!'

'OK, OK. I'll come home as soon as I can.' Jake phoned Sasha next. 'Hey, I've got to go,' he said, already halfway down the corridor.

'Go where?'

'I'm having a baby — can you call Grace if you need help?' He hoped Grace, the other medical registrar on call, wouldn't mind.

'Oh sure, good luck!'

'Thanks.' Jake exited into the darkness and began jogging towards his car. It was ten minutes past five.

Four hours later, or was it five — time seemed an abstract concept, something other people paid attention to — Jenny, the midwife, said, 'OK, we're still at five centimetres.'

'Is that normal?' Jake wished he'd paid more attention during his ob gyn rotation as an intern. Emily's cervix had been five centimetres dilated when they arrived, which basically meant there'd been no progress in the past several hours.

'It can be slow when you're a first-time mum, but I think it's time to start some Syntocinon to strengthen the contractions.'

Emily slumped against the pillows. 'You want to make these stronger?' Her face was flushed, her forehead moist.

'Usually we'd place an epidural before we do that, or it can be really painful.' Jenny glanced between Emily and Jake. 'That OK with you?'

Jake squeezed Emily's hand. 'Of course. What do you think, Em?'

'Whatever's best for the baby.' Emily winced and started sucking on the nitrous gas again.

Jake had never felt so useless.

'I'll call the anaesthetist.' The midwife left, her lime green trainers squeaking against the lino.

'I hope they're good at epidurals,' Emily said.

'They will be.' Jake hoped he wasn't making rash promises. For all he knew, the anaesthetist could be a newbie registrar. His anxiety was relieved when he heard a familiar voice in the corridor.

'Hey, Jake.' Tim Harrington, one of the anaesthetic fellows, pushed his thick-rimmed glasses up his nose. 'Heard you might be having a baby.' He extended his hand. 'You must be Emily.'

It wasn't long before Harrington had Emily bending over a table so he could insert a needle between her vertebrae. Jake decided not to watch. He didn't watch the midwife subsequently insert the urinary catheter either.

'Don't know why I didn't have the epidural earlier,' Emily said a few minutes later.

'Can you feel anything?' Jake asked.

'Just tightening when there's a contraction. Nothing like before.'

'You should go grab yourself something to eat,' Jenny said, and Jake realised the midwife was addressing him rather than Emily. 'Keep your strength up. Methinks it's going to be a while before this baby makes an appearance.'

'You go,' Emily said, so he did.

After ordering a double-shot latte and a panini, Jake walked outside, squinting into the mid-morning sun. If only he could lie horizontal for even half an hour. Perhaps he could steal away to the doctors' lounge.

No, he didn't dare. Once he fell asleep, he might not wake for hours. What kind of father missed the birth of his own baby?

He sat on a bench and devoured the panini before carrying his coffee inside to wait for the next lift. By the time the doors opened again, he'd consumed the rest of the coffee and was regretting not buying a second.

Still, as the midwife had said, plenty of time.

———

'Six centimetres dilated,' Jenny said three hours later, after yet another vaginal exam.

'Is that OK?' Jake was sitting in the armchair by the window, struggling to keep his eyes open. Gaps were beginning to appear in his consciousness, uncontrollable micro-sleeps.

'Sort of.' The midwife inspected the catheter bag. 'There's blood in your urine.'

'What does that mean?' Emily asked.

'It's usually a sign of obstructed labour.' Jenny stroked her chin. 'Sorry, hon, but I think you're heading for a C-section.'

Emily tipped her head back against the pillow. 'Whatever's safest for the baby,' she said. 'Right, Jay?'

'Absolutely.' Jake leaned forward to stroke her cheek. 'And you.'

Time seemed to pass quite fast after that. Twenty minutes later, perhaps less, Jake was sitting in a different chair, but in the operating theatre. A drape hung at the level of Emily's upper chest, shielding her abdomen from view, where the obstetric registrar was making the first incision.

'You all right?' Jake asked.

'I'm fine,' she said. 'Are you?'

'I'm great,' Jake said, his fatigue almost forgotten.

The registrar glanced over at them. 'Only a few minutes until you meet your baby,' she said. 'You'll feel some tugging, OK?'

'OK,' Emily said. And then, what felt like less than five minutes later, 'That does feel *really* weird,' just before the theatre nurse said, 'Welcome to the world, baby girl,' and there was a mewling cry and the registrar held the baby aloft, glistening and bloody and beautiful.

'Oh my God,' Emily said. 'Oh my God.' She was crying and smiling, and Jake was too, happiness and euphoria and relief flooding through him.

A healthy little girl. Our healthy little girl.

'You're amazing.' Jake kissed Emily on the forehead. 'You did it.'

'*We* did it,' she said, smiling back before they both gazed at their baby, their daughter.

We created that, he thought. *Wow, wow, wow.*

'You can hold her soon,' the nurse promised, before passing the baby over to the paediatric registrar. Jake followed the doctor to the cot in the corner, where, after a rapid check and Apgar score, he was allowed to hold his daughter at last, at last.

'Hello, little one,' he said, touching her button nose, stroking her damp, dark curls. Five fingers, five toes, so small, so perfect.

'We can put her on Mum's chest now, give her some skin-to-skin time,' the paediatric registrar suggested, and Jake heard Emily say, 'I don't feel very — I can't breathe,' and he turned and her skin was grey and clammy, just like when a patient was about to —

And he heard an alarm and the anaesthetist said *oh shit*, and Emily made a horrible gasping noise and Jake couldn't see her after that because suddenly there were more alarms and lots of people in the room and he was pushed aside and he heard *shock* and *hypoxic* and *bleeding* and all he could see was the bag of blood someone was squeezing to try and make it run as fast as it could in to Emily's veins. O negative, emergency blood, *what what what* —

And someone said, 'I'm sorry, we need you to wait out here.'

'But that's my wife.' Jake was in the theatre corridor, still holding the baby, their baby, and how had he got there, and what was going on, what the—

Then someone, the young woman, said, 'We'll update you as soon as we can.'

'But what's happening?' *And who the fuck are you?* They were alone, everyone else still inside the theatre.

'We don't know yet.' The woman spoke fast. 'It's possible she's had a PE.'

'A PE?'

He squinted. Her badge told him she was a house surgeon, told him her name too, a name he read and just as quickly forgot.

'Yeah, it's when the—'

'I *know* what it is.' A pulmonary embolism — a blood clot to the lungs. It could be life-threatening. It could be fatal. 'But why's she bleeding?'

'I don't know. Look, everything's just happened at once. It's probably best you take your little girl up to post-natal, OK?' The baby-faced doctor led him down the corridor and along to a brightly lit ward. 'Here,' she said, showing Jake into a single room with a freshly made bed, a cot beside it. 'Let the nurses know if you need anything. Would you like me to tuck her in?'

'Soon.' Jake sank into the chair beside the bed, holding the baby close.

'Have you got a name for her?'

'Um,' Jake said, his lips numb. 'Whetū.'

'That's pretty. We'll update you as soon as we can, OK?'

Jake nodded. The doctor left. Jake checked the time on his phone. Eight minutes past three, how could that be? He could have sworn it was closer to six pm. His skull felt tight, his tongue sandpaper-dry. There was a missed call from Emily's mother, an hour ago, and a text message: *Heard Emily was in labour, how exciting. Let me know when you have some news for me!* The message was accompanied by a smiley emoticon.

Ah God, what was he meant to say? Jake stared at Whetū, wondering if he was caught in a dream, his brain messed up by a week of night shift. He stroked the baby's tiny palm, felt her fingers curl around his pinkie. Her eyes opened, briefly, and he gazed into her blue-black irises, fighting the urge to cry.

Emily, Emily, are you OK?

An indeterminate time later he heard footsteps approaching and the low murmur of voices.

'Jake?' A rotund man with a greying surgical haircut, number one all over, entered the room.

'Yeah, hi.' Jake stood up, still cradling Whetū. The obstetric registrar was lurking behind the obstetrician, her expression unreadable.

'I'm Walter Chambers, obstetrician,' the man said, obviously not remembering Jake from his medical training. 'Have a seat.'

Jake held the baby closer. 'Is she OK?'

The obstetrician didn't nod. He didn't shake his head either.

'We tried as hard as we could,' Chambers said, and every word he said after that flew around Jake's skull like an out-of-control bird. *Shock, blood not clotting, uncontrollable haemorrhage, probable amniotic fluid embolism and in the end her heart . . .*

'Her heart,' Jake said, and the bird inside his brain began to batter against his skull, *no, no, this can't be true.* Whetū let out a small, sharp cry. He didn't move, just held her tighter, *no, no, no.*

'Her heart stopped,' Chambers said. 'We put out a cardiac arrest call. We tried.'

Tried, tried, tried.

But her heart, her heart, her heart.

And it was all a dream. A dream. It's all a dream.

Except it wasn't.

PART III

Chapter 43: Don't Dream It's Over

In the weeks after Emily's death (*she didn't pass*, Jake would say to anyone who dared to use that euphemism, she *died*), he wasn't sure he would cope. Probably wouldn't have, if he didn't have someone else to care for, someone who was completely and utterly dependent on him.

Don't get up tonight, Auntie Ngaire kept telling him. *I can feed her.* His aunt had come to stay as soon as she had heard the news. Three months later, and she was still there. *What else is a retired old lady meant to do?* Jake could think of plenty of other things he was sure she'd rather be doing.

Jake never let his aunt do the night shift, though. He couldn't sleep anyway, so what was the point of staying in bed? Usually he'd drift off while giving Whetū her bottle, and in those brief periods of sleep, he'd often dream that Emily was still alive. Sometimes, in those dreams, Emily would appear and tell him off for giving Whetū a bottle when she had breasts bursting with milk. Sometimes, in those dreams, he made love to her. Those were the best dreams, and the worst awakenings.

Q: How do you get over losing your double helix dragon?
A: You don't.

———

On the twenty-eight of March, three months since Emily had died (*no, she didn't pass, and I didn't pass either, because I failed her, over and over*), Jake gave Whetū a bottle and changed her nappy before tucking her into her pram. It was a Mountain Ranger, a brand Emily and he had chosen for its chunky wheels and easy collapsibility. The baby was asleep before they'd gone a block.

Jake took the same route he'd been using for the past several weeks — three blocks to St Clair Beach and along the promenade. The waves were close to perfect, glassy slabs with frothy peaks. He hadn't been for a surf in three months. Having fun seemed wrong, something he didn't deserve.

You'll destroy her.

You were right, Jim, but not in the way you thought. Are you happy now?

After ordering a takeaway coffee from a beachfront café, Jake powered up the hill, the sun hot on his neck. When he reached the top, he turned to gaze over the Pacific Ocean. The roar of the waves was barely audible. The horizon seemed very far away.

Whetū coughed and murmured, her eyes briefly opening. Her irises were dark, melting chocolate. She smiled at him, a burst of sunshine, and he smiled back. Jake began descending the hill and his daughter fell asleep again. He envied her.

At the completion of his circuit, he found Ngaire at the washing line, pegging out countless flannels, bibs and jumpsuits.

'Nice walk?' Ngaire asked, as she always did.

'Yep,' Jake said, as he always did. After parking the pram in the entranceway — Whetū slept well when she could hear the hum of the outside world — Jake went to check his e-mails on the laptop he kept on the dining room table. There were three from various online stores trying to push their wares, one from Dunedin Hospital asking when he thought he might return to work, and one from the lawyer.

More paperwork, he thought, unable to bring himself to open any of the messages. *More decisions.* He was so sick of trying to decide what to do; so sick of everything.

So, so tired.

Ngaire ambled in. 'Want a cuppa?'

'No thanks, I just had a coffee.'

'All right.' Ngaire flicked the kettle on and sat opposite him at the table, thumbing through the newspaper. 'Jakey, it's about time I went home.'

Jake pushed the laptop aside. 'Yeah, I know.' He couldn't expect Ngaire to stay forever. She had her own life up north.

'I've been talking to Huia, and she said she can come for a few weeks. Are you OK with that?'

'No.' Catching her surprised expression, Jake hastened to add, 'I mean, I don't think she needs to come. We're OK. We have to get used to it sometime.'

'What about when you return to work?'

'Well,' he said evenly, 'I'm not sure I *am* returning to work.'

'Really? I thought you loved your job.'

'I did. But it's too hard, with all the on call and unpredictable hours.' There was only so much help he could ask for from Lisa and Steve, who were both working too.

Also, every time he went anywhere near the hospital, his heart squeezed so hard he thought he'd pass out.

Her heart stopped. We put out a cardiac arrest call.

His aunt said, 'If you shifted up north, we could help out. You wouldn't have to worry about paying for day care or babysitters.'

'I know. But this is ours.' Thanks to Emily's life insurance. All he had to worry about was . . .

Everything, everything.

'You could rent it out.'

Jake massaged his forehead. 'Sure. I could.'

'Just think about it.' Ngaire moved into the kitchen. 'Are you sure you don't want a cup of tea?'

'I'm sure.' Hearing a hiccup from the entranceway, Jake said, 'Looks like the afternoon nap is over.'

'Let me get her,' Ngaire said before he could get up. 'Got to make the most of my cuddles before I go home.'

Returning to his e-mail, Jake saw a new message from Kylie.

> Hey Jake, just checking in to see how you are going. I've been thinking about you a lot. Ian and I were wondering if you'd like to bring Whetū over to the Gold Coast for a visit? You and Ian could hit the waves while I babysit. If you're free then we've both got a week off starting 17 April.

Call me if you want to talk — anytime. I can't promise I'll
know what to say, but I'm happy to listen (yeah, I do know
how to shut up sometimes, believe it or not). Anyway, I know
you'll be really flat-out looking after your little person so don't
feel like you need to write a long reply. If you don't feel up to
coming over then we understand.

Love K x.

Jake barely hesitated before typing his reply.

Hi Kylie

Thanks but I've never flown with a baby before . . . not sure I'd
cope with a three-hour flight.

Not to mention he should be saving his money. Not to mention he wasn't
sure how he'd cope with trying to act like he was OK around his friends
when he just wasn't. Not to mention . . .

'Ah, screw it,' he whispered and deleted the e-mail. He typed another
reply, hit send and booked return flights to the Gold Coast.

'Don't worry,' the elderly lady who'd had the misfortune of sitting next
to Jake said. 'You're much more distressed by her crying than anyone
else is.'

'I'm not so sure,' Jake mumbled, bouncing his daughter on his lap.
She just screamed even louder. The plane continued to rattle through the
clouds. *Jesus, could we just be on the fucking ground already?*

'It's her ears,' the lady said. 'Put your finger in her mouth.'

Ready to consider anything, Jake offered Whetū his pinkie. The baby sucked on it for a few seconds before spitting it out and resuming her attempt to break the sound barrier.

'Oh, there you go, that's better,' the woman said when Whetū threw up all over him just as the plane hit the tarmac. 'Must have been wind.'

Whetū let out a tiny belch and gave him a gappy grin.

'Yeah, good, I hate landing too,' Jake muttered, relieved to be on terra firma again.

'Have a nice holiday,' the woman cooed before beating a hasty retreat. After mopping up what must have been a whole bottle of semi-digested formula with his last baby-wipe, Jake strapped the baby to his front and got to his feet. He was busting for a pee. As for his daughter, she smelt really, really bad.

'Had a sore tummy, did you?' He asked once they'd exited the plane. The baby cooed, as if she hadn't been screaming for the past forty-five minutes.

Jake found a parents' room, where he peed with Whetū still strapped to his front, something he'd become accustomed to over the past couple of months, then changed her nappy.

'Stop looking so cute,' he said, and blew a raspberry on her tummy. Whetū giggled, so Jake did it again, forgetting for brief seconds about the gaping hole in the middle of his chest.

It's moments like that, he reflected as he exited the parents' room, *that stop me gassing myself.*

That thought was so real, so scary, that he had to take several deep breaths to control the rising, overwhelming panic he'd previously only experienced on a few occasions.

When we injected the insulin and Mum started having a seizure.

When we were coming in to land in Melbourne that time and the plane dropped God knows how many feet in a few seconds.

When they told me they'd lost her heart.

My heart, my heart.

Stop, stop, stop.

'You all right there, mate?' a passerby asked, and Jake realised he'd stopped walking completely and was standing with his palm on the wall, as if he were trying to stop himself flying off the face of the earth.

'Oh yeah, thanks,' Jake said, concentrating on putting one foot in front of the other again.

That was all he'd been doing for the last one hundred and seven days. Putting one foot in front of the other.

———

That evening, Ian treated them to his infamous Pad Thai and a selection of craft beer. They sat on Ian and Kylie's balcony in short sleeves, the April air still balmy.

'I know you don't drink much,' Ian said, clinking his bottle against Jake's. 'But I figured maybe you just hadn't found the right drop yet.'

'I still haven't forgiven you for my buck's night,' Jake said, trying to ignore the fresh jab in his gut at the memory of Emily tending to him the next morning. He glanced at Kylie, who was cuddling a sleeping Whetū. 'I can put her in the port-a-cot if you like.'

Kylie stroked the baby's crown. 'Are you kidding? I'm going to max out these baby cuddles as much as I can. Just relax and enjoy yourself.'

'Thought we could cruise up to Burleigh Heads tomorrow,' Ian said. 'There's a right point break with some mean barrels, guaranteed.'

'Sounds good.' Jake surveyed his surroundings, with the wide streets and palm trees, and the sliver of ocean visible between the apartment blocks to the right. 'This is a bit nicer than the box you had in Melbourne.'

Kylie picked up a fork. 'And only a few minutes' walk to a beach with some of the best surf in the world.'

'Paradise, yep.' Ian flipped the cap off another beer.

'Not sure why anyone would ever want to leave,' she continued.

'I didn't say *want* to.' Ian cleared his throat. 'I've had a job offer.'

Jake licked sauce off his thumb. 'Yeah? Where from?'

Ian tossed a bottle cap in the air and caught it. 'Switzerland.'

'Switzerland?' Jake squinted at Kylie. 'You're going to work in Switzerland?'

'*I'm* not.' Kylie shovelled another fork of noodles into her mouth. 'Considering I haven't even finished my ob gyn training yet, or even have a licence to practise in Europe.'

Ian gulped on his beer. 'We're just thinking about it.'

'*You're* thinking about it,' Kylie muttered. Whetū began to fuss and Kylie stood up, jiggling her. 'What's wrong, sweetheart, are you hungry?'

'Always. I'll go and make up a bottle.' Jake took off into the kitchen, glad of a chance to escape the impending argument, if that was what it was. He was testing the temperature of the formula on his wrist when Kylie hurried inside.

'OK, so she's really not happy now — oh. Cool.' She looked down at the baby, now sucking contentedly on the bottle. 'Thanks, Super Dad.'

'I can take her. You should eat your dinner.'

'I can cope with interrupted dinners for a week. Go on, have a beer, relax. I'll feed her, change her and put her to bed. Easy.' Kylie spirited the baby away, humming beneath her breath.

'Wow, how did it get so dark all of a sudden?' Jake asked, joining Ian on the balcony once more.

Ian pushed his plate aside. 'No dusk here, mate. Sun drops just like that. And then light again around six am.'

'Perfect for surfing.'

'Perfect,' Ian echoed and they fell silent for a moment.

Jake reached for his beer. 'So are you going to take this job in Switzerland?'

'I don't know.' Ian rolled his bottom lip between his teeth. 'Want to go for a walk?'

'Yeah, I dunno . . .'

'Don't worry about Kylie. She's in her element.' Ian moved inside and peered into the spare room. 'We're going for a wander, is that OK?'

'Sure, take your time,' Kylie called out.

Jake peered over Ian's shoulder. Kylie was sitting on the bed, cradling Whetū while the baby drank her bottle, her tiny eyes fixed on Kylie's face.

'Just ring me if she gives you trouble,' Jake said. 'We won't be long.'

'We'll be *fine.*'

Ian steered him out of the front door. 'Don't worry — what could possibly go wrong?'

Everything, Jake thought. But he accompanied Ian down the stairs and onto the street, strolling past Broad Beach's brightly lit sidewalk cafés and restaurants and apartment buildings, through the throngs of tourists chatting and laughing and eating and drinking and having fun.

Fun. I used to have fun, once upon a time.

And now . . . now he felt like a robot going through the motions.

The skyscrapers were clustered right on the beachfront, just as he'd seen in the photos. Hard to believe he was here at last. Jake kicked off his shoes. Why had he and Emily never come here? *Too busy thinking about having babies, that's why.* Blinking to clear his vision, he scuffed his feet through the sand, still warm from the twenty-eight-degree day.

Ian flicked a shell into the waves. 'This is like Dunedin on steroids, don't you reckon?'

'This is the complete opposite of Dunedin.'

'Apart from the surf and sand.' Ian stepped sideways to let a jogger go past.

'And the fact it's about fifteen degrees warmer.'

'You say that like it's a bad thing.'

'Not at all.' Jake waded into the sea. 'Whoa, this is like bathwater.'

'Yeah, no kidding. Want to go for a dip?'

Jake didn't answer. He was already dumping his t-shirt and shorts in the sand, and running at the waves.

———

Several minutes later, Jake sat on the tide line, catching his breath.

'What do you think?' Ian asked.

'That was great.' Jake blew salty water out of his nostrils, wiped his palm on his shirt. For a short time, he hadn't thought about anything other than the rhythm of the waves coming towards him and the sheer force of the water battering his body.

And it was really only for the briefest of moments that he'd thought about letting the ocean into his lungs, wasn't it?

Because who would look after Whetū then?

Plenty of people.

She needs you.

But what if the HD rears its ugly mug? What then?

Ian's voice broke into his thoughts. 'Should have brought our boards down.'

'Do you think the sharks come out at night?'

'Since when did you care about that?'

'I don't know,' Jake mumbled, the melancholy returning with full force. Used to be Emily who was scared of the sea, not him. Now he was scared of everything. 'If you like it so much here, why are you thinking of leaving?'

Ian groaned and flopped backwards. 'I love it here. But this is the job opportunity of a lifetime, you know?'

'Sounds like Kylie's not going to go with you though.'

'Sounds like.' Ian sighed. 'She wouldn't be able to work over there. Not that she'd have to, because they're going to pay me pretty generously. But she's not prepared to give up her career, which is fair enough. And . . .'

Jake waited. Ian said, 'Sometimes you need something like this to make you re-examine your priorities. You know?' He coughed. 'I mean, of course you do. I just think Kylie and I are going in different directions.'

'So you're going to break up?'

'I think so.'

'Right.' Unbelievable, but what else was he meant to say? *This year just gets better and better? Life shits on you and then you die?*

'I'm sorry, man.' Ian sat up again, showering sand over him. 'I don't want you to feel stuck in the middle or anything. It's just that Kylie and I have outgrown each other.'

'Hey, it's your decision.' Jake stared at the waves, driving relentlessly into shore. 'But, fuck.'

Ian got to his feet. 'Yeah, I know. Let's go home and get drunk, shall we?'

And Jake couldn't think of a reason why he shouldn't, so he said, 'Yeah, let's.'

Chapter 44: Let Down

DUNEDIN, JULY 2017

Jake showed the medical student into the doctors' room and waved at a chair. 'OK, doc, can you present your findings?' He waited for Tilly Anderson to sit down before sitting opposite her.

Tilly took a deep breath. 'Mr McCarthy is a forty-nine-year-old man who presents with a four-week history of back pain, and a three-month history of a dry cough. He has a past history of hypertension and diabetes.'

Jake gave her an encouraging nod. Tilly carried on, telling him all about her patient's medications and social history, right down to the fact that McCarthy had five daughters.

Five daughters? It was hard enough work looking after one.

Jake wondered what his daughter was doing right now. Probably having a nap since it was just after lunch. He gazed out of the window. Another grey day, pretty standard for July. It couldn't be much warmer than eight degrees outside.

'The blood test showed a normocytic anaemia, with a high calcium.' Tilly faltered, obviously sensing Jake's attention was wandering.

'Go on,' Jake said, focusing on her. With her wavy blonde hair and creamy skin, she bore a disconcerting resemblance to Emily at that age.

At that age? You're thirty-one, not eighty-one.

I feel eighty-one.

Jake crossed his legs. 'Great. What further investigations would you like?'

'Um, X-rays of the chest and back?'

'Good.' He swung towards the computer and brought up the patient's X-rays. 'What do you see here?'

Tilly squinted at the screen. 'This is a chest X-ray performed on Scott McCarthy on the sixth of July 2017, two days ago.' She bent forward. 'There appears to be a rounded opacity in the left upper lobe.'

'There *is* a rounded opacity in the left upper lobe. Have some confidence in yourself.'

'There is a rounded opacity in the left upper lobe.' She frowned. 'There's also something wrong with those ribs. I mean, there's a lesion in the fourth rib.' She glanced at him. 'I'd like to order a CT scan of the chest.'

'You got it.' Jake had just brought up the CT scan when his phone began to ring. 'Sorry, hang on. Hello?'

'Hi, is that Jake Heremaia?'

'It is.' He passed the mouse to Tilly. 'How can I help?'

'It's Nadia from Puffin Childcare here. Just calling to let you know that Whetū's got a fever of thirty-seven point nine degrees and a runny nose. She's looking pretty miserable.'

'Oh. Right. Do you want me to pick her up?'

'I think that would be a good idea. When do you think you'll be here?'

'Um . . .' *Shit, shit, shit.* 'Can I call you back in a sec? I've got to sort something out at work first.'

'Sure, talk soon,' Nadia chirped.

Jake ended the call, his mind even more scattered than it had been before. 'Go on,' he said to the medical student.

'Um, there's a spiculated mass in the left upper lobe measuring three centimetres. And multiple lesions in the vertebrae and ribs, consistent with lung cancer that has spread to the bones.' She peered closer. 'There also appear to be lesions in the liver.'

'Excellent. What would you like to do now?' His mind raced on. Perhaps Emily's mother would be free since it was the school holidays?

'I'd like to get a biopsy of the mass in the lung.'

'And?'

'Give the patient some treatment for their high calcium?'

'Definitely. And?'

Tilly hesitated. 'Refer to Oncology?'

'Well yes, once you have a biopsy result to prove it's cancer. But what are you going to tell the patient?'

'I guess I'd need to wait for the biopsy.'

'Sure, but don't you want to give them some warning?' Jake glanced at his watch. Nineteen minutes past one, eleven minutes to sort out Whetū and/or his clinic, crap.

'I guess . . .'

Jake stuffed his phone into his pocket. 'What are the chances this isn't cancer? Practically zero. So you need to warn the patient that there's a high chance this could be cancer, and if it is, then it's not curable.'

'Oh. OK.'

'No one likes giving bad news.' He stood up. 'But you need to be honest with the patient and tell them as much as they want to hear.' He smiled. 'You did really well, Tilly. I'll catch you on the ward round tomorrow.'

Jake waited until he'd exited the ward before ringing Lisa. The phone rang and rang before going to answerphone. *Double shit.* He left a hasty message and jogged down to clinic. The waiting room was jammed with patients already. Jake negotiated the obstacle course of walking frames and wheelchairs and ventured into the consultant's clinic room.

'Hi, Linda.'

'Hi, Jake,' the physician said, still typing. 'Looks like we've got a big list today.'

'Sure does.' Jake checked his phone. No messages or missed calls from Emily's mother. Bracing himself, he said, 'My daughter's sick. I have to go and pick her up from day care.'

Linda Davis swung around. 'Now?'

'Yeah. I'm really sorry. I can call around, see if I can find someone else to help out.'

'That would be *great*,' Davis said. 'Holy hell, my day just gets better and better.'

'Really sorry,' Jake repeated.

'It's fine.' Clearly it wasn't. 'And yes, if you can find another registrar for me, I would be very grateful. See you tomorrow, maybe.'

After twisting a fellow registrar's arm with a promise to return the favour — God knew when — Jake powered out of the hospital and to his car. He was driving down the one-way system when he noticed his warrant of fitness had expired two weeks ago. Damn it, there just wasn't enough time to do everything, not to mention trying to study for his fellowship exams.

He heard Whetū as soon as he walked into the day-care centre, crying the way she did when something was hurting.

'Hey, squirrel, what's wrong?' He scooped the nineteen-month-old up, noting her cheeks were flushed, her nose streaming. An ear infection, maybe?

'Daddy, Daddy.' His daughter snuggled into his shoulder, smearing snot all over his shirt.

Nadia passed him the baby bag. 'She's been inconsolable since lunchtime,' she said, her double chins wobbling.

'She feels really hot,' Jake said, all thoughts of work forgotten.

'We gave her some paracetamol at half-past twelve. Maybe you need to take her to see the doctor.' Nadia squirted alcohol wash on her palms. 'Oh wait, you are a doctor.'

'Not so much for little kids.' Jake slung the bag over his shoulder. 'Come on, squirrel, let's get you home.'

Once home, he stripped Whetū off and sat her in the bath, where she perked up for a while, splashing at the soapsuds with an intent expression.

'What can you see in there?' Jake asked, washing her soft curls with a flannel. 'Your reflection?' *The future? What does the future hold for you? Not HD, that's for sure.* He and Emily had made sure of that with a pre-selected embryo. *No manky HD genes for you, little star.*

'Daddy, up.' Whetū reached out to him. Jake picked her up and wrapped her in a towel, humming a tune he remembered his mother singing to him when he was little.

Hush little baby, don't you cry . . .

And he swore, then, that he would never ask Whetū to do for him what his mother had asked Jake to do for her.

I promise, I promise.

His phone rang seconds after he'd rocked Whetū to sleep, dozy with paracetamol and whatever virus was assailing her. Jake trudged into the kitchen, the phone to his ear.

'Hi, Lisa.'

'Jake, I'm so sorry I missed your call. Is Whetū OK?'

'She's OK, just a cold.' He checked the clock above the stove. Eight pm, way too late to think about making a proper dinner. Baked beans on toast again, then.

'Sorry I couldn't help out. We went to Ōamaru for the day. I can look after Whetū tomorrow if she's not up to going to day care, though.'

Jake leaned against the bench. 'Thanks, I'll let you know first thing in the morning.'

'No problem. I'll need you to pick her up by four o'clock, so I can make it to my yoga session.'

'Four, sure. Thanks.' He'd have to leave work at half-past three, half an hour before he was meant to finish. God forbid Lisa should miss her yoga, he thought, then felt guilty. It wasn't as if he could expect Emily's mother to drop everything to look after Whetū every time he needed it. He'd have to ask one of the other registrars to cover for him.

Sorry I need to leave early again. Frustration gnawed at him. He seemed to spend his whole life saying sorry to people. *Sorry I can't make it to your party, I can't get a babysitter. Sorry I can't come to work, my daughter's sick. Sorry I have to leave work at five fifteen on the dot so I can get to day care before it closes. Sorry sorry sorry.*

'That's fine. Let me know if you need me to take her to the doctor.'

'Thanks.' He took a can-opener out of the drawer. 'I'll call you first thing tomorrow.' After heating the beans, he poured them onto two slices of buttered toast. He was shovelling the first forkful into his mouth when he heard a hiccupping cry from above, then a wail. He waited. The wailing ramped up several decibels.

'Coming,' he muttered to no one in particular, and left his dinner to congeal on the table.

———

The following afternoon, Jake's house surgeon hurried into the doctors' room to tell him that Mrs Chen was passing blood from her rectum.

'How much blood?' Jake checked the time on his computer. Three pm. Shit, he needed to leave in exactly five minutes, ten at the most.

'Lots,' Karl said. 'She's passing clots and everything.'

Groaning inwardly, Jake got to his feet and strode down the corridor. 'Have you put a large-bore IV in?'

Jogging to catch up, Karl said, 'I tried, but she's got tiny little veins, and I can't even find those. Her blood pressure's dropped to eighty-five systolic.'

'Fantastic.' Jake smelt the blood as soon as he walked into the four-bedded room. The elderly woman was perched on a commode in a bed space by the window, propped up by a pair of nurses.

'How much blood do you think she's lost?' Jake asked, tightening a tourniquet above Mrs Chen's elbow and slapping the skin to raise a vein.

'Possibly five hundred mils,' the elder nurse said. 'I've called for some urgent units.'

'Good.' Karl was right, no veins. Mrs Chen slumped forward. 'Let's get her onto the bed,' Jake ordered. They took a limb each and heaved her onto the mattress before tilting the bed head-down. Jake slipped on a pair of gloves and pressed on the thready pulse in the woman's groin.

'Right,' he said to the house surgeon. 'I'm going to show you how to put in a femoral line.'

———

Once Mrs Chen had been rushed off for an urgent colonoscopy and he had washed the blood off his shoes, Jake ran two blocks to his car. Four o'clock already, wonderful. After firing off a text to Lisa — *Running late, sorry, leaving now* — he sped down the one-way system.

Twelve minutes later, Jake yanked on the brake and jumped out of his car.

'Sorry,' he said when he saw the front door open. 'There was a last-minute emergency.' Lisa was wearing leggings and blue sneakers, her hair in a ponytail. If he looked at her out of the corner of his eye, she almost looked like Emily.

Stop it, stop it.

'Never mind, I can go to the Friday session.' Lisa gave him a thin-lipped smile. 'Whetū's still asleep anyway.'

'Is she all right?'

'Yes, just tired, I think.'

'Thanks. I'd better get her out of your hair. I'm really sorry.'

'Ah well,' she said, closing the door behind him, 'it's not as if the patients know when your shift finishes, I guess.'

'No.' He walked into the kitchen. 'Where's Charlotte?' He had a soft spot for the twelve-year-old, who usually ran out to meet him.

'Steve's picking her up from her drama holiday programme at five.'

'Sounds like fun.' Jake plucked a baby bottle off the bench. 'Are you still OK to look after Whetū this weekend?'

Lisa frowned. 'This weekend?'

'Yeah, I'm on call, remember?' Clearly she *didn't*, or she wouldn't be looking at him like that.

'No, I — are you sure? I thought it was the weekend after.' She picked up her phone, presumably to scroll through her text messages. 'God, I'm so sorry. It's just that we've booked flights to Nelson.' Lisa looked up. 'Can you swap?'

Jake shook his head. *No, no, I can't, are you kidding? That's two days away. Everyone already thinks I'm super-unreliable. I might as well quit now. Jesus, I can't rely on anyone, on anything.*

'Never mind,' he said. 'I'll ask someone else.' He crossed his arms. 'I'll go and get Whetū, shall I?'

'You can let her sleep for a bit longer. Do you want a cup of tea?'

'No, if I don't get her up now then she'll never want to sleep tonight.'

Lisa stared at him. 'Are you saying I should have got her up sooner?'

'No, I'm not.'

'Really? I could have sworn that's what you were implying.'

'Well, that's not what I was saying.' Jake picked up the baby bag. 'I don't know why I thought I could go back to being a doctor anyway. It was always going to be impossible.'

'Jake, we're trying our hardest.'

Jake spun around. 'Are you? Could you not have written that weekend up on a calendar or something? Do you know what it means to do a shift with a doctor down? If I can't get a babysitter, then I'll have to call in sick and there's a good chance they won't be able to replace me. Do you know what that means for the patients?'

'Don't take that tone with me.' Lisa was shaking. He'd never seen her so angry. *Stop, stop, you need her more than she needs you.*

'I'm trying not to lean on you too much, but this is your granddaughter. She'll never know her mother and I'm just trying to make a life for us.'

Lisa clenched her fists. 'You think this is any easier for me? You're not the only one who lost someone. I lost my daughter, and I miss her every hour of every day. And I wake up all the time worrying about Whetū, about what would happen if you end up going the same way as — as —'

'As my mother?'

'Yes, as your mother.' She sank onto a bar stool. 'God, Jake, I didn't want to bring this up but I feel I have to. I need to make sure you've made a plan for Whetū, in case something happens to you.'

'In case I get HD, you mean?'

'I'm sorry to have to bring this up,' she repeated. 'But have you made a will?'

'I've made a start.' *In my head.* 'I will do it. Soon. I just need to sort out who would take Whetū if I can't look after her.'

'We'd be happy to, obviously.' Lisa's voice steadied. 'Although we're hardly getting younger, so if there's anyone else in your family or circle of friends you might think would be more suitable, then we wouldn't be upset if you chose them.'

'Sure. I'll get onto it.' If only Ian and Kylie hadn't broken up. *If only, if only.* 'And my advance directive too.'

'I'm speaking about hypothetical situations, Jake. I hope we never have to think about it.' She hesitated. 'But . . . what would you want, if you ended up with HD?'

Jake shrugged. 'I wouldn't want anything that would prolong my life if I were in the advanced stages. I don't want to end up like Mum did.'

'Of course you don't. I appreciate how hard that must have been on you.' Lisa hesitated. 'Jake,' she said, 'I think you know what I'm going to say, don't you?'

Jake swallowed. 'No,' he said. 'I don't.'

Lisa leaned forward, her tone softer now. 'I know what you and Emily did for your mother.'

'What do you mean, *did*?' Jake's heart began to thud. 'I did everything within my power for her.'

I promise, I promise.

'And you succeeded,' she said. 'Didn't you?'

'I don't know what you mean.'

Lisa looked at him, wordless, then stood up and left the room. *What the—?* Half a minute later, she reappeared and pressed an envelope into his palm.

'I found this when we were cleaning out Jim's wardrobe,' she said.

'Found what?' Jake asked, but he already knew, even before he'd tipped the empty insulin vial into his palm. He stared at it, his mouth dry.

'I know what you did,' Lisa said. 'You and Emily. It's a miracle you weren't caught. I guess, in a way, you were but I pleaded with Jim to keep silent.' Her eyes shimmered. 'For both of you.'

Jake opened his mouth, then closed it again. 'How long have you known?' He managed, his heart still firing rapidly.

'I've always known,' she said, and in the distance, he heard a faint cry, Whetū calling out for him. Lisa looked away. 'Go see your daughter, Jake. She needs you.'

Chapter 45: Broken Wings

20 September 2018

Hi Jake

How's it going over there? Bet you're finding it quite a change
of climate in Northland! I'm about to book flights across
the ditch for Christmas and was wondering if you could
accommodate a visitor for a few days? Would love to catch
up — it's been too long! How's Whetū? She must be nearly
three years old. Wow, time flies.

Anyway, let me know and no problem if it doesn't suit.

Kylie x

21 September 2018

Hey Kylie

I'd love to see you. Have 25 December until 5 Jan off so any
time then is cool — not doing much, apart from swimming and
surfing and running around after Whetū. She'd love to see her
godmother. Let me know when you're coming and I'll put you
on my calendar (because I have such a busy social life, ha ha).

Talk soon,

Jake

Hi Jake
Awesome. I've booked to fly into Whangārei on 30 Dec, will
forward my flight details. Can't wait!
K x

————————

Jake watched Kylie survey the lounge of the three-bedroom bungalow
he shared with Whetū.

'This is awesome, Jake.' She took a book off the shelf behind the door.
'How's this going?'

Jake shrugged. 'Not bad. It's kind of niche, I guess. We get a couple
of hundred dollars in royalties every six months.'

'I always loved how it ended.' Kylie flipped to the last page. A werewolf
surfer was tucked deep within the barrel of a mountainous wave. In the
night sky above him, a fiery double helix dragon emblem shone crimson
in the glow of the twin Blood Moons. The surfer's arms were spread wide,
his chest bared. *'Yaris faces the double helix dragon, once and for all,'* she read
from the curlicue text on the bottom of the page.

'And he says I am not afraid,' Jake murmured.

'It's a great last line.' She set the book down and wandered onto the
front porch. It was a year since he'd seen Kylie last, just before he'd left
Dunedin. Her fiery hair was shorter, swinging just below her ears, but her
clothes were as bright as ever. 'And the beach is what, five minutes away?'

'Yep. Half an hour's drive to work, but it's worth it. And Auntie
Ngaire's just down the road.'

Whetū tugged on the hem of Kylie's daffodil-yellow dress. 'Do you
want to play with my teddies?'

Kylie crouched beside her. 'I'd love to. What are their names?'

'Teddy.' Whetū gave her a thoughtful look. 'And Ted.'

'Great. What do teddies like to do?'

'They like swimming!' Whetū ran off, her pigtails bouncing.

'Oh my God, she's adorable. Are you all right out here by yourself?'

'I'm used to it. I'll come rescue you in ten minutes, OK?'

He packed a bag for the beach, listening to the chatter from his daughter's bedroom.

'My daddy's a doctor,' Whetū was saying. 'He gives people pills and makes them better again.'

'Oh, well I'm a doctor too.'

'Do you give people pills?'

'Yes. And I help babies to be born.'

Jake went to get some towels from the hall cupboard, but hesitated when he heard his daughter say, 'My mummy died-ed when I was born. So I don't have a mummy.'

'But you have a lovely photo of her right here, don't you? And she will always be your mummy.'

There was a clink, presumably from the cups and saucers that made up Whetū's tea set. 'Do you have a mummy?'

'Yes, I do. Everyone has a mummy.'

Jake cleared his throat and entered the bedroom. 'Who's ready for the beach?' Whetū and Kylie were sitting cross-legged on the floor, two teddies and a tea set between them.

'Me!' Whetū leapt up. 'Do you like the beach, Auntie Kylie?'

Kylie stood up, straightening the strap on her sundress. 'I *love* the beach. I'll go and put my togs on, shall I?'

'Stay here, squirrel.' Jake caught the small girl before she could run after Kylie. 'I need to put your togs and sunblock on.'

'I can do it.' Kylie winked at Whetū. 'We girls can get ready together.'

Whetū jumped up and down. 'Yay yay yay!'

Jake loitered in her bedroom for a short time after they'd left, staring at the photo on the dressing table. Emily was sitting on the sea wall at St Clair, her blonde locks swirling around her face, her hands curved over her pregnant belly. It had been cold that day, but Emily told him she had a little generator to keep her warm. She'd been twenty-eight weeks pregnant.

And ten weeks later, she was dead.

He turned away from the photo, away from Emily's trusting smile. Yesterday had marked three years since the worst day of his life. Time was no healer. He still missed her — every morning when he woke up, every night when he went to bed.

Alone.

———

At the beach, Jake dug a hole for Whetū to sit in with her bucket and spade before joining Kylie on the picnic blanket.

'So, how's Sydney treating you?' Jake took a strawberry out of the punnet between them.

'Sydney's fine. It's been a good place for training. And it's pretty easy to jump on a plane if I'm getting homesick.' Kylie squirted a stripe of sunblock down her leg. 'There's no way I could afford a view like this one.'

Jake slid his sunglasses over his nose. 'Me neither.' The waves were perfect today, forming cracking barrels he vowed not to let his daughter anywhere near until she was at least ten years old.

'Yet. How long until you get your fellowship?'

Jake took Whetū's hat out of the beach bag. 'Two years. Would have been one if I'd passed my exams the first time around.'

'It's amazing you passed them at all, considering. I guess there's no hurry.'

'No hurry at all. S'cuse me.' Jake went to put the hat on Whetū. Seconds after he sat down again, she threw it off.

Kylie laughed. 'That's what sunblock's for, right?'

'Yep,' Jake said resignedly.

'Have you heard from Ian?'

'Just what I see on Facebook. Looks like he's really getting into the skiing in Switzerland.'

She snorted. 'A replacement for surfing, I guess.'

'How about you, have you been in touch?'

'Not really. What's the point?' Kylie smeared more sunblock on her shoulder. 'Eight and half years together, and for what?' She glanced up. 'Well, you know.'

'I know.' Jake had become used to the awkward moments in conversation. 'Do you want me to do your back?'

'Yes, please.' Kylie swivelled around. She was wearing a two-piece swimsuit, lime green with white flowers. 'We've come a long way since Prof stood up in front of us and pretended to be a uterus. Remember that?'

'I am a uterus,' Jake intoned, squeezing sunblock into his palm.

'And these are my ovaries,' Kylie chorused with him, and let out a whooping laugh.

Smiling, Jake began to massage the lotion into her skin, sun-warm and covered with freckles. 'Didn't you get thrown out of class that day? For pretending to be a rectum?' She smelt like jasmine. A new perfume, perhaps, or maybe it was just he'd never noticed it before.

'Oh, yeah. That was classic.' She wriggled. 'Mmm, you've got good hands.'

'So they tell me,' Jake said, and there was another awkward silence. He hurriedly finished rubbing in the sunblock. 'You all right if I go for a surf?'

'Of course,' Kylie said, and he guessed she was hot, because her cheeks were flushed.

'Or you can go for a swim first, if you like?'

'No, you go for it,' she said. 'I'll play with Whetū.'

He was strapping his board to his ankle when his phone chimed, a message from Ngaire. *Does Whetū want a sleepover tomorrow night? Figured you might want to see New Year's Eve in adult style with Kylie.*

That would be great, he replied and went to face the waves.

———

Jake flicked his beer bottle. 'Can't remember the last time I saw New Year's in.' Apart from when he was on call at the hospital, which didn't count.

'Listen to you, an old man at thirty-three.' Kylie set her glass of wine down on the table between them and stood up to do a little twirl. 'I'll keep you awake until midnight, don't worry.'

'It's only half-nine,' Jake said, amused at the sideways glances from the diners at the table behind them. They probably thought she was drunk, but she was just being Kylie. Thank God some things never changed.

Kylie plopped back down. 'We can go for a walk on the beach.'

'A walk, sure.' He patted his stomach. 'Might be good to burn some of this off.'

'Because you're so fat, Heremaia. I could give you some if you want.'

'Come on, you're not fat.' *Just curvy.* And why was he noticing that now? Why?

'Hmm, I've put on two kilos since I broke up with Simon.'

'Simon? Who's Simon?'

'The surgeon I went out with a few months ago. It only lasted four weeks, hardly worth mentioning really.' She shrugged. 'The sex was good, though.'

Jake rolled his eyes at her. 'Sex, what's that?'

'Well, I hope you're not going to spend the rest of your life being a monk.'

'Ah, I don't know. I'm trying not to make life too complicated at the moment.' He drained his beer. 'Here, I'll get the bill.'

'But I was going to shout *you.*'

'Too late, I got in first,' he said and they argued all the way to the counter. Once Kylie had forced him to accept her counter-offer, they exited the restaurant.

'God,' Kylie said, glancing up the street, which sported a takeaway pizza joint and a dairy. 'Has there been an apocalypse or something?'

'If you're referring to the lack of people, I would say they've taken off to Whangārei to party. Fine with me.' He started towards the beach and Kylie fell in beside him.

'Have Emily's parents, I mean Lisa and Steve, been to visit?'

'Yeah, they came up in July.' His heart still missed a beat every time he heard Lisa's name. And yet, she'd never brought up their conversation again. His secret, it seemed, was safe.

'Actually,' he said when they stopped to take their shoes off, 'I meant to ask you something.'

Kylie skipped onto the sand. 'What's that?'

'I was going to ask you to be the executor of my will.'

'Whoa, is there something you're not telling me?' She grabbed his elbow. 'You're not . . .'

351

'No, relax, I'm fine. But that's exactly why I need to plan ahead, while I've still got a brain.'

'I don't know anything about executing wills.'

'You don't need to. I just need to choose someone who'd act in my best interests — someone who's not at least twenty years older than me.'

'OK, sure, if you think I'm the best person for the job.' They passed a group of teenagers, who were weaving and waving RTDs around. 'I'd be honoured.'

'And . . .' He glanced at her. 'I also need someone to be my EPOA.'

'Your enduring power of attorney?' She kicked her feet through the water. 'Sure. You need me to sign some documents, then?'

'Yeah. I'll sort it out soon, let you know.' He gazed up at the sky, his eyes automatically settling on the four stars that made up the Southern Cross. 'How many hours until midnight?'

'Ninety minutes, give or take. Come on, old man, let's go for a swim.'

Jake eyed the waves. 'A swim, OK.' Why not? For the first time in ages, he felt as if he could take a deep breath. 'You're not going to swim in your dress, are you?'

'Are you kidding? I don't have a death wish.' Before he could blink, Kylie had pulled her dress off and was running at the waves. Grinning, Jake stripped down to his boxers and did the same.

The first wave hit him chest-high, spun him around. He was ready for the next one, body-surfed it all the way into the shallows. When he stood up, he saw Kylie emerging beside him.

'Not bad for a Southern chick,' he teased.

She flicked water at him. 'You're a Southern man too, like it or not.'

It was true. He had spent most of his life in Dunedin. And yet over the past year he'd begun to feel as if he'd come home, at last.

Jake dived into the surf again, too buzzed by the hiss and roar of the waves to feel cold. After catching another wave in, he looked around for Kylie and spotted her diving beneath a white cap. Jake glimpsed her bob up, just before a much larger wave loomed behind her . . .

Shit. Jake swam in the direction he'd last seen her, diving beneath another looming white cap and *there* she was, her chin barely visible above the foam. Hooking an arm across her chest, he swam towards the shore, not letting her go even once they were standing in the shallows.

'You all right?'

'Of course,' she said, but she was shaking. 'Didn't realise how powerful the undertow was.'

'Me neither,' Jake said, transferring his hold to around her waist. He guided her into the soft sand and sat her down. 'Did you swallow any water?'

'No, really, I was fine,' she said.

'You're shaking.'

'I'm just cold.'

'If you say so.' Jake wrapped his arms around her. 'Think I should take you home for a shower,' he said, but wasn't too unhappy when she said, 'No, let's just stay here for a while,' her chin on his wrist. So he held her, breathing in the ocean scent of her hair, and she didn't stop him when he pressed his lips to her ear, let out a little squeak when he moved his mouth to the angle of her jaw.

'Jake.'

'Yeah?' His breathing was ragged, his heart all over the place. Kylie turned, cupped his face. And oh God, her skin was cool but the inside of her mouth was hot, and it had been so long, so long, that he let out a groan—

And when, after a couple of minutes where they kissed like teenagers, Kylie whispered, 'Shall we take this somewhere less sandy?' Jake said, 'Yes, let's.'

———

On the third of January, Jake drove Kylie to the airport. The sky was dark, even though it was only two in the afternoon.

'Storm front coming,' Kylie said, lifting her bag out of the boot.

'Sure is.' Jake climbed out of the driver's seat and peered into the back. 'Ah, she's fallen asleep.'

Kylie restrained him before he could open the rear passenger door. 'Don't wake her. I can see myself off.'

Jake wavered. He wanted to say goodbye to Kylie, but he didn't want to wake Whetū now she'd fallen asleep either. Chances were that Whetū would be super grumpy and make saying goodbye impossible anyway.

'It's fine,' Kylie said. 'I'll grab one of those trolleys over there.'

'I'll get it.' He trundled over to the front doors. When he returned to the car, he saw Kylie peering through the rear window.

'You all right?'

Kylie turned. 'Oh, yeah. I was just getting one last look at her.'

'Well,' he said, shuffling his feet, 'it won't be the last—'

'I mean the last look at Whetū aged three years and six days old. They grow up so fast, right? The next time I see her she'll look completely different again, and she'll probably know about one thousand more words, whereas I'll probably just have a couple more lines on my face.' She fingered the space between her eyebrows, still talking so fast Jake could barely keep up.

'Hey, um, I don't — Kyles?' He took her hand, lowered it to his hip. 'I didn't say I didn't want to see you.'

'No, I know. I get you need some time. I mean, God, we used to go out with each other's best friends.' She frowned. 'Actually, I was always closer friends with you than Emily, but you know what I mean. And I get it if you think this is all a humongous mistake except I'd really hate it if you stopped talking to me and I—'

'Kylie, stop.' Aargh, how was he meant to get a word in edgeways, let alone think with her burbling on like that? He kissed her. 'These past few days have been . . . fantastic. Confusing, but fantastic. I just need to sort a few things out in my head, OK?'

Kylie blinked at him. 'OK.'

'I mean, I've been putting one foot in front of the other for the past three years. That's how I've got through every single day. And now this has,' he swallowed, 'blown everything apart again. Not necessarily in a bad way,' he said quickly.

Ah Jesus, get it right, would you?

But how?

'You're allowed to move on, Jake,' Kylie said, her voice quieter than he'd ever heard it.

(Except when she whispered to me when I was moving inside her, that first

time, when she told me she thought she could fall in love with me and I couldn't say it back, and if only I could . . . if only . . .)

'I'm not sure you want to be the one moving on with me, though.' Her body was still pressed against his. He didn't want to let her go. He didn't want her to stay either. He just wanted to return to putting one foot in front of the other, return to his boring routine. It was safer that way.

'I'm not asking you for a long-term commitment,' she said. 'But if that happened, would it be such a terrible thing?'

Jake stepped away. 'I don't know,' he said. 'Flip a coin.'

Kylie narrowed her eyes at him. 'You know what I say to that?'

'What?'

'Fuck fate. If you want to spend your whole life worrying about what might happen, then you're missing out. We had fun, didn't we, these past few days?'

He exhaled. 'Of course.'

'And did we hurt anyone?'

Jake crossed his arms, looked away. He felt her hands on his wrists, her breath on his cheek.

'See you, Jake,' she said. 'But please, no matter what you decide, don't stop talking to me. I value our friendship too much for that.'

Then she was gone, walking across the car park, her hair and dress and shoes all so bright it hurt his eyes.

Chapter 46: Jigsaw Falling into Place

Jake opened the rear passenger door and frowned at his daughter. 'Whetū, why did you take your pants off?'

She pouted. 'They were wet.' Somehow she had managed to wriggle out of her leggings with her five-point seatbelt harness fastened.

'Oh man, really?' This toilet-training business was driving him batty. Whetū had decided she was too big for nappies, but her bladder hadn't quite caught up with that.

'I'm not a man, Daddy! I'm a girl!' She flounced out of the car and ran across the parched lawn. 'Koro, Koro!' She stopped to remove her t-shirt as well before continuing the sprint towards her grandfather, who was sitting on the porch, laughing.

'Naked as the day she was born!' He scooped her into his lap. 'And more beautiful every day. Did I ever tell you how much you look like your karanimāmā?'

Jake slung the baby bag over his shoulder, observing his father and his daughter out of the corner of his eye. Whetū did have a look of Christine about her, in a way he couldn't quite discern, but she had Emily's corkscrew curls and long limbs.

Three years and seven months since Emily had died, and it still gave him a physical pain to think about her. But he was no longer spending every waking hour thinking *what if, what if*. He had to move forward, even when it felt as though he was wading through poured concrete.

The little girl bounced on Willie's lap. 'Rain, rain, go away,' she said. It *had* started raining, large, intermittent drops that barely soaked into the summer-parched lawn.

'There are two changes of clothes in here.' Jake dumped the bag on the porch and peered beneath Willie's chair. 'Hi, Jimbo.' The old dog opened one eye, then closed it again.

'Clothes are over-rated,' Willie said, jiggling his granddaughter on his knee. 'Just don't mimi on me, will you?'

'I don't need to mimi,' Whetū said solemnly.

'Do you want a coffee, Jake?'

'No, I'd better —'

'Go on, just for ten minutes. Got something to show you.' Willie gently deposited his granddaughter on the porch and stood up. 'You could show me how to use that coffee plunger thing you bought me for Christmas.'

'OK, well, just ten minutes.' Jake stepped into the house's shady interior, which smelt like last night's fry-up. Whetū ran ahead of them, chanting, 'Rain, rain, go away.' In the distance, a faint grumble of thunder.

Jake made the coffee while his father entertained Whetū with a set of faded blocks that he'd found at the hospice shop.

'Here,' his old man said, once Jake had poured the drinks. Willie sat at the table, pushing a pile of junk mail aside, and passed Jake an envelope. 'Found these up the top of the pantry the other day, don't know how they ended up there.'

Jake slid the dog-eared photographs out of the envelope. One of them showed his parents standing in front of a Volkswagen Beetle, his mother cupping her pregnant belly. The next photo was of a young Jake running towards the camera. The photos were familiar but strange too, as if from another world.

'You were about the same age as Whetū is now in that one,' Willie said, tapping the young Jake. 'With a smile you could wrap around the world, just like our Whetū.'

'Little kids don't usually have too many worries, I guess.' Jake couldn't take his eyes off the photo, though. When had he lost the ability to smile like that? *Don't lose your smile, Whetū.*

That thought reminded Jake of the task he had yet to perform, the very reason why he'd asked his old man to look after Whetū for a couple of hours that afternoon. 'Better get going,' he said, after chugging down his coffee. 'I'll pick her up around four.'

'No hurry.' Willie nodded at the photos. 'You can keep those, if you want.'

'OK. Thanks.' Jake got up and gave his daughter a kiss. She was so absorbed in her block tower that she barely noticed. 'Be good for Koro.' He'd just set foot on the porch when he heard Willie say, 'Hey.'

Jake turned. His father shuffled his feet. 'So, I . . . You'll take care of those photos, won't you?'

'Of course.'

'And I, well, you know, I just wanted you to know that I was . . .' Willie took a cigarette out of his top pocket, stuck it in again. 'I didn't want you and Christine to go away. But I was scared, you know? And I was trying to work, to send you money, but I — And when I saw how she was the last time, how sick she was, I couldn't stand seeing her like that again.'

Jake leaned in slightly, inhaling. Had his old man started drinking already? There was no way he was leaving Whetū with him if he had. And yet, he couldn't detect the sickly fruity odour of digested alcohol on Willie's breath, and his speech sounded clear enough.

'And you, you looked at me like I was a stranger.'

Ah, Jesus. Jake stared out into the rain. 'You were,' he mumbled. There were so many things he could have said right then, but he swallowed them down. *Just keep moving forward, don't look back.*

'I didn't do the right thing, I know that,' Willie said.

Jake gripped his car keys. 'I didn't think I could forgive you,' he said, after a short silence. Willie lit a shaky cigarette. Jake chewed the inside of his cheek. 'Thanks for looking after Whetū,' he said, after a short silence. 'She loves coming to see you. I'll see you at four.' *Before you do start in on the turps.*

'Take as long as you need,' his old man murmured.

———

Take as long as you need. One week later, and Jake wasn't sure if any amount of time would be long enough for this next task. He chewed on his thumbnail, gazing into space. On his fridge, he spotted the *Get Out of Jail Free* card Gareth had posted to him a few months ago. *Don't know when you'll be in Melbourne next but I owe you one*, Gareth had written on the back. *Would love to catch up next time you're over, whenever that might be.* Next to the card was a photo of four-year-old Hannah.

Jake liked being a godfather, as inappropriate as it might have been. And he and Gareth had a lot more in common than Jake would have liked. Trying to focus, Jake looked at his laptop screen.

10 July 2019

> I, Jake William Heremaia, being of sound mind, voluntarily and willfully make known that my life should not artificially be prolonged beyond the circumstances set forth in this directive.

It was a standard form he'd downloaded from the internet, one that he could alter to his specific requirements.

> If I have an illness where there is no reasonable prospect of recovery and I am deemed permanently unconscious or permanently severely incapacitated, then I do not wish to receive any interventions to prolong my life.

Jake added in detail what those interventions were, such as CPR and being artificially ventilated and fed. All pretty standard stuff; nothing anyone would blink an eyelid at. But now it was time for the most important part of the document. He'd been thinking about it for months. *No, years.*

He began typing again.

> If I have a terminal illness where death is not imminent within the next few weeks but I am severely incapacitated i.e. unable to perform any activities of daily living for myself, then again, I do not wish to receive any interventions to prolong my life. This includes antibiotics (unless they are deemed necessary to alleviate suffering), CPR, artificial ventilation, intravenous fluids and assisted feeding.

He looked up. 'Can you read this? Does that make sense?'

Kylie unfolded her legs and got up from the couch, which was stained with Whetū's paint and the coffee he'd spilled a few weeks ago. After padding over to where Jake was sitting at the table with his laptop, she clasped his shoulders.

'I think so,' she said after a short silence. Her complexion, beneath her freckles, was milky-pale. 'Will you show this to Whetū?'

'Of course. When she's old enough.' He listened out for his daughter, in case the Northland gale had woken her up, but there was no sound from her bedroom. Rain battered the windows. He'd have to check the spouting soon, make sure it wasn't pissing water everywhere like last time. 'I love a good storm, don't you?'

'As long as it's gone before my plane takes off.' Kylie touched the screen. 'Do you want to say, *specifically Huntington's disease*? I think you should make it as clear as possible. For instance, what happens if you have a surfing accident and end up tetraplegic? Would you still want this?'

Jake hesitated. 'I don't know. It'd depend on whether I could communicate. Tetraplegia isn't a terminal illness.' He scratched his chin. 'Yeah, I see your point.'

'I just think you need to be really specific.'

'OK.' He began typing again, inserting *specifically Huntington's disease* after *if I have a terminal illness where death is not imminent with the next few weeks.*

'Few weeks is vague too.'

'True.' He erased *few* and replaced it with *two months.* 'How's that?'

Kylie chewed her lower lip. 'Not sure. Maybe think about it.' She sat beside him. 'Did your mum have one of these?'

Jake looked up. 'No,' he said. 'No, she didn't.'

'What about if euthanasia becomes legal here? Will you change it?'

He hesitated. 'I don't know. I'd have to think about it at the time. But from what I've seen, if patients have good palliative care, then most of them don't want that. And if I become a burden to everyone, then I'd be happy to be placed in hospital-level care.'

'Jesus, Jake.' Kylie looked on the verge of tears.

'I have to think of these things now. Before it's too late.'

'Hopefully you'll never have to. You might develop symptoms, but you might not, right?'

'Right.' Perhaps one day he'd tell Kylie exactly what he and Emily had done, exactly why this directive was so important. But for now, what he and Kylie had still felt new, fragile. Trust was a multi-layered edifice, layers of sediment.

He touched the pounamu around her neck, the one he'd sent her when he'd contacted her after two months of silence, neither of them knowing how to proceed.

I want to try, he'd said. *I want to start moving*. Not move *on*, no, he'd never completely move on, but to move. To breathe. To live. So they were trying, one small step at a time. First, a long-distance relationship. Next . . . Who knew what was next? He didn't want to dream too soon.

'One day at a time,' he said. 'Right?'

'Right.' Kylie shuffled onto his lap and kissed him once, twice, three times. 'Jake faces the double helix dragon once and for all,' she murmured. 'And he says . . .'

Epilogue: Jake

Heaven is bobbing out the back of a glassy swell, the first light of morning suffusing into the sky above. Heaven is the immensity of the water moving beneath me, slow and rhythmical, like the ebb and flow of the blood moving in and out of my heart, of the air moving in and out of my lungs. Heaven is what happens when I climb on top of my board and I am united with the wave and the universe and everything that tells me I am still alive, still strong, still loved.

Heaven is the life we make before we are released from our earthly bonds. Heaven is the love we give, and are given.

Heaven is a blue dawn, the world cracking open to let the sunshine in.

I am not afraid.

Support Organisations

New Zealand

Huntington's Disease Youth Organisation (www.hdyo.co.nz/)

Neurological Foundation (neurological.org.nz/what-we-do/awareness-and-education/brain-disorders-and-support/huntingtons-disease/)

Huntington's Disease Association (huntingtons.org.nz)

Health and Disability Commissioner (www.hdc.org.nz/mental-health-addictions/where-to-find-help-and-support/)

HealthEd (www.healthed.govt.nz/resource/helplines-and-mental-health-services)

Health Navigator (www.healthnavigator.org.nz/health-a-z/g/grief-loss/)

Mental Health Foundation (mentalhealth.org.nz/index.php/suicide-loss)

Call Healthline free on 0800 611 116 for health advice and information

Youthline 0800 376 633 or text 234

Australia

Brain Foundation (brainfoundation.org.au/disorders/huntingtons-disease/)

Health Direct (www.healthdirect.gov.au/counsellors-and-counselling)

Lifeline (www.lifeline.org.au/get-help/)

Suicide Call Back Service (www.suicidecallbackservice.org.au/)

Beyond Blue (www.beyondblue.org.au/get-support/get-immediate-support)

Griefline (griefline.org.au/)

For further information on Huntington's disease

Huntington's Outreach Project for Education (hopes.stanford.edu)

HD Buzz (en.hdbuzz.net)

International Huntington´s Association (huntington-disease.org/)

Acknowledgements

As noted in my dedication, thank you to my beautiful mother-in-law, Charlotte Merriman, who gave me a home when I was a second-/third-year medical student at Otago Medical School, and whose house I have borrowed for the Walsh family home. Thank you for being the best flatmate ever! As always, thank you to my friend and critique partner, Nod Ghosh, who critiqued a very different version of this novel in 2013 (*Red Sky in the Morning*), and then the completely revamped version as I sent it through, chapter by chapter, in 2019. Thank you to all of those who have offered advice on the surfing passages, some of which originally formed part of now-abandoned manuscripts, including James Russell, Ben Wheeler, Heather Matthews and Jackson Darlow. Thank you to my sister-in-law and obstetrician, Kim McFadden, for your advice on obstetric matters, and to the Auckland Genetics Service for their advice on genetic testing/counselling in Huntington's disease. Thank you to Julie Andrewes, Pip Lloyd, Colleen Lenihan and Vanessa Bailey for their advice on te reo and cultural aspects of the novel. I am eternally grateful to Harriet Allan, my fiction publisher, for keeping up with and publishing all of the manuscripts I keep sending through — the eighth novel in five years! Thanks to the amazing team at Penguin Random House, including Stu Lipshaw, Cat Taylor and Liz West, and to my agent, Nadine Rubin Nathan of High Spot Literary. Finally, I couldn't do this without the support of my beloved family — my husband Grant, and children Lachie and Maisie.

Eileen Merriman

Moonlight Sonata

A bitter sweet novel of forbidden love and family secrets.

A bitter-sweet novel of forbidden love and family secrets.

'Some secrets should never be told.'

It's the annual New Year family get-together. Molly is dreading having to spend time with her mother, but she is pleased her son will see his cousins and is looking forward to catching up with her brothers . . . Joe in particular.

Under the summer sun, family tensions intensify, relationships become heightened and Molly and Joe will not be the only ones with secrets that must be kept hidden.

'No one must ever know.'

Eileen
Merriman
The Silence of Snow

'Merriman certainly isn't afraid to explore territory more
timid writers might avoid.' — *Weekend Herald*

A compelling medical novel about facing one's demons, self-prescribing and finding the strength to carry on, even when it seems that all is lost.

Anaesthetic Fellow Rory McBride is adrift. Since a routine procedure went horribly wrong, he has been plagued by sleeplessness, flashbacks and escalating panic attacks.

Jodi Waterstone has recently started work as a first-year doctor at the same hospital, and the night shifts, impossible workload and endless hours on duty are taking a toll.

Both are trying to stay in control of their lives, but Rory starts to self-medicate with sleeping pills and sedatives to help him get through the nights . . . and the days. Before long, the sedatives aren't enough. Can Jodi save him from himself?

For more information about our titles visit
www.penguin.co.nz